second
Bride
down

second
Bride
down

NEW YORK TIMES BESTSELLING AUTHOR

GINNY BAIRD

Entangled Publishing, LLC
644 Shrewsbury Commons Ave., STE 181
Shrewsbury, PA 17361
Visit our website at www.entangledpublishing.com.

Amara is an imprint of Entangled Publishing, LLC.

Edited by Heather Howland
Cover design by Bree Archer
Cover art by VitaliiSmulskyi/Gettyimages
Interior design by Toni Kerr

Print ISBN 978-1-64937-369-4
ebook ISBN 978-1-64937-371-7

Manufactured in the United States of America

First Edition November 2022

AMARA

To my family,
for believing in me and my dreams.

CHAPTER ONE

"I'm going to marry Aidan Strong."

Misty Delaney stared at her best friend Mei-Lin, and her sisters, Nell and Charlotte, and waited for their reaction. The four of them stood in the service area of her family's coffee shop, Bearberry Brews. Her folks and their manager, Lucas, were in the kitchen running the roaster as they all prepped to start their day. Morning sunlight poured through the windows, glinting off framed black-and-white photos capturing several of Misty's favorite Majestic scenes.

Charlotte gawked at her and Mei-Lin pursed her lips.

"Misty, no." Nell's hazel eyes glistened. "Why?" Outside the thick stucco walls of their cliffside café, the ocean tumbled and roared, reminding Misty of the turning tides in her life. But she was tired of floating along. Ready to chart her own course.

"Because," she said, "I'm fed up with this dumb contest."

Without their parents' knowledge, the three sisters had made a wager. Whichever one of them hadn't found true love by the end of September, she'd be the one to marry their family's archenemy's son, Aidan, thereby merging their standalone shop, Bearberry Brews, with the larger corporation, Bearberry Coffee. And time was wasting. Today was September tenth. There were only twenty days left before Misty's parents' loan came due and they risked default, thereby losing this café and their family home which they'd put up as collateral.

Charlotte stroked the power crystal dangling from a leather strap around her neck. "Fed up or not, you can't just walk on our bet."

"She's right," Nell said. "That's not how a wager works."

Mei-Lin spoke under her breath. "Says the woman who's already won it."

Misty agreed. Nell had snagged her husband-to-be faster than Misty could ring up a double-shot latte — with foam. Not that Charlotte and Misty weren't happy for her. They all were. Nell and Grant were a great match.

Charlotte crossed her arms and the hem of her peasant dress flounced over the tops of her tall cowgirl boots. "Sorry, sis. One of us quitting this contest was not in the deal." As the middle child, Charlotte was all about fairness, but sometimes people didn't play by the rules.

Nell glanced toward the kitchen. "Charlotte's right. The *deal* was whichever one of us didn't find true love first—"

Misty frowned. "Easy enough for you to say."

"She *can* say it," asserted Charlotte. "Now that she and Grant are engaged."

"As published in *The Seaside Daily*." Mei-Lin's sleek dark hair slid over her shoulders. "Who knows?" She raised her eyebrows at Misty. "Maybe your news will be next?"

That was another condition of their wager, that any intended nuptials be announced to the whole town via the local paper. There'd be no fake maneuvering out of marrying Aidan then.

Coffee beans popped and crackled in the kitchen and the scent of roasting coffee filled the air. Today's special was toasted almond raspberry, and its smell was enough to make a person's mouth water. If they hadn't worked here nearly every day, so had become immune to the incredible aromas that routinely filled the berry-themed coffee shop.

"My news *will* be next," Misty stated stubbornly. "When my engagement to Aidan gets written up."

As much as Misty loved her hometown, she'd been thinking about leaving it an awful lot lately. After years of putting it off, she'd finally applied to the Rhode Island School of Design. It was probably foolish to believe that a scholarship would actually come through. At twenty-six, she was years older than the average beginning college student.

Still. The possibility lingered. And since she had her head around that option, it wasn't too huge a stretch to imagine moving clear across the Atlantic to marry some super-wealthy individual who could save her whole family from financial ruin.

Mei-Lin nudged her. "But what about school?"

"I'm sure there are tons of places I can go *over there*," Misty whispered back, before adding loudly for her sisters' benefit, "Once I'm married and rich." And anyway, it was just for five years. That was the deal the two moms had struck. There was some technicality about both families being able to divide their common property after that.

Charlotte scoffed. "I don't think that's been decided."

Misty's jaw tensed. Charlotte liked telling other

people what to do, but not this time. "Oh, I think it has."

"Misty," Mei-Lin said, pleading. "It's too soon to give up. You could still find your one and only. Your fated match. Think of love! Think of destiny! There's not a ton of time before your parents' loan comes due, but probably enough. Just look at Nell!" Everyone did and she blushed. "She landed Grant in only a week." Nell's color deepened, a diamond engagement ring glimmering on her left hand. That had been a feat, especially for quiet-natured Nell.

"I'm not giving up." Misty straightened her spine. "I'm being proactive."

She slipped her cell phone into her jeans pocket and sighed. The slew of incoming text messages had only made her more certain about her decision. Word had gotten around Majestic about the bet she and her sisters had made, and Misty's exes had come out of the woodwork, several volunteering to relieve her of the burden of marrying Aidan in favor of marrying them. Sadly, every one of her exes was the wrong guy for her.

Misty hadn't realized how hard it would be to find the perfect husband. She'd never exactly tried before, and had somehow thought it would come a whole lot easier than it had. She guessed she wasn't ready for the real thing. Not a super-serious relationship anyway, the now forever kind. She'd never met a guy she could imagine spending eternity with, so a placeholder marriage of convenience to bail out the family could work just fine.

Nell's cheeks sagged, her face an image of their dad's when he worried. Only, his complexion was ruddy while Nell's freckled skin was pale like her sisters' and their mom's. "Oh hon, you deserve your happiness, too." Her lower lip quivered. "I thought we'd all agreed?"

"Agreed to what?" a male voice asked.

Misty's gaze jerked toward the kitchen. Lucas Reyes stood in the doorway, his arms loaded with coffee bags. "It's um, nothing."

"Nothing?" Lucas's dark eyebrows arched above his intense gray eyes. "Is this about that deal you three made?"

"What deal is that?" their mom, Grace, asked, peering over Lucas's shoulder.

Bob Delaney chimed in from behind them with his faint Irish lilt. "If anybody's going to be making deals around here, they best be good ones!" The trio spilled into the service area behind the counter and Misty's dad glanced around the room. "Daughters?" he asked with a disapproving frown. "Is something going on?"

"No," Misty answered, maybe too quickly.

Her mom blew out a breath, sending a tendril of her graying hair spiraling. "Girls," she sighed. "Please don't say that your silly bet is back on?"

Their dad set his hands on his hips and scolded Nell. "I thought we got all of that settled after your situation with Grant."

"It is settled!" Nell said.

"Extra settled," Charlotte concurred. "We were just, um, planning Nell's surprise wedding—"

"Shower!" Mei-Lin improvised. "Which..." She grimaced at Misty. "Is not such a surprise anymore?"

"How super!" Nell grinned and ran her fingers

through her long auburn curls. "Thanks, guys."

Their dad smiled at Mei-Lin. "How nice. Did you think of it?"

"It…uh." She gave Misty the side-eye. "Was Misty's idea, actually."

Misty gaped at Mei-Lin, then refocused. "Uh. Yep!" She grinned at her folks. "Sure was." A party for Nell wasn't a bad thought. She'd totally earned it. "But it's more like an engagement celebration," she said, "since no wedding date's been set yet."

Lucas's gaze swept over Misty as he walked to the shelves by the register, and her heart thumped. Lucas had a strange way of seeing through her, even when she thought she was being craftily evasive. "A party," he said, as he began stocking the coffee shelves. "That's *sweet*."

Misty blinked at him, wondering if he'd figured her out. He seemed to guess that she and her sisters and Mei-Lin were covering something up. "We thought so."

"Will that be before—or after—your trip?" he asked, finishing his task.

Wait. What? Misty's pulse stuttered. So he *had* overheard some of their conversation from the kitchen. The question was how much and whether he would blab. But Lucas was generally chill, so hopefully not.

"What trip?" her folks asked, their words overlapping.

"Uh. No trip—yet."

Mei-Lin raced to the rescue. "Misty's just been thinking of traveling. A bit."

Charlotte pulled a convincingly concerned face.

"But we said now's not a great time."

"Right-o." Their dad checked his watch. "Probably best not to dash off anywhere at the moment." He chuckled warmly. "Opening in five."

Charlotte strapped on her apron. "This discussion's not over," she murmured.

From Misty's view, it was, though.

Nell adjusted her knitted scarf as she pranced by, heading for her office. "Far from it." Nell did their accounting while Charlotte was their marketing guru. Misty ran the register and made coffee, and she was pretty much over both things.

Lucas went to help Mei-Lin by righting the up-turned chairs that had been set on the tables and sliding them into place. All the while, he kept sending Misty questioning looks.

Charlotte stood beside Misty, unloading paper packages filled with the fresh baked goods and tidily arranging them in the glass-fronted pastry case. "You can't just call off our wager, you know," she said softly to Misty. "Not without giving things a try."

Misty kept her voice down, too. "I *have* tried."

"I mean, *really* try. With your whole heart."

"Ooh, you mean like you've been doing, Charlotte?"

Charlotte rolled her eyes. "I've been exploring my options."

"So have I, which has led me to believe there's nobody meant for me here."

"No one?" Charlotte shook her head. "In all of Majestic?"

"Nope." Did she imagine it, or did Lucas's neck redden?

"Well then, maybe you haven't been looking in the right places?"

"Oh I've looked plenty." Misty punched her access code into the register and began loading the cash drawer with bills after counting them out, the weight of her ponytail swinging behind her. She'd just changed the pink streak in her chestnut-colored hair to purple and liked this look better. She might try green next to match the thorny green stem on the rose tattoo on the underside of her wrist. Life was like that. Thorny. And her sisters' interference prickled at her more often than she liked. "You're not the boss of me, Charlotte."

"Spoken like a ten-year-old."

Misty stuck her tongue out at her annoying middle sister. Charlotte loved being in charge. She'd even told Misty which game piece to be when they'd played board games as kids. Like Misty couldn't decide things for herself. She wasn't that much younger than Charlotte. Only two years, and four years younger than Nell.

Charlotte huffed. "It's London, Misty. Not Portland, and you've never even been out of Maine." She'd moved on from banana muffins to orange and blueberry scones. There were molasses cookies, too, and fat round ones labeled "Pumpkin Spice" that looked delicious. Misty might sneak some of those later.

Charlotte and Nell both figured Misty for a health nut because she liked to pretend she went for morning runs and only ate organic products, which fit in with their café since even the treats at Bearberry Brews were made from all-natural ingredients. Misty had further encouraged their mistaken perception by fibbing about her penchant for healthy morning smoothies. She'd never been big into smoothies, but Nell and Charlotte didn't need to know that. Misty enjoyed having her little secrets, no matter how minor they were, and it was hard to keep secrets around her family. Only Mei-Lin knew about RISD and she'd promised Misty she wouldn't tell.

"Yeah, so?" she said about getting out of Majestic. "Then maybe it's time."

"Hmm. Maybe so." That sneaky gleam in Charlotte's dark blue eyes meant she was up to something. "Or maybe not?"

"Lucas!" their dad called from the kitchen. "Will you get the door?"

"Sure thing!" He made his way to the front of the store and flipped over the sign that said "open" on one side and "closed" on the other, then unlocked the door with his keys. There wasn't a line forming, but it was almost seven so their regular patrons would filter in shortly.

Mei-Lin took up her spot behind the counter, double-checking equipment and supplies. Charlotte did the same before switching on two coffee machines, one for their regular house brew and the other for decaf. They kept their cold brew in a small fridge behind the counter. A separate station with creamers, sugar packs, napkins, and coffer stirrers stood nearby.

Lucas passed Misty, his arm grazing her elbow as she tied her apron strings behind her. "You and I?" He nodded toward the storeroom. "Need to talk."

"What? Now?" The door chime rang and an older couple entered the café bundled up in sweaters. The

McIntyres owned the nearby market and stopped in for coffee every morning before opening their shop.

Lucas waved at the pair, before whispering, "As soon as you get a break."

CHAPTER TWO

It was all Lucas could do to keep his mind on his work until Misty got that break. He was supposed to be inventorying the storeroom but kept losing track by resetting his hand scanner each time he peered through the kitchen and out toward the register where Misty stood.

Misty's leaving Majestic?

To marry Aidan Strong?

No way.

Not happening.

His heart burned in his chest.

Not if I can help it.

Misty was smart. Maybe she'd listen to reason. He could try to talk her out of it. By what? Admitting that he'd worshipped her forever?

No. That would completely freak her out.

But he had. Ever since he'd started working odd jobs for Mr. Delaney after his dad died in that fishing accident when he was fourteen. His school nurse mom had needed the money, so she'd taken a second job at a bakery. His younger brother, Ramon, was destined for college, she was sure.

Mr. Delaney was a good man. Steadfast and kind. He'd sensed Lucas's predicament in wanting to help his mom put food on the table and had paid him to deliver coffee to local businesses. When Lucas had turned fifteen he'd trained him on the register. Misty was one year younger than him and came in to help out at the café sometimes. When Lucas first saw her, his heart had caught in his throat. He'd only been fourteen but he'd never seen anyone so beautiful, or met anyone as determined.

Misty's parents and sisters often made plans for her, but she tended to go her own way. Just like she had when she'd gotten that nose stud and her rose tattoo. She was energetic and fun and the high school guys had clamored around her, while Lucas had quietly stepped aside. Waiting. Hoping. That his turn might someday come. He'd thought of asking her out in high school, but Joe got there first. Then Misty began dating Richard. There was never much of a break between her many boyfriends, but obviously none of them had been right for her. Otherwise, she wouldn't have kept looking.

What Lucas wouldn't give to have her send one tiny glimpse his way, but Misty didn't see him like that. She never had. At least they got along as friends. That was something, but not enough. Not if she was now intent on moving to London. How could she even consider it? Misty was a homebody. What she knew and loved was Majestic. Fine if she wanted to travel. He'd take her anywhere in the world she wanted to go, as long as it wasn't to England to marry Aidan.

He ran a hand through his hair, his frustration building. He should have known something was up from the very first day of this month when he'd caught the three Delaney sisters huddled together in this storeroom, like they were plotting something big. And they had been, obviously. The three of them could claim one of them marrying Aidan was their mom's idea all they wanted, but they'd been the ones who'd decided to go along with it.

Apparently, the Strong family and the Delaneys hadn't been on speaking terms for many years, thanks to an underhanded trick John Strong had played on Bob Delaney. Strong had obtained international distribution rights to Bearberry Coffee, while leaving his old partner and friend with nothing besides this standalone café, Bearberry Brews. The Strongs had gone on to make their fortune after that, while the Delaneys struggled to get by.

It wasn't until after old man Strong died that his widow decided to reach out to the girls' mom, in hopes of making amends. Mrs. Delaney visited London and the two moms concocted a ludicrous plan about Aidan marrying one of the Delaney sisters in order to reunite the businesses. At first, Misty and her sisters had been opposed to the idea. Then, very plainly, they'd changed their minds. They'd all been in a race not to marry Aidan ever since, knowing that one of them would ultimately have to do it.

And Misty's, what? Caving? Throwing in the towel? Why?

"You wanted to talk?"

His chin jerked up and there she was, standing on the threshold to the storeroom. Heavy mascara lined her big hazel eyes, the ones that drove him so crazy. They were brownish green and her forest-colored apron brought out their mossy hues.

Lucas set down the scanner he'd been using to tally up supplies. "Ah, yeah. I did."

Misty peered over her shoulder as more patrons poured into the café.

"I probably just have a minute."

Yeah. He figured that.

He wedged his hands into his jeans pockets. "About what you said out there—"

"Were you eavesdropping?" She gasped. "From the kitchen?"

"Eavesdropping, no. But I overheard something you said." His gut tightened. "It sounded an awful lot like you'd decided to marry Aidan."

Misty's mouth fell open but then she closed it. "Shh!" She shut the door behind her. "Please don't say anything to my folks. They can't know, okay? Not until it's all sewn up."

"Misty, are you kidding me?" He gestured with his hands. "You moving to London? What? How did this happen?"

"Well, it's not happening yet." She folded her arms in front of her. "And won't happen at all if Charlotte, Nell, and Mei-Lin have anything to say about it."

"Maybe you should listen to your sisters and your best friend."

"Maybe they should mind their own business."

"Uh. Bearberry Brews is kind of their business and so are you."

"Me?"

"Yeah, Misty. You. Because people around here care about you." He swallowed past the raw knot in his throat. "I care, too, and I don't want you doing this."

Misty moaned. "*Et tu*, Lucas? Seriously?"

"Nobody wants you making a rash decision."

"It's not rash. I've thought it over carefully."

"Oh really? Since when?"

"Oh since…" Misty stared up at the ceiling and then back at him. "Yesterday."

Wait. "So. The day after Nell and Grant became engaged?"

"What?" She tried to look guileless but failed. "Oh yeah! Right. It was. But I didn't think of it like that." She frowned. "Exactly."

Misty and her sisters were super close. Always there for each other in good times and in bad. Nell's happiness over her engagement to Grant had been contagious. She'd come running into the café, all grins and flashing around the big rock Grant had gotten her. It had been impossible not to get swept up in her joy. Lucas had felt the buzz, too.

Misty scowled. "I'm not jealous of Nell for winning first, if that's what you're thinking."

He wasn't. Misty wasn't the jealous sort. She was caring, though, and worried a lot about her older sisters, even though they probably weren't aware of it. "The timing just seems coincidental. That's all."

She heaved a sigh and her shoulders sank. "What am I supposed to do, Lucas? It's down to me and Charlotte now, and Charlotte can't go to London. What would Mom and Dad do without her? Where would the business be without her?"

It was true Charlotte's marketing talents had bailed the café out before. When things had seemed bleak financially, she'd always found them a way. Some glitzy new promo like "Two-for-one latte Sundays" and "Frappy Hour" to drive up business during the late afternoon lull. Unfortunately, she hadn't been able to think up a quick fix for her parents' current bank loan problem. Lucas was still a little stunned she'd agreed to the anti-marrying Aidan bet along with her sisters, but not half as surprised as he was to learn Misty had jumped in on it, too.

"She could probably still keep her hand in things from over there."

"No, because her contacts are here," Misty said stubbornly. "Charlotte knows everyone in Majestic, from the Managing Editor at *The Seaside Daily* to every last advertiser in town, and they all totally love her. I'm not sure she'd be able to arrange so many of her great deals at huge discounts from a distance. She has a way about her in person."

"I'll concede Charlotte's persuasive."

"Well, she's not persuading me to change my mind."

He edged closer. "Maybe I can persuade you then?"

Misty sighed. "Lucas, please."

"It's not like you've got to give up today anyway. It's only the tenth. September's still got twenty more days left."

Misty set her hands on her hips. "Oh, and you think that's a good thing? Drawing this whole situation out even more? It's unfair and anxiety-producing to let this go on, Lucas. Why drag this stupid bet out when there's such an easy way to stop it?"

"By you marrying Aidan and moving to London," he said deadpan.

"Yes."

"Look. This is your decision." Lucas softened his tone. "But hey, if you want to talk later—"

"I won't," she said, but emotion flickered in her

eyes and he could tell she was tempted to spill. Misty often claimed she didn't want to tell him things, before she wound up doing that anyway. He didn't mind being her sounding board. He'd listen to Misty any day.

"In any case." He shrugged. "I'm here."

She considered him a moment, but her expression was appreciative and not adoring. More like she counted on him as a big brother or a trusted cousin. Not exactly the sort of vibe he wanted to elicit. "You've always had my back, haven't you?"

"Never doubt it."

She exhaled slowly and rolled back her shoulders. "Thanks, Lucas."

"Just promise me one thing." He closed the rest of the gap between them and took her hands.

Her trusting look shot a searing-hot arrow straight through his chest. If only she trusted him more. As someone more significant to her. Someone she might open her heart up to.

But no. That was asking too much.

"What's that?"

"That you'll sleep on this. Give this whole I'm-marrying-Aidan idea twenty-four hours to sink in. If you still feel the same way tomorrow"—and man, how he hoped she wouldn't—"then I'm with you one hundred percent. I want what you want, Misty, and if you decide that's London," he said bravely although his heart was breaking, "then London it is."

He took some small comfort in the fact that it wouldn't be a real marriage, more like "in name only." Still. That would chew up five good years of Misty's life before she'd be free again. Maybe even free to finally be with him? Then again, that was a lot of time overseas, spent getting used to a glitzy lifestyle with lots of expensive perks. Ones that someone like Lucas could nowhere near provide. Then another—even scarier—thought hit him.

What if Aidan Strong wasn't really so terrible, after all? What if he was a genuinely nice guy? Someone smart, talented, and funny? Someone who would take one look at Misty and know she was the kind of woman he should never let get away, setting aside the whole crazy way their union had started?

Lucas's stomach soured.

Only one thing would be worse than Misty moving to London and marrying Aidan.

Her legitimately falling in love with him and deciding to stay.

A smile trembled across her lips. "Thanks, Lucas."

"You'll sleep on it, then?"

She hung her head and then looked up at him. "Okay."

The best he could do was stall for time. Maybe she would wake up and realize the whole notion of marrying Aidan and moving away was a major mistake. While it was torture seeing her every day and not being able to admit his feelings, not seeing her at all would be so much worse.

She laughed sadly. "I'm really going to miss you. Miss all of you."

Lucas's heart panged. His own feelings aside, someone like Misty wouldn't be happy leaving her family and friends behind, even if it was only for a few years. Her heart was in Majestic.

But if her sisters and Mei-Lin couldn't talk her out

of this, what chance did he have? He'd have to be a heck of a lot more than a friend to pull heavier weight in her decision. But that would mean coming clean about his feelings. The romantic feelings he'd harbored for her all these years. And what would that accomplish? Only serve to mess with her head and give her one more problem to worry about, since she clearly didn't feel the same way about him.

He tightened his grip on her hands. "Let's see how you feel in the morning, hmm? And if you've changed your mind, no shame in that. We all do and say things we think we mean at the time, but then later we think better of them. Maybe you don't have to go. Don't have to marry Aidan. Maybe none of you do. Maybe there's another way."

"Before this place faces bankruptcy and my parents lose their house?" Her shoulders sank. "I don't think so."

"Maybe we can think of something?" He swallowed hard. "You and I together?"

She lightly shook his hands in hers. "You've always been the greatest. So there for me."

"I *am* here for you." The words burned in his throat. "Anything you need."

The storeroom door pushed open and Lucas dropped Misty's hands.

"There you are, child," Mr. Delaney said. "Lucas, too." He gave them each a quick once-over then got back to business. Beyond him, Lucas spied a throng of customers crowding the counter and the register where Mei-Lin and Charlotte worked furiously trying to keep up. "I'm afraid we could use a hand." He nodded at Lucas. "Two hands." He shook his head and chuckled. "All hands on deck. If you don't mind."

"Yes, sir," Lucas said. "Right behind you."

• • •

Misty gave the customer his change, willing her hand to stop shaking. It was hard to stay cool about everything given Lucas's extreme opposition to her plans. Not that she always listened to Lucas, but he generally gave great advice. Her sisters hadn't been totally enthused about her going to England, either. You'd think Charlotte would hug her, not scold her, for taking the Aidan bullet. But no. She'd gotten all uppity about Misty making up her own mind.

Still. It was the right thing to do. She didn't have to listen to any of the others. Bigger things were at stake here.

"Here you are, sir. Enjoy!" Mei-Lin passed the double-whipped strawberries and almond cream macchiato across the counter to the man who'd just paid for it, then whispered above Misty's shoulder, "You look like you need a break."

"I took one thirty minutes ago."

Mei-Lin lightly touched her arm. "Then go take another."

Misty stared into Mei-Lin's light brown eyes.

"It's okay to make a statement," she said. "It's also okay," Mei-Lin said under her breath, "to withdraw it. It's a big step, moving to Europe. Maybe Charlotte's better suited—"

"To what? Travel? Marry rich?"

Mei-Lin sighed. "Misty—"

"Someone's got to do it," Misty told her. "Might as

well be me."

"Hey, Misty!" Charlotte called from beside the microwave. "Say cheese!"

Misty blinked when Charlotte held up her phone. "What for?"

Charlotte tucked a lock of her ebony hair behind one ear. "Maybe Aidan would like a preview pic of his future bride?"

Mei-Lin frowned but Misty didn't mind taking the bait. "Ha-ha, very funny." She untied and removed her apron. Then set it aside before beaming at the camera, one hand set sassily on her hip. Charlotte was just playing around. She wouldn't really send this to Aidan, not when she was all opposed to Misty marrying him in the first place. "Like this is so enticing," Misty said. "Me at the register at Bearberry Brews."

"Some guys are into baristas," Mei-Lin said. "Speaking from personal experience."

"Love it!" Charlotte snapped a photo and then another.

Misty adjusted her ponytail band and then preened some more.

She stopped suddenly, wondering if Charlotte was being serious. What if she really did send a primer to London? Misty's pulse pounded, then she told herself to calm down.

What would that really hurt? Aidan hadn't seen any of them in years, and they all looked all right. Unlike him, apparently. The man's image was posted nowhere online, which could only mean one thing. He was as freakishly geeky as he'd been as a kid. Maybe worse.

At least the business-arrangement marriage was

guaranteed to be platonic. Misty's heart softened. Maybe she should take pity on him? Not too much pity, though. Not physically. Ew. An image of his childhood face came back to her in a flash with his broad bucked-tooth smile.

He couldn't exactly help being pasty.

But he might have tried harder not being such an utter pest to her and her sisters.

Misty reined in her uncharitable thoughts, committed to being kind.

Spiritually kind. She had to set her limits.

Poor Aidan likely needed a friend. She'd heard of his type. Super successful in business, but a failure in the personal relationship department.

Misty inhaled deeply, centering her positive energy.

She was claiming a separate bedroom for sure. Maybe even a whole different wing of the house. If it was a gigantic house, which it probably was, that could work nicely.

Yes. She was going to be a kind and patient wife-in-name-only to Aidan.

Charlotte flipped through the shots she'd just taken. "Nice. These will do!"

"Do for what?" Misty asked warily. "You're not honestly sending those to Aidan?"

"I don't know," Charlotte taunted. "Maybe I should?"

Misty's panic spiked. "Charlotte," she said. "I was just kidding around. Delete those!"

"Delete?" She examined her phone screen and grinned. "No can do."

"Let me see then!"

"Nu-uh." Charlotte held her phone away when Misty grabbed for it. "They're not edited. Plus. I'll need to pick the best one."

"Best one for what?"

"Maybe I'm planning a little surprise?" Charlotte's smug tone made her nerves skitter. Now that she'd thought it over, posing for Charlotte had been a bad idea. More apt to send the wrong signals to Aidan than assert this was a hands-off arrangement. Maybe she could find a way to nab Charlotte's phone and delete those pics before Charlotte did something evil with them?

Huge problem was, Charlotte always kept her phone on her.

Misty sighed and glanced toward the kitchen. Lucas stood in the doorway, having observed the photo shoot. "Taking up modeling now?" he asked when Misty walked past him.

"Hardly." She intended to eat the sandwich she had in the kitchen fridge for an early lunch. For whatever reason, she was starving. "Charlotte was just being goofy."

"Goofy," Lucas said with a suspicious edge. "Right."

Her parents were at a back table, going over supply orders, and Nell sat in her office with the door partially ajar. Misty saw Nell's red ballerina flats under the edge of her desk before she pushed the door open further.

"Oh hey," Nell said, looking up. She'd been studying her laptop while making notes on a ledger beside it. She had a pencil clenched between her teeth, which she removed. "Is something up? I mean. Other than…" She dropped her voice. "Your wild notion about going to London?"

"It's not so wild." Misty sat down in a chair. "To me, it seems logical."

Nell shot her a haughty stare. "To me it sounds like cheating," she continued in a whisper. "Worming your way out of our bet."

Now if that wasn't the pot calling the kettle black. "You're the one who bought a plane ticket to London."

"Right." She cocked her head. "But I didn't go."

"Because Grant stopped you."

"So?"

"So, Nell." Misty set her elbows on her knees. "How is this any different?"

"I'm the oldest," she said, like her pulling rank made sense.

"Yeah, well. I'm the youngest, so—"

"You still have your whole life ahead of you."

"Charlotte does, too," Misty said. She sat back in her chair and crossed her arms. "Besides all that. It's only five years. I'll be done by thirty-one."

Nell heaved a breath and shut her laptop. "We never should have made that bet."

"What were our alternatives?"

"Don't know." Nell twisted a lock of her auburn hair around one finger. "Maybe we should have tried harder to find a different way to solve the café's money problems. Like that fake fundraiser idea we told Mom and Dad about."

"Yeah, well, we didn't," Misty said. "And there's not a lot of time left now."

Nell frowned. "No."

"At least you're okay." Misty surveyed her oldest sister. Though Nell was only thirty, she'd always looked after Misty and Charlotte in a motherly way. "I mean, more than okay. Look at you! Getting married!"

"It is kind of unexpected." Nell giggled. "And amazing. I just wish the same could happen for you—and Charlotte. You know, that you could meet your perfect matches."

"With this clock ticking?" Misty said. "Seems unlikely."

"I thought Grant and I were unlikely, until we happened."

"Yeah." Misty grinned. "So glad you did."

"You're telling me!" Nell rolled her eyes. Then her face took on a dreamy cast. So dreamy that she appeared lost in some awesome memory. Nell had been a little out of it ever since Friday and announcing her engagement. Misty'd caught her scouring over wedding cakes on Pinterest and perusing wedding gowns on her phone. Misty completely understood her being besotted with happiness. She'd crushed on Grant for so long, she was probably still in shock that her wildest dreams of being with him had actually come true.

"Okay," Misty said, breaking Nell's stupor. "I guess I'd better go."

"Wait!" Nell snapped to attention. "Not to London?"

Misty stood. "It's not like I'm leaving today."

Nell leaned across her desk. "Great. So then, you haven't told him yet, have you?"

"Aidan? No." She was still working out the best way to do that. She didn't want to pull a Nell and claim she was coming when she wasn't. Maybe better to announce once she was there. On British soil. She could text Aidan to send a car to pick her up or something like that. At least then there'd be no mixed messaging. She'd let him know when her decision was a done deal. Which it would be…very shortly.

Misty walked toward the door. "Don't worry. I'll be telling him soon."

"No rush." Nell held up one hand. "I mean, take your time—until you're sure."

"I am sure," Misty said, weirdly not feeling it.

She totally wasn't having second thoughts.

Or third ones.

Or fourth ones, either.

She was just beaten down from having to defend her position so hard. Lucas had probably been right to encourage her to sleep on things. He was always so wise. When she woke up tomorrow, she'd know better what to do about approaching her parents and then reaching out to Aidan. Meanwhile, she was done with discussing the situation today.

With Nell, Mei-Lin. Lucas. Everyone.

"Sweetheart?" her mom said, when she reached into the refrigerator. "Are you all right?"

"Yeah," Misty said, somewhat distracted. The turkey on rye she'd slapped together didn't look nearly as tasty as the delicious wraps and subs that Nell used to fix her, but it was good that Nell had stopped making lunches for her and Charlotte. Misty and Charlotte weren't kids any longer. Like they'd been when their parents had needed to go to work super early, leaving Nell in charge of getting them all on the school bus.

She peered at her mom. "Why?"

Her parents frowned at each other and then her dad asked, "This isn't about Aidan?"

Misty forced a little laugh, knowing she'd have to tell them soon. But not yet. She needed to get everything straight in her head and her heart first. "Nope! I'm just…" She pulled her sandwich from the fridge. "Thinking about my future."

"Thinking's always good," her mom said.

Her dad's light eyes twinkled. "If you'd like to talk? About those plans?"

"No thanks," she said. "I'm good."

Misty closed the refrigerator door, deciding to eat outdoors in the sunshine. There was a spot on a low stone wall beside the shop that overlooked the ocean. It was her favorite place to ponder things of importance. And you couldn't get any more important than a decision that would impact her whole life.

• • •

At long last alone, Misty was grateful for the calm and quiet. She shut her eyes and turned her face toward the sky. Warmth bathed her cheeks and wind swept her bangs aside, sifting through her ponytail behind her, which swished to and fro like the tail of a fluttering kite. She held her arms out at her sides, her palms kissed by the sun.

Late morning in early September was still warm enough in this part of coastal Maine, though she appreciated the loose knubby sweater she'd tugged on over her T-shirt and jeans.

Misty loved walking barefoot along the beach in

summertime and collecting seashells all year through. Fall was a great time for shell collecting around here, but surely there were seashells and beaches in England. They just might not be as beautifully familiar. And people probably talked differently. She'd have to get used to spending time at the "seaside" rather than the beach. But whatever. She'd manage.

She licked her lips, tasting the salty sea air and letting the seagulls' calls carry her out with the tide. Now she was going to marry Aidan Strong, a man she hadn't set eyes on in twenty years. But she was cool. She was centered.

In control.

Yes, that.

Five years would go by in a flash, then she'd return to Majestic. Or maybe move somewhere else and put her new skills and training to work.

She wouldn't miss her sisters that much.

Or Mei-Lin.

Or her parents.

She'd miss Lucas least of all.

Tears bubbled up inside her, stinging her throat, and Misty opened her eyes.

She was lying to everyone and she knew it.

Including herself.

CHAPTER THREE

The next morning, Lucas approached the outskirts of town on Highway One and jammed on his brakes. His pickup fishtailed sideways, then dragged to a halt.

An enormous billboard stood illuminated against the purplish dawn. Misty's pretty hazel eyes stared down at him, as she beamed at the camera with one hand on her hip, a green rose stem barely visible on the underside of her wrist. Judging by her new purple highlights, the pic was taken yesterday.

A light bulb went off in his brain.

What a *sneak*.

Misty had wrinkled up her nose but then she'd participated in Charlotte's impromptu photo session anyway. Putting on her cutest ham face. Having *absolutely no idea* Charlotte would put her image on a billboard for anyone driving by to see. He stared at the slogan written in huge swirly letters to the right of her head.

Marry me: Misty!
Request for Proposals by 9/30
Find me at Bearberry Brews!

The text was all wrapped up in a bright pink lipstick-looking heart.

Lucas's head pounded at the memory from yesterday at the café.

"What are you going to do with that, Charlotte?" Misty had asked her.

Charlotte had shrugged and said something about a little surprise.

Nuh-uh. This was a big one. Huge.

Charlotte was the marketing person with ties to all the advertisers in town, but overnight seemed awfully fast for a new advertisement to be commissioned and put up. He thought hard trying to recall what was on this billboard previously.

Oh yeah. He stared up at it and remembered. A pitch for Grant's camping store, Blue Sky Adventures. Which meant…

No way. But yeah. Grant was in on this, too. He had to be. Because Nell had probably convinced him to go along with letting Charlotte supplant the space. She'd probably sweet-talked somebody into erecting this billboard late last night. Bearberry Brews had done billboard ads before, so she undoubtedly had connections.

She was also good with Photoshop. Obviously. Misty had been standing at the register when she'd snapped this pic, and clearly not on a beach with a fancy wedding altar erected behind her and in front of the ocean. There were even two rows of white folding chairs in the background like wedding guests were expected at any second, and loads of flowers were everywhere. He was kind of surprised Charlotte hadn't given Misty a bridal bouquet.

Lucas groaned and ran his hands through his hair while dark clouds hovered in the sky. It was doubtful Misty had seen this since she lived in town and the ad was brand-spanking new. He snagged his cell off his console, determined to warn her. Then his phone *dinged*.

It was too late.

Lucas, help!

Weird crowd at Bearberry Brews!

He didn't doubt it. Nothing this exciting ever happened in Majestic. Suddenly their hometown girl was a Highway One celebrity. Maybe they could find a way to get this billboard taken down before it did too much damage.

He wrote right back.

Where's Charlotte?

She and Nell bolted for the storeroom.

Chickens.

Your folks?

Not here yet.

Raindrops speckled his windshield, then came down harder.

He grumbled and flipped on his windshield wipers.

On my way.

Keep things locked up tight.

• • •

Misty pounded on the storeroom door. She'd had to enter Bearberry Brews through the back alley due to the strange commotion out front. Unfamiliar vehicles and people clogged the drizzly cobblestone street. Not entirely true. She *had* recognized someone. The short brunette with the leopard print umbrella was Allison Highsmith, the woman who wrote the dating blog. *Two* someones. The guy in the weird floppy hat and trench coat was Darcy Fitzpatrick from *The Seaside Daily*. *Nooo.* Had her sisters squealed to the paper about her marrying Aidan already?

They might have at least asked her first.

"Charlotte! Nell!" She banged on the door again, trying its knob. Since the storeroom didn't lock from the inside, someone was holding onto it. "What's going on? Let me in!"

Her sisters had been strangely secretive yesterday afternoon. Mei-Lin had acted off, too.

That couldn't have had to do with this, could it?

She heard a muffled discussion, then the door cracked open. It was Nell and her hand was on the knob. Who knew she was so strong? Maybe she'd buffed up from all that wood chopping at Grant's cabin.

"Sorry. We panicked." She got that motherly look in her eyes. "Are you okay?"

Misty huffed. "Want to tell me why those people are here? Including Darcy from *The Seaside Daily*?"

Charlotte peered over her shoulder across the service area and out the glass front door. "Oh *yeah*. That is him. Good deal." She sent him a wave and Misty grabbed her wrist.

"Isn't that Allison Highsmith?" Nell asked. "The one with the dating blog?"

"It is," Charlotte said, wide-eyed. "She's been bugging me for a scoop on our contest ever since the whole Aidan thing broke and you went off to Grant's cabin with him."

Nell's face flushed. "I wouldn't mind sharing my story."

"Well, I'm not sharing mine," Misty said. "Besides which." She squared her shoulders and dropped Charlotte's wrist. "There is no contest any longer. Game over. Remember? I called it yesterday."

"Well, they didn't get the memo," Nell said, staring at the street. A couple of guys stood by Allison and Darcy, both strangers in town as far as Misty knew, and she knew pretty much every person in Majestic. One of them appeared businesslike and the other wore a Stetson.

Wait.

Who was the old man with a mustache teetering his way up to their shop? He held a bouquet in one hand and wielded a cane with the other. A slew of raindrops speckled the shoulders of his raincoat and silvery gray hair.

"Mr. *Mulroney*?" Nell asked on a gasp.

Matthew Mulroney was as sweet as the day was long, but he was also ancient. He'd run the Majestic B&B with his late wife Eugenia for years before she passed. He still operated it on his own, in deference to her memory, but had cut way back on accepting reservations and was advertising for extra help.

"He must be pushing eighty," Charlotte said. "But isn't that adorable?" She winced, and Misty knew that she'd caught her red-handed at something.

"What did you do?" She advanced on her sister. "Does this have anything to do with that photo you took yesterday?"

Charlotte took a giant step backward. "I'm thinking…yes?"

Nell raised a hand. "Let's consider the positives—"

"Positives?" Misty asked aghast. "Like what?"

Charlotte tugged on the power crystal that she claimed kept her focused and calm, but that nervous habit of hers never seemed to calm her. "I never thought things would happen this fast. But okay. Fast is good. Given that there are less than three weeks left before Mom and Dad's loan comes due, press coverage couldn't hurt."

"Where did you post that photo, Charlotte?" Misty asked, her anxiety growing. "Somewhere online?"

"Not online, no."

"She was a lot more innovative than that," Nell said. "And a little old-school to tell you the truth. But, you know, retro is good."

"What did you *do*, Charlotte?"

"I, um…advertised."

Advertised? Misty's pulse skittered nervously. "How?"

"She put up a billboard." Nell nodded like this had been a very good idea. "North end of town."

That's what Charlotte had used that photo for? *Nooo.* No, no, no. "Saying what?"

Nell's strawberry-blond eyebrows perked up. "Marry me: Misty!"

Misty goggled at the group. This was so much worse than she thought. "I've got a 'Marry me: Misty!' personal ad up on Highway One?"

Nell nodded. "And it's drawing traffic from the looks of things."

"A little slow at first," Charlotte said. "But it will pick up."

"No." Misty set her chin. "It's going to stop. Now!"

"What the hey is going on?" Mei-Lin appeared in the doorway and took one look at Misty. "The billboard? Oh no." She glanced at Charlotte, who grinned tightly while Nell bit her lip. "Or maybe, yay?"

Misty sighed. "I can't believe you were in on this, too. Seriously, Mei-Lin?"

Mei-Lin gripped her shoulders. "A loveless marriage, Misty? No. That's not what I want for my best friend. You deserve more than that. The real deal."

Misty's head swam. How had Mei-Lin signed on for this? How had her sisters come up with it in the first place? Okay, it had to have been Charlotte who thought this up. Charlotte and her big marketing ideas! What was Misty supposed to be? The café's special of the day?

"Ladies?"

Lucas stood on the threshold. Thank goodness he was here.

He walked into the storeroom, appearing somehow less shell-shocked than the rest of them. "My sisters and Mei-Lin have done something crazy," Misty said on a breath.

Lucas flashed his cell at the group. "I saw." A pic of the billboard filled the screen.

Misty's eyes nearly popped out of her head.

How had Charlotte done that? A bridal altar, really? And that sand was so white, definitely not like a rocky beach in Maine. Not with that turquoise water in the background. The backdrop resembled Bermuda or somewhere farther away than that. Maybe Fiji?

"Hey! It looks pretty good." Charlotte preened and Misty wanted to kick her.

Mei-Lin smiled at Misty. "You do look great, it's true."

"Love the lipstick heart," Nell said. "Nice touch."

Lucas sighed and addressed Misty. "So, what? Want me to tell those folks to go away?"

"*Yes*," Misty said at the same time her sisters and Mei-Lin said "no."

"I mean, think about it, Misty," Charlotte urged. "Maybe the media coverage will help? You said you'd exhausted your man possibilities in Majestic. So what better way to bring in more candidates?"

Misty *tsk*ed. "You mean strangers?"

"They're not all strangers." Nell peered past Lucas's shoulder. "Look! Here comes Jordan!" she said, mentioning her fiancé's handsome friend and camping store manager.

Lucas shoved his hands in his jeans pockets. "I'm pretty sure he's headed this way for a coffee."

Misty scrunched up her face at her sisters and Mei-Lin. Could they really believe they were helping with this?

She sighed.

Yeah, they probably did.

Lucas thumbed toward the street. "Just say the word."

He was such a good guy. Her hero. "Word!"

Charlotte's brow furrowed. "Let's be reasonable. Maybe if you gave one live interview it wouldn't hurt? It could run on social."

Misty rolled her eyes. "Awesome way to let Mom and Dad know the Aidan bet is not off. Let them find out on Facebook."

"They were going to know that anyway when you

announced going to London."

Misty jutted out her chin. "I wasn't planning to tell them until everything was sure."

"Okay then." Charlotte held a stubborn gleam in her eyes. "Then let's cut a deal. We'll say no to the media but yes to the guys."

"She's right," Nell chimed in. Then she glanced at Charlotte, playing the diplomat. "But Misty's right, too. We don't want too much publicity yet—"

"Yet? I'm on a billboard!" Misty fumed at Charlotte. "Which is coming right back down."

"Let's not be hasty." Charlotte held up her hand. "Maybe we should—"

"Take names!" Mei-Lin jumped in. "Develop a roster. Then you can take your time and look through them."

"I'm not looking through anything," Misty said as Mr. Mulroney knocked on the café's front door.

Lucas surveyed the group, his gaze landing on Misty's. "Should I—"

Misty blew out a breath. "Yes. Please. Go and see what he wants." Because he seriously couldn't be there for her. She shuddered at the knowledge that all of the others were, though.

And that there were likely more of them on the way.

• • •

Lucas walked to the door and cautiously cracked it open. Phone cameras flashed.

He held up his hands. "Sorry folks! No news here!"

"But—the bet!" Allison said. "I guess it's back on?"

Darcy inched closer, holding up his smart phone. "We heard the deal got canned when Nell and Grant became engaged?"

Allison held up her cell phone, too, clearly filming. "Yeah," she said. "But it's pretty obviously not." She sent a combative look at Darcy and tried to move past him but he blocked her approach with his elbow, edging nearer himself.

"Can I get a statement? Maybe even an exclusive?"

"Sorry, Darcy," Allison said sourly, scooting in front of him. "I've got dibs." She and Darcy had dated in high school, and it hadn't ended well. It didn't take a genius to detect the bad blood between them. Each still blamed the other for their subsequently dismal dating histories and divorces. That was a long way in the past to reach back for excuses. Fifteen plus years.

"I'd like to see Misty," a man in a tweed jacket announced. "Is she here?"

The cowboy tipped his hat. "Begging your pardon, fella, but I'm ahead of you."

Word was spreading like wildfire about that billboard. And here came the town's most gossipy couple to pour fuel on the flames. The McIntyres scuttled down the sidewalk wearing cable-knit sweaters and sharing a huge golf umbrella. They pushed their way past Jordan, who goggled at the scene.

"Does Misty's mother know she's done this?" Mrs. McIntyre asked Lucas stodgily. "Because I doubt that she'd approve."

Jordan raised his eyebrows at Lucas, who sent him a signal about telling him later, while shielding himself with the door. He tried to close it, but Mr.

Mulroney shoved his bouquet through the opening.

"Please give these to Misty. From me."

"Uh. Sure." Lucas took the flowers, wondering what *that* was about. Mulroney couldn't really believe himself to be in the running? Darcy and Allison hopped up on the stoop on either side of Mulroney. Before they could speak, Lucas shut and locked the door. Beyond them, Jordan pulled up the hood of his rain jacket and strode away.

Lucas handed Misty the pretty bouquet of sunflowers. Each shiny yellow petal held an assortment of raindrops that glistened like dew, and a damp red ribbon was tied around the cellophane and tissue paper cradling the flowers' stems. "Mr. Mulroney asked me to give these to you."

Misty gave him a weird side-eye. "That was nice of him, but why?"

"He is a little old for her," Nell told Charlotte.

Charlotte tugged on her crystal. "Beggars can't be choosers."

Mei-Lin leaped in. "Misty's not a beggar!"

"Wait," Nell said, pointing to the flowers. "Look. There's a notecard attached."

Misty opened the rain-splattered envelope and withdrew the notecard from inside it. Her sigh signaled relief. "Looks like Mr. Mulroney doesn't want me for himself. The sweet older guy was only trying to help me."

"Well," Mei-Lin said. "What does it say?"

Misty recited the message out loud. "True love can't be found on a billboard."

Lucas could have told them that. Then again, nobody asked him.

Charlotte wrapped an arm around Nell's shoulders like the two of them were a team. And they seemed to be. Teaming up on Misty. "Mr. Mulroney means well," Charlotte said, "but he's mistaken."

"Charlotte's right," Nell said, trying to sound upbeat about it. "You never know."

Lucas attempted being the voice of reason. "Mr. Mulroney may have a point. The billboard move was a little extreme." A muscle in his cheek flinched and he set his jaw. "Don't you think?" He stared at Charlotte, then at Nell, and finally at Mei-Lin, waiting for them to apologize, or back down. Something. But they didn't.

Charlotte crossed her arms. "Extreme times call for extreme measures."

Nell nodded like she agreed. Still, her face was beet red.

Mei-Lin gritted her teeth and glanced at Lucas while sheepishly avoiding Misty's gaze. "It's only because we love her." She gave Misty a pouty-frown and mouthed, "*We love you.*"

Misty sighed and rubbed a hand over her heart. "I know." Then Misty turned her big hazel eyes on Lucas and his pulse spiked. From the way she was looking at him, she was hoping he would do something but he had no idea what.

That billboard going up was only one part of this very messy equation involving Misty maybe marrying Aidan. That thought had been hard enough for Lucas to take. But the town suddenly teeming with lots of new groom-to-be choices? That was really too much. Lucas didn't like this new turn of events one bit, and from the freaked-out expression on Misty's face, she didn't like it, either. She seemed completely over-whelmed.

A motorcycle puttered down the street, slowing in front of Bearberry Brews. Then a service truck appeared. A guy stepped out of it and he and the motorcycle dude had a short chitchat with the cowboy and the businessman under the awning in front of their shop. Allison and Darcy joined their circle, gesturing as they spoke and rain dribbled off the sides of Allison's umbrella. They appeared to be explaining things to the newcomers, and preparing to disperse.

The cowboy tipped his hat and Charlotte hurried toward the door. "Maybe I should take some names before anybody leaves."

"For yourself, Charlotte?" Misty asked, as Charlotte grabbed her rain jacket off a hook. "Because I'm all good."

"Stop that, Misty." Charlotte shrugged into her rain jacket. "You're *not* going to marry Aidan, and you know it."

Lucas never paid much attention to signs of any kind, unlike Mei-Lin and Nell, who were always going on about them at work. If two people showed up accidentally at the same place and time, or liked the same music, or had similar tastes or hobbies, those were clear "signs" they were meant to be together. But all of those sounded like silly superstitions or coincidental occurrences to him. He was far too practical to view the world that way.

But this situation…if there'd ever been a time for a sign, that billboard going up was it. And he was reading its signals loud and clear. He had to do something to help Misty. No one else was available. Not even Mei-Lin, who'd clearly gone along with her sisters in this scheme.

"You're right," Lucas said. "She's not." Not if he had anything to say about it. And he hoped he would, if Misty would only listen. He hadn't totally had her ear before, but he could try again. Maybe, by what? Stepping in? Now, there was an idea. His neck warmed at the thought of him playing her boyfriend. Just temporarily to get her sisters off her back, and to ward off those billboard guys.

She'd like that, wouldn't she? Probably even thank him? The ruse would also buy him the precious time he needed to prove to Misty, once and for all, that he could actually be the guy for her. That she didn't need to go hunting for rainbows elsewhere, when she might have a buried treasure right in her own backyard. He'd certainly treasured her for an eternity. Was it too much to hope she might change her mind about how she viewed him? Lucas saw two things very clearly. One, he needed to get Misty out of her current fix, and two, he owed it to himself and his own sorry heart to pull out all stops and really give things with Misty a try.

Misty frowned, like she was trying to read his mind, but couldn't. "Right," she told the others. "I'm *not* marrying Aidan because…" She widened her eyes at Lucas.

Lucas cemented his decision then and there. "Misty's already seeing someone."

She sucked in a gasp, getting it. "Yeah!" Pink spots formed on her cheeks. "I am."

Lucas broke a sweat. He hoped he was doing the right thing. For Misty. For himself. For the two of them. Finally giving them their chance.

"Seeing someone?" Nell's face was a blank page and so were the others'.

Lucas reached for Misty's hand and she squeezed his, holding on extra tight. At least that was comforting, and felt really good and right. Him and Misty together. Yes, they'd get through this, and somehow— oh how he hoped, hoped, hoped—would wind up together on the other side.

"Yeah," Lucas said, grinning at Mei-Lin and Misty's sisters. "Me."

CHAPTER FOUR

Misty's breath hitched. He...we...*what*? She'd had no idea where Lucas was going with this until he'd said it. It made perfect sense, though. If her sisters thought she was involved with Lucas, they'd lay off about the billboard guys, and maybe pull back on discussions about Aidan for a bit, while she got her head together on all of this.

Lucas's grasp was reassuring and strong, a lifeline on choppy seas. Just seconds ago she'd been about to go under, drowning in the billboard situation and her hidden reservations about going to London. Now, thanks to steadfast Lucas, she'd been granted a reprieve. She held his hand tighter, like she was hanging on for dear life, and in some ways she was. Her life had never felt so totally mixed up until now. But she'd fix it. Having Lucas right there beside her gave her that much more confidence she would. And, with his sound support and advice, she'd fix things in the right way.

"It's true," she said solidly. "We made things official last night."

Nell fanned her face with her hand, and Mei-Lin's mouth fell open.

Charlotte blinked. "Wow," she said to Lucas. "You and Misty? Who knew?"

Lucas kissed the back of Misty's hand. "Yeah," he said. "Isn't it great?" Goose bumps skittered up her arm, then she tingled all over. No wait. This was

Lucas. Friend-zone Lucas. She couldn't…wouldn't…
even think of him that way. Their friendship meant
too much to her for her to ever risk it. Those were
probably just tingles of relief. No. Not probably.
Definitely. He was only doing this to help her. He really did have her back. One hundred percent.

Nell's shoulders sank. "Oh hon, why didn't you tell
us?" She didn't sound mad, just disappointed not to
have been in on the big secret. That made two of
them. When had Lucas decided this? It had to have
been spur of the moment, and maybe because he felt
his hand had been forced by this new billboard blast.
He'd already made it clear he didn't want Misty moving to London. It was just as evident he wasn't thrilled
about her dating random guys brought in by a
Highway One sign. Neither was she.

Misty's spirits lifted further. Because seriously, this
fake relationship ruse presented a great opportunity.
A way to keep her sisters from insisting she check out
Aidan alternatives while she figured things out. She
was still conflicted over RISD. Part of her really
wanted to go, but it seemed like such a longshot for
her to get in. And even if she did, how could she
abandon Bearberry Brews if Charlotte was the one
leaving to marry Aidan? "Er, there hasn't been time,"
Misty said. Heat swept her cheeks. "It's all so new."

Charlotte glanced at the street. "Wait! People are
leaving."

Mei-Lin grabbed a notepad and a pen. "Maybe we
should get some names like you said." She tried not
to look at Misty. "You know, as backups."

Misty gaped at her. "Way to have faith in our relationship, Mei-Lin."

Charlotte eyed the couple suspiciously. "Your very new relationship. Hmm."

Lucas slid his arm around Misty's waist and tugged her in close. His body heat seeped into hers and warmth pooled in her belly. Wait. What was that?

No. They were friends. *Friends*.

She was just all mixed up from this rapid turn of events.

One day she's marrying Aidan. Reluctantly, but still. The next, Charlotte's erected some huge billboard ad making Misty look desperate for a groom. And she *was* desperate. Just not to get legitimately married. Being seriously involved for real was the last thing that she wanted. Opening up her heart? Making herself vulnerable? No deal. That's why the in-name-only marriage to Aidan had looked so good. Until it didn't. What she wanted most of all right at this moment was to climb out of this big black hole she'd fallen into and obtain some clarity and light. Maybe, with Lucas's help, she'd get there.

"So, then." Charlotte crossed her arms. "It's not like you're engaged?"

"Not yet," Lucas replied smoothly. "But by the end of this month? Who knows?"

"That's giving Charlotte a lot of leeway," Mei-Lin pointed out. "To lock down a husband first."

Nell raised her hand. "True love and a husband! It has to be real."

"Exactly," Lucas said. "Certifiable. Which is why—" He held Misty closer. "I'm moving into her place."

"What?" Misty tried not to sound surprised. "I mean, yeah." She swallowed hard. "We talked about it."

His gray eyes twinkled. "We need some one-on-one time to be extra sure. That's why we're shacking up together."

Misty slapped his chest. "Platonically!"

"Not too platonically, though," he told the others. "We're just saving certain parts until after marriage."

"It's just for a week!" Misty added. As much as she appreciated Lucas's gallant gesture, she couldn't put him in this position forever. Half the month would be gone by then, and if Misty was biting the bullet and moving to London, she'd need to go ahead and make herself do it. She was also supposed to hear from the admissions committee sometime this week. So once she knew more about school, she'd be better able to weigh her options.

He studied her, attempting to read her eyes.

Misty arched her eyebrows and he got it.

"Uh, yeah," Lucas told the others. "A week is what we agreed on. By the end of that, we'll know what's what."

Misty grinned. "And whether or not we're really meant for each other."

The whole billboard thing should have died down by then, too. Hopefully. In the meantime, maybe having Lucas at her apartment wasn't such a bad idea, just in case one of those dudes decided to track her down and show up.

"Well, Lucas. Misty." Nell appeared lost. "I don't know what to say."

Misty shrugged. "Congrats maybe?"

"Sure," Charlotte said. Doubt tugged at the corners of her mouth, causing fine wrinkles to appear and making her look like their mom, but younger.

"Congrats."

Lucas's gaze snagged on Mei-Lin's notepad. "Want me to come with you?"

"That's okay," she said, glancing at Charlotte. "We've got it." She put on her raincoat too.

As they left, Nell shouted after them. "Maybe see if anyone wants coffee?"

When Misty stared at her she said, "What? It's not like we can't use the business."

Charlotte opened the front door and waved her arms, capturing people's attention. "I'm sorry, everyone! It's over! Misty's already spoken for!"

The guy in the Stetson spoke up. "What?" The rain behind him pitter-pattered on the sidewalk as the man beside him in a reflective vest stepped forward. "Already?"

A burly guy with a tattoo sleeve held a motorcycle helmet under one arm. "Wait. That billboard just went up last night."

The man in the tweed jacket and square glasses nodded. "He's right."

"Yeah, sorry." Mei-Lin winced. "But we will be taking names for the waitlist."

This seemed to appease them somewhat, even though they grumbled.

Allison and Darcy hurried in their direction. They'd been discussing something below the Mariner's Restaurant's overhang, but now sensed new action.

Darcy reached Charlotte first and shook out his dripping hat. "So what's the story?"

Allison steadied her umbrella with one elbow and started recording with her phone again. "And who's the guy?"

• • •

By the time her parents arrived at the café twenty minutes later, the street had cleared.

"You all got to work early," their mom said with a smile.

Their dad removed his fleece. "Top of the morning to everyone."

They all said their hellos then their mom spotted Mei-Lin's notepad.

"Inventory?"

Mei-Lin picked the notepad up and held it against her chest. "Uh, yeah."

Their dad shook his head. "We've got electronics for that. Lucas will show you."

Mei-Lin grinned tightly. "Sure."

Misty held back a giggle. Now that the moment had passed, it seemed so ridiculous. She was still annoyed with her sisters and Mei-Lin for concocting the billboard scheme, but she couldn't stay mad at any of them. She knew they'd only meant well. Since Lucas had gotten her off the hook from seeing any of those guys, she felt even better.

"Well, I'm glad that part's over," Misty said, happy that her parents hadn't been the wiser about what had gone on with the billboard and those early morning visitors. Maybe if Charlotte could get the billboard taken down quickly—and Mrs. McIntyre didn't blab—they'd never have to know. Charlotte and Mei-Lin hadn't told anyone who Misty was involved with. They'd just said it was someone she'd known for a while, and who had stepped forward.

Which was actually true. Just not in the way those people probably assumed.

Their parents walked into the kitchen and Mei-Lin peeked at her notepad and her dark eyes twinkled. "We did get a good start on a list, though."

Lucas laid his hand on Misty's arm and spoke in low tones. "So?" he rasped quietly. "How are we going to play this?"

"Let's talk after work," she whispered back. It was too risky to discuss things here with so many busybodies around.

"I can drive you home."

"Sounds good."

Lucas disappeared into the kitchen and Nell approached Misty, handing her an envelope.

"What's this?" Misty asked. She opened its flap and withdrew a sheet of paper. It was an itemized list of some kind, numbered from one to ten, and all typed up professionally. Not handwritten.

Charlotte was at Nell's side. "Your dating to-do list."

"My what?" Misty studied both her sisters, then Mei-Lin joined them, strapping on her apron.

"Your make or break list," Mei-Lin whispered. "For making a go of things."

"Making? A? Go?"

"Yeah," Nell said. "We thought you could use it with those billboard guys, but since they seem to be out of the picture..." She shrugged. "Now you can use it with Lucas."

"I don't need instructions"—Misty's nose twitched—"on how to date anybody."

"It's not that," Mei-Lin said. "We want you to be

sure that the guy that you settle on is your one."

"Right-o," Nell said. "No faking it."

"Oh sure." Misty scoffed at her oldest sister. "Like you faked things with Grant?"

"We didn't fake things," Nell said, sounding indignant. "It was a battle of wits till the end. Wills, too."

"Yeah, but." Charlotte stuck out her chin. "While you were up at his cabin, you did kind of tell the whole town that you and he were engaged."

"No, Charlotte." Nell's eyes flashed. "You and Misty did that. You took what I said and misconstrued it."

Charlotte laughed. "Fine if that's what you want to believe."

"The important thing is," Nell said in placating tones, "everything came out okay." She examined her engagement ring, waxing dreamy. "I mean, really, really super."

Mei-Lin cleared her throat as if to remind them. "The list?"

"Oh yeah." Charlotte nudged Nell, who nodded, and Misty shook out the page.

Top Ten Ways to Prove that He's Your One

"The idea is," Nell said, "you go through each dating idea with the guy you pick. In this case, Lucas."

"If you work your way through the list and feel nothing," Charlotte said, "then nothing is there. Things aren't meant to be."

Mei-Lin slid back her glasses. "Because it will be absolutely impossible to do all these romantic things with the person meant for you without the two of you falling in love."

"And if you do fall in love." Nell grinned triumphantly. "Then, you'll have found your one."

Seriously. Like it was that easy.

"So, what if this doesn't work?" Misty asked.

"Then you go on to the next guy," Charlotte said. "Then the next."

"But where—"

Mei-Lin cocked her chin toward the notepad she'd set on the counter.

"Oh." Misty inhaled deeply.

Okay. Here we go.

1. Ride bikes to Lookout Point.

That sounded harmless enough.
Good way to get started.

2. Beach picnic.

No problem.

3. Share a sunset.

Aww.

4. Stargazing at midnight.

Hey, these were easy! Except Misty never ever stayed up until midnight. But just this once, she could wing it.

Wait.

5. Get physical.

"Physical, as in—"

Nell laughed. "As far as you want to take it, Misty."

Mei-Lin jumped in. "Just exercise together or something."

"Sure," Charlotte teased. "Break a sweat."

6. *Discover one shared passion.*

She stared at her sisters and Mei-Lin.

"Six is a little vague."

"You'll know it when you find it," Nell said.

"And if you don't?" Charlotte warned.

Mei-Lin frowned. "Maybe you take that as a sign."

"Yeah." Nell's eyebrows knitted together. "A bad sign that things aren't really meant to be. Come on, Misty. If you're going to marry the man, you've got to have some shared interests, or at least one important one."

Okay, fine. She could try.

As long as it didn't involve sweating.

7. *Slow dancing in the rain.*

Now, that sounded romantic.

"Whose idea was seven?"

Two pink dots formed on Charlotte's cheeks.

"Whoa, Charlotte," Misty said. "Didn't know you had it in you."

"What?" Charlotte puffed out her chest. "Romantic thoughts?"

"We all have them," Nell said.

Mei-Lin giggled. "Yeah, some of us more than others."

"Maybe some of us just aren't as vocal about it." Charlotte smirked.

8. Get frisky in the kitchen.

"Frisky? What?"

"Do something fun together," Nell urged.

Mei-Lin nodded. "Like couple's cooking."

"That's not 'frisky.'" Charlotte chuckled. "Unless you're cooking *au naturel*."

Misty flushed at the insinuation.

Her and Lucas in nothing but aprons?

Nope!

She focused hard on the list so she could stop thinking about that because, honestly, Lucas was nicely built. He wasn't a big guy but he was solid.

He also had pretty adorable curly hair and killer gray eyes.

Plus—just once or twice—she had caught a glimpse of his very cute butt in jeans.

Hang on. She wasn't helping herself.

Next!

9. Making out at the movies.

Misty's chin jerked up. Uh, no. That wasn't her.

"I don't know about the movies thing."

Mei-Lin met her eyes. "You've got to give things a try, Misty. A real try."

"She's right," Charlotte said. "You can't marry a guy without kissing him."

"Yes, but seriously?" Misty recoiled slightly. "Does it have to involve PDA?"

"Everyone in town should know that you're a couple," Charlotte said.

"Yeah, well, fine." Misty shifted on her feet. "But maybe not that explicitly."

Mei-Lin wiggled her eyebrows. "Don't knock it until you try it."

Misty gasped. "Mei-Lin! You'd never."

Mei-Lin chuckled. "Maybe I wouldn't. Doesn't mean that you can't, though."

She tapped on the page, prodding Misty to finish.

10. Breakfast in bed.

"Oh, no. No, no. And no."

"It only says breakfast," Nell pointed out. "Things don't have to get racy."

Mei-Lin grinned. "Unless you want them to."

At least she wouldn't have to worry about wanting to with Lucas. She'd never thought about him in that way. She recalled the intense look in his eyes when he'd tried to warn her off of marrying Aidan in the storeroom, and a weird flutter settled in her belly. Her and Lucas? No.

She shut her eyes trying not to think about it, but then she did.

The two of them in their jammies, snuggled down under the covers. He was whispering something tender and she felt all happy and warm inside. At least that was a cleaner image than the aprons-only-in-the-kitchen one.

Misty's eyes flew open.

Wow. That was weird.

"You okay?" asked Mei-Lin.

Nell leaned toward her. "Keep reading. There's one more."

"I thought this was a 'Top Ten' list?"

Mei-Lin grinned. "Extra credit."

11. Spill your biggest secret.

Ahh. No. Misty didn't keep secrets from Lucas.

Okay, except for about RISD, and a few other things. None of which she was prepared to tell him, especially since their "relationship" was just pretend.

"What's the value of number eleven?"

"You shouldn't marry someone without really knowing them," Nell said. "Inside and out."

"Which means," Mei-Lin added, "you're privy to their dreams and they know about yours." She sent Misty a pointed look. "If it's important to you, it should be important to the other person."

"Exactly," Charlotte said. "Whether that secret is personal or professional doesn't matter. What matters is you've got to trust your partner enough to share it, because if you don't—"

"You might not be fated," Mei-Lin said.

"And you'll want to be sure." Nell rubbed Misty's arm. "That you're written in the stars."

"Fine." She folded the list and shoved it in her pocket. If playing along would get them off her back for a week, it would be worth it. But she'd have to make an actual effort with most of these things because her sisters would likely demand proof she was going through the list. Like with photos or texts or something. "I'll do it."

"Lucas will have to participate, of course." Mei-Lin grinned smugly. "Not that I think he'd mind."

Nell glanced toward the kitchen and giggled. "No. He'll be all-in."

Charlotte tilted her head in thought. "If you're going to do all that in a week, though that could take a lot of time."

Nell gasped. "You're right. She can't come in." She turned to Misty. "Neither can Lucas."

Misty's heart thumped. "We can't do that and leave you short-staffed."

"You must do that," Mei-Lin insisted. "Charlotte and Nell are right."

"But how will you get by?"

"I can help out during business hours here," Nell offered, "and finish up bookkeeping stuff at home."

Misty's heart went out to her for her kindness but no. "I can't ask you to do that."

"You're not asking, I'm volunteering." Nell flipped back her curls. "Besides which, you and Charlotte did the same for me. Covered while I was in the mountains with Grant."

"Yeah," Misty replied. "But with Lucas out, too, you'll be doubly short-staffed."

"Not if we call in Sean!" Charlotte said, having the idea.

"That's right," Mei-Lin agreed. "He's always looking for odd jobs and ways to fill in. He's barista'd for us before."

"Which means I can do Lucas's job temporarily." Charlotte grinned. "I always did have a managerial spirit."

"If by managerial, you mean bossy…" Nell rolled her eyes and everybody laughed, including Charlotte because she knew it was true.

"So great!" Charlotte said. "It's all settled? You and Lucas will take this coming week off to work on the list?"

Misty felt awkward about not coming in. "Maybe

we could still do that and come in half days?"

"No days," Charlotte said firmly. "As the fill-in café manager, I make the schedule."

Take-charge Charlotte. Maybe she really *was* suited to the role.

"I'll help out extra, too," Mei-Lin said. "Whatever it takes for you to make *all* the right decisions, Misty."

Charlotte scanned their faces. "So, who's going to tell Lucas?"

"About the list and time off?" asked Misty. "I think that should be me."

Nell grinned from ear to ear. "Super."

Lucas came back out of the kitchen to unlock the front door, and they all got busy at their respective stations, pretending that they hadn't been talking about anything in particular, least of all him.

Mei-Lin turned to Misty once Nell and Charlotte had stepped away. "Is there a reason you didn't tell me?" she whispered. "About you and Lucas?"

Misty avoided Mei-Lin's eyes. "Like I said. This all happened really quickly."

That was the understatement of the year.

Mei-Lin got that sage twist to her lips that said she didn't buy it. "You know what I think?"

"No. But I suppose you're going to tell me."

"I think this sudden new 'relationship' has got something to do with that billboard going up."

Misty sighed. "I seriously can't believe you were in on that."

"For your own good. Look, Misty, I'm not trying to tell you what to do—"

"Oh yes you are."

Mei-Lin chuckled. "Okay, just a little." She made a

pinching motion with her thumb and forefinger. "I'm just worried about you, that's all." Her face fell. "I know you had hopes. Dreams."

"Who says I still don't have those?"

Mei-Lin whispered, "So RISD?"

"Shh! It's still on the table, at least until I hear one way or another."

"Well good. That's good. But what about Lucas?"

"What about him?" She was dying to tell Mei-Lin the truth about the fake boyfriend deal. She'd always told Mei-Lin everything and it was so hard not telling her this.

Mei-Lin studied her a long moment, then understanding lit up her eyes. "Wait. One. Second. This whole thing with Lucas?" She dropped her voice further. "It's not even real? Oh my gosh!"

Misty hushed her again. "Not a word to my sisters, okay? I really, really need time, Mei-Lin. Time to get things sorted. In my heart and in my head."

"You don't really want to go to London, do you?"

"I don't want to not go."

Mei-Lin screwed up her face. "What's that mean?"

Misty bit her lip. "I feel so mixed up about everything. But thanks to you and my sisters—and Lucas—I'll have the next seven days to clarify my choices."

Mei-Lin's grin sparkled. "And if you get into RISD?"

That was almost too wonderful to think about. Getting into design school would be her dream. And also add one more complication to her currently complicated existence. "Let's just take this one step at a time."

Mei-Lin squealed quietly and hugged her. "Still.

That would be so fab!" An instant later she frowned. "Okay," she said, pulling back. "What about those billboard guys? More will likely trickle in before that billboard comes down. Even if Charlotte takes it down soon."

"Can you run interference? Say I'm not interested?"

"That seems like an awfully big waste."

"Not if someone works out for Charlotte."

"Yeah." Mei-Lin chuckled. "That's true." She winked playfully. "The cowboy was kind of cute."

"For Charlotte maybe, not for me."

"No, I suspect your type is more short, dark, and handsome."

Misty swatted her arm. "Lucas is not short. He's taller than I am. Maybe five ten."

Mei-Lin's eyebrows arched. "You've been thinking about it then? You and Lucas for real?"

"What? No." But even as she said it, Misty recalled the warming look in his coal gray eyes when he'd told everyone they were dating. And the way she'd tingled all over when he'd kissed her hand. But she wasn't attracted to Lucas. She just wasn't. What's more, he wasn't attracted to her. Not like that.

When Charlotte and Nell returned, Misty said, "So Charlotte. How about you? Are you planning to use Nell's little list, too?"

"You bet I am. I've got my own copy." Charlotte grinned. "Once you're busy with Lucas, I'll be off on my own pursuits."

"Maybe you should give *yourself* the week off?" Misty joked.

"Don't need it." Charlotte shook out her raven

tresses. "I'm a really great multitasker. I can run the café and find my own last-minute groom at the same time."

"So you're not giving up, either?" Mei-Lin clucked her tongue. "Interesting."

"Nobody's giving up, all right?" Nell said. "The bet is still on—for everyone except me." She made a flashy show of her engagement ring and the others sighed.

"I'm really glad that you're happy," Charlotte said.

Misty's heart gave a small twist of joy. "Yeah," she told Nell. "Me too."

"There's still time for things to work out for you two," Mei-Lin said to Misty and Charlotte.

"Yeah. No." Misty rubbed the side of her nose that didn't have the stud in it. "Probably not for *both* of us."

She was still a little stunned by Charlotte's sudden turnaround, but maybe she shouldn't be. Just because Charlotte erected that billboard didn't mean that she'd taken herself out of the running. Charlotte was so darn competitive, she'd just meant to ensure a fair competition. Just like when they were kids, and Charlotte had refused to let Misty forfeit at checkers—or later, at chess, even once it was obvious that she was losing. But this time maybe Charlotte wouldn't emerge victorious. Misty squared her shoulders. *This baby sister is upping her game.*

"Right," Charlotte said. "Probably not both. Someone's got to marry Aidan."

"That someone could be you," argued Misty.

Charlotte turned up her nose. "Also could be you, Misty. I mean, if this thing with you and Lucas doesn't work out—"

"Maybe it will?" And if it didn't, which Misty knew it wouldn't, she would just make other plans! Staying holed up with Lucas would give her time to work on those, then Charlotte would see which one of them would get the best of the other.

For once in her life, Misty was not letting Charlotte come out on top. She probably should have her head examined for briefly believing she should rush off to London to marry Aidan. England wasn't what she wanted. At least, she didn't think so. She wanted RISD, or somewhere like it. Plus her own life as an artist. Finding true love along the way would also be nice, once she was ready for that. Which, in all honesty, was probably not now. But Misty would cross that bridge when she came to it. Like when she was, ohhh…thirty.

Charlotte jutted out her chin. "Maybe we'll see?"

Misty set one hand on her hip. "Guess so."

Charlotte stuck out her arm and shook Misty's hand. "May the best woman win."

CHAPTER FIVE

Misty and Lucas opted to leave through the alley since some out-of-towners were still milling about on the street in front of the café. Mei-Lin said they seemed harmless enough, but—even so—Misty didn't want to put up with the face recognition and the questions. She was tired enough from hiding out all day. Various guys had wandered into Bearberry Brews after seeing the billboard, some of them questioning if it was for real. Others apparently seriously interested. Mei-Lin had steered them all away, while surreptitiously jotting down names without alerting her parents.

Meanwhile, Misty'd spent a lot of time taking sudden trips to the private bathroom near the office. So much so, her mom even asked if she was experiencing stomach problems. Yeah, she was. Her gut was in a solid knot from the events of the past few days.

"Good night, Mom and Dad!" she said to her folks as she and Lucas cut through the kitchen. She knew she'd have to tell them about Lucas moving into her place but wanted to be careful about how she put it. Her parents weren't that old-fashioned and they did like Lucas, but they'd wonder where this sudden urge to cohabitate had come from. She and Lucas hadn't even been dating as far as they were concerned.

"Good night, kids," her mom said. "See you in the morning."

"The front door's not locked yet," her dad said, seeing them head out the back way.

"Ah yeah," Lucas said, thinking fast. "But my truck's parked closer to here."

"And Misty's going with you because…" Her mom let that question linger.

"We have things to discuss," Misty said.

"That's right," Lucas agreed. "About Nell's party."

Her dad smiled warmly. "What a fine idea. When will that be?"

Misty and Lucas stared at each other. Thinking fast, she said, "No date set yet. Maybe, er. Early October?"

"All right," her mom said. "Keep us appraised of your plans. Maybe you'd like to have the party here? Or back at our house?"

Her dad frowned sadly and Misty guessed he was thinking about that bank loan they might not be able to repay. Even if they went into default, surely they wouldn't lose Bearberry Brews and their house that quickly? Still, they'd probably not feel much like celebrating with those prospects hanging over their heads.

Guilt swamped through her and Misty questioned her taking more time to decide on Aidan. Maybe she should march back into the other room and tell her sisters to forget about the stupid bet. Just like she'd done yesterday, before Charlotte had gone all crazy with her billboard antics. She bit her lip, fearing what other schemes Charlotte might concoct if Misty tried to call their bet off again.

No. Better to let Lucas help buy her time. Charlotte claimed she'd be out there looking for her own guy, and maybe she'd find him. If she became engaged first, Misty would still go off to London, but because she'd lost to both her sisters fair and square. Not because she'd walked on their agreement, which was one of the things Charlotte and Nell had become upset about.

"None of the details have been decided yet," Misty told her folks. "About the party. Once we work out more, we'll let you know." She spied her dad's baseball cap on a hook by the back door. "Dad, mind if I borrow your hat?"

"Sure, love," he said. "Go right ahead."

Misty tucked her long ponytail underneath it and Lucas handed her his aviator-style sunglasses. "Here. Why don't you put these on, too?" He slid off his jacket. "And wear this."

"What? Why?"

"It will be big on you. Disguise your girly figure."

"What am I supposed to do with my denim jacket?"

"Just wear mine on top."

"What about you?"

"I won't be cold," he said. "It's just a short walk. Besides that, the rain's let up."

When they reached the end of the alley, a small cluster of men huddled around a lamppost outside the café's front door. She really wanted to avoid them if she could. She was worn out from her day and not wanting to deal anymore—

Wait. Was that Mr. Mulroney? He seemed to be saying something to the others and had their rapt attention. Which meant this was a great time for Misty and Lucas to bolt for his truck.

Misty huffed as she hurried along. "Charlotte has got to *fix* this."

"Yeah," he said as they climbed into the cab and shut their doors. "Want me to talk to her?"

"No, thanks. I'll do it." She set her chin, annoyed with her middle sister. She'd gotten over things this morning when she thought the problem was solved, but apparently the issue was ongoing.

As Lucas backed out of his parallel parking space on the street, one of the guys pivoted their way and pointed. Mr. Mulroney turned toward them as well.

Lucas reached out and pushed down on Misty's baseball cap.

She slid down in her seat and he drove away.

"Wow." Lucas checked his rearview mirror. "Persistent."

Misty had out her phone and was texting Mei-Lin and her sisters.

"What are you doing?"

"Warning them because of Mom and Dad."

"Good idea. I'm sure they won't be thrilled about the billboard. All day long I kept half expecting Mrs. McIntyre to stop by."

"No joke. Me too."

She sent her text to Charlotte.

Billboard. Down. Now!

Charlotte wrote right back.

Okay, okay. Working on it!

Misty spun in her seat before they rounded the corner. Charlotte and Mei-Lin were already in the street taking down names and numbers, judging by

Mei-Lin's notepad. They'd had the good sense to steer the group toward Mariner's, though, and away from the front of the shop.

"I guess Nell must be inside talking to my parents," she told Lucas. "Keeping them distracted until those guys can be driven away."

"Yeah," he said. "Good thing they live south of town like Nell does."

Misty gasped. "You do think it's only the one billboard? Not more?"

"Yeah," he said. "It's just the one. I went out on my lunch break and checked."

Misty sighed. "Thanks, Lucas. And thanks for coming to my rescue with that whole made-up boyfriend thing."

"It was kind of a genius move, huh?" He grinned and her pulse fluttered. *No wait. Why?*

She removed the baseball cap, trying to ignore the sensation while also trying not to look at Lucas. "Yeah, that was very cool. How did you know that would be the right move?"

He shrugged. "Manly intuition."

She laughed. "That is so not a thing."

"Sure it is. Don't be sexist."

"I'm not being sexist, I'm just—" She turned to face him as he caught a glimpse of her.

"What?" A playful glimmer sparkled in his eyes. "It's an equal-opportunity world."

"I know it is. Or. Um. Should be."

He pulled up alongside her apartment building and parked his truck. "Well, I'm glad I didn't make a mistake anyway."

"Your story about us dating wasn't a mistake, it

was perfect."

He grinned. "Sure surprised your sisters."

She decided not to tell him they suspected he'd crushed on her for a while, because she'd never believed it. Until now, when she held a sliver of a doubt that he might kind of like her. But it was only super tiny. He wasn't *seriously* into her, which was exactly for the best. And she wasn't into him, despite that weird tension in her stomach.

He glanced up at the window to her living room on the second story of the brownstone.

"So? You're actually cool with me moving in?"

"Of course I'm cool." Her nerves skittered momentarily but then she calmed down. This was Lucas. Her buddy. He always made her feel better no matter what was going on. Given the huge life choices she was about to make, it would be great having him around. He steadied her. "I guess you'll be in the guest room, if that's okay? It's really basic."

"I'm fine with basic. So." He thumped on the steering wheel. "In private we're still friends, but in public we're a couple, yeah?"

"If you don't mind?" Her eyebrows rose. "I know it's a lot to ask, but it's only for a short while."

"Anything that helps you to make the right decision. This whole Aidan thing is a very big ask. A lot to ask of any of you."

"I know. But in a way we've asked it of ourselves. And it will be okay," she said, but still her heart wrenched. She thought it was on account of London and the thought of moving so far away. But something niggled at her soul saying it wasn't. Like there was something deeper going on she didn't understand. "No matter who has to go, me or Charlotte."

He frowned. "I'd rather that it was neither of you, but if it's got to be someone then I'd pick Charlotte."

"If she lands a fiancé before the month ends, I'm afraid it *is* going to be me, and not her."

He peered into her eyes. "How do you know you won't find a fiancé first?"

Her cheeks warmed and she laughed to deflect her embarrassment. She knew he couldn't be talking about him, but he couldn't really believe she'd find someone to marry on such short notice? "Seriously? I can't imagine who."

"Dunno." He rubbed his chin. "Maybe someone in Majestic? Someone you haven't thought of?"

But no. She'd already contacted all her exes, the available ones anyway, and none of them had panned out. Maybe Lucas was hinting about her most recent situation. "I already broke things off with Sean if that's who you were thinking."

He shook his head. "I'm sure that if Sean had been a possibility you would have taken things up with him directly, rather than announcing your intentions to marry Aidan."

"Yeah. That's true." He was so astute about everything. "Lucas," she said, taking his hand. "Thanks for doing this. I'll try my best not to make the situation any harder on you than it has to be. You can still do your own thing pretty much. I mean, when we're in private."

"It's not a burden, Misty," he said softly. "I'm glad to help."

"So then," she said. "Maybe tomorrow after work?"

"Are you sure you'll be safe until then? What if one of those guys learns where you live, and decides to come around? Your apartment's not very far from the coffee shop."

"Oh yeah." She chewed on her bottom lip. "That wouldn't be good."

Even if the billboard guys were basically harmless, that would be a little creepy. Unnerving to have one of them show up at her door when she was home alone. And maybe not all of them were harmless anyway? If she'd been thinking clearly, instead of in a desperate rush to subvert Misty's plans to fly to London, maybe Charlotte would have considered that.

"I can go home and get some stuff and come back later this evening?"

Her spirits lifted. "Could you?" Maybe she needed him to lean on more than she thought, because the idea of being alone tonight didn't sound half as good as having her trusted friend—and potential body-guard—around.

"Of course. No problem."

Lucas hadn't been gone more than ten minutes when someone knocked at Misty's door. She opened it thinking he'd forgotten to tell her something and had come back, but instead of Lucas she saw a kindly older man with a mustache standing in the stairwell.

"Mr. Mulroney?"

He smiled and wrinkles furrowed his brow. A swath of silvery hair sat slightly askew above it. "I'm sorry to intrude." He shuffled on his feet. "I just wanted to be sure you got my message."

"With the flowers, you mean?" She motioned for

him to come inside and have a seat. He took the armchair beside the sofa and nodded, settling himself in with the help of his cane.

"Aye. The bouquet. I'm not much into cell phones and such."

She knew that he wasn't. All reservations at the Majestic B&B had to be made the old-fashioned way using his landline. He didn't even provide a method for booking online. The inn was small, with only three guest rooms that shared an upstairs hall bath, and Misty suspected Mr. Mulroney wasn't super interested in keeping them all booked up. He seemed to be on the verge of shutting his business down.

"That was nice of you to bring the flowers." Misty sat on the sofa. She'd arranged his bouquet in a vase and set it on the coffee table. "I mean brave, maybe." She chuckled. "Considering you had to get past the press."

"Considering this is Majestic," he quipped, "the media isn't much. One reporter? The lady who writes the romance blog?" He waved his broad hand. "Nothing." He shook a scolding finger. "Those contenders, though. They merit keeping an eye on."

"I'm hoping they'll be gone before long," she said.

Mr. Mulroney rubbed his cheek. "That billboard out there on Highway One," he said. "That wasn't your idea, was it?"

Misty shook her head. "It was Charlotte's."

"Figured as much." Mr. Mulroney rubbed his cheek. "So," he said after drawing a breath. "I heard about your wager."

Misty sighed. By this point, who in town hadn't?

"When Nell got engaged, word was you'd called

the bet off." His thick eyebrows rose. "But apparently not?"

Misty crossed her arms in front of her. "Mr. Mulroney, I know you're trying to help." By sticking his nose in her business, which was so Majestic, and so typical.

"Your mother is my godchild, you know." Mr. Mulroney's late wife, Eugenia, had been best friends with Misty's late grandma, Nonna. "So, her worries are my concerns, too, and I've got to believe—just know—she wouldn't want any of her daughters moving to London to marry this Aidan fellow."

Misty decided not to mention the fact that the whole scheme had originally been her mom's idea. Hers and Mrs. Strong's. She sighed. "There's a lot going on over at the café that you don't know about."

"That may be so, but that doesn't mean that one of you girls should do something so drastic. Marry an old family foe to save Bearberry Brews."

"I appreciate your concern, really I do." Misty glanced at the flowers. "But I'm afraid this is something my sisters and I need to work out for ourselves."

Mr. Mulroney harrumphed. "That's fine. As long as you and Charlotte work things out the way Nell did." He grinned. "Meaning, you hold out for your special one."

Everyone in Majestic seemed to be singing the same tune. First her sisters and Mei-Lin, then Lucas, and now even Mr. Mulroney. "I know that you mean well," she said, "but there's nothing to say my 'special one' can't come along later."

He tapped his cane on the floor. "Or sooner!"

"Yes, well." Misty grinned tightly. "I've already

exhausted my choices in Majestic."

The old man leaned toward her. "Have you?"

He pinned her with his clear blue eyes and Misty's heart caught in her throat. What was he getting at? That she'd overlooked someone obvious? She hadn't.

His gaze flitted to the spare bedroom, and where Lucas would be sleeping. Mr. Mulroney couldn't think—

"I saw you and that Reyes lad driving away in his truck," he said. "I always liked him and his family. Hard workers. Honest folk."

"Yeah. Lucas is great."

"So. Maybe he is great for you."

Misty's face heated. "Oh, no. Not in that way. He and I are just—"

"Yes, yes. Heard it before. Friends."

Mr. Mulroney stood with difficulty, steadying himself with his cane.

"My Eugenia and I started as friends in grade school, you know," he said. "And just look where we winded up. Fifty years together, each of them golden."

That was endearing and probably true. "Lucas and I," she said. "We're not like that."

"Perhaps not yet." Mr. Mulroney scrutinized her. "Give it time."

Misty bit her lip, because time was the one luxury they didn't have. Not bunches of it anyway. Besides that, Mr. Mulroney was dead wrong. Still, his heart was in the right place. She noticed the shadows falling outside her windows and his frail hobble. "You okay getting home?"

"Oh yes. It's only round the block."

"Take care on the stairs then."

He turned before he left and said with a serious look, "Take care with your heart, Misty. You've only got one of those to give." He winked. "You'll want to make sure it lands in the right place."

• • •

Lucas reached his mom's house just as she did, arriving home from her job at the school. She wore powder blue nurse's scrubs and had on a sweater. "Lucas?" she said, stepping out of her car. "What a nice surprise. I hope you can stay for dinner?"

"Probably not tonight," he said. He took her canvas bag holding her work supplies, including her purse and water bottle, from her and helped carry it indoors. "I've got some place to be later."

She smiled, her dark eyes shining. "You boys stay so busy these days. What am I going to do next year when Ramon goes off to college?"

He shrugged then teased her. "Don't know. Start dating?"

She laughed. "Like that's going to happen."

"It's never too late they say."

She unlocked the front door and let them in. "It is for this old lady."

"Mom." He sighed indulgently. "You're only in your fifties." She still looked good, too. As a nurse, she watched her nutrition and kept herself in shape. Being on her feet so many hours throughout the day also helped with that. Lucas hated seeing her work so hard. Her life should have taken its toll on her smooth facial features, but somehow it hadn't, and she still appeared relatively youthful in spite of her age.

"Yes, but." She looked down at her swollen ankles. "Tell that to my feet."

"If Ramon gets a good financial package, maybe you can give up that second job."

"But I love working at the bakery," she said. "Think of all the perks! Free cinnamon rolls for one. Ooh. I brought some home with me today. They were made fresh this morning. Would you like one?"

"Maybe I can take two back with me, if that's okay."

Her eyebrows shot up. "Two?"

Ramon breezed past them in the hall wearing shorts and a tank top and carrying a basketball under one arm. Ramon was shorter than Lucas but bullish like their dad. Stocky and built like an ox. His hair was curly like Lucas's but a lighter brown like their mom's.

"Hey, bro!" He grabbed Lucas's hand in a fist-grasp. "That Delaney chick. Whoa." His voice held a teasing lilt. "She's advertising!"

"Advertising?" His mom glanced at his brother then at him. "What does Ramon mean?"

"I guess you haven't heard," Lucas began tentatively. "Charlotte put up a billboard at the north end of town."

Ramon grinned. "Says 'Marry me: Misty!' 'cause she's looking for a honey."

Their mom folded her arms and frowned. "Sounds like she's searching for more than a boyfriend to me." She stared at Lucas. "What do you know about this? You work with her and the two of you are friends."

"Uh, yeah." Lucas shifted on his feet. "About that—"

"No way!" Ramon grinned. "You're going to do it!" He fake-whispered to his mom, "Lucas has always had a thing for Misty."

"I have not." Lucas cleared his throat. "Had a thing."

Ramon thumbed at him, speaking to their mom. "Could have fooled me by the way he looks at her."

His mom studied Lucas a moment. "You know, Ramon has a point." She gasped. "Wait. Is this true?"

"No, not exactly. The point is Misty was very surprised by the billboard. Terrified, really. The gimmick was not her idea at all." He blew out a breath. "Can we sit down?"

His mom motioned toward the living room and Ramon glanced out the window. He was apparently waiting on someone who hadn't arrived. "This, I've got to hear."

"Yes," their mom said. "Me too." She took a seat on the sofa and Ramon and Lucas each grabbed a chair.

Lucas ran a hand through his hair. Where to begin? "This all started on the first of the month."

"This month?" his mom asked. "September?"

Lucas nodded. "The Delaneys' business is in bad straits. They had these old family friends that helped them start their business. The husband, Mr. Strong, cheated Mr. Delaney out of international interests in the bigger corporation."

"I remember hearing something about that rift," his mom said. "The Strongs used to live in Majestic, but that was years ago."

Lucas nodded. "Anyway, now that Mr. Strong has passed, his widow wants to make amends for her late husband's wrongdoing. Their son feels guilty, too, so had agreed to help."

"Help how?" his brother asked.

"By merging the two businesses back together again. That will help save the café and also the Delaneys' home, which they put up as collateral on their loan."

His mom nodded. "That was nice of Mrs. Strong and her son."

"Yeah, but. There's one small stipulation." Lucas rubbed his palms together. "In order for the companies to merge, Aidan—that's the son's name—has got to marry one of the Delaney sisters."

Roman's eyes went huge. "Is that even legal?"

Lucas laughed uncomfortably. "If they agree to it, yeah. And it appears that Misty and her sisters have decided that one of them is going to do it—they just haven't settled on which one. They kind of made this out-there bet. Whichever one of them can't find a better husband of her own by September thirtieth, she'll be the one to take the hit and marry Aidan."

His mom frowned. "Why is it a 'hit'? What's wrong with this young man?"

"I don't think anything officially. He's obviously very successful and runs Bearberry Coffee now. He doesn't exactly want a real wife, either, so is okay with a business-arranged marriage. It only has to last five years, then the estate can be divided equally."

"*Ay, ay, ay.*" His mom's shoulders sagged. "This sounds like a big mess to me, and a way to make war between the sisters. I thought they always got along?"

"They have and still do. There's just a bit of a competition going on."

"*Not* to marry Aidan?" Ramon hooted. "Seriously dude. What a mess is right. I guess it's a good thing you're staying out of it."

Lucas shifted uncomfortably as Ramon and his mom stared at him.

His mom's forehead rose. "*Hijo*, you are staying out of it?"

"Misty's my friend, Mom." He exhaled sharply. "I can't just leave her out there on a limb with all those billboard guys coming after her."

"I saw some new plates around Majestic today when I passed through," Ramon said. "Wondered what that was all about."

"Plates? What?" She focused for a moment. "You mean out-of-towners?" Ramon nodded and she addressed Lucas. "If Charlotte's competing against Misty, then why did she put up the billboard?"

"The Delaney sisters and their relationship are a little complicated," Lucas said. "Misty had called off the bet, willing to sacrifice herself to go to London where Aidan lives—"

"There's a move involved?" his mom said. "That does complicate things. Even more."

"Yeah, well." Lucas cleared his throat. "The thing is Misty's sisters didn't want her to give up that easily without at least trying to find a fiancé of her own first."

"Which is where you step in," Ramon ribbed him. "Like a knight on his steed galloping to her rescue."

"Stop it. It's not like that," Lucas said. Even though it kind of was. He'd do anything to prevent Misty from making the huge mistake of marrying Aidan. Even riding a white horse if he had to.

"So Charlotte and Nell are still in the running then?" his mom asked.

"Not Nell," Lucas said. "She just got engaged to Grant Williams."

"The Blue Sky Adventures guy?" Ramon asked. "I like him."

"Oh yeah," his mom said. "Now that you mention it, I saw the blurb in *The Seaside Daily*." She fiddled with the hem of her sweater. "So, Lucas. What exactly is it that you've come here to tell us?"

"That I'm…" He swallowed hard. "Moving in with Misty."

"Moving in?" his mom asked, aghast.

Ramon just grinned. "Nice way to shut out the competition."

"Mom." He could already see her mind spinning and counting up all the candles she'd have to light at church. "It is not what you think, okay? Nothing lurid going on. I'm helping Misty buy some time, and also truthfully"—he squared his shoulders—"offering her some protection from those billboard guys."

"So you'll stay in separate rooms?" she asked.

"Absolutely."

Ramon smirked. "Right."

Lucas *tsk*ed at his little brother. "Don't be so quick to judge, Ramon. You'd do the same if you felt the way—"

"Aha!" Ramon's dark eyes danced. "So you are hung up on her, aren't you?" He clucked his tongue with satisfaction. "Nailed it."

"Lucas?" his mom said. "Is Ramon right?"

He dragged a hand down his cheek. "Mom—"

A horn sounded outside and Ramon glanced at

the SUV that had pulled up in front of the house. "That's my ride. Sorry." He stood, nodding at his mom and Lucas. "Got to go."

"You will be home for dinner?" their mom asked.

Ramon headed for the door. "Sure thing." He shook a finger at Lucas like he was the older brother. "Don't do anything I wouldn't do." Then he winked and shut the door.

Lucas got to his feet. "I need to push off, too. I told Misty I'd get my things and come over."

"Separate bedrooms?" his mom asked again, obviously still wrapping her head around it.

"Yeah, Mom. Yeah."

She seemed to process this, then make a decision to live with it. Since Lucas was twenty-seven, she didn't have a whole lot of choice. Still, he hadn't wanted to upset her. Which is why he'd come to give her some advance notice, in case she learned about the situation elsewhere. Majestic was a tongue-wagging town.

"Well, will you at least take some cinnamon rolls?" she finally said, sounding resigned. "They were made fresh at the bakery today."

He stood and hugged her tightly, because she'd never let him down. He'd never want to let her down, either. She was the best. "Thanks, Mom."

CHAPTER SIX

Misty lived above the Mermaid Tattoo shop, because she'd made friends with the owner and he'd cut her a special deal. If she didn't fuss about the state of her dilapidated apartment, he wouldn't charge much rent. All fine by her. The turn-of-the-last-century building sat near the top of a hill, one block back from Kittery Street, where Bearberry Brews was located. Because of the positioning of her unit behind the row of businesses in front, you could still see a sliver of the ocean from here and appreciate the tune of those rowdy waves slamming against the shore. Misty loved the ocean. It was fierce and untamed. Sort of like she was.

She'd miss it if she went to RISD, where she wouldn't be smack-dab on the sea but close enough to Narragansett Bay. In London, it would be even worse. She could always make day trips to the beach. But visiting and living right on top of it were two separate things.

Lucas unloaded the last duffel bag from the back of his truck and carried it up the stairs to her apartment. She shut the door behind him as he scanned the living room. Despite its broken-down state, Misty's place was surprisingly roomy with tall ceilings and peeling plaster columns decorating the hall. Had it been in better shape, or renovated like most of the other buildings on this block, the apartment would have been out of her reach income-wise. But given its dated condition and the fact that its laidback owner had neglected to raise the rent for years, she was pleased to be able to afford it.

This front room overlooked the street and held a small sofa, along with a couple of secondhand armchairs. Misty's trumpet case rested in the corner, leaned up against one wall. She'd had it since she was thirteen and had never been able to part with it, hanging onto it for sentimental reasons. Music was her secret passion and she played nearly every day at sunrise, though very few people knew it, except for her nearest neighbors. She did play with a mute in though, so trusted that her music wasn't too disturbing.

"What you got in the case?" he asked, noting her eyes on it.

"Oh that!" She waved her hand. "My old trumpet. I've had it since way back in the day."

His eyebrows rose. "Which day?"

"Middle school jazz band."

"That was some time ago." He chuckled and ran a hand through his hair. "Still play?"

Misty bit her bottom lip. "Um, not so much."

He scrutinized her a beat. "There's no dust on the case."

How did he always *know* things? Misty laughed. "Okay. I play sometimes. Like once in a blue moon." She paused, then decided to add a joke. "Or when the moon is full." She tried to minimize it like it was no big deal. Otherwise he might ask her to play something, which would be hugely embarrassing. Misty hadn't performed for anyone other than the sunrise outside her window for years.

"Howling at the moon with your trumpet." He

rubbed his chin. "I guess I can see it." He nodded toward the living room windows overlooking the street. "Bet they can hear you all the way down on Kittery."

Misty grimaced. "Hope not."

"Are you really that bad?"

"Actually, I used to be sort of good, but that was so long ago." And also before she'd met Lucas so maybe that's why he didn't know about her musical bent. He'd gone to the private Catholic school where his mom worked as a nurse before entering the public high school, so he and Misty hadn't crossed paths until he was fourteen and she a year younger. That was after his dad passed, and he'd started doing deliveries for her parents' café.

"Jazz band, whoa," he said. "That's impressive. I'd like to hear you play sometime."

Eek. There he went. Just like she'd hoped he wouldn't. "Don't get your hopes up."

"Do you have a favorite?"

"What?"

"Song."

She did but it was sappy and sentimental. Something by Fleetwood Mac that she would never play in front of Lucas. Talk about sending the wrong signals. "Not really, why?"

He shrugged. "Most musicians have favorites they play."

"I wouldn't exactly call myself a musician."

He glanced at her trumpet case and then lowered his eyebrows. "I think the evidence speaks to the contrary."

Misty laughed. "I always liked 'What a Wonderful World.'"

"Yeah, Louis Armstrong is great. I went to his house once, you know."

"Seriously?"

"Yeah. It's where he used to live in Queens. It's all done up like a museum now, but a bunch of his stuff is left in place, just like he had it when he was living there, including his studio. You can see his record collection and everything."

"Cool!"

"Yeah." He grinned at the memory. "It was awesome."

She knew Lucas had an uncle in New York, his mom's brother, who he sometimes visited. He and his mom and Ramon went down to the city a few times a year.

"I think you'd like New York."

It sounded kind of huge and overwhelming to her. All those people crowding into public transportation. "I'm not sure."

"Plenty of nice museums there," he tempted.

What was this? "Are you trying to entice me on a trip?"

He chuckled. "Probably not right now." He shifted on his feet. "But maybe someday. You'd like it. It's artsy, like you."

"I'm small-town artsy, though."

"Says the woman who was about to jump on a plane to London."

"Okay. All right." He had her there. Her shoulders sank. "I did think better of it."

"Good."

She was happy about that, too. Running off to marry Aidan now was premature and uncalled for.

Her sisters and Mei-Lin were right about her honoring her bet with Nell and Charlotte, but she didn't need added assistance from any of those billboard guys.

He handed her the sweet-smelling box he held in his hand.

"What's this?" She noticed the logo from the local bakery where his mom worked.

"Cinnamon rolls from my mom."

"Your mom? Oh?"

"I needed to stop by. Tell her what was going on here. Otherwise, she might have heard rumors and worried."

"So what did you tell her? The truth?"

"Of course." His face hung in a frown. "Did you want me not to?"

How could she ask him that? She knew he and his mom were close. Especially after losing her husband, she, Ramon, and Lucas had formed a really tight family unit. "No. It's not that. That was fine. You were good to say something. But what about—"

"Don't worry. They won't say anything to your sisters. Not that they even see them much."

It wasn't really Charlotte and Nell she was worried about. She was more concerned about her own parents. Since Lucas had leveled with his family, she'd feel bad now not telling her mom and dad the truth. But she couldn't ask them to keep things from Nell and Charlotte. More importantly, she couldn't have them guessing that the bet with Aidan was back on. And that was the whole reason Charlotte had put up her billboard to begin with. And the reason Lucas was moving in. She sighed.

Lucas slid the strap of his heavy duffel off his shoulder. "Should I put my stuff in…?"

"Uh, yeah," she said. "That one's fine."

The other spare bedroom was mostly empty, except for a folding card table and a chair, where she sat to work on her designs. She had some art stuff in there and a low cabinet with deep pullout drawers where she kept her drawings. Misty's room was across from the bathroom and down the hall, next to the kitchen.

Lucas walked into her guest room and dumped his duffel bag on the single bed with a maple wood frame and headboard. Not much else fit in there besides a side table and a basic chest of drawers. It all matched at least. She'd inherited the set from her late grandmother.

He surveyed the cramped room. Its one meager window didn't afford much light and the sun was already setting. "This is perfect, thanks."

Misty wondered for about the billionth time why he was doing this. "You really didn't have to move in," she said.

He crossed his arms. "You would have maybe preferred someone in a Stetson?"

She laughed. "Right."

"I've got to give you credit." His eyes gleamed. "You did kind of cause a stir."

"Fourteen guys on the list is hardly a stir, Lucas."

"Fourteen and counting."

She laughed. "You're not supposed to count Mr. Mulroney."

"I didn't. Still. Counting all the others…" His mouth twitched. "For Majestic, that's epic. Fourteen's a mob."

She laughed hard and shoved his arm. "Stop. It wasn't on account of me. It was all due to Charlotte."

"Charlotte wasn't on the billboard. You were."

"Yeah." Misty sighed. "Good ol' Charlotte." Her stomach rumbled and she realized it was getting late. "Hungry?"

"A little."

"I don't have a ton to eat. We could make eggs. Toast. That kind of thing."

"Breakfast food sounds good. Got anything to go in an omelet?"

"Uh."

"Onion? Cheese? Ham maybe?"

"Oh yeah, I've got all that."

He chuckled at her blank look. "All right, okay," he said. "I'll cook."

She heaved a breath. "Thanks, Lucas. I'm not much with—"

"Cooking, I know."

"Do you? How?"

"You told me." His gray eyes shimmered. "You've actually told me a lot of things."

True. She just hadn't imagined he'd recall every single one.

"I like your apartment," he said, following her back toward the kitchen. "It's cozy." He pulled his bedroom door closed and the knob came off in his hand. Lucas stared at it when Misty blushed. "It's no biggie. I can fix this." He set it down on a bookshelf loaded with seashells of every kind. Misty had collected them forever.

"That's quite a collection you've got there."

"Yeah." It was funny to think of it now, but he'd

never been to her place. There'd never really been much reason.

"I like shells."

"Do you?" she asked, because he'd never told her that. He'd actually never told her tons of stuff. Or maybe he had and she hadn't been listening.

"Yeah." He shoved his hands in his pockets. "Don't collect them, though." He smiled and her heart fluttered a little. *Whoa. Why?* "I like yours. They're pretty."

Misty swallowed past the awkward knot in her throat. "Ah, thank you."

He scanned the whole living room but she wasn't sure what he was looking for. "So. Where do you keep your books?"

"What?" Misty darted a glance at the bookshelf loaded with seashells and laughed. "I truthfully don't own a ton of those." She shrugged sheepishly. "I'm not a huge reader. But I do keep some art books in my work space." She rubbed her chin, wondering about his question. "Why? Do you stock a library at your house or something?"

He laughed. "No." He shook his head. "I do read a little, though. Biographies mostly."

She mock-frowned at the seriousness of it all. "That sounds…intellectual."

He chuckled. "Of baseball players, Misty. Soccer stars. Some celebrities. Musicians, and the like."

The air *whooshed* back into her lungs. For some reason she thought he was judging her, but he wasn't. He'd just been curious.

He shrugged. "Some other nonfiction, too."

"I like nonfiction," she said eagerly, wanting to

feel more a part of this discussion. "I listen to tons of podcasts."

"Those are cool. What sort?"

"Self-help and wellness. Meditation. That kind of thing." She'd always had a stress edge but these practices seemed to soothe her. She'd been really big into self-awareness this past year, which was one reason she'd decided to finally pursue RISD.

"Sounds like valuable stuff." His lips twitched. "And all this time, I thought you were listening to K-pop on your lunch hour."

She smirked playfully. "Happen to like that, too, but no. Generally, I'm learning to become more mindful."

"Of?"

She beamed brightly because she believed her efforts were working. "Myself."

"Well, good for you!" He grinned as she beckoned for him to follow her. "Maybe I should try that sometime."

"It's probably good for everyone." She motioned down the length of the hall. "Kitchen's this way."

They hadn't talked much about how they were going to handle this, beyond setting the general parameters of him sleeping in the guest room. It seemed a little awkward mentioning Nell's romantic dating list. Then again, if they weren't seen in public doing at least a few of those couple-y things together, her sisters might get suspicious about her and Lucas's supposed romantic involvement.

"How about I make us some dinner and we chat while we eat?"

They reached the kitchen and she switched on the

light revealing a Formica table with a blue-speckled top and two metal chairs. The outdated appliances had likely been here for at least twenty years.

Lucas washed his hands at the sink and opened the refrigerator. Misty stood beside him, handing him things like the eggs, milk, and butter. He set everything on the counter.

"Got a frying pan?"

"I think there are a few of them under the stove." At least she hoped she still had cookware down there. She hadn't checked in a while honestly. Every once in a while, she got in a flurry clearing things out.

He pulled out the drawer but the only item in it was a cookie sheet. He met her eyes and grinned. "Nope."

"The box!" she said, suddenly remembering. "For charity!"

"Where's that?"

"Hall closet," she said. She took off in that direction. "I'll get it." Besides the two frying pans, she had other cooking supplies in there. A partial nest of mixing bowls. A few saucepans with lids. A large rectangular baking dish.

Lucas laughed when she returned with a frying pan in one hand. "You really don't cook much, do you?"

She shrugged shyly. "It's never really been my thing."

He noticed the blender by her toaster oven. "Too busy making smoothies?"

Of course, he had to remember that. She'd more or less told her sisters she started each day with a power shake. She hadn't known that he'd been listening, but maybe she should have figured. She'd made such a point of bragging about her healthy habits to Charlotte and Nell. "Ah, yep! Smoothies are my thing." Although she had a hunch she'd like those delicious-smelling cinnamon rolls even better. She picked up the box and took a peek. Their deep swirls oozed with melted cinnamon sugar. She couldn't wait to try these in the morning.

"Maybe we should go shopping," he said. "The fridge looks a little bare."

"Plan to," she said. "First thing tomorrow."

"You're working tomorrow," he said, "but it's my day off. I can go if you'd like?"

"Lucas," she said, meeting his eyes. "We both have the day off."

"What?"

"More like the week."

He ran a hand through his hair. "I don't know what you're talking about, Misty. We can't possibly—"

"But yeah, Charlotte says we can. She's taking over as café manager."

He blinked.

"But only temporarily. Charlotte and I filled in for Nell when she was with Grant up at his cabin. Now they want to give us the same chance." Her face warmed and she wrinkled up her nose. "I mean, fake chance. No. Real chance for our fake relationship. Oh boy." She chuckled uncomfortably. "I'm really blowing this."

"Not at all." He winked and she felt a happy buzz of warmth. "Still. How will they manage?"

"Charlotte's calling Sean, Mei-Lin says she'll work extra, and Nell says she'll do her books at home."

"All for us?" She nodded and he laid a hand on his heart. "I'm actually kind of touched." His voice was a little husky which made her feel emotional, too.

"I know. It's super generous of them. I told them they didn't have to."

"But they insisted. Yeah. Sounds like them." He set the frying pan on the stove still stewing over their impromptu holiday. "It's going to feel a little weird not working at all. How about we go in half days?"

"I already suggested that," she said. "They said no."

He shrugged. "Well, if that's what they insist on, we'll do it. I mean, maybe it will be good for you to take the extra time to sort things out."

"And you?"

"I'll need the extra time to support you," he said with a cheerful grin. He motioned to a chair and she sat down, as he started to work. "Bowl?"

She loved how easy he'd made that awkward conversation.

That was so Lucas.

"Left cabinet."

He pulled out a drawer and found a fork which he used to whisk the eggs after he expertly cracked them. "We need a plan to deal with the billboard guys."

"Yeah, and my primary plan involves having Charlotte remove that ad." She set the cinnamon roll box back on the counter. "She's promised to get it taken down tomorrow."

"Good. That's something."

She nodded.

"In the meantime," he said, "let's hope none of

them winds up here. If they do, I can steer them away. Luckily, I don't think anyone knows your address. It's not listed anywhere?"

"Like in the phone directory, or something? No."

Lucas seemed satisfied with that answer. He put a pat of butter in the frying pan and it sizzled. Next, he added the onions he'd chopped. Savory goodness filled the air and Misty's mouth watered.

He added the eggs, meat, and cheese to the pan and then looked up. "You're not still thinking of going to London? You told everyone yesterday morning you'd completely made up your mind."

"I thought I had. Only." She sank back in her chair. "This morning I woke up feeling differently. Conflicted. Then the billboard thing hit and well…"

"That's okay." The low rumble in his voice soothed her. "Nobody's making you decide anything today. That's why I'm here. To buy you time."

She sighed. "You don't know how much I appreciate that."

He lifted the skillet off the stove and flipped the omelet perfectly.

"Wow! Where'd you learn to do that?"

"Mom taught me."

"I like a man with skills."

His neck colored. He served them both some of the omelet and set their plates on the table. Then he grabbed the silverware from the drawer.

"Want something to drink?" she asked him.

Lucas rubbed his hands together. "Got any beer?"

She shook her head. "No. Sorry."

"Wine?" His forehead rose and she grimaced. "It's all good." He laughed warmly. "Water's fine. Thanks."

"Let me get it," she said, standing. Maybe she couldn't cook but at least she could do that. "Ice with it?"

"Sure."

But when she peeked in the freezer, she saw that she'd forgotten to refill the ice tray. She pulled it out and set it on the counter, staring at it.

"You know what?" he said. "Regular old tap water is good."

She served them both a glass and returned to the table. "Sorry. I wasn't exactly expecting company."

"It's all right," he said. "I'm a pretty low-maintenance guy."

She couldn't help but grin. "You really are pretty easy to be with."

"Some say." He took a bite of his food and motioned at her plate with his fork. "Aren't you going to try it?"

"Oh, right. Sorry." She took a bite and nearly shimmied with happiness. "This is amazing, Lucas."

"Glad you like it," he said, sounding pleased. "So, about Aidan."

Misty frowned. "Yeah. About him."

"You're going to have to decide sooner or later."

"By the end of this week."

"You could take the rest of the month if you wanted."

"And let Charlotte beat me to the punch by finding a husband first? No, thanks. Whatever I decide I want to choose on my own terms. That's why I announced I was going to marry Aidan before. I'd rather make up my own mind about things than have others push me into it, and my sisters have been pushing me for years. Especially Charlotte."

"I want you to take enough time to be sure you're not making a mistake." He locked on her gaze and she felt tender and raw inside. Like he could see into her soul and every dark corner. He wasn't judging her, but he was caring about her. Genuinely concerned about her doing the right thing.

"I won't go unless I'm sure."

"Won't you?"

She shook her head.

"Then good."

She was kind of embarrassed to mention the list but figured she ought to. "In the meantime, I'm not totally certain my sisters believe us."

"What? About you and me?"

She nodded. "Mei-Lin knows the truth. I mean, I told her."

"Not surprising."

"But Charlotte and Nell were...doubtful. They wanted insurance. Sort of." Her face burned hot. "That you and I are seriously trying."

Lucas took a sip of water. "What kind of insurance?"

"This." Misty handed him the list and he stared at it. "It's actually kind of lame. I don't know how they came up with it. I mean, Nell. I think it was mostly Nell."

He unfolded the paper. "Riding bikes? Watching a sunset?" He met her eyes and she blushed. "Some of these are really sweet."

"Uh-huh. Yeah." She squirmed in her seat. "Still. There's no reason we have to—"

"Why not?"

Misty's mouth hung open. "We can tell them we did without—"

He hooted and gripped his sides. "Frisky in the kitchen?" He looked up and Misty wanted to sink through the floor.

"Nell said we could just cook together or something!"

His mouth twitched as he kept reading.

"And anyway," she rushed to continue, "there's nothing saying we have to do all of them. My sisters will probably never know. Just one or two maybe to—"

He ignored her, still reading. "Hmm. Oh. Uh-huh. And that, too? Well, all right."

She bit her tongue and waited for him to make some comment, but he didn't. He just glossed through the items like none of them was a super big deal. Still. The tops of his ears turned a little red a few times.

"This is great." He finished reading and handed her the page. "I think we should totally go through with it."

"But—"

"Come on, Misty. What have we got to lose? And some of those outings are pretty public. Having people seeing us out and about picnicking and whatnot... That will only look good, right? More convincing?"

Her pulse fluttered nervously. "I...um, guess so."

"Time is what you want and playing along with your sisters' list can help buy it. Keep them out of your hair. And the rest of the town, too. It will be hard for any of those billboard guys to hang around if it's general knowledge that you and I are together."

He had a point there. "Mei-Lin said the same thing."

"Mei-Lin's a good woman." He smiled. "I always really liked her."

Misty shrugged. "We don't have to do each one. I mean, with some of these, who's to know?"

"You're right," he agreed. "We can pick and choose. So where do you want to start?"

"Maybe with the biking?" she said. "That will get us out there in public view."

"Good plan." He glanced around the kitchen. "Have you got a bike?"

"No. You?"

He shook his head. "But I've got an idea where we can rent some."

"I can get the groceries while you get those."

"How about I get both?" he said. "The store is on the way back from Blue Sky Adventures, and that will give you a chance to check on your sisters and Mei-Lin at the café."

"Good idea," she said. "Maybe I can pitch in for a few hours."

"I'll do the same the next day." He chuckled. "If they'll let me."

CHAPTER SEVEN

Misty woke up the next morning feeling better about the dilemma she was in. She didn't have to decide about Aidan today. Not tomorrow, either. Lucas was such a sweetheart, stepping in like he had. She recalled the playful interest in his eyes when he'd teased her about those billboard guys, and for an instant she questioned whether Mei-Lin and her sisters were right.

Could Lucas actually have a thing for her?

No. He would have said so already.

He'd had years to say something.

But he hadn't.

She tugged on her jean jacket, glancing around her apartment. The door to the room where Lucas was staying was barely cracked open. The lump of blankets on the bed indicated he was still sleeping. She'd never figured him for one to sleep in. She'd been up for over an hour.

Misty checked the time on her phone knowing she needed to get going. The one thing she didn't feel great about was skipping out on work. With increased business at the café, they could probably use one more hand.

So she slipped quietly out of her apartment and shut the door, slowly turning its deadbolt lock until it jolted into… Wait. Ugh. There it went sticking again. She shoved her key in harder and then jiggled it and turned. Finally! The door locked.

She'd left her spare key in the kitchen for Lucas with a note. He'd said he'd be going out this morning and had volunteered to get the rental bikes with his truck. So surreal that they were going through that list. She had no issues with most of it. Other parts though…

Misty paused halfway down the street. The rising sun cast shadows between the three-story buildings. Most were connected Victorian townhomes and the majority of them had been restored. Her building had been, too. It just hadn't been updated since before she was born. She searched in both directions but only saw a kid paper carrier riding his bike along and tossing copies of *The Seaside Daily* onto various businesses' front stoops. The street was largely commercial, though these brownstones had once been occupied as private homes.

Still. She had this eerie feeling that she wasn't alone.

She clutched her denim jacket more tightly around her, hugging it over the crisscross strap of her tiny leather purse, and picked up her pace. The faster she walked in her low ankle boots, the more she thought she heard someone behind her.

She stopped short and spun quickly around. But the street behind her was empty.

Seagulls soared overhead traveling toward the ocean, its raucous sound growing louder as she rounded the corner onto Kittery Street.

She stopped stock-still in front of Mariner's, which was just two doors down from Bearberry Brews. Something rustled behind her and she wheeled around with a shout. "Hey!"

A black-and-white cat skittered into the alley.

Great. She really was being paranoid.

But then she spied that Stetson, hovering above the upper rim of a dumpster.

Seriously? It wasn't even seven o'clock.

Heat burned in her cheeks as she stomped her way into the alley. "Hey, you! Cowboy!"

The brim of his hat appeared and then a pair of startled green eyes. "Morning, Miss Misty."

She squared her shoulders assuming the bulldog stance that had never failed to terrify any of her ex-boyfriends. "Were you following me?"

"No ma'am," he said but he looked called out. He stepped around the dumpster with his hands outstretched and held high, like he half expected her to wield a weapon.

His jaw was rugged enough and a touch of his short sandy hair was visible below his hat. He wore jeans and a flannel shirt and was decently built like he did lots of physical work.

"At ease, cowboy."

"Sorry." He lowered his arms to his side. "Didn't aim to shake you up," he said in a subtle western twang. "I just wanted a word." He tugged on the brim of his hat. "My name's Dusty. Dusty Lane."

"Dusty for Dustin?"

"No, ma'am. The real name's Spencer. My brothers laid Dusty on me when I was a kid. That came with the cattle wrangling."

"I...see." Even though she didn't, she could roughly imagine it. Dusty at home on his range with his lasso.

"I know you're Misty Delaney, and all. The one

from the billboard accepting propos—"

Misty stopped him in his tracks. "Sorry, but I'm already taken."

"That's what he said. That guy." He peered out of the alley, maybe to make sure Lucas wasn't with her. "I just wanted to hear it from the horse's mouth myself."

"Look, I'm sorry about the billboard." She relaxed her posture. "That was my sisters' idea and not mine. And anyway." She eyed him curiously. "Are you really that desperate to marry?"

He blinked. "Um. No. Are you?"

She shrugged. "Maybe?"

He shook his head. "A woman like you shouldn't have to settle. I'll bet you're bright."

"Thanks. I like to think so."

"So then." He took a few steps closer and Misty inched back. "What's your big rush?"

"What's yours?"

He set his hands on his hips and looked down. "The old man's not well and he'd really like to see me hitched, like my brothers."

"Oh? How many of those have you got?"

"Four."

"Whoa. All married?"

"Yep. With kids. Every last one of 'em 'cept me."

"Well, you shouldn't be in a race with your—" Misty stopped herself. Who was she to dish out this kind of advice? She shook her head. "Never mind."

"And your reason?" he asked. "For the rush?"

He didn't need her life's story. "It's complicated."

She considered his scuffed boots and the big brass belt buckle that seemed really out of place in

Majestic. "What brings you to Maine?"

"I was headed up Portland way for a cousin's wedding. He met a girl from there and they're getting married next week."

"Is your cousin from Texas, too?"

"Not Texas, ma'am. Big Sky Country. Wyoming."

"So. What made you stop here?"

"Don't know." He removed his hat and ran a hand through his hair. "I saw that billboard and maybe took it as a sign." He sounded just like Mei-Lin. Always looking for signs everywhere. Misty didn't see signs. She saw coincidences or events that happened on purpose.

"Well, I'm sorry that it wasn't," she said. "Maybe you'll meet somebody at the wedding?"

He placed the hat back on his head. "Suppose that could happen."

She started walking and he followed her like a wayward puppy dog.

"I ah…have to go in to work."

"Yes, ma'am. I guessed that."

"So, why are you—"

"Wouldn't mind a cup of coffee before I hit the road."

"We don't open till seven," she said when she reached the door. Through its glass panel she saw Mei-Lin and Charlotte inside. Lately, Nell ran late. Ever since her engagement to Grant.

He stood back a polite distance and tipped his hat. "No problem," he said. "I'll wait."

Misty ducked in the door only to be greeted by Charlotte's unwelcoming glare.

"What are you doing here?"

"Yeah," Mei-Lin said. "You're supposed to be with Lucas working on that list." She wiggled her eyebrows but Misty ignored her.

"It's his day off, not mine. I thought I'd help out, at least for just a few hours."

Charlotte touched her arm. "You shouldn't be here, Misty. You should be home with him."

"Right-o," Nell said, waltzing in the door. "We'll cover for both of you!"

"You can't," Misty said. "Unless you clone yourselves."

Nell frowned. "Sean's coming in at nine and was very happy to help out." That was mainly because he was always short of cash, thanks to his general lack of a job. His artistry was writing country music, and his parents basically supported him by letting him live in the space above their store.

Her cell buzzed. Weirdly, it was Sean. Like he'd sensed them talking about him.

You didn't even think to ask me?

I might have said yes, you know.

Yeah, she kind of did. Which was why she hadn't.

Misty decided not to answer Sean. She'd said all she had to say to him when she broke things off the night before last. It wasn't like they'd ever been that serious anyway. They'd only been casual-level dating. Not even exclusive.

Nell locked the door, gazing through it. "Whoa! Still drawing a crowd."

"What?" Misty goggled at the group that had gathered around Stetson guy. There had to be a dozen or more of them. "Oh no!"

"Hmm." Charlotte bit her lip. "I wonder if these are new ones or repeats?"

Mei-Lin stood up on her tiptoes to peer over Nell. "I recognize the cowboy."

"I set him straight," Misty said. "He's only waiting on a coffee. Which reminds me…" She turned to Charlotte. "I thought you promised to take that billboard down.

"I did! And it will come down. Just as soon as the ad run's over."

Wait a minute. What?

Charlotte's forehead creased. "I paid for two whole weeks."

"Well, un-pay then."

Charlotte frowned. "Doesn't work like that."

"Charlotte! Seriously! This can't go on. I want that photoshopped image of me off that billboard, and I mean like yesterday."

"Okay, all right. Don't get shouty. I'll see what I can do." She tucked a lock of hair behind her ear. "But these things take time. It's not like you can make a work order happen overnight," she said, sounding all huffy.

Mei-Lin, Nell, and Misty stared at her. Making a work order happen overnight was precisely what she'd done in getting that billboard up in the first place.

"Okay." Charlotte held up her hands. "I'll see what I can do."

"You shouldn't have spent the money, Charlotte." Misty sighed. "Not with things being so tight around here." She chastised Nell. As their accountant she was supposed to exercise financial responsibility. "I'm surprised you let her do it."

Nell rolled her eyes. "As if I could ever stop Charlotte from doing anything."

"For your information, ladies." Charlotte raised her chin, indignant. "I paid for the billboard out of my own funds. Savings. Not a penny came from Bearberry Brews."

"Wow, Charlotte. You shouldn't have," Misty said. "Seriously. Shouldn't have."

Nell tugged at the circle scarf draped around her neck. "Since Lucas isn't here to shoo those guys away," she said, glancing toward the street, "I'll do it."

"Wait!" Mei-Lin said. "I'll help you."

Charlotte spoke up. "Don't forget to get any new names for our waitlist. Also, ask them in for coffee." She giggled. "So I can scope them out."

"I'll suggest the coffee for sure." Nell beamed at Misty. "You should have seen Dad yesterday, after I tallied our receipts. There was a new spring in his step."

Well, at least something good had come out of Charlotte's wacky idea.

Nell spoke to Charlotte. "Still. Misty's right. That billboard needs to come down pronto. It's not fair to mislead people about Misty and her availability. Not with her being with Lucas."

Charlotte sighed. "Okay, fine. I'll get on it." She cocked her head at Misty and gave an order. "In the meantime, you go home."

"What? Now?"

"The clock's ticking, Misty. For you and Lucas. You tell him he's not coming in tomorrow, either. Not even for a little bit. You guys can't afford the time."

"What about your time?"

"I'm not wasting it," Charlotte said smugly. "I'm seeing Dave tonight."

"Dave?" Misty asked dumbfounded. "Who's Dave?"

"The nerdy guy in the coat and tie from yesterday," Mei-Lin whispered.

"He is *not* a nerd," Charlotte answered. "He's just well put together."

"Where did he come from?" Misty asked.

"Belfast. He's a banker."

"Oh! Well." Misty licked her lips. "Okay." So Charlotte *was* using the waitlist for her own gain. Good for her! "Where are you going?"

"Out to Mariner's."

"Fancy."

"I suggested coffee first." Charlotte shrugged. "But after I explained the situation, he said why not step things up?"

"Wait." Misty gulped. "You actually told him?"

"Told who what?" their mom asked, pushing in the door and past Nell, who sent a wide-eyed glance at the others.

Their dad came in next. "Quite a bunch of fellows out there," he said. "Wonder if that has to do with Charlotte's new coffee special? That first-timers' discount she dreamed up yesterday." He turned his blue gaze on Misty. "Or does this new uptick in business have something to do with you?"

Their mom frowned. "Mrs. McIntyre told us about the billboard, girls. But your father and I had to see it with our own eyes."

"Mom. Dad." Misty's voice squeaked. "I had nothing to do with it. Promise!"

"We weren't born yesterday," their dad admonished. "And we're very disappointed, honestly. We thought that whole Aidan thing was done."

Charlotte's face turned red. "We were only trying to help you and Bearberry Brews."

"This isn't the way," their dad told them. "And you know it."

"But wait!" Charlotte blurted out. "Things are already good! Misty's with Lucas!"

Misty's parents turned to her.

"Lucas?" her dad asked. "Is that true?"

"I, er…" Misty hedged. "Yeah."

"They've moved in together," Mei-Lin said. Then she added very quickly, "But into separate rooms!"

Her mom's scored face softened. "What's this about, Misty?"

"Lucas, he—"

"Didn't want her making a mistake," Mei-Lin supplied. She nodded, a knowing expression on her face. "Because he loves her and always has."

Misty's dad snapped his fingers. "I knew it." His eyes twinkled at his wife. "Didn't I tell you, Grace?"

Their mom clasped her hands together. "Yes." She gave a happy gasp. "Yes, you did. I thought so, too." She beheld her youngest daughter. "Do you feel the same?"

Misty's head spun. Did everyone believe this about Lucas? Was it possible it was true?

"I'm, um. Trying to make sure?"

"Which is why she's going home right now," Nell said. "To keep spending time with Lucas, before

Charlotte finds a guy of her own." She pursed her lips, realizing she'd blabbed.

Their mom's eyes flashed. "So your bet *is* back on."

"Daughters," their dad said wearily, inspiring guilty looks all around.

"The marriage only has to last five years," Misty argued. "And whichever one of us goes, the results will be so, so worth it." Her folks glanced at each other and shook their heads.

"We can't let you do this," their mom said.

"Maybe it's too late to stop them?" Mei-Lin ventured, then she winced. "Sorry. I'll stay out of it." Although she was almost like family, she technically wasn't. "I'll just go outdoors and um, take names."

Their mom's eyebrows arched. "Names?"

"We'll let Charlotte explain," Nell said, hustling out the door with Mei-Lin. "It was all her idea!"

"Which part?" their dad asked.

Mei-Lin snagged Misty by the elbow and whispered, "You're coming with us."

"The billboard!" Nell called before she leaped out the door.

Charlotte grumbled. "Thanks one heck of a—"

Nell tugged the door shut and stepped into the crowd, which immediately focused on Misty.

The cowboy stepped forward to intervene. "Misty's already spoken for."

A hipster in a man bun contended, "Says who?"

"Says Misty!" the cowboy said. His gaze fell on Mei-Lin. "Oh, hey there, pretty lady. I remember you." He tipped his hat. "You're the list-taker, right?"

"List?" a guy in a naval uniform asked. "There's a list?"

"Nobody told us about that," a construction worker complained.

The cowboy answered, "That's because you weren't here yesterday."

"Nobody panic!" Mei-Lin waved her notepad. "I can still take everyone's names."

Nell shoved Misty's arm while the group was distracted. "Go. Go!"

Misty gazed at the crowd and then into the café where her parents were berating Charlotte. No way was she going back in there. "Okay," she whispered to Nell while scooting away. "Thanks!"

• • •

Lucas entered Blue Sky Adventures hunting for Grant. He ran into Jordan first. Jordan had been moving camping equipment from the back room onto the sales floor and his dark complexion glistened with sweat.

"Hey man," Jordan said. "Help you with something?"

"Ah yeah." Lucas looked around, seeing nothing but outdoorsy adventure equipment and clothing. "I heard you guys rented bikes?"

Jordan pulled a hanky from his pocket and wiped his forehead. "Motorized or not?"

The idea of motorized hadn't occurred to Lucas, but he kind of liked the thought. "What kind of motorized?"

"Not serious motorcycles, but we've got mopeds."

Grant came in through the front door. He pushed his sunglasses up and into his wavy blond hair. "Oh hi, Lucas!" He grinned and his dark eyes shone against his suntanned skin. "I heard you were taking a little time off."

"Moved in together," Jordan chirped. "Yeah. I heard, too." He chuckled. "That have to do with this billboard thing?"

Lucas shifted on his feet. "Might have had some influence."

"Nell said the café was slammed."

"With good reason," Jordan said. "That was a great shot of Misty."

Every shot of Misty was great, as far as he was concerned. Though he didn't exactly like other guys thinking that. "Well, Misty's off the market now."

Grant scrutinized him a moment. "Glad you finally made your move, dude."

Finally? "What's that mean?"

Jordan cleared his throat. "It's just that some of us around here might have noticed your um, interest in Nell's baby sis."

Lucas wanted to groan. No way. Had it been that obvious?

"Yeah." Grant laughed. "Everyone but Misty."

"Ha. Yeah." He shoved his hands into his pockets. He was ready to get out of here. Being read so easily made him feel foolish. Transparent. Had Misty honestly missed his crushing on her, or did she have her suspicions too? "So," he said in casual tones. "About those bikes—"

"Want to see what we've got?" Grant asked. "They're in the shed around back."

"Sure."

Grant led the way while Jordan hung back to man

the store.

"So. Really great about you and Nell," Lucas said. "I don't believe I've seen you to say congrats."

"Yeah." Grant smiled and for an instant he seemed far away. "Great how things worked out."

"Pretty intense bet those Delaney sisters made."

"Definitely a little out there, but I suppose they've got their cause."

"They do love their family and the business," Lucas agreed. "They'd do just about anything, I guess."

They reached the shed and Grant grinned. "Yeah. How about you?"

"How about me?"

"Where do you stand in all of this?"

"I stand on the side of whatever's best for Misty."

Grant slapped his shoulder. "Good man."

CHAPTER EIGHT

When Misty returned to her apartment, Lucas was up. She peeked through his open bedroom door. Whoa. He'd made the bed and tightly tucked in all the corners. It almost looked like you could bounce a coin on it. She knew that Lucas was organized from work, but not that he was so meticulous in his personal life. Misty was, too, about certain things, like taking care with the details in her artwork. Her bedroom, though? She didn't keep that so tidy, and rarely made her bed. What was the point when you were only going to get back in it later?

She shrugged out of her jacket and carried it back into her room, dumping it on her rumpled comforter. Her parents had tried to instill certain good habits in her. Making the bed never stuck, though. Charlotte always made her look bad by making hers, since they'd shared a room. Charlotte also always did her homework on time. Misty had been good with coming up with excuses. Most of her teachers had bought her stories and let her off easy for her tardy assignments. Nell claimed that was on account of her charm, but Misty wasn't so sure about that. She didn't feel like a charmer most days.

She strode back into the kitchen hunting for Lucas in there. "Hello!" she called.

No answer.

"Lucas?" She stepped into the kitchen and that was empty as well. The glistening coffee pot sat turned upside down in her dishrack. Incredible, but Lucas had washed it. It probably needed a decent scrubbing about now.

He must have gone out on his errands. She was glad one of them was buying groceries because she was starved. Maybe she should have snagged some of those pumpkin spice cookies from the shop before being shooed away by Mei-Lin and her sisters. What she wouldn't have given to be a fly on the wall and hear what her folks were saying to Charlotte!

She caught a scent of something tempting in the air, then saw that the oven light was on. She peeked inside it and her stomach rumbled. Lucas had left those yummy-looking cinnamon buns in the warm oven after heating them up. He'd clearly had one himself.

She removed the tray using an oven mitt and set the cookie sheet on the stovetop, goggling at the gooey goodness. Melted cinnamon sugar and butter seeped deep into the crevices of thick doughy spirals. Okay, she was going in.

She tested a large swirly roll with her finger. It was nice and warm but not too hot. Just right. She picked it up, the stickiness coating her fingers, and took a big bite.

Oh yeah. Utter deliciousness.

Maybe it was good she was taking a few days off to spend with Lucas.

That way she wouldn't have to face her parents again for a bit.

Her phone buzzed in her pocket and she scanned the text from her mom.

Your dad and I are not so thrilled about Aidan.

I'm going to talk to Jane and call the whole thing off.

What? No! She couldn't do that.

Misty punched the call back button with her free hand and her mom picked up.

"Well, this is a surprise."

Misty swallowed her bite of cinnamon roll, then took another. "Mom."

"You could have told us, Misty," she said. "According to Charlotte, you announced yesterday that you were bound for London."

Traitor. Why did Charlotte have to blab?

Probably in her own defense for setting up that billboard.

"That's true, but—" Misty chewed quietly, holding the phone out away from her.

"But now she's off with Lucas," Misty heard her dad in the background say.

"Yes," her mom said as an aside, clearly speaking to her dad. "She might have told us about him, too."

"Maybe she didn't want us interfering?"

"Bob! We're her parents."

Misty took another bite of her treat, surveying it. She'd probably finish it completely before this call was done.

"Uh," she said. "If the two of you would like to talk—"

"No, no," her mom answered. "The one we want to talk to is you. All of you girls, actually. We're calling a family meeting."

Uh-oh. Misty knew what that meant and it was

never good.

"I'm a little indisposed."

Her mom gasped. "With Lucas?"

Next, her dad chimed in. "Maybe we should give those kids their privacy, Grace? Charlotte says their relationship is brand new."

"New? They've known each other for years!"

Misty rolled her eyes at the ceiling. "Oops! Sorry! Burning the toast. Gotta go!"

"Toast?" her mom asked. "What toast?"

"And pul-eeze, Mom. Don't call Jane. Not yet!"

"Why not?"

"Because…things are still being worked out."

"Well, your dad and I don't like the way they're working."

She had to talk to Charlotte and Nell ASAP. She dropped her mostly eaten cinnamon bun back in the box and hurried over to the sink, turning on the water and rinsing off her gooey hand.

A family meeting? No. She wiped her hand on a dish towel.

She'd call a sisters' meeting first.

"Nothing's been done yet!" she told her parents, while rapidly texting Charlotte and Nell.

ER meet-up!

Serious hitch!

Charlotte answered, guessing. *Mom?*

"Nothing?" She could envision her mom's squint. "Is that what you call the billboard at the edge of town? And what about Nell and Grant?"

Yep. Her!

Nell suggested a time and place. *7:30 p.m. Mariner's.*

Misty sent a thumbs-up.

Charlotte did, too.

Great. They were on.

"We like Grant, though," her dad chimed in. Then he spoke a little louder, clearly angling toward her mom's phone. "Lucas, too! Of course!"

Misty sighed. "Let me call you later, okay? My toast is burning."

"Burning? Oh no."

"Uh yeah. Uh-oh."

"What?"

"Fire!" Misty shouted. Then she ended the call.

Lucas dashed into the kitchen. "Misty! What's"—he glanced around the room, then stared at the stove. The toaster oven next and then the disassembled coffeepot—"going on?"

Misty sank down in a chair. "That was my parents."

He studied her anew. "And why aren't you at the café?"

"Everyone sent me home to work on our list."

"Figured they might." He joined her at the table. "What did your folks want?"

"They kind of saw the billboard—and told Charlotte to take it down."

Lucas nodded. "The more people Charlotte hears that from the better. I mean, she's already got that waitlist. How long is it now?"

"Mei-Lin says close to fifty."

His eyebrows shot up. "Wow."

"One of the guys—the cowboy. He followed me in to work today."

"Followed?" He set his elbows on the table. "How?"

"A little creepily at first, but I think he's okay. Dusty just wanted to talk."

"So you're on a first name basis now?" A muscle in his jaw tense.

"It's not like that. Come on."

Lucas hung his head and then looked up. "You're sure?"

Misty laughed. "Sure I'm sure! *Lucas*," she said. "I'm not interested in any of those guys. They're strangers!"

"Like Aidan?" he said, nailing her.

"Ah. Aidan…" Misty gathered her poise. "Is an old family frenemy. He's not a stranger entirely." She slapped her forehead. "And get this! Mom wants to call his mom to cancel the whole deal."

"Would that be such a bad thing?" He took her hand and Misty's heart jolted. Then she felt all fuzzy and conflicted inside.

"Yes!" She squeezed his hand and released it.

"Sorry. I—"

"No. Don't be."

He dove into her eyes and Misty's heart reeled. She tried to tell herself she didn't see him that way. And she didn't. She really didn't.

"Thanks for being here for me."

"Anytime."

She and he were just pretending—for her sisters. But if that was the case, then why did her heart thump each time he got that certain look in his eyes?

"Bottom line. I'm helping you out." He sat back and folded his arms. "Don't worry, Misty. I get that this is all make-believe." His gray eyes twinkled and Misty laid her hand across her belly to quell its nervous flutter.

Her smile trembled. She had no problem acting with Lucas.

Despite the fact that he was a *very* nice-looking guy.

She normally didn't see him on his days off and his slight beard stubble added a sense of ruggedness to his persona somehow. Not that he needed anything extra. Lucas was already tough enough. Otherwise, he probably wouldn't have survived working at Bearberry Brews all these years around her quirky parents and meddlesome sisters. Though they rarely meddled with him. It was Misty's life that they interfered in, mostly. Still. He'd witnessed his fair share of her family's drama and it hadn't scared him away.

"It *is* make-believe," she said. "But we've got to be convincing to buy more time."

"For you to make your mind up about Aidan?"

"That, and…other things."

"Oh yeah? Like what?"

But she wasn't ready to tell him about RISD. What if that didn't even come through? "I'm just sorting things out."

"Good to know," he said, which was how he responded when she was being evasive on a topic. "Good to know" from Lucas was his way of pointing out that she hadn't actually told him anything. And she hadn't about certain things. About others, though, she'd spilled a ton.

"Hungry?" he asked, changing the subject.

"Just a little. I don't normally eat much in the morning."

He eyed the open cinnamon roll container and its demolished contents.

She giggled. "Okay, busted! I do enjoy a sweet treat once in a while. Just normally don't buy them. Those cinnamon buns are delicious, by the way."

"Yeah. They're really tasty." He frowned. "I'm sorry you filled yourself up, though, because I'd planned a breakfast surprise. I stopped by the market and picked up some groceries."

"Thanks, Lucas." She hated to disappoint him, since he'd gone to extra trouble. She could probably squeeze in a bit of French toast, or pancakes or... "I'm not *that* full. I'm sure I can fit a little more something in."

He grinned. "Great."

"Just let me know how much everything was and I'll pay half."

"You don't have to."

"It's only fair."

"All right." He paused and then said, "Also went by Blue Sky Adventures to get those bikes. I thought we could head out later but since you're already here, how about we pack a picnic lunch and ride out to Lookout Point?"

That sounded like a lot of fun and she said so. It would also knock an item off their list.

"But first, let me grab the grocery bags from the living room. I dumped them on the couch when I thought the place was on fire."

"Sorry." Misty went to help him retrieve the bags. There were three paper sacks and they all looked pretty full.

"Whoa, Lucas. You got a ton of stuff."

"We're going to have to eat while I'm here," he said reasonably. "And we're going to start with one of your favorites right now."

"Favorites?"

"Smoothies." He winked. "I got the best fresh seaweed. Hemp hearts, chia seeds, and acai berries, too."

"Seaweed? Oh!" Her stomach roiled a little. She had no idea what acai was, but if it was a berry she'd probably like that. "Nice."

"I didn't know what went into those drinks, truthfully," he told her. "Did a little research on my phone."

"Right there in McIntyre's Market?"

"Yeah. Sean helped, too."

Sean? Figured. He was always eating really weird stuff and insisting that Misty try it. She had once or twice, and that had been enough. "Did you tell him you were buying for me?"

"No." Lucas's face was a question mark. "Should I have?"

"Uh, no!" She puffed out a breath hauling the heavy grocery sack, which also felt cold, the paper sides of it chilling her arms. "Not really." What did he have in there? Gobs of popsicles?

"Got a five pound bag of ice too," he said. "Considering your ice situation."

"Oh great!" She peeked into her sack, spying the ice below a spinach box. There was a huge tub of plain yogurt in there, too. "Thanks, Lucas."

"You didn't want raw egg?"

Raw? Egg? Her nose wrinkled up even though she didn't mean for it to. "Um. Probably not."

"Didn't think so," he said, unloading his bag. "Given that we had omelets last night for dinner." He'd bought strawberries and oranges, and loads of mason jars that looked like they'd come from the organic section of the shop. Fortunately, he'd also gotten some normal food, like deli cold cuts and sandwich bread. Although the bread was whole wheat. Which was cool. Misty didn't mind whole wheat. She was still worrying over the seaweed.

He pulled a chip bag into the air with a flourish. "Ta-da!"

Misty viewed its gold-and-brown packaging. "What's that?"

"Oven crisps! They're baked," Lucas announced, pleased with himself. "Not fried like potato chips, but of course you know that."

"Er. Right." She really would have preferred the potato chips. But okay. She could deal.

Lucas was busy sorting the unpacked groceries into two piles: one for making smoothies and one not. "How about you put things away while I whip up?" He already had the lid off the blender and had plugged it in.

He was really focused on this. Trying hard to be so thoughtful. Might have been better if he was whipping up a big chocolate milkshake, but maybe the smoothie wouldn't be too bad. Especially once he included those whatchamacallit berries.

She picked up a wad of dried seaweed bound

together by a narrow string and smelled it, then sti-
fled a gag. Its briny scent was disgusting. If she
wanted sea-to-table dining, she would have gone to
Mariner's and ordered an entrée. "This from around
here?"

"Sean said everything is local-sourced. Perfect for
a healthy-minded woman like you." He grinned and
her chest warmed because he was trying so hard.

"Cool."

• • •

A short time later, Misty finished up her "breakfast"
while Lucas wrapped their sandwiches. "I'll toss these
in my daypack," he said. "With the chips and a couple
of waters." He studied her bloated cheeks. She was
trying to swallow this last bit. She really was. But, as
much as he'd blended, the seaweed still came out a
little stringy. *Ooof.*

Lucas sent her a worried look.

"Everything okay?"

She shut her eyes and gulped down the contents
of her mouth. It wasn't terrible, but also definitely not
her first choice for a breakfast smoothie. She might
have preferred strawberries and bananas or something. Not that she'd ever tell him this and hurt his
feelings.

"Oh yeah." She wiped her mouth with a napkin
and smiled. "It was delicious!"

She was going to get Sean for this. If she ever saw
him again. Which she certainly would in tiny Majestic.
Population 2002, according to the sign beside the
billboard. She hoped—at this moment—that

Charlotte was in the process of having it taken down. Otherwise, Misty was going to kill her. Twenty-four hours of this had been enough.

They got ready to go and Lucas suggested she put on her jacket. "Might be a little breezy when we're riding along."

Misty blushed at him being so considerate. "Good idea, thanks." She grabbed her windbreaker from the coat closet and followed him down the narrow stairwell. He'd parked his truck by the curb on the street. Two mopeds leaned up against it. Each had a helmet draped from its handlebars. Misty brought her hands to her mouth. "Mopeds!" She glanced at Lucas. "I thought we were riding bikes."

"These *are* bikes." His gray eyes twinkled and warmth spread through her chest. "They just move a little faster than the other kind."

Misty laughed, totally pleased with the situation. She hadn't been on a moped in years. Not since she was a teenager. "I guess we'll see if I remember how to ride."

"You'll do fine," he said, and his confidence in her gave her a boost.

He had his daypack over his shoulders and handed her a helmet. "Which one do you want? Red or green?"

"Red," Misty said decisively. They appeared roughly the same size and a little high off the ground. She hoped that she could manage. Then again, she'd been able to handle one of these back in the day. Gulls called overhead and Misty glanced at the sky. It burned bright blue with big billowy clouds hanging low. Auras of sunshine surrounded them. The breeze was a brisk but not uncomfortable. She was glad she'd worn her jacket.

"Looks like a great day for riding," he said, strapping on his helmet.

Misty put hers on, too. "Yeah, this will be fun."

She couldn't remember the last time she'd done something out of the ordinary. Most of her life was so routine. Like going in to Bearberry Brews for work, or out for a beer with Sean. Oh yeah. There *had* been her application to RISD. That had pushed her out of her comfort zone. Completing all those short and long essay responses and submitting her portfolio had been a major task. Then there was all that financial aid paperwork to get through.

Mei-Lin had been a huge help in the cheerleading department. Meaning, Mei-Lin texted, called, and dropped by repeatedly to check up on Misty's "progress"—complimenting her at every finished step—until Misty was finally done and her slides had been turned in.

But her RISD application had been different than this. That had exerted pressure and anxiety, while this outing with Lucas just seemed fun. He climbed onto his moped, grasping the handlebars. "You remember how to get this going?"

"Think so." She studied her controls. "Turn the key while braking." She squeezed the brake levers on her handlebars, trying them out. They tensed and released in her grip, the experience coming back to her. She flipped on the bright red kill switch, as an emergency measure.

"You all good, or you want me to walk you through it?"

"I'm all good." Misty nodded, feeling giddy. Even though this seriously wasn't a big deal, at least it would give her a break from thinking about Aidan and that looming bet. She and Charlotte used to ride a ton when they were younger. Nell had never been much into it. Funny, now that Nell was marrying such an adventuresome guy.

"All righty then." Lucas grinned. "Let's get going." He released his brakes, revving the engine.

Misty positioned herself on her seat, getting ready. "We headed out to the lighthouse?"

"I thought we might have lunch out there, but it's still a little early." He turned and glanced over his shoulder. "Is there anywhere else you'd like to go first?"

. . .

Misty gaped at the oversized billboard. This was way worse than she'd imagined and her imagination was really good. "I can't believe Charlotte did this."

She undid her chinstrap and removed her helmet.

"It's a pretty good likeness of you though."

"Because it *is* me." Misty huffed. "You think she might have asked me first."

"Who? Charlotte?"

She read his eyes, knowing he had a point. Charlotte always did pretty much what she wanted, even when people told her not to. In some ways, resistance to her ideas made her defend them all the more.

Misty sighed. "You're right. She wouldn't have listened."

The one small mercy was that the billboard was in the process of being taken down. Two men wearing hard hats and reflective orange vests were there with a ladder bucket truck, backing it up to the billboard. One guy was in the cab and another on the ground, waving and shouting at him and giving directions.

"I don't get it!" the guy called out the cab of the ladder truck. "We just put this thing up!"

"It's got to come down though," his co-worker said. "Today!"

A man in a black sedan slammed on his brakes and his vehicle screeched to a halt. He slowly backed up on the empty stretch of highway, pulling over. "Uh-oh," Lucas said. "That's the newspaper guy."

Darcy Fitzpatrick stepped from his car just as a bright orange Land Rover pulled up behind him. Allison Highsmith exited its driver's side with a combative air.

"Looks like somebody tipped you off, too," she said, striding toward him.

He held up both hands. "Allison, look…"

The rest of their conversation was muffled, then the bucket ladder dude on the ground motioned for the other one to halt. "Is there some sort of problem?" he asked Allison and Darcy.

"No," she said. "We just heard—"

"Wait!" Darcy nudged her, turning Misty and Lucas's way. "Look! There they are."

The sign workers pivoted, too. "Is that her?" one of them asked. "Misty?" He shot a glance at the partially taken-down billboard, but enough of her face remained in clear view.

"Maybe she'll talk this time?" Darcy said to Allison.

Her voice was a little breathy. "And maybe that's her secret guy?"

"Hey you!" Darcy called. "Wait up!"

Lucas slapped on his helmet and buckled his chinstrap. "I think we'd better bolt."

Misty was already ready to go. "Yeah, like now." If there was one thing she didn't want to do today it was talk to the local press, as meager as it was. This was her time to be free of all that pressure. She chided herself for having to see the billboard in person. Maybe she should have skipped this.

Allison hurried in their direction with Darcy right on her heels. "Misty! Please! Just a minute!"

"Two!" Darcy yelled. "Save one for me!"

"You go first," Lucas said. "I'll be right behind you."

Then they spun their mopeds around and took off.

"Turn to your left!" Lucas bellowed into the wind.

She stared across the sandy field covered with tall seagrasses. A narrow path wound through it.

"It's a shortcut!" he told her.

Misty lowered her shoulders and picked up her speed, riding faster and faster. Sharp winds nipped at her cheeks and her ponytail flew behind her. She was invincible and free. They'd also lost the guys from the highway, leaving them in their dust. Woo!

She peeked behind her and Lucas motioned for her to turn around.

"Careful! Misty!"

Wait! What was that?

She hit a bump and then another.

Her front tire reared up then came down hard, hitting a rut in the sand.

Her front wheel went one way and the back went another.

The next thing she knew, she was flying over her handlebars.

CHAPTER NINE

Lucas watched the action unfold right in front of him in painstakingly slow motion, and it was horrific. The forehead section of Misty's helmet smacked the ground first. A split-second later her hands made purchase with the earth, hitting the sand heels first as her body jettisoned forward, faceplanting her in the earth. *Misty! No!*

Lucas cut his engine and leaped off his moped, discarding it as he went, and raced over to her. The engine on Misty's moped had cut automatically and it keeled on its side.

"Misty! Are you all right?"

She pushed herself up on her hands and winced. "I—think so."

He knelt beside her, helping her roll into a sitting position. "Take it easy. Just catch your breath."

She wheezed in some air, then exhaled in rapid puffs, maybe hyperventilating.

"Easy," he cautioned. "Deep breaths."

She inhaled fully, then let it all out before stretching her arms out in front of her. Her hands and wrists were scraped and one of her windbreaker sleeves was torn, but she had no visible gashes anywhere. "How's your head?"

"Throbbing." She unlatched her chinstrap and Lucas gently removed her helmet.

"You're probably going to have one helluva headache." He hoped that was all.

"Guess it was lucky I was wearing that," she said when he set it down. "Hit the ground pretty hard."

"Lucky for you it was sand and not pavement."

"Yeah." Her breath still came in fits and starts.

Lucas rubbed her shoulder. "Anything else hurt besides your head?"

"My hands." She examined the mild abrasions. "And wrists mostly." She rubbed those next.

"Knees?"

"Probably okay. My jeans prevented any scrapes, thankfully."

"Maybe we should clean you up with some water from one of the water bottles and napkins?"

"I'll be okay," she said but her voice shook.

"How's your back?"

She righted herself in a sitting position. "Seems fine."

"Neck?"

She moved it around and rolled back her shoulders. "All good. Maybe a little stiff."

He frowned. "Maybe we should take you to the clinic."

"No, Lucas. Really. I'm sure that I'm fine."

"Well, the moped riding is sure done for the day."

She jutted out her chin in that stubborn way he found so adorable. "Says who?"

A few strands from her ponytail had broken loose and a purple wisp of hair spilled across her forehead, partially shielding one eye. He tenderly reached out and tucked it behind her ear.

"Says me," he answered in a low murmur. "We need to get you cleaned up and—"

"Then what about the lighthouse?"

He couldn't believe her persistence but maybe he should have. "It will be there tomorrow, I hear."

Misty pouted. "Tomorrow's supposed to be rainy."

Lucas checked the clear blue sky. "Could have fooled me."

"I saw it on my weather app." She shifted and bent up her knees, resting her arms on them. He watched her carefully but didn't note any further signs of distress. Maybe she had gotten off easily. He thanked his lucky stars for that.

"Want to try standing?" She nodded and he held out his hand.

She stared down at her injured palm. "Ugh."

"Here," he said, grabbing her under her elbow. "Let me help this way."

She made it to her feet setting her weight on one side and then the other, attempting to stand on each foot while he kept her stabilized. "All good?"

She nodded.

He stared down at her moped and then over at his. Even though she wanted to, he doubted her ability to ride safely with those battered hands. "I don't think you should get back on yours," he said. "Not like" — he glanced at her hands — "that."

She sighed. "You're probably right about me keeping a grip on the handlebars, but I can probably push it along just fine."

His gaze swept the field. They were only a few hundred yards from the far end of town. The bakery where his mom worked wasn't far from here. They kept a first aid kit on hand. Besides that, his mom had training as a school nurse. "We're pretty close to Dolphin Donuts," he offered. "Maybe we can pop in there?" He released her gradually, making sure that she was standing steadily. "I was thinking we'd check in with my mom."

"I honestly don't think I need medical attention, Lucas."

"She might give us some donuts, then? For a discount."

"Not free?"

He chuckled and his heart felt light. Which was about a thousand times better than it had felt a few minutes ago, when it had been clenched clamshell-tight with fear. "I can ask her."

Misty shot him a playful smirk, the one that always made his heart beat double-time. "In that case," she said, "I guess we'd better stop by."

. . .

So much for feeling reckless and free.

Misty pushed her moped along over uneven ground locking her shaky knees. She was fine. She could do this. She'd taken a baby spill. So what? No bones were broken. No serious damage. She could have been hurt much worse.

"You're doing great," Lucas said. "Almost there."

They pulled out of the sandy field steering onto the sidewalk. Dolphin Donuts & More was just a few doors down. Its fancy painted front window showed a dolphin diving through a chocolate-iced donut with red, white, and blue sprinkles. An image of a fluttering American flag had been stuck on top and made to look like it was held in by a wooden toothpick.

The donut shop owner's daughter Jill had been in

high school art classes with Misty. She'd painted the
design for her dad one Fourth of July as a promo and
he'd never changed it. He liked it that much. Jill lived
in New York now and did something artistic. Not in
the visual arts, though. It was more like theater.

Lucas's mom, Consuelo, looked over when she
saw them enter the shop. There was only one other
customer at the moment, a man carrying a big box of
donuts who Misty didn't recognize. She ducked behind Lucas as they passed him, in case he was a
billboard guy.

"Lucas!" His mom's broad grin lit up her face, her
dark eyes sparkling. "Misty! How good to—" Her
cheeks sagged when she noticed Misty's scrapes. "Oh,
honey. What happened?" She stared at Lucas and
then out the front window. Their mopeds were parked
by the lamppost. Luckily, hers hadn't sustained any
damage.

"Lucas and I were riding," Misty said. "And I hit a
little…bump in the road."

"Or the field, really." Lucas's eyebrows knitted
together. "We're lucky it wasn't worse."

His mom scooted around the counter, her forehead furrowing. "Is it okay if I take a look?" She had
a kindness about her that was soothing. Misty'd always liked Lucas's mom. She was a nice person who'd
had a lot laid on her shoulders. Losing her husband in
her forties among them.

"Sure," Misty said, extending her arms, wrists up.
The abrasion on her left wrist had spared her tattoo
and she was grateful for that.

Mrs. Reyes gently placed one hand on the underside of Misty's arm while tenderly grasping her

fingers with the other. She lifted Misty's arm up and down and manipulated this way and that. Then she did the same with the other. "None of this hurts?"

"The moving?" Misty asked. "No. Just the raw parts."

"I've got something in my first aid kit I can put on that." She smiled warmly. "We'll need to clean you up first."

"With soap and water?"

Lucas chuckled at her wide-eyed response. "Come on, now. Be a big girl and cooperate with the nurse."

"Yeah," Mrs. Reyes teased. "My rates are much better than the clinic's."

"I'm really sorry to bother you."

"Don't be silly," Mrs. Reyes said. "I'm always happy to see you. Only." She frowned. "Sorry it's because of this."

Misty followed her into the kitchen where she was told to wait by the sink. Mrs. Reyes returned from a back room a short time later carrying a plastic box with a medical cross emblem on its top. She turned on the water and scrubbed her hands under the faucet. Then she reached for Misty's arm. "This may sting a little but it will be worth it."

"No risk of infection?"

"High risk of donuts."

Misty laughed despite the light cleansing.

"You can pick your flavor."

"Probably something with chocolate."

"We've got plenty of those." Mrs. Reyes used clean paper towels to pat her dry. "Now, hmm." She fished through her medical kit. "Your hands don't look so bad. We can try a bandage on that deeper scrape on the heel of your right one and another on that spot on your right wrist." She wore her wavy dark hair in a short cut. It spilled forward as she worked, gleaming in the fluorescent light. "But," she said, "I'm going to spritz on a little antibiotic spray first."

She applied a few quick bursts of antibiotic spray and Misty held her breath.

The sting wasn't really too bad and it dissipated quickly.

Lucas had inherited his charcoal-colored curls from his dad, as well as his dad's gray eyes. His mom's eyes were very light brown, bordering on amber. The fine lines surrounding her mouth and eyes deepened when she smiled. Mrs. Reyes was in her fifties, Misty guessed, about ten years younger than her parents, who'd gotten started on their family later.

"I heard about your billboard," Mrs. Reyes said while opening a bandage. She pulled back the top layer of its wrapping without looking at Misty. "It's really caused a stir." She wasn't judgy when she said it. Her tone was more like…curious.

"Ah, yeah. About that—"

Mrs. Reyes looked up. "I know it wasn't your idea."

"No. It was Charlotte's."

She applied the bandage, then prepared to open another. "That somehow didn't seem like you," she said gently.

It touched Misty that Mrs. Reyes thought well of her, then she wondered why Lucas's mom had an opinion of her at all. Did he talk about her to his mom? Maybe he talked about everyone who worked at Bearberry Brews? He'd worked there forever.

Funny thing was, he never talked about his home life.

"When is that billboard coming down?"

"Coming down as we speak." Misty sighed. "It never should have happened." Mrs. Reyes raised her eyebrows. "But Charlotte only meant well. She and Nell and Mei-Lin."

Mrs. Reyes's tender gaze poured into her and Misty found herself opening her soul. "Mei-Lin was opposed from the start," she confided. "Never wanted me to give up on true love and marry Aidan Strong. But, I mean, Mei-Lin. You know. She's such a romantic. So's Nell! They believe in that stuff, fated matches."

"And you don't?" Mrs. Reyes opened a medicine bottle and gave Misty two tablets. Then she handed her a small paper cup of water. "Take two of these, then two more in four hours. Trust me. Your head will thank you. The rest of your body will, too."

Misty did as she was told, considering the question. "Fated? I don't know. I've never experienced that vibe, but others do. Just look at Nell and Grant! But me? No." She shook her head. "I can't see it. That's why I'd given up and had decided to go to London, because it was the right and honorable thing to do."

Mrs. Reyes gave her the medicine bottle to tuck in her purse. "Keep it," she said. "I've got more." The compassion in her eyes carried Misty along on this gently rolling wave. It was like she couldn't help spilling more. "You were saying—about fated matches?"

Misty blew out a breath. "I mean, really. Do you think they exist?"

"They did for me and Lucas's father. Probably for your mother and father, too."

"I don't know. Maybe." She shrugged. "But I never thought that would happen to me. I'm twenty-six, Mrs. Reyes, and I've never even fallen in love."

She looked surprised. "Never?"

"I mean, sure I've dated guys. Lots and lots of guys. Some super-hot ones, too—"

Misty cupped a hand to her mouth, horrified.

What am I doing?

Completely unloading to Lucas's mom!

Nooo. Why?

Misty swallowed hard. She knew why. Consuelo Reyes had that same "tell me all about it" look that Lucas sometimes wore. The one that made Misty want to confess her deepest darkest secrets.

Despite her better judgment.

Like now.

"I'm really sorry." She puffed out a breath. "I shouldn't have said all that."

Mrs. Reyes cleaned up the trash and closed the first aid kit. "It's all right. Sometimes it's good to talk about things. Get them off your chest."

Yeah, sure. She just didn't need to go unburdening to her fake-boyfriend-for-the-moment's mom. Telling her all about her troubles.

Mrs. Reyes frowned sympathetically. "Sounds like you've been under a lot of stress."

"I have been, yeah. Lucas has been incredibly helpful."

"He's a really great guy, my Lucas."

"You raised him so well!"

"Thanks."

"I mean it, though." Misty thought of what a considerate apartment guest he'd been. "He's kind. He cooks! He makes the b—"

Mrs. Reyes's demeanor shifted. "Bed?" She blinked.

Misty's cheeks burned hot. "His bed, Mrs. Reyes."

"Ahh."

Her face steamed hotter. "In his very own room."

"Everything okay back here?" Lucas asked. Misty whipped toward the door as he walked through it. "You've been gone a while."

"Lucas." His mom waved him along. "Can we talk?"

He shifted on his feet. "Um. Sure."

Misty slipped out to the customer area of the bakery but she could still overhear their hushed discussion. Especially when she stood close to the kitchen door and cocked her head a certain way. She plucked a laminated menu off the pastry case and pretended to be studying it. Just in case Lucas and his mom suddenly reappeared, or somebody else happened into the shop, she couldn't exactly look like she was eavesdropping. Which she wasn't. It was only that they were whispering so loudly.

"I'm worried about you. You and Misty. How long do you plan to keep up this charade?"

"Not long. A few days. One week tops."

"And what do you expect to happen by then?"

"For her to make up her mind. Once and for all."

"About what? About Aidan? About you? I don't want you to get your hopes up, *mijo*," she said quietly. "She seems like a very nice girl. But Lucas, she isn't ready for a serious relationship."

"How do you know?"

"If she was, she wouldn't be conflicted."

"Yeah, and she also might be on a plane to London." His voice cracked like that was the most heartbreaking outcome imaginable.

"But that relationship would be fake, Lucas. Maybe even much more than yours is with her."

"What's that supposed to mean?"

She studied his eyes, then her face fell. "Oh *hijo*, no." Her tone softened. "Ramon was right, wasn't he? You're in love with her, aren't you?"

"Mom. Shhh!"

Misty dropped her menu and it fluttered to the floor.

No way. Her sisters and Mei-Lin were right? The revelation was a little embarrassing but hugely flattering, too. Did he really feel that way about her? And was this new, or something he'd felt before?

"Misty?" Heat flooded her cheeks when Lucas caught her crouching by the pastry case. "Um. What are you doing?"

She picked up the menu and waved it in her hand, taking care with its sharp edges and her scrapes. "I, er, just dropped this!"

She stood only to be caught up in Mrs. Reyes's curious stare. "I promised you donuts, and donuts you'll get!" She took up her station behind the counter, clearly viewing Misty with new eyes. Maybe as a potential daughter-in-law and the mother of her grandchildren, if she believed what she guessed about Lucas to be true. But weddings and babies took two parties to happen. Misty's heart thumped. She wasn't in love with Lucas. Of course she wasn't. What would she do without him if she let herself fall and things went wrong? As great as he was, and he was pretty amazing. Super amazing. Maybe more amazing than she knew. She couldn't risk it.

"Chocolate you said?" Mrs. Reyes's eyes danced like she was in on a big secret. Now, Misty was in on it, too. She rolled her gaze toward Lucas, standing there all innocent like.

"We'll pop them in my daypack," he said about the donuts, "unless you want to eat them here?"

While she knew she risked ruining her lunch, the fact that the donuts were still relatively fresh and warm was too tempting. "I don't know about eating a whole one since they're so big, and after that awesome smoothie. Do you want to share?"

"Don't see why not," Lucas said.

"I can make you some coffee to go with," Mrs. Reyes volunteered.

Misty grinned. "That would be amazing!"

Lucas motioned toward the street. "Let's sit at one of those umbrella tables outside."

Once they were settled with their coffee, Misty weighed what to say. She couldn't admit she'd overheard Lucas's conversation with his mom. That would be embarrassing. It was also a little unsettling to know that he felt that way about her, and probably had for a while.

Sunbeams streamed under one end of the umbrella creating a magical sparkle in his deep gray eyes. Misty's skin tingled and her heart did a funny dance.

It was Lucas who was into her, though, and not the other way around.

He opened the donut bag and took out the giant treat, tearing it down the middle and handing her one half. It had to be all the adrenaline she had going on after seeing that billboard and the biking accident, because she was actually pretty hungry. She was also eager to wash that smoothie taste out of her mouth. She'd tried by brushing her teeth and using mouthwash but that hadn't quite done it. Maybe it was the seaweed part. That had tasted kind of bitter and this donut was sweet revenge.

"Thanks, Lucas."

He grinned. "The donuts here are pretty hard to resist."

"Mmm." She sunk her teeth into the tasty treat, savoring the sugary warmth of its doughy cake. And, OMG, that milk chocolate icing was to die for, and obviously homemade, just like the rest of everything at Dolphin Donuts & More. Everyone in town loved the shop, including her parents who had a regular standing order to stock the pastry cases at Bearberry Brews.

Some people thought they made their own confections at the café but they didn't. Her parents had decided long ago to specialize in one thing and do it exceptionally well. They did serve a few basic breakfast and lunch items, but those were outsourced, too, and brought in from the deli section at McIntyre's Market.

Lucas glanced down the street, which remained relatively quiet. Majestic wasn't precisely a touristy town. They got some visitors here but mostly those were folks passing through on their way to some of the popular beaches. Charlotte's billboard had drawn a bigger influx of outsiders than the tiny town had seen in a while.

"I'm glad that billboard's coming down," he said. "We don't need a repeat of what happened this morning."

"No joke." Misty shook her head. "I'm guessing my folks gave Charlotte quite an earful."

"What's she planning to do with that waitlist?"

"She claims she's going to use it herself."

Lucas guffawed. "Seriously?"

"She's already going out with some random guy named Dave."

"The suit and tie dude with the glasses?"

"Yeah, he's a banker."

"I remember him, but not some of the others. The cowboy excluded." His cheek flinched. "He's the one who tracked you down."

It charmed her somehow that he seemed protective or maybe even slightly jealous. Although Lucas had absolutely nothing to worry about. Misty wasn't into Stetsons and spurs. She was into... Well, she wasn't totally sure what but not Dusty, anyway.

"I'm sure he's well on his way to Bar Harbor by now," she said.

Lucas finished his donut and wiped his fingers on a napkin. "Yeah. Good thing."

She studied him a moment in the sunshine, wondering about his motives. While it was true he was trying to help her, she hadn't realized Lucas wasn't being entirely altruistic. He was hoping she'd come to care for him, too.

She considered this concept a moment, rolling around the idea of her and Lucas as a couple in her brain. Physically, as a pair, they looked nice enough together. But did they have things in common? Could they form that kind of bond? The sort that would last forever?

She wished that she could say yes, because that would solve her Aidan problem. No way would she go off to England to marry him if she was desperately in love with Lucas.

Lucas was a good guy. The best guy. A friend and trusted confidante.

Someone she could fall in love with, though?

"So," he said after a lull during which they both finished their coffees. "I was thinking we might drive along the coast for a bit, then head on over to the lighthouse. If we're not hungry for lunch by then we can save it to eat back at your place. Or we could always eat half."

Lucas was so great at solutions. "Why don't we play that by ear?"

He nodded and gathered their trash and they both stood.

"The only thing is"—she glanced at her hands— "I'm not sure about me driving."

"Hadn't planned on that. Not with those hands." His eyes twinkled. "I was thinking we'd leave one of the mopeds here and that you could ride with me."

Which would mean she'd have her arms around him and be holding on tight. Her stomach swooped and the niggly voice inside her said the idea of them being together seemed slightly exciting.

"If you'd rather not, though," he said, "we can walk the bikes back to your place and relax. Or, we can leave the mopeds here and I'll come back for them with my truck. I got that ramp to load them."

"What?" Misty cried in mock protest. "And miss going to the lighthouse?"

"We are supposed to bike out there together," he said.

"There's nothing on that list about us taking separate bikes." Misty shoved his arm playfully and he pressed her bandaged hand to his arm.

"No," he said. "Nothing at all."

Misty's heart fluttered at his intense look, the one that generally meant he could see into her head. If he could right now then he'd know what she was thinking. And that was her heart and head felt pretty mixed up right now.

She saddled up behind him on the moped and leaned in close, smelling his spicy masculine scent. It wasn't heavy like cologne. More fresh and clean like bodywash and its aroma washed over her like a tingly rain shower.

"Just hang onto me," he said. "And we'll go for a spin."

She settled her arms around his waist, molding herself up against him. His body felt solid and strong pressed against hers, leaving her a little breathy. "Sounds good," she said, tightening her grip.

"Ready?" he asked over his shoulder.

But, honest to goodness, she wasn't sure.

For all her wishful thinking about the future and having an artistic career, there was one thing she'd never planned on.

Having designs on Lucas.

CHAPTER TEN

Lucas roared along the high beach road, wind whipping against his face and sunglasses.

With Misty behind him and the ocean thundering below, this was heaven. She clung to him, her warmth seeping into his. The day was balmy but not hot. Ideal mid-September weather. They hadn't even needed their jackets. So, after their coffee and donut, they'd tucked them in his daypack. He'd tied that to the rear bumper of the moped with the bungie cord he kept in its zipper pocket.

"This is so cool!" she called over his shoulder.

"Yeah," he agreed, keeping his gaze ahead of him. That one accident this morning had been plenty. "Perfect day!"

She snuggled against him, pressing one side of her helmet against his back and he deduced she was staring at the sea. He caught snippets of the view in his peripheral vision.

Diving seagulls.

Dancing white-capped waves.

Wind-swept deep purple flowers curtseying on a hill.

The diamond-patterned lighthouse stood up ahead of them, perched on a man-made outcropping and was surrounded by a wrought-iron balustrade. Park benches ringed its perimeter and a lookout station was established by the railing. For a couple of coins you could use the hefty hand-tilt binoculars for a better view of the sea, and maybe catch a glimpse of a dolphin.

A small crowd of visitors waited in line to tour the lighthouse, which limited capacity due to the narrow width of the steep spiral staircase inside. Lucas slowed to a stop as they approached and set his feet on the pavement. He cut the engine and Misty hopped off, removing her helmet. He got off next and smiled at her.

"What do you think?" His gaze swept the lighthouse's front door. The tail end of the line had just disappeared inside it. Now might be a good time to take advantage. "Want to go up?"

Her grin spread all the way up her pretty hazel eyes, making them sparkle. "You bet I do."

By the way she scampered up those lighthouse steps, it was hard to believe Misty'd been thrown off her moped only a few hours ago. She stopped short behind a gaggle of tourists. Six middle-aged couples wearing shorts and long tube socks. A few of them had binoculars draped around their necks. They'd paused to hear one of the men dramatically deliver the punchline of his joke. Once he had, they all laughed then soldiered ahead.

Misty turned and rolled her eyes at Lucas. "Think we'll be like that one day?"

He chuckled at her fake worried expression. "Hope so."

"What?"

"Seems like they're having fun to me."

Misty shrugged and continued on her way. By this time, they saw the opening at the top with sunlight spilling onto the staircase's landing from outdoors.

Lucas followed Misty onto the platform where she stretched out her arms beside her. Next, she closed her eyes and tossed back her head, extending every finger on both her hands.

"What are you doing?"

"Shh!" She silenced his query, her face smooth and serene. After a few moments she said, "Feeling the wind."

He shot her a quizzical look just as she opened one eye. Then she opened the other. "Maybe you should try it?"

Lucas glanced around at the older couples who were observing the water and a mom and dad who were each holding hands with one of their young kids. No one was paying attention. So.

He stepped up beside her, a little closer to the railing, and held out his arms.

She giggled. "Not so rigid. You look like the Tin Man."

"Hey!"

She laughed again and stepped behind him lightly shaking his upper arms and loosening up his elbows. "Now," she instructed. "Palms toward the sea."

He cracked a grin. "Did you invent this?"

A mischievous gleam filled her eyes. "Maybe."

He held his palms forward and she took up her spot beside him, mimicking his pose.

This felt pretty silly but—

"Now," she said. "Close your eyes and turn your face up to the sun."

Lucas peeked at the others and now they were watching. "Misty—"

"Lucas. Just try."

He cleared his throat, ignoring the strangers' curious gazes, and shut his eyes, leaning his head back slightly. "Now what?"

"Just feel the wind."

He waited and a light breeze swirled around him. Then—whoa—a huge gust ripped across his chest. "Keep feeling," she urged softly. So he did.

Gulls cried. Surf crashed and the murmurs of the others faded away.

Rip. Whoosh!

His whole torso was engulfed in a rotating torrent.

Lifting him up, up, up above the earth.

He felt almost like he was flying.

Soaring.

Like a bird.

As the sun kissed his face.

So warm.

"Cool, Daddy!" a child's voice said. "Can we try it?"

Lucas opened his eyes to find Misty beaming at him. She shot a sidelong glance at the family and both kids; a little boy and his older sister were feeling the wind with eyes closed as their parents kept watch behind them.

"I think you've started a trend," he said in a husky whisper.

"Well?" she asked in a self-satisfied way, already knowing the answer. "Did you like it?"

He couldn't help but grin. Her happy energy was contagious. "Yeah. I kind of did."

"I started doing that when I was a kid," she said, eyeing the children. "About their age, I guess."

"Yeah? What make you think of it?"

"Not sure. Maybe it was the ocean or the beach. Something about nature here and wanting to become a part of it."

"You are a part of it. We all are."

"That's not exactly true." She set her chin. "We all live here, but not everyone's aware. Not everyone communes."

He chuckled at her choice of words. "Communes, hmm. Sounds very new age."

She cocked her head and her purple highlights shimmered in the sunlight. Most of her ponytail had worked loose during the moped ride, and now wind-blown tendrils framed her pretty face. She looked more gorgeous than he'd ever seen her.

"What?" she laughed self-consciously.

Lucas smiled. "Nothing."

"Nothing?" She shot him a sassy smirk, then turned toward the sea, pulling the ponytail band the rest of the way out of her hair. Coppery-brown strands whipped back behind her shoulders, shimmer-ing in the sun. She never wore her hair down, and her beauty stunned him.

He stepped up beside her to stare out at the hori-zon.

"New age, hmm." She rolled her eyes at him and his neck burned hot. "Not sure if that's meant to be bad or good."

"Where it concerns you." His voice went a little husky. "It's always good."

She bit her lip, but he could tell she was pleased. "Is that a fact?"

"Yeah." He fell into the depths of her mossy brown eyes, then had to plow his way back to the surface for air. "So," he asked. "Did your sisters do that, too? The wind thing?"

"They don't even know about it and you won't tell them, either." She arched one eyebrow and he laughed at her stern glare.

Lucas laid a hand across his chest. "You have my word."

"And your word is good, right?" She said it more like a statement than a question, like that's what she believed already, and he was glad.

"Yeah."

They both turned and looked down at the beach where different folks ambled along, some alone and others in small groups or in pairs. A woman in a sun-hat and a pail in her hand paused to collect seashells. The kids near them had stopped feeling the wind by now and were headed back down with their parents. The older couples had already left.

"Lucas?" she said. He turned to her. "This has been really fun."

"I know. I think so, too. I mean." He frowned. "Apart from the billboard thing and your accident."

She studied her upturned hands and the few bandages his mom had applied. "It really wasn't too bad. I know it could have been a lot worse."

"How are you feeling?"

"Really hungry. You?"

He chuckled when her stomach rumbled. "Yeah, I'm hungry, too. Want to have our lunch on one of those benches down there?"

"Sure."

"That will knock two items off that list."

Misty shook her head. "Picnic on the beach was

one of them. Not picnic at the lighthouse. It was ride bikes out to the—"

He laughed at her correction, not minding it at all. Having ten more excuses to do date-like things with Misty sounded fantastic to him. "You're right! We'll have to do an official beach picnic later. But Misty?"

She stared at him.

"We probably won't have to do every single item on that list if you don't want to."

"I know." She shyly lifted a shoulder. "We can pick and choose." Her cheeks turned pink, and he wondered which items she was considering keeping and which she wanted to cast aside. "A bunch of them are really harmless anyway."

"My thinking exactly," he said, although it wasn't. Because he was hoping. Oh he was hoping at least a few of the things they did together would have a very big impact on Misty's heart.

As they ate their sandwiches, Lucas hunted for a topic of conversation that didn't have to do with that list. Since both of them were pretty obviously still thinking about it, it would be uncomfortable to bring it up again. So he didn't intend to—unless she did first.

"Great sandwiches," she said. "Thanks for fixing them. The smoothie, too."

"Got plenty of supplies for more."

She wrinkled up her nose in a way he couldn't read. "Oh really? That's, ah, awesome! But I'd…hate to put you to so much trouble."

"It's no trouble making breakfast for you." He handed her a bottle of water from the daypack and she thanked him, uncapping it to take a swig. "This is nice," he said. "It being just the two of us. Doesn't often happen that way."

"I talk to you at work," she said. "Sometimes in private."

"That's true. But we almost never see each other outside it."

"Not true. I've seen you at Mariner's before." She thought on this. "And at McIntyre's. Even at the bakery."

He shook his head. "I meant on purpose. Running into each other by accident doesn't count."

"What about those family dinners at my folks' place?"

"That's just it. We're always in a group."

She sat back against the bench, munching happily. "Hmm. I guess you're right."

Things got a little quiet after that. Maybe he shouldn't have called attention to the fact that they were nearly never alone because now it felt weird. They could practically hear each other chewing, which was kind of ick. "Ah, Misty?"

"Yeah?" Her eyes widened eagerly. She apparently hadn't liked that awkward silence either.

He shifted on the bench, unsure of how to proceed. He was actually kind of blowing this. If they couldn't fill a simple lunch hour with congenial conversation, how were they supposed to enjoy each other's company over the course of a lifetime? "Um. What should we talk about?"

She surveyed their surroundings. "The weather?"

"It's gorgeous."

"Yeah. But supposed to rain tomorrow."

He frowned. "Right."

Another bout of silence ensued and Lucas wanted

to kick himself.

Why am I so bad at this?

Misty sat up straighter but then she slouched. "No. We probably shouldn't talk about that."

"What?"

She winced. "The billboard?"

"Agreed," he said. "At least it's coming down."

"And we can't talk about Aidan," she added firmly. "No thanks. Not today."

He was cool with that. Today and every day, really. "Or that bet with your sisters."

"Definitely." She nodded. "Off-limits."

"This is our fun day," he asserted.

"Yes! Let's talk fun!"

They both stared at each other and then stared harder.

Finally, she blinked.

Great. That wasn't working, either.

"You know what was funny, though?" he said, re-calling an incident. He reached back into familiar territory. Common ground they shared between them. "That time those guys walked into the café and tried to order up some beers."

She laughed. "They thought Bearberry Brews was a pub!"

"They were so not amused to learn it was a coffee shop. They'd driven out of their way for a cold one and fish and chips."

"At least we steered them to Mariner's."

"Yeah. That was good of us."

"Sure was." Misty shook her head. "Charlotte's marketing idea of a 'frappy hour' caused similar con-fusion."

"Oh *yeah*." Lucas chuckled. "Are you talking about the dog thing? When what Nell wrote on the outdoor chalkboard looked like 'Puppy Hour' and just about everybody in town showed up with their hounds?"

Misty giggled. "The McIntyres even brought theirs!"

Lucas shook his head, but he was chuckling, too. "That was some scene on Kittery Street."

Misty rolled her eyes. "Nell's handwriting is so bad! It's a good thing she uses her computer most of the time."

"At least your folks were good sports about it."

Misty nodded. "They gave extra discount coupons to all those dog owners." She rubbed her chin. "Remember that tourist that came in from Bar Harbor that time? The lady who wanted to see the kitchen."

He raked a hand through his hair. "Wait. The one in the big floppy hat with a huge purple flower on it?"

"Yes. That's the one. She insisted on knowing how we got the berries into our coffee and wanted to ob-serve the process."

Lucas's mouth twitched. "She was probably a spy."

Misty gently nudged him with her shoulder. "Yeah. Right."

"I'm serious." His eyebrows arched. "Maybe even had a camera hidden in that big flower thingy of hers." He wiggled his fingers over his head like he was wearing a hat, and Misty hooted. Lucas leaned back against the bench, enjoying the sunshine and this moment. Being out here joking around with

Misty. "A *corporate spy* sent to do reconnaissance by the competition." He took a swig of water. "Bear-berry Coffee."

She swatted his arm. "Not funny."

He cracked a grin at her. "No? Because I think I'm generally hilarious."

She smirked. "Remind me to come see you do stand-up."

"All right. When I get my first gig, I will."

She chuckled at yet another memory. "Do you re-member the customer who accused Charlotte of not whipping up enough foam?"

Lucas cracked up. "*Not* the dude with the ruler?"

"A math teacher, I think, yeah!" She exploded in chuckles. It had looked fairly ridiculous, the way the guy had actually measured the top peak of foam. "I'd forgotten all about him."

"That was years ago."

"Ten at least."

They both sat back against the bench and sighed. Then Lucas remembered another story. Misty laughed and came up with one next, and somehow another couple of hours flew by.

He wanted more of this. More time alone with Misty. More chances to connect. But how many more chances would he get with only a week to prove that he was the one for her?

CHAPTER ELEVEN

After a fun lunch at the lighthouse, Lucas gave Misty a ride back to her apartment. He used his truck bed ramp to load the moped in his truck and drove over to the bakery to pick up the second one they'd left with his mom for safekeeping. While he was off returning the rentals, she changed into clean jeans and a dressier shirt, getting ready for her meetup with her sisters.

The three of them really did need to talk. They couldn't have their mom reaching out to Mrs. Strong to call off their deal with Aidan. It was between them and Aidan now. Well. Between Aidan and Misty or Charlotte now, anyway. She ran a brush through her hair, remembering how Lucas had looked at her at the lighthouse and heat flooded her face. After hearing what he'd said to his mom, a lot of other things were falling into place.

Maybe by coming to her rescue from those billboard guys, he'd also been hoping to win her approval. And not just in a friendship way like she'd first imagined. She tried again to wrap her head around it. Then an image came back in a flash of him standing there atop that lighthouse feeling the wind.

Lucas normally stayed so serious and under control. And yet, he'd opened himself up for that one amazing moment. She could still see the look on his face. Like he was in his zone. His element. Maybe even experiencing peace for the first time. Watching him had taken her breath away for a moment.

Her phone buzzed on her dresser and she picked it up. It was Charlotte.

Can we meet earlier?

Have nighttime plans.

Misty checked the clock on her nightstand surprised to see it was four thirty. She and Lucas had stayed at the lighthouse much longer than she'd expected, but she wouldn't trade the afternoon for anything. She'd already gazed at the selfies they'd taken in front of the lighthouse five times since she'd gotten home. Her favorite was the one of them on the moped just before they left, her cheek pressed to his back and her eyes shining, and the warm smile on his face as he glanced back at her over his shoulder.

It was the best conversation—no, the best day— she'd ever had with a man.

Nell texted next, responding to Charlotte.

When do you want to meet?

Can you and Misty do five?

Charlotte liked the text in reply and Misty typed in a quick okay.

If Lucas wasn't back before she had to go, she'd leave him a note.

Something told her she'd be thinking about getting back home the whole time.

"What's going on?" Nell asked once the three sisters were seated on barstools. "Why the 9-1-1?"

"Yeah," Charlotte said. "That billboard came down. See!" She flashed her cell at Misty and then at

Nell, showcasing the billboard with its pre-existing ad for Blue Sky Adventures. That was one thing to be grateful for anyway.

"It's not about the billboard," Misty whispered. "It's about Mom. She wants to contact Mrs. Strong about calling off our deal."

"With Aidan?" Nell gasped. "No."

Charlotte's mouth hung open. "What? Now?"

"I know it's a terrible idea," Misty told them. "We're already in this deep."

Nell shrugged, looking sheepish. "I'd have a hard time explaining to Grant if all of a sudden the entire thing fell through. I mean one reason he cut me some slack was—"

"Nell," Charlotte said. "Wouldn't be your fault."

"Exactly," Misty said. "And besides that, you and he are perfect for each other. Now that the two of you know it, nothing's going to change that."

"Yeah." Charlotte nodded. "You and Grant are sewn up. Committed. Engaged!"

Nell sighed a dreamy sigh. "I know."

Misty leaned forward over the bar and her sisters angled toward her. "The point is it's almost mid-September so we're already pretty close."

"To one of us landing Aidan," Charlotte said. She shot Misty a stubborn look. "Meaning, most likely you."

"Me?"

"You volunteered."

"Yeah, but that was before."

Nell gave an excited little giggle. "Before the billboard—or Lucas?"

"Yeah," Charlotte asked huskily. "How's that going?"

"We're off to a great start," Misty said.

The bartender leaned forward. "What can I get you ladies?" He was Charlotte's age with sinewy tattooed arms and an alarming grin. He also had incredible blue eyes. Unfortunately, for the purpose of their bet, Misty knew he was married. With kids.

They all ordered light beers and the bartender turned away to get them.

Nell's gaze stayed glued to his broad shoulders and Charlotte nudged her. "You're getting married, remember?"

"Ah, yeah! Right!"

Misty rolled her eyes at Charlotte. "Nothing wrong with looking." She raised her hands. "And not touching."

Charlotte hooted and Nell shook her head.

Nell clasped a hand to her heart, displaying her pretty diamond. "There's only one man for me and his name is Grant Williams."

"Right," Charlotte said. "And now Misty's got Lucas."

Misty gave a thin smile, deciding not to comment. Clive was really nice to look at, it was true. But there was something about him that just didn't do it for her. Apart from the married and taken already part, obviously. Maybe he was too flirty. Not that she minded flirty too badly. She'd dated those sorts of guys. But once she settled down for real, it would be kind of nice to be with someone who only had eyes for her. Someone more loyal seeming.

Like Lucas.

Heat flushed through her body.

She was not thinking of Lucas in a happily ever

after way. Was she?

Their beers arrived and their glasses were frosty and cold. Misty took a sip of hers. Ahh. Good and delicious. The fried fish aromas filling the air were pretty savory, too, except to Nell. She covered her mouth and nose briefly with her napkin pretending not to notice.

"What's the special tonight, Clive?" Charlotte asked.

"Fried clams and chips."

"I thought you were going out tonight?" Nell said when Charlotte looked tempted. Nell clearly wasn't. Of the three of them, only she wasn't a huge fish fan.

"I am," Charlotte said. "But not until later."

"Who ya seeing?" Misty asked her.

"Dave." Charlotte's cheeks reddened. "He's very sweet."

Nell scrunched up her face. "Sweet enough to marry, though?"

Charlotte huffed out a breath. "Time will tell."

"Time's running out," Nell reminded them all unnecessarily.

She and Charlotte gazed at Misty. "So," Charlotte said. "You going to dish or what? What's happening with Lucas and that list?"

"We've crossed one item off it." She took out her phone displaying the lighthouse selfie.

"Only one?" Nell whined. "He's been there two days."

"One and a half," Misty corrected.

"Well then, you need to work faster," Charlotte said. "Because after Dave, I'm seeing Paul."

Nell's eyebrows shot up. "Who's that?"

"He just rolled into town this morning." Charlotte tugged at her crystal. "Showed up at the café."

They all gaped at her.

"What?" Charlotte complained. "I have a lot of ground to make up and no time to waste. Misty's known Lucas forever!"

"We still haven't solved the problem about Mom," Nell said.

"Someone should talk to her." Misty nodded then she stared at Nell. Charlotte did, too.

"Oh, *nooo*. Why *meeeeee*?"

"Why not you?" Charlotte asked. "You're basically removed from the picture, so impartial at this point, now that you're engaged to Grant."

"It's true," Misty said. She set down her beer. "Besides that, Mom will listen to you. She always does."

Charlotte nodded. "Even if she pretends to disagree at first."

Nell sighed. "Fine. I'll go in and take the fire." She glanced at her sisters. "What do you want me to say?"

"Maybe that you had your chance with Grant," Charlotte offered.

"And now Charlotte and I are in a race for it!"

"In the race not to marry Aidan, yeah."

Nell frowned. "Mom will just view that as another reason to stop the contest."

"Not if you can convince her more good will come of it than bad, and not just from the deal with Aidan and about saving their house and the café." She rolled her eyes toward Misty. "You can say that Lucas and Misty might have a chance. He probably wouldn't have stepped forward right now otherwise. If it weren't for the billboard guys and Aidan."

Misty conceded to herself that was probably true.

But if not because of those things, when would he have ever stepped forward?

"Without a doubt," Charlotte said and Nell nodded.

"How do you feel about Lucas?" Nell asked. "Is there anything there?"

Misty's neck burned hot and then her whole face steamed.

"I…ah, have always thought of him as just Lucas. You know?" She shrugged. "A friend. But lately? Things are changing. That's why, after our um…amorous night together, he decided to move in."

"Oh?" Nell's eyebrows arched and so did Charlotte's.

"You had an amorous night?" Charlotte asked with a sultry edge.

"Kissing!" Misty drank from her beer. "Just kissing!"

She'd never thought of kissing Lucas before, but now a moving picture reel of that scene filled her brain. They looked kind of like old-fashioned movie stars. Super dramatic. And their kisses were in slow motion.

Her heart thumped.

Nell picked up her mug and took a dainty sip. "Well, I'm glad you're finally seeing him in a different light."

"Right. And you'd better keep your eye on the ball." Charlotte hoisted her mug in the air. "Before I beat you to the finish line with that list."

Nell twisted her long curls in a heap, tossing them

behind one shoulder. "Do you really think you will? With Dave? Or Paul—"

"With someone." Charlotte set her chin, still elevating her mug. She winked at Misty in a challenge. "May the best woman win."

Misty didn't like the way Charlotte said that, like she was sure the best woman would be her. Why not Misty this time? For once. Charlotte was always taking charge, bulldozing her way over the rest of them. Yeah. Well. Maybe not this time.

Misty clinked her mug against Charlotte's. "May the best woman win."

They each swigged from their beers and turned to Nell.

"Now," Charlotte said. "About the parents."

Misty stared at Nell. "Specifically Mom and Mrs. Strong—"

"Okay. All right." She blew out a breath. "I'll do it. I'll talk to Mom and beg her not to interfere."

"Dad too," Misty said and Nell sighed.

"If I have to."

Misty knew she should feel relieved but still a weight hung on her soul. If Charlotte found her special one that would leave Misty to marry Aidan, even now knowing that Lucas had feelings for her, and that just felt wrong. But could spending a few more days with him really cement things in her mind? And if it did, then what? What about her dreams of design school and RISD? She hadn't been willing to give her career ambitions up, even in her plan to marry Aidan. She wouldn't want to forgo that dream on account of Lucas, either.

Misty stared out of Mariner's front window,

hoping to see things more clearly because right now her emotions were in a foggy jumble.

"Wait!" Charlotte said, following her gaze. "Is that Mei-Lin?"

Nell gawked at the apparition and then Misty's jaw dropped, too.

It most certainly was Mei-Lin in a cute short dress patterned with daisies under the leather jacket that matched her boots. She sashayed down the sidewalk with a long, tall cowboy in a Stetson.

Charlotte's blue eyes twinkled. "Mei-Lin and Dusty?"

Nell giggled. "Seriously?"

Misty was going to text Mei-Lin pronto to find out.

The only thing was when she did, Mei-Lin didn't answer.

"Probably turned off her phone," Misty informed her sisters after tucking her cell back into her small purse. Mei-Lin and the cowboy? How had that happened, and when?

"I'm sure she'll tell you all about it," Charlotte said lightly.

"Yeah," Nell agreed, finishing her beer. "Soon enough."

Misty returned to her apartment, placing her key in the front door lock and preparing for the struggle. Wait. The deadbolt slid open smoothly. Huh. That was different. Maybe it had naturally loosened up, or had somehow fallen into place?

She found Lucas sitting on the sofa with his laptop on his knees. "Oh hey!" he said, looking up. "Have a good time with your sisters?"

"Oh yeah, the best."

His forehead furrowed. "They're both all right?"

"Yeah, fine. We, um…just needed to talk."

"I hope they weren't pressuring you about that list or Aidan?"

"I think we're all on the same page now."

Misty removed her denim jacket and hung it in the coat closet. She shoved it shut expecting the door to catch without settling in its frame like it always did, but it closed smoothly, its latch clicking seamlessly into place.

Okay.

She opened the closet door again, then once again shut it. It closed like a charm.

She studied Lucas who was watching her. "Did you fix the closet door?"

He nodded. "And the guest bedroom doorknob."

She stared at the door to the room where he was sleeping, and sure enough he had.

"And that sticky window."

"In the kitchen?"

He nodded.

"Yes! Now I can get it all the way open when I burn toast."

He chuckled. "Which is often?"

"Very."

"Noted." He wore a teasing grin. "I'll be sure to check your fire detectors next."

"Wait." Her mouth fell open. "The deadbolt on the front door?"

"Yep. Took care of that, too."

"But how?"

"I keep a small toolbox in my truck just in case."

"Just in case what?" she asked. "Some stranger asks you to be a good Samaritan and repair their screen door?"

He laughed. "I do handy work at my mom's house once in a while. Used to be when I stopped by she'd say, 'Lucas, do you mind looking at such and such?' Then I'd have to promise to take care of it next time when I had my tools. Finally, I learned my lesson and started keeping a mini supply in my truck."

"Ramon's not handy?"

"I'm sure he could be, but so far he's been focused on his studies and blowing off steam with his buddies. And honestly that's okay. I don't mind doing things for my mom. Makes me feel"—he shrugged—"useful."

Misty's heart warmed with admiration. "Well, you've sure been useful around here, and I didn't even have to ask." Which made his efforts extra special. He'd thought to help her on his own.

"It was no trouble. Seriously. Took me all of ten minutes." He shut his laptop and settled back on the sofa. "So tell me. What's the word from Mariner's?"

"Charlotte's dating billboard guys. Multiple," Misty said, still unable to believe it. Although Charlotte had threatened to do that, it was amazing that she'd followed through. She apparently didn't want to lose that Aidan bet now that it looked like Misty might win with Lucas.

"What? Really?"

"Believe it or not, Mei-Lin's dating one, too." She pulled a face. "I saw her with the cowboy."

"That's so random." He set his laptop aside. "Don't think I would have called it."

"I know, right?" Misty shook her head. "I tried to text her but she didn't answer."

"Where were they headed?"

"Down Kittery Street toward the dock area."

"There are some good places to eat there," he said. "And that new microbrew."

"Yeah."

She glanced around the darkened room and switched on some lights. "I'm sorry it's so late. You're probably hungry."

"We had a late lunch, so I've been good."

"Want to get a pizza or something?"

He grinned. "Pizza sounds great. We can order delivery."

"It would be good to stay in," Misty said, feeling suddenly like part of an old married couple. She giggled at the idea.

"What?" he asked, perplexed. "What is it?"

"Nothing. It just seems like we're settled old folks or something."

"We are not settled, Misty. Or old, by any stretch." His gray eyes twinkled and a faint flame sparked in her soul. She tried to fan it out but that only made it burn brighter.

She tried to ignore the weird emotion. Her and Lucas married? No. Whatever in the world had made her even think of that?

Other than the fact that an engagement to him would spare her from marrying Aidan.

Right.

She sat down and yanked off her boots, sinking into her big comfy armchair and tucking her feet beneath her. "You want to call in the pizza or me?"

Good. This was good. Focus on food and practicalities. That would take her mind off of how great Lucas looked sitting there on the sofa in that black short-sleeve T-shirt of his. It draped just right, outlining the contours of his solid chest and upper arms.

"I'll do it." Muscles rippled as he snagged his phone from an end table. Misty's heart pitter-pattered.

"Everything, right?" he asked. "No anchovies, no onions?"

She gasped. "How did you know?"

He chuckled. "I've heard you put in orders at Majestic Pizza before. From the café for you to pick up on your way home."

"Oh yeah," she said and then she laughed. "Whew. For a moment I thought you were clairvoyant." Which would be terrible about now with her sizing up all his attributes, including that one deep dimple that etched into his left cheek when he grinned. Had it always been there?

"Nope, not that. Just a good listener, that's all." He was a great listener and he'd always been. After overhearing his talk with his mom, now she had an extra inkling as to why.

She hung her head to hide her blush and then looked up, rubbing her cheeks so he wouldn't notice their color. "So," she said about as casually as she could. "Maybe we can watch something when the pizza gets here? A show or maybe a movie?" Anything to get her staring at something else instead of him.

His face brightened at her suggestion. "How about an oldie but goodie, like one of the ones you like?"

"Wait. What?"

"Didn't Mei-Lin drag you to that Cary Grant film fest last spring?" Dragged was right. Mei-Lin had been gushing about Grant as a handsome leading man and was all about his romances, *An Affair to Remember*, *Bringing Up Baby*... It wasn't until Misty discovered Grant's more thriller-like films that she became hooked, too.

"Yeah and it was great." She adored Majestic's historic theater. It was in an ancient building that had been completely restored to its former 1920s glory. Heavy red curtains framed the huge single screen and its chairs were covered in plush red velvet. Misty loved going.

Lucas nodded. "I remember you commenting afterward that you'd really gotten into some of his tenser films. I'm a fan, too."

"Who else do you like?" She was happy to be on safer ground and talking about something as benign as movies. That way she could focus on iconic idols like Cary Grant, and keep her mind off of Lucas. Although she could kind of see him in a picture with his swath of charcoal curls and those stunning gray eyes.

He shrugged. "Jimmy Stewart."

Misty knew of him but thought he only did westerns. "I'm maybe not up for watching any cowboy flicks tonight."

He hooted at this. "Okay. Fine. No cowboys. I'm with you."

"Not Christmas, either. Didn't Stewart do *It's a Wonderful Life*?"

"Yeah, but he made lots of other stuff, too. He was in four Hitchcock films. Mysteries. Or more like psychological suspense."

"Ooh, those sound cool." One thing was sure, she wasn't watching any *romance* with Lucas. That would be awkward with her knowing what she knew about him, without him knowing that she knew it.

Not that he'd likely suggest it. Misty wasn't much into modern-day rom-coms herself. Oh, she watched them occasionally with her sisters and Mei-Lin. She stole a peek at her phone again, but Mei-Lin still hadn't answered. Mei-Lin was supposed to be *deflecting* those billboard guys from Misty, not dating them herself! That was Charlotte's role. Although there actually were plenty of them to go around.

"Cary Grant worked with Hitchcock, too," Lucas said. "*North by Northwest*?"

"Oh yeah, that was fab."

"*Suspicion*," he continued. "*Notorious—*"

Misty perked up. "What about the one where he was the cat burglar?"

"*To Catch a Thief*?" Lucas said. "Yep. That was great."

This was awesome! Amazing! She had no clue Lucas knew all about those old movies. "So Stewart—?"

"*Rear Window*, *The Man Who Knew Too Much*, *Vertigo*…" He stopped and snapped his fingers. "Of course. *Vertigo* has a bell tower scene. Not exactly a lighthouse, but reminiscent. Given our adventures today—"

"That might be just right."

"People aren't exactly going to be feeling the wind, though."

"If it's suspense, I'd guess not." Misty laughed. "Maybe we should watch that one?" she said. "Do you think you can find it?"

"Yep." Lucas peered at every corner of the living

room, maybe hunting for a television which she didn't have. "No TV?" he said. "No problem. We can watch on my computer. I've got a very cool app that gives me access to tons of classic films, all remastered."

"Nice!"

Misty didn't mind needing to sit closer to Lucas, like right next to each other on the sofa. That would be fine. They were friends. No biggie. Especially since they weren't watching anything romantic. It would be more like a friend date than a real date and Misty was actually looking forward to it. Pizza and a suspense film sounded fun. Especially an old film. Those were a whole lot less graphic than thrillers made today, and Misty didn't like graphic, or violence on the screen. She did enjoy the tension, though, and the excitement of trying to unravel a mystery.

Lucas pressed a button on his phone. "I'll call in the pizza, then see if I can find it."

Misty relaxed in her seat, feeling like a pampered princess. "And what am I supposed to do all this time?" She stretched out her hands like she had long, painted fingernails, which she didn't. Since she worked with her hands all day and then created designs with them in her spare time, she kept her nails trimmed short and almost never wore polish. She did have a cool ring of some sort or another on almost every finger, though. A few were copper. Others silver. All were bands with different designs on them and none had any gemstones. Her favorite was the one with a Celtic knot.

"How about you get us something to drink?"

Misty hesitated, wishing she'd thought to stop and pick up a bottle of wine. Even though that seemed date-like, and this wasn't a date exactly. They were just hanging out, her and Lucas. While pretending to be dating so she wouldn't have to marry Aidan. It was good that she and Lucas were just pretending, because otherwise that could be a problem in light of her plans to attend RISD. Assuming she even got in.

Now, with Charlotte determined to win their bet, things were even more twisted. Misty could be forced to go to London to marry Aidan if she lost to Charlotte, even if—after thoroughly thinking it through—she decided that was the very last thing on earth she wanted to do. What a messed-up situation. Definitely called for wine. The only thing was she didn't have any.

"I bought some chianti this afternoon on my way back from Grant's," he said, surprising her. He had his phone pressed to his ear and was waiting for the pizzeria to pick up. "A chenin blanc, too."

"Fancy!" she said. "You know your wines."

"I know a little about wine." His mouth twitched. "Leonardo at the wineshop had some recommendations." He held up a finger and spoke into his mouthpiece. "Ah yeah!" he said. "I'd like to order a large pizza."

Ooh good. Large. Misty couldn't wait. "Ask for extra cheese!"

He cocked his chin and grinned. "All right."

Misty's heart fluttered at the cute sparkle in his eyes. She swallowed hard, reminding herself she was just pretending. But a sneaky little part of her didn't seem to agree.

CHAPTER TWELVE

Misty sat so close to Lucas her warmth nearly seeped into his skin. He wouldn't mind moving closer but didn't want to push his luck. It felt pretty great being here with her and enjoying the movie. He'd propped his laptop on the coffee table in front of them and both held plates in their laps. His only held the remainder of a pizza crust. Misty was munching on her third piece. He appreciated her healthy appetite and guessed she'd earned it by starting out her day so super healthy with that smoothie.

He'd tried some of the concoction he'd made her and it was not tasty—at all. But as long as she liked it, he was happy to make her more. He'd fix her another bright and early in the morning. He wanted to get his run in first. He'd missed going these past two days and wanted to get those kinks out of his joints and stretch his legs.

"Wait. Wait." She slid her plate onto the coffee table. "Can we pause it here? I want to go grab more pepper flakes."

He chuckled, not having known Misty liked her pizza so spicy. "Sure." He lifted the wine bottle, noticing they'd both drained their glasses. "Want another shot?"

She glanced back over her shoulder. "Just a little more."

He watched her walk away in her cute socks that had multicolored thick stripes on them. Her jeans and sparkly purple stretch top fit her snugly, accentuating her petite but curvy figure. The top had a scoop neck in front but Misty didn't wear any necklaces. She never had. She had double-pierced ears and a nose stud, though, and always had plenty of rings on her fingers, so clearly she wasn't opposed to jewelry. Would she wear an engagement ring? Most women would but then Misty wasn't most women. She was her own unique self.

She returned to the sofa with her pepper-flake-doused slice of pizza.

"You're going to burn your mouth off," he joked.

She rolled her eyes and his heart danced like it always did when she was playful. "No, I won't. I've conditioned myself to it."

His eyebrows rose. "Conditioned?"

"Yeah, by eating plenty of jalapenos." She took a big, whopping bite, seeming to enjoy it immensely.

Lucas chuckled. "Jalapenos don't sound very Irish."

"My folks don't cook with them. I do."

"I thought you didn't cook?" He picked up his own pizza, still warm and melty, and bit into it.

She chuckled. "I mean I add them to things, like sandwiches and such."

"Gotcha."

She shot him a curious stare. "You don't like spicy food?"

"It's fine." He shrugged. "I've just never fixed a lot of it."

"How about your mom?"

"Oh no. Puerto Rican cooking is all about Caribbean flavor, but without heat."

She stared at him in surprise. "What? No jerk chicken?"

"You're thinking Jamaica."

"Oh. Sorry." She took another bite of pizza. "So what did you eat growing up?"

"A ton of plantains." He laughed. "Cooked every which way. Baked, caramelized, fried—"

"Ooh, caramelized, like candied?"

The thought of kissing the sticky caramel off her lips left him distracted.

He cleared his throat. "Exactly," he said, snapping himself back to attention. He took a sip of wine. "Those."

"Yum. I'd love to try some." She sat back in her seat looking happy and content. In her element, her home. Her space. And truthfully, he loved being in it with her.

"All right," he told her, setting down his wineglass. "I'll make you some. My mom taught me how."

"Ooh that would be great." Her eyes twinkled with delight. "Did your dad cook?"

"Not one thing." Lucas shook his head, recalling his dad's staunch stance on his role in the kitchen, which was basically eating in it. Only. "He worked really hard. Fished a lot. Rain or shine, summer heat and in wintry cold. By the time he came home, he was done."

"I can't say I blame him."

"Yeah, me either. And anyway, back then, Mom didn't mind. She was raising me and Ramon was just a baby." He glanced at his computer. "Ready for me to turn the movie back on?"

"Sure," she said, chewing happily. "Gosh. I don't

know why I was so hungry."

Lucas patted his belly. "For my part, I'm stuffed. I'm going to have to run extra tomorrow."

"Good for you."

He studied her profile, getting an idea. "Hey, would you like to come with?"

She blinked. "You mean, exercise?"

He raised his eyebrows. "Exercising together is on that list."

Misty groaned but she was clearly teasing. "Okay. I'll try it. As long as we don't go too far."

Lucas restarted the movie, looking forward to that morning run on the beach even more than he had before.

"Look!" Misty shouted, her eyes glued to the screen. "It's her! The blonde! No, no!" she cautioned Jimmy Stewart. "Don't follow her to the mission!"

But of course, Mr. Stewart raced right up those bell tower steps after her. Then, the woman jumped.

Misty set down her plate and picked up her wine. "OMG."

Lucas itched to reach out and take her hand, but now wasn't the time.

Soon, though.

He hoped.

The film ended after its dramatic climax and Misty heaved a sigh. "That was awesome. Really great. So much intrigue! I never would have guessed the twist."

"Yeah. It's pretty fun."

She stood up and picked up their dishes and then yawned, covering her mouth with one hand.

"Here," Lucas said, relieving her of the plates. "I'll take care of those."

"I can't let you."

"Of course you can," he said. "Because you'll do the dishes tomorrow."

She nodded. "That sounds fair." Then she yawned again. "Sorry. Not much of a night owl I guess."

He checked his phone and chuckled. "Turn into a pumpkin at ten o'clock?"

"Something like that, yeah."

"Why don't you get ready for bed then, while I clean up in the kitchen? There isn't much there. Just the rest of the pizza to put away."

Her forehead rose. "You sure?"

"Sure, I'm sure. Now scoot!" he instructed. "You'll want to get your shut-eye for our run."

"What time were you thinking of heading out?"

"Six too early?"

"Not for me." His heart hammered at the thought of seeing her every morning from here until eternity. If things worked out, maybe he'd get that lucky.

"Great. Then set your alarm."

"Don't need one." She sent him a flashy smile and heat warmed his neck. "Never have."

• • •

Misty crawled under the covers, worn out from the day but still floating on air from the fun. She checked her scrapes, which still hurt a bit. She'd cleaned them again when she'd washed up for bed and had applied fresh bandages where they were needed.

Her fall from the moped had been frightening at first, but once she'd realized she wasn't hurt badly, she'd started feeling better pretty quickly. Having

Lucas fussing over her had helped. His kindhearted mom had helped her, too. Then their climb up the lighthouse had been amazing and their lunch together really, really great.

She and Lucas got along so well, but then they always had. She stared up at the ceiling without switching off the light, trying to imagine a new life in London. Would Charlotte really become engaged first? That seemed so unlikely, but just look at Nell! Of course, Nell had had her eye on Grant since high school. Charlotte would be starting with someone from scratch. Not that Charlotte wasn't up to the task. She was single-minded when she put her mind to something.

Misty sighed, thinking of Mei-Lin. As if thinking of her conjured it, Misty's phone buzzed on her nightstand.

Finally!

Sorry. Just seeing your text!

Yes, went out with Dusty. He's a hottie!

That was followed by a kissy-face emoji.
Wait. There had to be more.

Mei-Linnnn!!! HOW did this happen?

Did he ask you out? You, him?

Where did you go?

We mutually decided, and Anchors Away.

You went for beers? What else?

Mist-yyyy!!! Dinner! Duh.

SO. When are you seeing him again???

There was a long pause and then a text.

He's still here.

Misty's mouth hung open and she set down her phone. Mei-Lin, that little minx! She was such a fast mover! She had to get the scoop in person.

Let's do lunch. I'd love to talk!

Mei-Lin answered:

I can sneak out tomorrow for a few.

OK. Meet you then!

Misty didn't say where because it was assumed they'd connect at the café and then grab a bite nearby. Mei-Lin and the cowboy! She sank back against her pillow. Who knew?

"Night!" Lucas called from the hall. He'd apparently seen her light still on under the door and knew she wasn't sleeping.

"Night!" she called in return. "See you tomorrow!"

Of all the times she'd said that to Lucas, they'd both been at work. It felt strange saying that to him here. But truthfully, in an odd way, it was also a little exciting. Nerves flitted about in her stomach. Was she finding Lucas extra attractive in a very non-friend way all of a sudden? Definitely.

Misty saw her closet door was ajar and shut it, her gaze snagging on that boyfriend box on her closet shelf. She'd kept stuff for years from former boyfriends, going all the way back to her first sort of serious one in high school. Handwritten notes passed at school, cards attached to floral bouquets, movie tickets…some old photos. She didn't even know why she still had it. She hadn't added to it in a while. It had really been a teenage thing. But still. It was hard to think of throwing it away.

Misty climbed into bed. She'd always figured that once she found her *forever guy*, she'd get rid of it. She'd have to really fall in love, which she'd never let herself do completely. Every time before, she'd always held a special part of herself back: her heart.

She pulled the covers up to her chin and sighed, thinking of Lucas.

She had eyes and wasn't stupid. At least she was more enlightened than she used to be. Meaning, that she had been *very obtuse* for a while. But still, it was impossible to say how this would end. She or Charlotte had to help her parents. And, if Charlotte kept picking up the pace of this contest like she'd threatened to do at Mariner's, then the last bride standing—*and* the one left to marry Aidan—could very well be her.

Was she ready for that? She'd thought so before. But that was *before* she'd begun having doubts. Also *before* this new thing with Lucas. And she still hadn't heard from RISD. Her heart wrenched and she clasped her hands to her chest.

Now, she wasn't so sure.

CHAPTER THIRTEEN

Lucas entered the darkened living room at a little before six the next morning. Misty sat in the big chair by the glowing lamp, lacing up her running shoes. She had on a sweatshirt and exercise leggings. He wore his running shorts and an old T-shirt.

"I guess you were right about not needing that alarm," he said.

She paused to adjust the band on her ponytail. "I've gotten up at five thirty ever since I was a little kid. Used to drive my parents nuts! Especially at Christmastime, because I'd wake Charlotte and Nell up, too, so we could all go see what Santa brought."

He chuckled, trying to imagine her little girl face.

"And your parents wanted to get up with you?"

"Had to," she said. "Mom and her pictures. She documented everything when we were small. You should see our baby books."

"Yeah? I'd like to see yours."

Her face twisted up in a weird expression. "Some of it's kind of scary."

"What? A baby book?"

"I was born really early. Eight weeks premature." She shrugged. "So some of those early pictures are of me in an incubator."

"Oh no." His heart clenched at the thought that she might not have made it. Might not be here today. "Your parents must have been really worried."

"Yeah, they were. I was taken away from them

pretty immediately and sent to the big hospital two hours away. They stayed in a hotel nearby so they could be close at hand and visit as much as was allowed. I guess things were dicey there for a while, but I pulled through. They claim I was a tough little nugget."

She still was in his mind. Determined. A fighter.

It was interesting to know she'd always been that way.

"What about your older sisters? Who looked after them during that time?"

"My grandmother, Nonna, watched them back at my parents' house."

"I didn't realize you had an Italian grandmother?"

She nodded. "On my mom's side. Her mom."

"That's kind of cool. Did she speak Italian?"

She smiled softly, as if falling into a memory. "It's *all* she spoke."

"Did she live in Majestic?"

"No. Chicago. I don't remember her too well. She died when I was little, but my mom hung onto her stuff when she passed. Kept a lot in storage. I eventually got the bedroom set in the room where you're staying. Nell got her piano."

"And Charlotte?"

"Her dining room table. It's a huge one with lots of leaves and chairs. My mom waited until we were older with places of our own, then doled some of Nonna's things out. Charlotte was really the only one of us who cooked. I mean, seriously. Gourmet style. So naturally, she got the dining room stuff."

He laughed. "It's never too late to learn, you know."

She finished with her shoes and looked up.

"To cook." He shot her a teasing stare. "That is one of the items on our dating to-do list. Couple's cooking."

"You might convince me if I get hungry enough on this run." She glanced into his bedroom at his made bed. "Such a tidy guest."

"Mom beat cleanliness into me like a rug."

She giggled at his funny expression. "What? With a broom?"

His mouth twitched. "Didn't want to cross her and find out."

"Hmm. Maybe not." She stood and did a few stretches bending and extending her knees to each side. She stretched out her arms. "You don't seem to sleep in much," she said. "I mean, apart from yesterday."

"With the job, I generally can't. Sometimes do on my day off, though."

"Not me." She grinned, rolling back on her heels and then standing up on her toes while balancing herself with arms outstretched. "I've never slept past six o'clock."

"Never?"

She rolled her eyes toward the ceiling, thinking. A split-second later she set her pretty hazel gaze back on him and placed her hands on her hips. "Nope!"

He chuckled, glad to know she woke up so chipper. He wasn't exactly a morning grouch himself, but it did take him a few minutes to get started.

"Do you still wake up extra early on Christmas, even though you know there's no—"

"Shh! Don't say it! I don't want you to jinx my Christmas luck."

He crossed his arms, amused. "You've got Christmas luck?"

"I do. When I look out the window just right, I make it snow."

He shook his head at her assertion. "So, now you're magic?"

"I used to think it was Santa helping me out. Later, I determined it was the power of my will."

"Helps that it snows a lot around here in December."

"Doubter."

"I mean." He shrugged. "Your odds are pretty good."

She lifted a book from the low table beside her, threatening to lob it at him, and he laughed, not the least bit afraid.

"What's that you're reading?"

She flipped it over and stared at its cover. "It's just a textile design book."

"Textiles? Like fabrics?"

"Yeah. I like looking at the designs. There's something very…I don't know…soothing about the repetition."

He'd seen Misty doodling on notepads at work and she did draw lots of patterns. He'd thought that she'd just been bored. He didn't understand she'd been creating those patterns on purpose. "Yeah, cool. I guess I can see what you're saying." He paused. "Ever think of designing something of your own?"

She shyly ducked her chin. "I've got a portfolio."

"Will you show it to me?"

"Er." She bit her bottom lip. "Not sure."

"No pressure."

She studied him. "You're a very easygoing guy. Bet you didn't bug your parents on Christmas morning to get up early."

He chuckled. "No. I saved that for Three Kings Day."

"What's that?"

"A Puerto Rican tradition. They come on January sixth. The idea is like when the three wise men visited baby Jesus bringing gifts."

"Ooh, that sounds kind of cool. Did they have reindeer?"

He shook his head. "Camels. Some people say horses, but it was camels for sure in my house."

"So, wait. You didn't have Santa Claus?" Her eyes widened in concern.

"Oh no, we had him, too."

Misty clucked her tongue. "That's double-dipping!"

"Worked out pretty well for me." He shrugged. "And anyway, the Three Kings only brought trinket stuff to me and Ramon. Santa brought the bikes."

"But not mopeds, though," she teased.

"Nope. Not those."

And he was glad, because Misty's tumble aside, he much preferred the memory of riding mopeds being tied to the feel of her pressed against his back, laughing into the wind.

• • •

Misty trudged along behind Lucas holding her side but he shot out ahead of her. "Slow down!"

He stopped and glanced over his shoulder and

then pivoted around on bouncing steps, still jogging as he returned to her. His calf muscles tensed beneath his toned thighs. "You doing okay?" His face wrinkled up. "You look winded."

"I *am* winded," Misty gasped as she tried to catch her breath. "You're going too fast."

"Oh." He ran a hand through his hair, looking abashed. "Sorry."

The sun was fully out of the water, casting a glistening glow across the waves. But the sky wasn't blue, it was dusky, like it was when bad weather was coming. Misty scooted back toward the dunes to avoid the encroaching tide and Lucas followed her.

"Want to take a break?"

"No break." Misty held up her hand. "Just a breather."

He laughed at her choice of words, then his feet stopped moving. "Your call." He set his hand on his hip. "Maybe we should turn around?"

Misty stared back at the steps they'd descended from the road. They'd barely gone a football field's length. Her lungs seized up but then relaxed a little as she drew in slow deep breaths. "No, no. I'm good. I'd hate to spoil your run."

"You're not spoiling anything," he said. "It's great having you along." The warm glimmer in his eyes said he meant it. "If you weren't such a slowpoke—"

"Hey!" She dashed into the waves and sent him a blast of chilly morning spray. Ouch. The freezing saltwater kind of stung her hand, too, but the stunned look on his face had been worth it.

"Oh, you—" He came after her and she dashed aside, outmaneuvering his grasp.

"Who's the slowpoke now?" she called behind her, running away. She picked up her speed and Lucas came after her, calling her name.

She wasn't stopping though. She was running free, sprinting and sprinting along while kicking up sand and spray. She passed a lady walking a dog and waved hello. Then she heard Lucas's steady footfalls pound-pound-pounding behind her.

In the next instant his arm shot around her and he had her by the waist. "Come here you," he said in a husky growl.

Gooseflesh rose on her arms and skittered across other parts of her body.

He tugged her back against him, and she giggled, crying out. "Lucas! Let me go!" His arm was around her middle as she squirmed to get away.

"Not until I do…this!" He reached down with his free hand and sent a shower of cold ocean water blasting in her direction. Misty yelped and broke free.

"You're going to pay for that," she said, shaking her finger.

His gray eyes danced. "Oh yeah? I'd love to see how."

She squatted down, cupping both hands in the water, as the surf crashed over her feet, soaking her shoes and ankles in an icy eddy. Then she hurled a huge thrust of saltwater his way.

He jumped back in time to avoid the soaking.

Darn it.

Then he came after her!

"Noooo!" she shouted but she was laughing when he caught her again.

"You think you're so, so funny, hmm?" His sexy

whisper tickled her ear. He dipped his hand into the surf, sending a palmful of spray her way again. It hit the side of her neck and was—*brrr*—freezing.

She wheeled on him but he caught both her wrists in his hands.

"Lucas," she yelled. "Let me go!"

He held her arms up in the air on either side of his shoulders. Her sweatshirt sleeves were soaked and icy trickles raced down her bare arms below it.

"I don't trust you." He leaned toward her and suddenly Misty didn't trust herself. Oh wow, he smelled great and looked so sexy. Damp streaks ran down his T-shirt, molded to his chest.

"That makes two of us."

She wiggled in his grasp but he held on tighter, the fingers of his left hand circling her tattoo. He stroked his thumb against the painted thorny stem. "Why did you get this?"

"Because I wanted to."

His eyebrows rose. "Didn't happen to be on account of a guy?"

Misty caught her breath. Why would he assume that?

"No," she said defiantly. "It was on account of me. I wanted to do something for myself. Something that no one could take away."

He surprised her by bringing her wrist to his mouth. He gave her rose petals a satiny soft kiss and Misty nearly fainted. "Then you made the right choice."

Lucas dropped her arms and she stared at him, her heart thudding. So hard.

The satiny caress from his lips still lingered on her skin.

"Sorry." He stepped back. "I shouldn't have—"

"No, really," she said, locking her shaky knees. "It's all right."

But it wasn't all right. Not all right at all.

In one tiny instant, everything changed. She couldn't keep lying to herself about whether she felt something. Because in that tingling instant she definitely had.

Lucas looked up and checked the sky. The horizon was still clear, but dark clouds gathered in the west. "Maybe we should head back. I think rain's coming."

But nothing could compete with the thunder churning in her soul.

Her and Lucas?

She could almost see it. Feel it.

Her falling into his arms. Or him falling into hers. Maybe better, both of them holding each other.

But no. She couldn't do it. Open her heart for real to a guy. Any guy. What if things didn't work? What if he let her down? It was so much easier to be the strong one and in control. If she let down her guard, she'd be raw. Vulnerable. She'd never loved anyone with her whole heart, not romantically.

Keeping her emotional distance had worked great for her so far. She'd dated and had fun, but when the guy wanted more, she'd always backed away. Why then did she find herself getting pulled toward Lucas, gravitating in his direction more and more?

If she let herself fall in love with Lucas and things went wrong, "heartbroken" wouldn't begin to cover how she'd feel. He wasn't just any guy. He was a good friend. Someone she trusted. A person she could lean on. She couldn't bear to imagine having all of that taken away.

Thunder rumbled in the distance and Lucas turned toward her. "Misty?"

She stared down at her saturated feet and then up at him. "You're right. We'd better head in."

"First let's get that photo for your sisters."

"Great idea," she said, and they did. Misty texted it to Nell and Charlotte and Nell sent back a smiley face. Charlotte just gave a thumbs-up. Good. At least they believed she was trying. And she was, too. She just never expected the feelings that kept bubbling up to the surface each time she got closer to Lucas.

The sky clouded over as they jogged down the beach, reaching the steps to Kittery Street. Most of the shops hadn't opened, but the lights were on at Bearberry Brews. People needed their morning java fix. Pings of rain dripped from the sky as they rounded the corner to Misty's street.

Lucas opened the door to the stairwell when they reached her building, letting Misty in first. Then they both ducked indoors seconds before the sky opened up, dumping a broad curtain of rain. "Whoa," Lucas said, shaking the damp from his hair. "Made it back just in time."

Misty peeled off her wet sweatshirt on the way up the stairs, revealing her tank top underneath. "Want to grab a shower first?" she asked. "I can make us some coffee."

Lucas nodded and shut the door behind them. "Coffee sounds great."

Misty entered the kitchen and pulled out her phone to see who'd been texting her. It was Nell messaging privately, without Charlotte in the loop.

You'd better work quickly.

Charlotte's stepping up her game.

Nell forwarded three Charlotte selfies. Charlotte and Dave picnicking on the beach. Charlotte and Dave toasting to a sunset with full goblets of wine. Charlotte sitting propped up against some pillows and her headboard, grinning and holding a breakfast tray.

Wait.

No way. She wasn't! Going through that list, and twice as fast as Misty?

Sneaky Charlotte hadn't warned Misty, either. She'd only sent her pics to Nell.

Misty set her jaw and her face burned hot. So Charlotte was seriously in this to win.

But with Dave? She didn't even know Dave! Although she was obviously getting to know him better. Nell forwarded one more pic.

Misty groaned.

Charlotte and Dave at the gym???

Majestic didn't even have a gym, so they must have gone to the next town over. How had Charlotte even had the time?

What's going on? Isn't Charlotte coming in?

No. Sean's covering for her.

Mom is, too.

Mom?

A string of baby dots indicated that Nell was answering. At last her text appeared.

She feels guilty for starting it all. Wants you and Charlotte to be happy by finding your forever men. Then no one will have to marry Aidan.

Misty rubbed her tight forehead with her fingers, understanding she'd painted herself into an impossible corner. She didn't want to marry Aidan herself, but she was petrified of actually falling in love with Lucas, then possibly losing him forever. She'd never fully given her heart to anyone, and this seemed like a very risky place to start, with the marriage-of-convenience timeline ticking.

Still, she couldn't stand the thought of Charlotte winning the wager with someone else. Not after her tricky billboard stunt. But someone had to lose their bet and move to England. Otherwise, what would become of her parents and their café? Their family home, too? Misty's spirits sank so low she couldn't imagine finding a way to bring them back up again. There seemed to be no way out of this messy quagmire involving Aidan. And then there was RISD…

Her stomach clenched. She'd wanted that dream so badly. Could she really let it go?

She made up the coffee and walked into the third tiny bedroom she used as a studio. Then she sat down in the metal folding chair at her card table to think. Rain streaked outside the alley window fogging up the glass. That's exactly how she felt, all muddled up inside. She was glad to be seeing Mei-Lin today at lunchtime. Maybe she could text her and they could meet up a little earlier. She definitely needed a shoulder and some girl talk. Like, soon.

CHAPTER FOURTEEN

"So, what's going on with the cowboy?" Misty removed her rain jacket while Mei-Lin shook out her umbrella. They'd just walked into the Dockside, a shack-style eatery in the section of the docks where the fishing boats came in. They served the best fried fish sandwich made with the catch of the day, along with fries cooked in peanut oil. Misty was always tempted to try something else, but then fell back on her old standby. It was just too good.

"Gee," Mei-Lin joked. "Don't we even get to order first?"

"I already know what I'm getting."

"Of course you do."

They took a seat at a small table beside a window. A choppy gray sea churned outside, jostling small fishing boats on roiling waves as a cloaking fog hugged the water. Misty thought of Lucas's dad and how he'd held that job, rain or shine. Misty hadn't known Mr. Reyes well. He'd been quiet-natured but had seemed kind and gentle. A lot like Lucas.

"Why mess with perfection?" Misty answered. "What do you think you'll have?"

Mei-Lin picked up the menu wedged between a napkin holder and a catsup bottle. "Hmm, probably the fried clam po' boy."

"I'm going for the fried fish sandwich and chips." Lucas had tried to fix Misty another smoothie this morning but she'd declined saying she'd grab a power bar since she and Mei-Lin were lunching early. It was eleven thirty-five and the Dockside had just opened its doors to lunchtime customers. Already, the place was filling up. It was a hugely popular spot for locals.

"You never change."

"Oh yes, I do."

A ponytailed guy in an apron took their orders. Both also got coffee which sounded good on a dreary day, and it arrived in short order.

Mei-Lin grinned above her coffee mug. "What about you and Lucas? Things going well?"

Heat flooded Misty's face. "Better than expected."

"What?" Mei-Lin gave an excited whisper. "Mistyyy! You're going through the—" She paused and frowned. "Wait. What happened to your hands? And wrists?"

Misty sipped from her coffee mug, then set it down. "They're fine. I just fell off a moped."

"A moped?" Mei-Lin gasped. "Oh no! Were you hurt?"

Misty shook her head. "Not other than this." She turned over her palms and the scrapes were so much better and she only still needed one bandage. She was surprised Mei-Lin had noticed anything.

Mei-Lin tasted her coffee, too. "Were you with Lucas?"

"Yeah. Riding bikes out to the lighthouse."

"Oh, those kind of bikes." Mei-Lin chuckled. "Bet that was fun. Until you fell off."

"Yeah, it was." Misty sipped from her coffee. "Before and afterward."

"What happened afterward?"

"Lucas and I had lunch, and we talked. Talked a

lot actually, but not about anything important. Mostly about work."

Mei-Lin rolled her eyes. "Boring."

"I know it sounds that way," Misty confided, "but it kind of wasn't."

Mei-Lin angled forward. "No?"

Misty's heart fluttered at the memory of sitting in the sunshine with Lucas, and especially at the way he'd looked at her at the top of the lighthouse after they'd been feeling the wind. "I'm scared that something's happening."

"Okay. Define happening?"

"I'm not really sure. It's just that Lucas…" Misty bit her lip. "He's not exactly how I thought he was. In some ways he's more."

Mei-Lin's eyebrows waggled. "More sounds good."

Misty blew out a breath. "More sounds confusing to me." And it was. She wasn't ready for serious with a guy. She'd told herself that from the beginning. That's why the short-term marriage to Aidan had looked okay.

Mei-Lin reached out and touched her arm. "Look. Whatever's going on, I'm sure you'll figure it out. Try not to stress so badly and just, you know." She shrugged. "Enjoy the ride?"

Misty sighed. If only things were that easy. "That's kind of hard to do with the Aidan thing still hanging over my head."

Mei-Lin frowned. "I know. I just hate to see you not giving Lucas a chance."

Misty gasped. "Mei-Lin! Lucas and I aren't real."

"Yet." Mei-Lin dropped her voice in a knowing way.

Misty willed herself not to dwell on that right now. She had other priorities like worrying about what her mom might do next. "I met up with my sisters," she told Mei-Lin. "Mom was getting out of control. Wanting to contact Mrs. Strong to call off our arrangement with Aidan."

Mei-Lin grimaced. "I hope she didn't."

Misty shook her head. "Nell intervened."

"Good. Your mom always listens to Nell, except when she doesn't."

Misty chuckled. "I know."

"So!" Mei-Lin sat up straighter. "What else have you been doing with Lucas? Come on." Her eyes sparkled. "Give me details."

Misty sighed at how considerate he'd been. "He made me a smoothie."

"A good one?"

"No." Misty wrinkled up her nose and Mei-Lin laughed. "He tried, though—so hard, and I didn't want to hurt his feelings, so I said it was delicious."

"Uh-oh," Mei-Lin teased. "I see more smoothies in your future."

"Stop!"

"I mean it," Mei-Lin said. "The sure way to get more of something from a guy is to fawn over how fantastic whatever it is is."

"Is *is*?" Misty chuckled and Mei-Lin did, too.

"You know exactly what I mean." Mei-Lin's forehead rose. "Anything else?"

"Well, yeah…" Misty weighed how to frame this. "I kind of overheard. I mean, after I fell off the moped we went to Dolphin Donuts. Lucas's mom is a nurse and he wanted her to check out my injuries, which were pretty minor, honestly."

"That was thoughtful of him. Caring."

"Lucas is very caring," Misty assured Mei-Lin.

Mei-Lin smiled warmly. "Aww. Do tell."

Misty groaned. "Oh, Mei-Lin. I don't know. I'm so mixed up. He is so nice and well, we get along. You know? Lucas is easy to be around. He's always been. Only, I think you and my sisters were right." She lowered her voice in a whisper. "I overheard something he said to his mom about why he was staying at my place, and, Mei-Lin, I think Lucas really *likes* me."

"You don't say." Mei-Lin wryly twisted her lips. "I could have told you that ages ago. Charlotte and Nell, too. In fact, we all did, but you didn't listen."

"I know, I know. The point is, I believe you now."

"And? How do you feel about him? He's caring like you say and *very* handsome."

Misty swatted her arm. "Mei-Lin!"

"I mean, for you, not for me. I've already got my eye on someone."

"No joke." Misty grinned at the vision of Mei-Lin and Dusty walking down the street. "Why didn't you tell me?"

Mei-Lin chuckled. "It's all so new!"

"And you're seeing him again?"

"He's invited me to his cousin's wedding."

"What? When?"

"This Saturday. In the meantime, he's hanging out a few more days in Majestic. He's gotten a room at the Majestic B&B."

Misty viewed her friend in awe. "I'm so impressed with you, Mei-Lin. Pursuing this new relationship with gusto. I didn't even know you had a thing for cowboys."

"I've got a thing for anyone who says 'yes ma'am' and calls me 'little lady' even though I'm five foot nine." She laughed. "But probably a particular thing for Dusty. He's not just anybody. He's like really special, Misty. I just feel it."

Misty scratched her head. "I honestly didn't see this coming."

"Maybe you've never known my type."

"I've met lots of the guys you've dated. Actually, pretty much all of them."

"Yeah, but no one from Wyoming's ever come to Majestic before." She shrugged. "Not that I'm aware of." Mei-Lin got a flirty look on her face. "He's got real cowboy boots, you know."

"Yeah, I saw."

"I have a confession to make." Mei-Lin's whole face colored. "I've had a thing for cowboys for a long, long time."

"But you never said a thing."

"Nell knows," she said timidly.

"Nell?"

Mei-Lin pursed her lips, then whispered, "She started loaning me her books when I was fifteen."

Misty gawked at her. "Romance novels?"

"Yeah." Mei-Lin giggled. "Including the steamy ones."

Misty giggled and held Mei-Lin's hand. "I always knew Charlotte was sneaky. I never guessed Nell has a sneaky side, too."

"She wasn't trying to be sneaky. She just knew I liked to read and could never keep enough books on hand. She bought so many used novels at the thrift store, she built up a big collection."

"She still has one. Only now, it's mostly in ebook."

"Yeah, well, back then, those weren't as big, and actually I'm glad. I loved staring at those cowboy covers!"

Misty laughed and released her hand.

The waiter brought their food and refilled their coffees. Everything was hot and looked delicious, and they dug into their lunches.

"So, enough about me," Mei-Lin said between bites. "Let's hear more about you. Have you heard from RISD?"

Misty paused while eating a french fry. "Not yet. I checked their website this morning and my scholarship application is still pending."

"No news is good news."

"I'm hoping that's true."

Mei-Lin blew out a breath. "I'm so glad you're not going to London. I'm not sure if I could bear it."

"I don't think that's been decided. Charlotte's not giving up."

"But I thought when she dreamed up that billboard—"

"What? That she'd committed to marrying Aidan herself?" Misty took a bite of her sandwich. "Yeah, I thought so, too. But then she learned about Lucas moving in with me, and she changed her mind."

"Charlotte's so competitive," Mei-Lin said. "She's always been that way."

"I don't think she can help it, honestly. Nell's competitive, too, but not like Charlotte. More like with board games and such." Misty shook her head. "That's never been me. I don't care who wins most days, as long as everyone is having fun."

Only she did care now, more than she was ready to admit. Because if Charlotte won this bet, Misty would be stuck marrying Aidan. Misty didn't like competing with her sisters, she really didn't. But one way or another, they'd basically forced her into it.

Mei-Lin adjusted her glasses. "So that's where she was this morning! With Dave." She shook her head at Misty. "Charlotte called in sick."

"Uh-huh, yeah. Right." Misty took a sip of coffee before adding, "But I think my mom is on to her, according to Nell."

"Your mom knows about that list?"

"No, don't think so. Not about that. But she does understand that Charlotte and I are looking to…settle down." Misty winced when she said the words, because they sounded so wrong for contemporary women. Outdated. Old-fashioned. But still. This was all for the good, and nobody was going to marry anybody they honestly didn't want to. Except for maybe Aidan, and that liaison was finite at least. Only five years before the entire business could be divided equally between the two families.

"Mom worried our panicked husband hunt was all about Aidan and that bet," Misty continued. "But Nell convinced her it's not. It's more like Charlotte and I see Nell's happiness and we want that for ourselves. I think Mom was kind of relieved in the end. She's been fretting over us meeting 'eligible men' for months now."

"All those attempted fix ups."

"We didn't understand she was doing it because she feared Bearberry Brews could go under and we might all lose our jobs. In any case, she seems happy enough that Charlotte and I are both seeking our respective partners now. Plus, she and Dad have always really liked Lucas."

"True. He's almost like part of the family. Your marrying him would just make that legit."

"It's not just that, Mei-Lin. Lucas is more than family." She couldn't say he was her best friend because Mei-Lin was. Lucas was special in a different way. "He and I are—" A lump wedged in her throat.

Mei-Lin reached out and held her hand. "I know how he's there for you." Understanding glimmered in her eyes. "How he's always been. But Misty? Can't you see that maybe Lucas can be there for you in another way, too? Still as a friend and still supportive. But…" She lowered her voice and added gently. "Also as so much more?"

Misty recalled Lucas's kiss on her tattoo and a tingling sensation hummed through her. Her and Lucas? Forever? If he could make her feel like that, then maybe. Maybe, yes.

Mei-Lin leveled her a stare. "You can't let Charlotte win," she asserted firmly. "Not when Lucas is destined to be your one."

"You don't know that, Mei-Lin."

"Don't I? Because I think I do." Her eyebrows arched. "I think you do, too."

• • •

Mei-Lin's words hung over her as Misty walked back to her apartment through the rain and the fog. Was Mei-Lin right? She'd seemed so certain that Lucas was Misty's one. But, if that was the case, shouldn't

Misty have tuned into that earlier? Or maybe she couldn't have known until now, because the conditions hadn't been right.

One thing she knew, she didn't want to make a mistake, and—above all—she didn't want to hurt Lucas. He'd always been there for her and was such a caring guy. She already loved him for that. But could she fall *in* love with him? Had she already started?

Misty took care with her footing on the slick cobblestones that made up the streets in this older section of town. Even though the heels on her ankle boots were low, they caused her trouble sometimes on the uneven ground and she didn't need to go falling again anytime soon. Steady streams of rain pummeled her from above and she cinched the tie on the hood of her raincoat, wishing she'd thought to bring along an umbrella like Mei-Lin had.

She glanced down Kittery Street as she crossed over from the dock area, catching a glimpse of Bearberry Brews at the end. Warm light poured through its windows and glass front door, spilling onto the gloomy sidewalk as Mei-Lin hurried inside. Rainy days were always good for business, so the place was likely packed with customers ordering hot berry-flavored beverages and delicious treats. Misty wondered who was running the register right now. Maybe Sean, or perhaps one of her folks had stepped in while Mei-Lin had gone on her lunch hour.

It felt strange staying away from the café for so long, but maybe it was good to take a break. Her whole life hinged on the decisions she'd be making shortly, and it was important to have space to think things through. What was she going to do about

Lucas, though? She just didn't know. Maybe if they kept working their way through that romantic date list, an earth-shattering answer would come to her. She couldn't decide to marry him based on murky feelings. She needed a hot certainty that burned in her soul. Lucas deserved no less than that. Having a wife who would love and adore him fully. It would be wrong of Misty to commit to him otherwise, and better for her to go off to London.

Lucas had so much to offer. He was kind, steady, and achingly handsome. He needed someone who was as equally into him as he was into her. Though Misty didn't have experience in giving her whole heart, she'd dated enough to know that emotionally imbalanced relationships were never satisfying for either partner. They definitely didn't lay the right foundation for a marriage. Though some people made that mistake and married anyway, thinking that love for one of the parties or the other would eventually come along, Misty wasn't going to do that to Lucas. She cared about him too much to ask him to take that kind of risk.

She found him at the kitchen table eating leftover pizza for lunch. "How's Mei-Lin?"

"Good. Dusty's taking her to his cousin's wedding."

His eyes widened. "Whoa. When?"

"This weekend."

"That sounds—serious?"

"It sounds something, doesn't it?" She fixed herself a cup of coffee from the nearly full pot and joined Lucas at the table.

"I saw some of your designs in there," he said with

a nod of his head.

Misty's heart pounded. Had he been looking around her spare room? What if he'd come across her application stuff for RISD? No. She'd stashed that away in a bottom drawer. It was unlikely he'd looked in there.

"I wasn't snooping or anything," he said, reading her expression. "It got a little stuffy in here with the rain, so I went to open a few windows, and some of your sketches on the card table blew onto the floor." He met her eyes and the fact that he was telling the truth was so transparent. "Sorry about that. I put them back and shut the door."

"Oh no. No problem."

"You know," he said. "They're very good."

"What? Really?"

"Misty. You've got talent." He smiled softly. "I mean real talent. I could see those designs on sofa cushions or something. Shirts even. Tote bags. Neckties? Anyway. They were all pretty cool."

She was touched by his faith in her. "Thanks, Lucas."

"I mean it. Maybe you should pursue it? Try to do something with design?"

Heat rose in her cheeks. "I, um…"

"Wait." He scanned her eyes. "Don't tell me you already have?"

"No, no! It's not that." Her forehead felt hot and sweaty so she dabbed it with a napkin. "You're right. It is a little muggy in here."

Lucas stood and pushed the kitchen window open a little farther. A cool breeze blew in, carrying along the scent of the rain.

"So what then?" he asked, returning to the table. "You've thought of maybe going to school?"

"School?" She forced out a laugh. "Ah. Yeah. That would be awesome, but also so expensive. You know?"

"There are scholarships, though."

Misty swallowed hard. "I've heard."

"It's not too late to follow your dreams," he said. "You're still in your twenties."

"Yeah. So are you."

He chuckled. "Yes. And?"

"What about your dreams?" she asked him. Suddenly, she was embarrassed she'd never thought to ask Lucas about much of anything before. Mostly, they always talked about her. Or, more like, she'd talked and Lucas had listened and sometimes had given advice. "Have any?"

His mouth twitched like he was pleased by her interest. "A few."

"*Like?*" she said, leading.

He chuckled at her persistence. "Like, opening my own bookstore someday."

"A bookstore? Really?"

"I was thinking used books and a coffee bar, something like that."

"You'd be competing against your former employer then."

He laughed. "Not really. My coffee wouldn't be berry-themed. No fancy whips, frappes, or lattes. Just plain old organic served with your choice of cream. Maybe regular drip and cold brew. Possibly pour-over, too. But nothing that's a mouthful to order."

She giggled. "That doesn't sound like much of a

coffee bar."

"Sure it does. But the emphasis will be more on books than on the coffee. I was thinking of having a snack wall."

"A snack wall? What's that?"

"You know those bulk bins they have in grocery stores?"

"Yeah."

"So, here's what I'm thinking." His eyes lit up. "I'm thinking of having a selection of easy-to-grab goodies. Things that can be served into a cup, like small candied chocolates, nuts, dried fruit, yogurt-covered raisins, and so on."

She could be on board with a wall of snacks while she sipped coffee and read a book. "And, what? People would pay per ounce for those?"

"I wasn't thinking quite so formal. Whatever they could fit into a designated container. I might offer a small, medium, or large paper cup. Think of it, Misty! People could hang out for hours. Work on their laptops, spend time with friends. Buy and read books. Discuss them."

Her vision shifted from reading to working on her designs while the happy buzz of others working floated around her. "That does sound pretty cool, honestly."

"I want it to be a family place, too." He oozed this happy glow while talking about it. "Somewhere people can bring their kids and not have to leave them at home. I'd even have a play corner with wooden toys and those beady-things, maybe. You know those wire abacus deals that you see in doctors' office waiting rooms?"

She nodded.

"Yeah." He sat back in his chair, looking satisfied. "Like that."

"I imagine you'd draw tons of young parents."

"Sure. They could get out of the house and be social, and their kids could be social, too. I'd like to fill it with comfy furniture. Sofas and overstuffed chairs." He pursed his lips. "I'd need to find a way to stop the kids from sneaking the candy, though."

She laughed at this. "I'm sure you'll think of something."

"Yeah. Probably will."

"Maybe have the bins and levers all up high?"

He nodded. "Great idea. Maybe I'll ask for your suggestions."

"I'd be happy to help if I can." Even though this was a faraway dream, she was honored to be included in Lucas's fantasy project. It sounded terribly ambitious and like it could go off so well in Majestic. Like a mecca for the younger crowd and possibly for older folks, too. Seemed like Lucas intended to make everyone feel included. That was so *him*.

"In the meantime." He set his hands on the table. "Someone promised to show me her portfolio not too long ago."

"Are you seriously interested?"

He winked and warmth spread through her chest. "I am."

• • •

Lucas flipped through Misty's designs, in awe of the intricate patterns. She was so meticulous in her work, amazingly precise. "You drew all this freehand?"

"With colored pencils, mostly."

"Using a straight-edge?"

"Sometimes." She ducked her chin, and Lucas guessed that she didn't need to use one often. She was one of those rare talented individuals who could draw a straight line.

"This one with the geometrical designs is really fun." He smiled at the bright and bold colors. Their assertiveness on the page reminded him of her.

"Thanks. That's one of my favorites. I sent it in with…" She bit her bottom lip.

"With?"

"I was, er…thinking of putting together an application someday to a—jury."

"Like an art jury, you mean? To get your work in a show?"

"Yeah, something like that."

Lucas liked that idea. Misty getting more exposure for her awesome work. It didn't quite look like stuff you'd exhibit in a gallery, though, or even in a café. Its uses seemed more industrial somehow. Like the designs were meant to go on other things like she'd explained to him, not stand alone as art. They were all masterpieces, though, in his eyes.

He closed the large flat portfolio case and zipped its long zipper. "Well, I think you're very talented. Thanks for showing me your work."

"Thanks for asking to see it." She blushed. "You didn't have to."

"No, but I wanted to, because it's important to you."

"What do you do in your spare time?"

In a shocking way, he realized this was a question

she'd never asked him. "Read mostly, and plan for my future. Now that Ramon is in his senior year of high school, I've got more time. He's super busy with his friends and doing all that last-year stuff, and the pressure's off a bit with all his college applications in. Until that got done, I spent a lot of time being his tutor."

Surprise washed over her face. "Wait. I thought Ramon is super smart? Hasn't he gotten two Ivy League acceptances already?"

Lucas's chest puffed out with pride. "He has and he *is* super smart, but he has test phobia issues. I mean, for standardized tests, he freaks out. So I helped him with a lot of practice and preparation for those college entrance exams, including his APs."

She beamed brightly. "You are such a great big brother."

"I'm not that great. I used to yell at him sometimes when he was little."

"What?" She sounded surprised, and he got why. She'd never even heard him raise his voice, because he really wasn't the shouty type any longer. "You?"

He shrugged, not exactly proud of memories of his teenage temper. Thankfully, he'd outgrown it. "Ramon used to want to follow me everywhere. A few times, I caught him spying on me and my dates."

She giggled. "What were you guys doing?"

"Nothing too racy. Watching shows. Making out on the sofa in the den."

Her face turned red and then she quipped, "So then. I guess he got his education."

Lucas laughed. "Not that much of one, come on."

"So, other than tutoring Ramon? Reading and

planning your future?"

"I like to cook. When I lived at home I used to help my mom sometimes with dinner. She's worked two jobs these past ten years. When she gets home, she's beat."

"That's why you're so good in the kitchen."

He shrugged. "I try."

She opened a long drawer in a deep cabinet and put her portfolio away. "I'm not expecting you to cook for me every night."

"No. You let me order pizza."

She swatted his arm. "I can also order in. Italian or Chinese."

"The options are endless," he teased. "Only not. Especially not in Majestic."

She chuckled, appearing happy and relaxed in his company, and he enjoyed having this effect on her. He also regretted asking her about her tattoo this morning. That had probably been none of his business.

"Misty," he said, "about our run this morning."

She jutted out her chin. "I did better than you thought, huh?"

He couldn't help but laugh. "Yeah. Yeah, you did. But that's not what I wanted to say. I wanted to apologize—"

"Apologize? For what?" She widened her eyes but then narrowed them an instant later. "You did get a little forward with that kiss." But the way she said it was a little flirty, rather than offended, which got him thinking that maybe she hadn't been so opposed to the move.

"Yeah. Sorry." He shifted on his feet, because he

wasn't entirely sorry about kissing her beautifully painted wrist. He'd more or less fantasized about doing that ever since she'd gotten that rose tattoo.

She reached out and touched his arm. "Lucas. You were right." Her gaze went a little weepy and he ached to hold her.

Patience. Patience.

His dad's voice came back to him.

Good things come to those who wait.

"When you asked about the tattoo," Misty said. "I did get it after a breakup, but it was me who broke it off and not the guy."

"Things just weren't...right?"

"I wasn't right in my head or heart about it. I hated letting him think that I was. I mean, I didn't lead him on intentionally. But then he started getting serious and assuming more."

Lucas studied her. "What made you pick a rose?"

Misty shrugged. "Some days I feel that's all I am to guys. Something nice they think they want to reach out and hold. But they can't, you see." Her lips twisted wryly. "Because I've got a stem and it's thorny."

"Ahh. Like a protective moat."

"Who's got a moat?"

He laughed in surprise. "Well, I do, I guess. It's how I protect my castle." He thumped his chest. "In here."

"So, your castle is made of sand?" she teased, but he didn't mind it.

"Yeah," he answered, "but the moat's filled with sea water. And alligators."

Misty laughed. "Alligators don't live in salt water."

"Mine do." Lucas turned to look at her. "And

anyway, how do you know all men are averse to
thorns? I mean some of us kind of dig them."

She laughed and shoved his shoulder. "Come on."

"Well, I wouldn't be put off." Her hazel eyes met
his and he caught his breath. "By some silly old
thorns."

She stood up straighter. "And I'm not afraid of
moats, either."

"No?" He stepped toward her. "What are you
afraid of?"

She blew out a small breath. "Messing up and
making the wrong decision."

"Well then." He pursed his lips. "We'll just have to
make sure you make the right one, won't we?"

A pink hue swept her cheeks.

"You deserve more, Misty. More than those guys
who can't put up with a few thorns. I mean, come on.
Life isn't perfect. People aren't perfect. But I still like
to believe that there are people out there who are
perfect for each other." She stared into his eyes and
he fell down into their depths. "I mean." He licked his
lips when his throat went scratchy. "That's how it
should be."

"That is how it should be," she said. "You're right."

"That's the way it is with your parents," he told
her. "You can see it."

"I know. They're very sweet. Coming up on their
thirty-fifth anniversary next week."

"That so?"

"Yeah." Her eyes sparkled. "And my dad's got a
very big secret. He's giving her a diamond ring."

"What? How?" Given the Delaneys' financial
problems, now was probably not the best time for

such an extravagance. Though he did find the notion romantic. Mrs. Delaney never wore an engagement ring, only a simple wedding band. Lucas had surmised when she and Mr. Delaney had married, they hadn't been able to afford a diamond.

Misty spoke in an excited whisper, although it was just the two of them. "He inherited an old family ring from his mom and has had it in a lockbox for a lot of years. Because of their money problems, he at first thought he might sell it, but then he decided he couldn't let it go. He's friends with the jeweler who cut him a deal for resetting the stone. Dad's been paying for the new ring on layaway, ten dollars every week, for the past eight months. Mom has no idea."

"That gift is going to bowl your mom over."

Her pretty smile blew him away. "I know."

Lucas's heart warmed, then it skipped a beat when he found himself imagining doing something similar for Misty. Giving her a special gift. Maybe even a ring, if that's what she wanted. Some day when the moment was right.

CHAPTER FIFTEEN

Lucas was seriously impressed by Misty's work and he told her so again over dinner. He'd been to the market while she was with Mei-Lin and bought supplies to make them pork chops with Adobo, Sofrito black beans and rice, and caramelized plantains.

Misty eagerly dug into her food. "This is really delicious. The plantains are so sticky and sweet."

"Yeah, they go great with the black beans."

"They go great with all of it." She sliced a bit of her thick pork chop off its bone and popped it her mouth. "I love this. Thank you."

"You're welcome."

She frowned and toyed with her glass of red wine. "Lucas?"

"Yeah."

"There's something I didn't tell you earlier."

"Oh? What's that?"

"It's about Charlotte and that list. She's got a copy, too, and is going through it."

"Wait. With who?"

"His name is Dave."

"The banker?" When she nodded, he asked, "What have they done so far?"

"The beach picnic, the sunset…breakfast in bed. She even went to the *gym*."

He whistled. "Charlotte worked out?" he said because she typically didn't do this.

"That's what I said." Misty set down her wineglass.

"Maybe she's serious about him."

His jaw tensed. "We don't know anything about this guy. Do you really think she can fall in love with a stranger in a week? It was different for Nell"—and he hoped him and Misty—"because she'd known Grant for years."

"My thoughts exactly." She bit her bottom lip. "If it doesn't work out, Charlotte would be okay in London, don't you think? She's worldly. She spent time in Scotland in college."

Misty was the only one of her sisters who'd never gotten a higher education. She'd never been interested as far as he knew, and that was her call. He'd done community college himself, business classes. He figured those would come in handy someday when he opened that shop of his own.

"She's got a head for marketing," he said. "She'd be an asset at the top."

Misty nodded. "And then could chart her own course after that."

"After the five years is up, you mean."

"Yeah."

They fell into silence. If what Misty feared was true, Charlotte still might win the bet. The only way Misty could prevent that would be to get engaged first.

"So, what are you going to do?" he finally asked. "Run out there and find someone to marry first?" He tried to make light of it, but his heart ached at the joke.

"Lucas. I'm not going anywhere yet." She set her chin. "Besides that, I don't just want some random guy."

"No? Then who?" It was risky asking directly but he still wanted to hope.

She shrugged, avoiding his gaze. "I'm still figuring things out."

"Hey." His voice came out a low murmur. "I know you are. Sorry. I didn't mean to push you."

"You're not pushy. In fact, you're one of the most patient people I know." Her eyes glistened with the greenish sheen that always swept him away. If only he could carry her along with him.

"What do you want to do then?" he asked. "In the meantime. While you're figuring?"

She glanced at the list. "Maybe we should work on that?"

"For your sisters' sake? To keep up the ruse?"

"Yeah, sure."

He honestly didn't care what excuse she gave him. He was just happy spending time with her. He surveyed the eleven items, thinking out loud. "Not much of a chance for a sunset tonight," he said, peering out the rainy window.

"Storm's supposed to lift before dawn. So maybe tomorrow?"

"Want to try the beach picnic and then the movies late afternoon?"

She blushed.

"We don't have to do the making out part, Misty. Maybe I'll just put my arm around you and give your cheek a light peck." If she decided that she wanted more, though, he'd be more than happy to oblige her. One thing he knew, he wouldn't push. With Misty, that would only backfire.

Her color deepened. "As long as we make it out of

there by sunset."

He chuckled, loving the sound of their day. "That can be arranged." Nell's list, them doing these things together, could only bring them closer, and closer with Misty was exactly what he wanted.

He stood and reached for her empty plate. "Want any more?"

"No thanks, I'm stuffed. Thanks again for the Puerto Rican dinner. It was so, so good."

"No problem."

She got up to help him and they tidied up the kitchen together like they'd done it a million times before. Lucas liked how easy it was to be with Misty. They just fit like a hand in a glove.

"What about tonight?" he asked her. "Feel like streaming another oldie?"

She cracked a grin, looking prettier than ever in her sparkly purple top and purple-streaked hair. "Yeah, that would be fun."

He thought back on that list and grinned. "Hey, I just thought of something. Our love of old movies—"

"Yes!" Her eyes shone. "Our one shared passion!"

He shrugged happily. "Never know. Maybe we'll discover more?"

She blushed but didn't look away. "Maybe so."

• • •

Misty wasn't sure which movie she liked best, *Vertigo* or *The Man Who Knew Too Much*. Both were exciting, but she suspected she might like *Rear Window* even better. Since they were going to the cinema tomorrow, they decided to put off watching that until

Friday. Afterward, they might select another classic star to watch, or stick with their director's theme and stay with Hitchcock.

Lucas shut his laptop when the credits rolled. "We should probably save *Psycho* for Halloween, though. It's pretty spooky."

Misty shivered. "Not sure if I can take that one. I don't do spooky."

"I promise to protect you." His eyes sparkled and it occurred to Misty that she always felt sheltered and cared for around Lucas.

"I bet you would." She tried to imagine spending Halloween with him, and then other holidays as well, like that Puerto Rican one he'd mentioned, Three Kings Day. "Do you think you'll want to continue your family's traditions with your own kids someday?"

He blinked like he hadn't expected that question. "Ah, I'm not sure. I mean, I guess most of them are pretty nice. Some of it would depend on my wife, though." He cleared his throat. "She and I would probably discuss it. Decide together what's best."

Lucas was always so fair, wanting to be balanced and respecting the other person's opinions. That was something she appreciated about him.

"But you want kids?" she asked.

"Sure. I mean, I think so. It would be nice. How about you?"

Misty bit her bottom lip. "I always kind of have? But I'm not totally sure I'm maternal, to tell you the truth. That's more like Nell's style, so nurturing. And Charlotte's such a mother hen. Always telling others what to do."

He chuckled. "I'm sure you'd do just fine if you decide to have kids down the road."

Her heart warmed at his faith in her, but she was curious. "What makes you say that?"

"You're a good-hearted woman. Some say that's all it takes with parenting, having your heart in the right place. My dad used to say everyone makes mistakes. He admitted to making them, too. But he said he did the best with what he knew, and my mom was the same way. I always understood that they loved me."

"Yeah." Misty sighed. "Same with my sisters and my parents."

"Family's pretty important, you know." He paused and then said, "To me."

"To me, too."

She put two and two together and her heart did a happy dance. "Our love of family?" She met his eyes and he grinned.

"Another shared passion. Yep."

A vision filled her head of her and Lucas with little children dressed in cute Halloween costumes and she repressed a grin. It was kind of a heartwarming picture. Lucas would definitely make a great dad.

Lucas studied her a moment. "I know you and your sisters always do a big family Christmas with your folks," he said, roping her back into the conversation.

She nodded. "Thanksgiving, too," she said. "My dad's oyster stuffing is amazing."

"Legendary, I hear." Though Misty's folks had asked him over to dinner, he'd never come for a holiday. He had his own mom to think of, and his little brother who relied on him. It was interesting how couples made it work, sharing holidays between their families. Misty didn't imagine that could ever be a problem with Lucas. In some ways, he was like part of the Delaney clan already. Her folks were warm and welcoming and would always clear more space at their table. She was betting they'd make room for Mrs. Reyes and Ramon, too.

Wait. What on earth was she thinking? Kids? Family holidays?

The rain beat steadily outdoors, thudding against the windowpanes. They'd had to lower all the windows until they were mostly shut, but they were open enough for a cool breeze to flutter in, carrying the musky scent of the rain on its wings.

"Still coming down in droves." Misty stared out the darkened window and Lucas did, too.

"Not a fit night out for man nor beast," he joked.

Misty remembered an item on the list. "Dancing in the rain. Ha. Guess ol' Charlotte didn't think about lightning."

He glanced out the window. "None of that happening now."

"True."

He thought a moment. "Is there still that awning-thingy on your roof?"

"Awning?" Then she remembered. It was some old-fashioned hand-crank deal that you could extend partway across the rooftop to create shade. Her landlord, Jared, had set it up a few years ago. When she'd moved in, he'd showed her how to work it and said she was free to use the patio furniture there. She'd almost never been up there and definitely never in the rain. "I believe so. How did you know about it?"

"After you got this apartment, you showed us pictures on your phone at the café. You were pretty proud that you had access to the rooftop."

Misty laughed. "I guess I kind of forgot about having that perk."

"You don't use it?"

"It's not in use much. Jared hosts parties up there sometimes."

His eyebrows rose. "Bet there's nobody else up there now."

"Lucas, I can't believe—"

"What? You want Charlotte to finish the list before you do?"

"No, of course not."

He winked. "If we do this one more thing tonight, we can probably pull out into the lead tomorrow."

She giggled, liking the sound of that. "You're right."

Lucas grinned. "So then, you're not opposed to a little rain?"

She wasn't, especially around him. It wasn't like she needed to worry about looking any worse than normal. He'd seen her first thing in the morning now with none of her makeup on, including her heavy eyeliner, and he hadn't mentioned a thing. Like he didn't even notice the difference. When he looked at her, it was like he saw straight through to her insides, appreciating her soul.

That was so, so different from Sean and all the others, always commenting on her short and shapely figure. In some ways she found their compliments depressingly reductive. Lucas wasn't like that, though.

"No," she answered. "Not opposed. I won't melt."

His eyes twinkled. "That's the Misty I know. Always up for adventure."

"Always up for beating Charlotte," she said with sass.

"All right then." He nodded, appearing game. "Let's get to it."

• • •

Misty couldn't believe she was doing this. Going up to her apartment building's rooftop to dance with Lucas in the rain. They both wore rain jackets and Lucas carried a flashlight. Somehow this seemed more like a weird adventure than anything romantic. But anyway, it was a way to cross one more item off her list.

With her luck, Charlotte had already knocked off four more items by now.

Misty seriously wanted to meet this Dave and give him her okay. Nell had seemed a little worried about him, too. Why would a stranger want to move so fast? What was in it for him? Other than marrying gorgeous Charlotte, which was a very big prize, given how smart and accomplished she was. From Charlotte's perspective, though, what did she stand to gain, apart from avoiding marrying Aidan?

Misty didn't want Charlotte to win, but she also didn't like the idea of her becoming engaged to someone for the wrong reasons. Grant and Nell were different. They'd known each other a while, and Nell had always dreamed of being with him. Now Misty knew Lucas had felt the same way about her for eons. It wasn't like they were strangers. Not like Charlotte and Dave.

They reached the heavy exterior door and Lucas shoved it open, guiding the way with his flashlight. Rain poured down on them, dousing their faces. He wiped his clear with the back of his hand. "Man, this is torrential."

"Maybe not such a good idea then?"

He located the awning crank and handed Misty the flashlight to hold steady for him. "Why don't we see if this works?" He gave it a turn, then leaned into the crank, exerting more effort. Finally it turned, then turned again—revolution after revolution giving a whiny squeak. Its green-and-white canvas covering bloomed above them, forming a protective barrier over their heads.

Misty held out her upturned palms. No raindrops fell into them. "It works!"

He came and stood beside her as they both absorbed the panorama. The building in front of Misty's was a little lower, so from this bird's-eye perch they had a view of the tumultuous sea, its thundering waves darkened in the storm. Winds whipped toward them, tussling through Lucas's curls and tugging loose strands of Misty's hair from her ponytail band.

She looked around, enjoying the dramatic scenery. The salty scent of the sea wafted toward them in cold crisp blasts of ocean air. "It's kind of cool up here."

"It is," he agreed. "I like it."

She looked over at him and grinned. "I like it, too."

I also like being with you, Lucas.

It was hard not to feel comfortable with him. Lucas was like a cozy sweater that was easy to slip into. He made her feel fuzzy and warm, even in the wind and the rain.

He set the flashlight on the outdoor side table beside the fake rattan sofa with faded weather-resistant cushions. He turned it faceup, its beam casting a circular light on the canopy above them.

"Nice," Misty said. "Almost as good as disco lights."

Lucas chuckled at this. "You don't see much of those in Majestic."

It was true. To get the club life, you had to go to a much bigger town. London probably had plenty of dance places, but at the moment Misty didn't want to dance anywhere but here. She also didn't want to dance with anyone else.

He held out his arms and the sleeves of his raincoat crinkled. "Not the best clubbing clothes."

She grinned up at him. "I think you're dressed just right."

A smile warmed his lips. "Yeah. So are you."

Misty's heart fluttered and then it pounded harder when he took her in his arms. "I guess we have the music of the rain." His breath heated her neck and all her senses tingled.

She settled her arms around his neck. Then she remembered about Charlotte. "Wait," she said, looking up. "The selfie!" She unzipped her rain jacket pocket and took out her cell phone.

He held out his hand. "Let me do it. My arms are longer."

Misty passed him the phone and they half embraced like they were dancing. The rain-streaked rooftop formed the backdrop behind them.

Lucas took a series of pics. "I'll let you choose the best one later," he said, handing her back her phone. She put it away, acutely aware of each *pitter-patter* and the cadence of heavy waves hitting the shore. The rain picked up and then slowed down, moving in sweeping movements across the rooftop as Lucas took her in his arms once again.

They swayed together gently and he tightened his grip. "This is nice."

Misty's breath hitched. "Yeah."

He pulled back to gaze into her eyes, tucking a loose strand of hair behind her ear. "This is like a dream come true."

"Is it, Lucas?" Misty dared to ask him. "True what the others think?"

His gray eyes bathed her in an aura that filled her soul with endless sunshine. "I don't know. What do they think?" One side of his mouth turned up higher than the other and warmth pooled in her belly.

"That you…like me as more than a friend?"

He supported her in his arms, taking another slow turn around the rooftop. "I definitely like you as more than a friend. I have for a while."

A shiver of excitement and anticipation tore through her. "Since when?"

"Oh, since about the first time that I saw you."

Misty laughed, embarrassed. "Lucas—"

"I mean it, though."

He held her gaze in an adoring way and Misty experienced a light buzz of current. Then a mild humming thrummed through her veins. She'd never had any guy see her—really see her—the way Lucas did, and she was starting to see him like she never had before.

Sexy, strong, brave. Someone not afraid to share his feelings.

"You're pretty special, Lucas."

"Do you really think so?" He took another turn and the motion drew her closer. Her heart hammered and her face burned hot. She could barely whisper the words.

"I do."

He cupped his hand to her face. "I'm glad."

Suddenly, their dancing stopped.

But now the entire world spun around them as she fell into Lucas's eyes. His kind, sultry, and—ooh, ooh, ooh—unbelievably hot eyes. They were like low-burning embers leaving a mark on her soul and opening up her heart. She'd kept it closed down to outsiders, all icy cold. But now Lucas brought the heat like a glowing hearth during a snowstorm. Misty was ready for the frostbite to end. She was all toasty warm with Lucas. He had her.

"I know you've had some trouble trusting guys. Believing there was no one you could count on." He traced her cheek with his thumb. "But things are different now. I'm here."

Yes. She saw that.

Felt it.

"Nobody else was ever right."

"It's sometimes hard to know what 'right' is." He tugged her even closer and Misty's pulse skittered. "Until you find it."

He dipped his chin toward hers and said on a husky breath, "I'm here for you, Misty. I won't let you down."

"Lucas, wait." Guilt swamped through her when she thought of RISD. What if that came through? She'd be letting him down by leaving Majestic, and not to marry Aidan but to attend school. "Maybe we shouldn't. I don't want to be unfair to you."

"Why don't you let me decide what's fair?"

"But there's so much going on." She licked her lips. "My future's up in the air."

His lips brushed over hers and she melted. "I get that."

"But you and I... I can't promise—"

"Then don't," he said. "Let's just see how things go."

He kissed her again and every last bit of her tingled. "This okay?" He nibbled on her lip and she moaned.

"I...didn't know how you really felt."

"It's all right." He kissed her again, lightly at first with silky warm brushes of his lips. Then deepened his kisses and rasped, "You know now."

Misty whimpered and clung to him, kissing him back—again and again.

"Oh, wow." He groaned and held her tighter, cradling her head in his hands.

Misty's raincoat rippled in the breeze, fanning out around her as wind whistled through the rain, kicking it up and splashing it sideways.

But she stayed warm in Lucas's embrace, his kisses carrying her over the rooftop and up through the rainclouds, into a twinkling night sky.

Where the sparkling stars met a shimmering moon.

And the world was at peace in the heavens.

CHAPTER SIXTEEN

Misty woke up with a song bursting in her heart. Her senses came alive, tuning into the world in an exquisite and unusual way. Everything was precise. The scent of last night's dinner lingering in the air. The delicious weight of her warm duvet, blanketing her from the chill seeping through her slightly cracked window. The dark, shadowy space teaming with light ushered in by the waning moon.

Misty wrapped her duvet around her and padded barefoot to the window overlooking an alley. The rain had completely stopped and cool breezes rippled through the air. The sky outside was in the process of shedding its thick black coat and replacing it with the purple garment of dawn. The world was a beautiful place.

What a moment that had been on the rooftop with Lucas. Dancing with him and then kissing in the rain. She'd never guessed she'd feel this way about him.

But she did.

He made her soul smile and her heart sigh. But, most of all, he made her not want to worry about anything for once.

Not her parents or the café.

Or Charlotte, or Aidan.

Not those random billboard guys, or even RISD.

No. What she wanted for today was to feel this good all day through. She wanted to picnic on the beach and go out to the movies…

Maybe even—okay—make out a little. She bit her lip. Or maybe *a lot*. And get transported to the moon once again by Lucas's wildly sexy kisses.

She grinned, humming a special tune. "Fly Me to the Moon" had been one of the trumpet solos she'd taught herself, and it was super romantic. The lyrics spoke of taking each other away just by the touch of a hand. She'd been a bit embarrassed to like something so sappy, but it wasn't nearly as sentimental as her all-time fave, "Songbird" by Fleetwood Mac.

Misty's fingers twitched and she stretched out her hands, laughing.

"Oh no you don't," she scolded her grabby hands, because she knew what they wanted.

She hadn't played in days, and she'd never played for him. She'd given up playing in jazz band when she'd transitioned from middle school to high school, where the audition competition was tougher. So she'd been afraid to try out. She'd also started gravitating toward art back then, and found herself enrolling in more and more visual arts type classes, leaving less time for music anyway.

Privately, though, she kept playing the trumpet, but only with no audience. The instrument had been expensive, even secondhand, and her parents had sacrificed to buy it, so she felt an obligation to keep using it somehow. She enjoyed the buzz of the mouthpiece against her lips, and when she mastered the notes just right, the results were thrilling.

The trumpet was bold, powerful. Not dainty like a stringed instrument. While those certainly elicited beautiful tunes, there was something wild and unfiltered about a horn. Densely beautiful. Exciting. Hard charging and powerful. Like her.

Her fingers twitched again and she shook her head.

It was super early and the neighbors might not appreciate it.

Then again, this street was hardly residential.

And the folks on the next street over, and the one after that?

Misty grinned.

Maybe they wouldn't mind a little wake-up call?

• • •

Lucas opened his eyes to a low, wailing tune. He recognized it at once.

"What a Wonderful World" by Louis Armstrong.

Misty was playing her trumpet!

The melody carried through the small apartment, sound resonating off the high ceilings and paint-chipped walls. He got out of bed and walked toward the living room in his camp shorts and T-shirt, like someone dazed living a dream. He reached the threshold and caught his breath.

Misty was a vision in her leggings and sweatshirt surrounded by natural light. Sunshine poured through the open front window in ribbony cords of orange and gold, glinting off the side of her brass instrument as she played, her ringed fingers nimbly working its valves. Her hair fell loose around her shoulders, her purple highlights sparkling in the sun as she played out the window to the world, filling Majestic with her song.

And then Lucas saw it in his mind's eye. The green

trees and blooming roses that Armstrong described, and the sparkling rainbow lighting up a sky.

His heart warmed, full to bursting.

She stopped playing and lowered her trumpet, peering over her shoulder.

"Oh, hi there." A blush swept her cheeks. "Good morning."

"Don't stop on account of me."

"I'm sorry if I woke you." But her playful smile said she really wasn't.

"Misty," he said. "You're fantastic. I had no clue."

She grinned. "Thanks."

"I mean it. That was beautiful. I've never heard it played in that key."

"Wait." Her eyebrows knitted together. "You know trumpet?"

He chuckled because he'd never actually had lessons. "I wouldn't exactly say 'know.' I mean, we're acquainted, but not close or anything."

She set her trumpet down in the armchair. "Lucas Reyes." She grinned. "You've been hiding something from me."

"I didn't exactly hide it. You never asked."

"So wait." Her mouth hung open. "You play? Seriously?"

He shrugged. "I knock around with it once in a while. I've got my dad's horn."

"That's so cool that he used to play."

"Yeah. He was in a band with my uncle in New York. They played Latin tunes and everything. That's how my mom met my dad. She was in the city with a friend and met him when he was playing at a restaurant. I think she slipped him her number."

"Your mom?" She clasped her hands to her cheeks and then she giggled. "Who knew?"

"Yeah. So. After that," he continued, "they started dating long distance because she lived here. Eventually, Dad gave up on the music dream and took a job at my abuelo's fishing company. Abuelo helped get him outfitted with his own rig and everything, but Dad viewed it as a loan. He eventually paid everything back—with interest."

"I had no idea about your dad being musical. So that's where you get it from, I guess."

He nodded and Misty set her hand on her hip.

"Ever take lessons? Play anywhere?"

"Nope. Only for myself sometimes. I've picked up a few tunes over the years."

Misty lifted the trumpet and shoved it toward him. "I want to hear one." Her forehead rose in the most darling fashion. "Please?"

Lucas chuckled, deciding to indulge her. "All right." He thought a few minutes about what he might play and then belted out a fun and upbeat choice. From a kids' movie even, but oddly one of his favorites. He hoped she wouldn't find his selection too goofy. Then he decided he might as well risk it. It was a fun wake-up tune.

"No way!" She laughed and clapped her hands when he began the intro. "'The Bare Necessities' from *The Jungle Book*?" He paused to answer but she nudged his arm. "No, no! Keep playing! I'll dance!"

He chuckled, stumbling over a note, then picked it right back up again, belting his heart out in song.

"I LOVE that song!" The joy on her face was unmistakable as she danced around the room like a little kid, singing along. "That's what I'm all about today," she said. "Forgetting about my worries and my strife."

He laughed again but remained focused enough to finish the piece. He ended with a flair and then lowered his trumpet with a hearty, "Yeah!" mimicking the big bear Baloo from the film.

"Oh, Lucas!" She threw her arms around him. "That was incredible!"

He stared down into her amazing greenish hazel eyes. "You're incredible."

Her gaze washed over him like a warm ocean wave. "Thanks. So are you."

He gave her a kiss and then studied her outfit, down to her athletic shoes. "You look all dressed to go somewhere."

She grinned up at him. "Aren't we going running again?"

"I'd love to run with you."

Already, she was running away with his heart.

He thought he'd loved her before, but maybe that had been a crush. Now was different. These emotions were effervescent and overpowering, but in the best possible way.

Because, from the look on her beautiful face, Misty was experiencing them, too.

Misty and music? Another shared passion. This was incredible. He'd never known this about her. Now all he had to hope was that the greatest passion they would share would be about the two of them becoming a couple, and maybe even lasting forever.

• • •

A short time later, Lucas chased Misty down the beach as big billowy clouds caressed the deep blue sky. "Slow down! Where are you going?" She'd tied her hair up in a ponytail and it was flying behind her.

"To get there first!" she called over her shoulder.

There? He had no idea what she was talking about until she led him to a sandbar. She pointed from the shore across a deep eddy. "See that? Over there?"

"Yeah? What about it?"

"Look harder."

He did and mounds of seashells glistened in the sun. "Wow. Those must have been turned up by yesterday's heavy rain."

"I know." She grinned. "It's exciting. I might even find my perfect conch."

"There's such a thing as a perfect conch?"

"Yeah, there is." She lightly shoved his chest and he laughed. "You just have to know where to look for it."

"And you think that's over there?"

"I've found some of my very best shells in this location."

"But never your perfect conch?"

"Not yet." She shook her head. "They've all been broken."

He rubbed his cheek. "We'll need to take our shoes off to get out there, and wade through this puddle."

She dropped down on the sand onto her bottom and began untying her shoes. "Uh-huh. I know." She pushed up her leggings above her knees and stood. She shot him a flirty grin and his neck warmed. "Coming with me?"

He wasn't about to let this new sexy and flirty Misty go anywhere without him. "Don't see why not."

Chilly water nipped at his feet and toes, swirling around his ankles, and crushed shells pricked his insteps, but Misty held onto his hand, tugging him along. "I wish I'd brought my bucket," she said. "Or at least a small tote bag."

"I've got a few pockets in my shorts."

She shook her head at his offer. "Thanks, Lucas. But I don't think we'll be sticking a big old conch in there."

His ears burned hot, when he realized how that might look. "Right."

She giggled at his expression. "I'll use my hoodie pouch." She patted the giant pocket resting low on her stomach.

"That works!"

By the time they'd been on the sandbar for ten minutes, Misty's pouch was working really well. She looked like an adorable kangaroo, filling her midsection with tiny treasures. She *ooh*ed and *ahh*ed over each one. "This one is an olive shell. See its pretty purple color?"

He smiled. "It matches your hair."

She held it up beside one ear. "Maybe if I find another, I'll make some earrings… Ooh, look! A sand dollar! And—yes! Some green sea glass!" She was so engaged in her collecting, she didn't spot the partially buried specimen beside her left foot.

But he did.

Lucas bent down and gingerly picked it up, shaking loose some sand.

Its creamy tan center glistened against the sheen

of the water, the conch's corkscrew spiraling clock-
wise. Its top was adorned in a circular, pointy-tipped
crown. He turned it over, looking for cracks or missing pieces.

It was perfect.

"I think I've found your conch," he announced
proudly.

Misty swung around, her palms loaded with shells.

She stared down at his hand and gasped. "You did
it!" Her eyes gleamed with delight as she bounced on
her bare heels. "It's so pretty!"

Then she wrinkled up her nose and hurled an ac-
cusation. "Did you plant it?"

He laughed in surprise. "What? No."

She narrowed her eyes just slightly. "But then
how—"

"Just fate, I guess. Could be I was meant to find it."

"Meant to? Hmm."

"Uh-huh." He grinned. "So I could give it to you."

"That's sweet, but I'm not sure I believe in fate."

"You know, I didn't used to, either," he said, "but
now I've kind of changed my mind." He'd sure taken
Charlotte's billboard as a sign to finally step up and
pursue Misty, and he'd never in his lifetime regret it.
The only thing he'd regret was if he hadn't given this
his best try.

"Yeah? What changed it?"

"This." He held up the conch, using it as a prop.
"You said you've searched and searched forever for
your perfect conch, and then there it was! Right down
below you. You know what I think?"

She laughed. "No, what?"

He smirked playfully. "That it's a sign that I'm

your good luck charm."

She rolled her eyes. "Lucas Reyes. Don't tell me you've started believing in signs?"

"Why not?" he asked, baiting her. "Others do."

She cocked her head. "Sounds a little superstitious to me."

"Says the woman who believes she can will it to snow."

Misty held up her index finger. "That's only at Christmas."

"Yeah." He chuckled. "Not superstitious at all."

She tucked the shells in her hands into her sweatshirt and Lucas passed her the conch. She viewed it every which way, holding it gently in her hands. "This is amazing. It's all intact."

"It's a big one, too. How did a conch get all the way up here?"

"Doubt it's that kind of conch," she said. "Not a legit one from the Caribbean. This here is technically a whelk."

He'd heard that word before. "The guys that attach themselves to lobster cages?"

"Sometimes." She stared at her prize. "But I've never seen one grow so big. Not only that, it's a leftie."

"A what?"

"Most have openings on the right and spiral counterclockwise," she told him. "This one goes the other way."

"Probably happened because I'm left-handed."

"Lucas." Misty giggled. "You did not change the shape of this shell just by touching it."

"How do you know I'm not magic?"

Her eyes twinkled. "I don't," she said and his heart

pounded. "Maybe you are."

He stepped toward her and took her in his arms. "You make me feel that way. Like I could do anything."

"You found my perfect conch."

"I thought you said it was a whelk?" he asked huskily.

"Same diff." She smiled. "And anyway? It's just what I was looking for."

He jostled her toward him, holding her closer. "What should we do today?"

"I was thinking of maybe a picnic?" She playfully batted her eyelashes. "Then going to the movies?" Even though they'd previously discussed these plans, it was fun acting like they were coming up with date ideas off the cuff. Almost playful. Like they were acting out a scene in a film.

He pressed his forehead against hers and tightened his embrace. "How about watching a sunset afterward?"

She grew a little breathy. "That would be nice."

"*This* is nice."

Her lips parted slightly and a hunger tore through him. So fierce. Untamed. Every muscle flexed as he dove into her eyes. Those gorgeous green meadows inviting him into her private world. Her soul. And— oh, how he hoped—her heart. She reached up and touched his cheek, running her silky soft fingertips against his morning stubble. Then she traced the line of his bottom lip.

"Kiss me, Lucas," she whispered.

He brushed his lips over hers and her breath was hot on his.

Heavenly.

"Harder."

She wasn't going to need to ask twice.

He claimed her beautiful mouth with his, devouring her with deep, wet kisses and she sagged in his arms. The conch fell from her hand, plummeting into the sand, but he had no fear of it breaking against the soft cushion of the shore. All that mattered now was Misty, with the wind circling all around them, and seabirds singing their beautiful tunes. And the waves crash-crash-crashing to the rhythm of their wildly beating hearts.

He bolstered her up against him, holding her tighter.

"I've got you," he rasped before kissing her again.

She pressed her palms to his face and his heart grew wings. "I've got you, too."

CHAPTER SEVENTEEN

When they got back to her apartment, Misty's heart was still pounding.

What Lucas did to her.

How had she never guessed this was possible?

Him and her? It had all seemed so foreign and faraway. Like something miles in the distance that you couldn't make out through a hazy fog.

But now those clouds had lifted and everything was crystal clear.

Lucas was just so, so...*everything*. He made her laugh. He made her smile.

He had her playing the trumpet for him!

And he played trumpet, too!

How cool was that?

Very cool, honestly. She'd always had a thing for musicians.

Especially since now.

Besides all that, he'd found her the perfect conch shell.

Misty sighed but then she shot him a sidelong glance as he headed for the shower. She'd told him to go ahead first, because truthfully she couldn't wait to text her sisters and tell them all about it. She and Lucas were falling in love!

Or, at least in heavy like.

Her whole body tingled when she recalled his heated kisses.

A girl could get used to those.

Oh yeah, she could.

No way was she going to London now to be saddled with some distant British guy who had all the finesse of a clunky kettledrum. No. She wanted a man who played a trumpet. Who blared out his intentions in red-hot sexy song.

Okay. A Disney tune was maybe not so sexy.

Even though "Bare Necessities" did have the word "bare" in it. She giggled thinking of both her and Lucas being bare. Then her face burned as hot as a blow torch.

She'd never been super modest with any other guy.

But Lucas.

She sighed.

She wanted to make everything right with him.

No more letting him do all the cooking and whatnot. She'd be taking her turn. It would be terrible for her to finally fall for him, and then have him walk out on the deal. Though, based on his ardor on that sandbar, that was doubtful. They'd practically scorched the ocean, and setting fire to water was nearly impossible to do. Okay. Maybe totally impossible. Didn't matter. That wasn't the point.

Misty strolled into the kitchen, looking forward to a cup of coffee. She'd drink some and text her sisters while—

Hang on. What were all those text alerts on her phone?

She picked it up.

Noooo!

There was Charlotte in sort of a shadowy pic, and she was dancing in the rain! It was hard to tell where she was exactly. Down at the docks maybe? Some lights shone in the background through a grainy gray film of raindrops falling.

It looked kind of like the outside of the Dockside, but she wasn't sure.

Charlotte had her hands up in the air above her head and was swiveling her hips like she was doing a line dance or something. Only there was nobody else in line.

Misty frowned and flipped to the next photo. There were more!

Charlotte sitting at a restaurant table by a wine bottle and holding a red rose by its stem.

Misty glanced at her wrist, liking her rose better. It seemed extra special now that Lucas had kissed it.

Charlotte sitting at her kitchen counter and very clearly x-ing out the items on her "Top Ten" list.

With a Sharpie.

Way to do overkill. Drama. Drama. Drama. That was Charlotte. She wasn't a colored pencil sort of girl. Her statements were BOLD.

Misty squinted at her phone.

All but one of Charlotte's items were crossed through. Everything but going to the movies.

No way! She'd shared some deep secret with Dave? What?

Also. Honestly. What could the two of them have in common? What shared passion? Misty and Lucas already had three—besides each other.

Misty's gut clenched.

How could Charlotte have made so much progress?

"How we doing? Pretty good, huh?" Lucas entered

the kitchen, all cleaned up for the day and wearing a grin. He saw her staring at the list and frowned.

"What is it?" His brow creased. "What's wrong?"

"It's Charlotte," she said. "She and Dave have pulled out ahead of us."

His jaw dropped. "They danced in the rain?"

Misty scanned back through the photos and flipped her phone around, showing him the dancing pic.

"Uh. That looks like *Charlotte* dancing in the rain. Where's Dave?"

Misty shrugged. "Taking the picture, I guess."

"Mind if I take a look?" He thumbed through the ones Nell had sent her, too. "Doesn't look like she's done everything."

"Almost, though." Misty retrieved her phone to open the group chat she'd received this morning. "Here. There are more."

Lucas perused the pics and shook his head. "Looks like she really doesn't want to marry Aidan." He laid her phone on the table and she set her chin.

"Well, neither do I." Misty's eyes grew hot and she rubbed the side of her nose.

"Hey." Lucas stepped toward her and took her hands. "Misty." She hung her head but he urged gently. "Look at me."

When she did, he said, "No one's going to make you marry Aidan, all right? Not happening." The way he said it was so reassuring. So steady. Like him. "And anyway. It's not like you don't have choices." His eyebrows arched in an adorable manner and Misty hugged him.

"Oh Lucas," she said. "I choose you."

"I was hoping you might." He swatted her backside and Misty jumped. "Now go get your shower," he commanded with a twinkle in his eye. "We are *not* letting Charlotte and Dave beat us to the finish line."

Misty felt instantly better. Lucas always knew the right thing to say and how to make sense of a messy situation. She grabbed her phone and took it with her to the bedroom, where she went to get her clothes.

She texted her sisters, responding to Charlotte's latest.

Her reply was short and sweet.

Game's not over, Charlotte.

Not yet.

The hot shower did her a world of good but when she came back to the kitchen, Lucas cut her off at the pass. "Nuh-uh, can't come in here." He grinned. "I'm making you a surprise."

Misty's stomach rumbled. "Breakfast?"

His gray eyes gleamed. "Woman. Go get back in bed."

Misty gulped. "What?"

He chuckled at her stunned expression. "So I can serve you breakfast, Misty. It's on the list, remember?"

"Oh, right!" She giggled. What had she been thinking? That Lucas was making some big move? No. That wasn't him. He wasn't like that. He'd never push her in that way. "Can I at least grab more coffee?"

She tried to walk around him, but he blocked her path with his solid frame. "I'll bring it to you."

She returned to her bedroom and pulled back the

duvet, scooting underneath it and fluffing some pillows behind her back. Lucas appeared an instant later and handed her a mug.

"Coffee," he said, appearing pleased with himself.

"Thank you."

He held up a hand. "Don't go anywhere. Be back in a bit."

Misty couldn't wait to see what he was cooking up for her. After getting up so early to play the trumpet and then their fun excursion on the beach, she was famished. She eyed the pretty conch shell on her dresser. With the mirror situated behind it, she could see it from both sides and it was beautiful. She couldn't believe Lucas had found it, but she was so glad he had.

She sighed at the fact that he'd hinted it was a sign.

Though she claimed she didn't believe in those, maybe she was beginning to in some weird way. She'd wanted a perfect conch forever, but as much as she'd searched she'd never found one. Then, suddenly, one was right there. Just below her feet.

Almost like Lucas had been right under her nose all these years, and she'd never noticed how very special he was until now. She turned her ear to the kitchen, listening for the sound of frying eggs or sizzling bacon. She heard the whir of a blender instead.

Noooo. Not another smoothie?

Mei-Lin was right. She had to tell Lucas she didn't really drink those things. But when he entered her bedroom with a tray, looking all pleased with himself, she just couldn't. Not today.

"I hope you like it," he said, setting the tray on her

lap. "I added extra seaweed."

"Oh, er. Great!"

"After our busy morning, I thought you'd be really hungry, so I made a big batch. There's more in the blender."

"Oh, nice." She took a sip and tried not to gag. "But you really didn't have to go to so much trouble."

Nasty. Nasty. Nasty.

"No trouble."

A delectable smoky scent filled her senses. Then she heard an amazing crackling sound. "Wait. Is that bacon?"

"Yeah. I thought I'd fry some up to throw on our sandwiches."

"Huh?"

"For our picnic?"

"Oh right. Only." She rubbed her tummy. "It smells so, so good."

He chuckled and crossed his arms. "Would you like some now?"

She practically sprang out of the bed and her breakfast tray wobbled. He leaned forward and studied her smoothie glass. "That would be…uh…great." She added a bit sheepishly, "Could we also maybe have some eggs?"

His eyebrows rose and then he ran his hands through his hair, getting it. "Oh wow." He shook his head. "You don't really like these power drinks, do you?"

She winced. "Sorry."

"Why didn't you say something earlier?"

"I didn't want to hurt your feelings."

"Honey," he said. "It's okay. Seriously. But why

did you— Oh," he said, getting that part, too. Lucas was so great at putting things together. "This is about your sisters, hmm? When you told them about the healthy way you start your day, you were just showing off for them."

She lifted a shoulder. "Maybe?"

He laughed really hard, then picked up her break-fast tray with one hand. He grabbed one of her hands with his free hand afterward. "Come on, princess."

She tossed back the duvet and pushed it aside. "Princess?"

"Yeah, you."

"Where are we going?"

He tugged and she set her feet on the floor.

"To the kitchen, so I can make you a royally big breakfast."

She grinned from ear to ear. "Can I have toast with that?"

He winked and her pulse fluttered. "Anything you wish."

Lucas visited with Misty as he prepared their breakfast of bacon and scrambled eggs, with buttered rye toast. He carried two plates toward her where she sat at the table, then kept walking. "Lucas?"

He glanced over his shoulder. "It can't really be breakfast in bed if we eat in here, can it?"

She blushed. "My bed or yours?"

"Yours is bigger," he said, referring to the fact that hers was a double and his was a twin.

"Right."

They went into her room and sat on the bed, their bare feet resting lazily on the duvet. It was warm enough not to need the covers, especially with

Lucas's body heat beside her. "Oh!" she said, remembering. "Selfie!" She snagged her phone off the nightstand.

She lifted her phone in front of them, its camera trained on them. He leaned toward her, and their shoulders bumped. "Sorry."

She giggled. "It's okay. Say…something!"

He grinned at her phone. "Something!"

Misty nudged him. "Very funny."

"Let me see." She showed him the pic and he nodded. "That's a good one. We look sweet."

"We *are* sweet."

"Yeah."

He settled back against a pillow and took a heaping forkful of eggs while she munched on her piece of toast. "Thanks for not making me drink that smoothie."

He laughed. "I'll pour it out when we clean up." He studied her a moment. "I was kind of wondering how you could stomach the stuff."

She slunk down against the headboard. "I honestly like bacon and eggs better."

"Hmm." He nibbled on some crispy bacon. "Me too."

With any other guy this might feel weird, having breakfast in bed together in such an innocent way. But it wasn't strange with Lucas. It just seemed natural, like they'd done this all their lives.

"Thank you for the breakfast," she said. "It's super delicious."

"You going to send that selfie to your sisters?"

"You bet I am, but I'm going to wait until we've got a few more to add first."

"Let's not forget about that at the picnic."

"No. At the movie theater, either."

He set his plate down in his lap and sighed, wrapping his arm around her. "You know what I think?"

"No, what?"

"That this is a pretty good way to start the day."

She laughed. "We actually started it much earlier."

"You really are an early bird, aren't you? You must have been up at five o'clock."

She nodded. "Woke up extra early today."

"Why's that?"

Heat flooded her face. "I was happy."

Lucas took her hand and then kissed the back of it. "I woke up happy, too." He glanced toward the window, which was streaked by sunshine. "I'm looking forward to our picnic on the beach. I'm packing all your favorite foods."

She blinked. "How do you know my favorite foods?"

"I've been paying attention." He rubbed his cheek. "Though I admit to messing up with the smoothies."

"You did not mess up. I should have told you right away. And anyhow, it touched me that you'd go to the trouble." She studied his handsome face. "What are your favorite foods?"

"We have some of the same ones. I like big, loaded subs with turkey, avocado, and bacon."

"Yum! Is that what we're having for lunch?"

"Among other things."

"You've got to seriously stop treating me so well. You're spoiling me."

"I don't mind spoiling you." His eyes danced.

"Besides that, you're making me dinner."

Misty panicked for a moment but then she recalled their discussion about takeout. "What will it be? Italian or Chinese?"

"You choose."

"All right," she said smugly. "I will."

She took another bite of bacon and finished up her eggs, thinking of the Louis Armstrong song she'd played this morning. What a wonderful world she'd landed in, for sure.

And she was *not* letting Charlotte snatch it away from her.

CHAPTER EIGHTEEN

Misty reached for the old-fashioned picnic basket on the top shelf of her coat closet. She'd gotten it at the thrift store because it looked cool, but she rarely used it. As she and Lucas packed up their lunches in the kitchen, she noticed a pastry bag from Bearberry Brews.

"What's in there?"

"Pumpkin spice cookies." Before she could ask, he added, "I saw you drooling over them when they came in. They'll make a nice dessert."

"So did they hound you?" she asked. "When you went in?"

"Nobody said much except Mei-Lin. She said to tell you hi."

Misty wanted to see Mei-Lin again before she took off for the weekend and Dusty's cousin's wedding. So much had gone on between her and Lucas and things were changing fast.

She handed him their water bottles from the fridge. "You think of everything, don't you?"

"Not everything. But I've been able to think more since having time off."

She chuckled at his reply. "I've been able to breathe more without my sisters watching me with their eagle eyes, and my parents trying to figure us out."

"I think they did figure you out, if you're talking about Aidan."

But she didn't want to talk about Aidan today. She'd already decided that. She also didn't want to think about RISD so she pushed that to the back of her mind. Every time she got an email alert on her phone her heart jumped a little. Lucas had been so encouraging about her designs. Would he be as supportive of her going away to school? And how would they make that work? Lucas was rooted here, between his job and sort of looking after his mom.

He sure wouldn't want to move up to Rhode Island. She guessed they could try long distance but then there was that engagement stipulation in her bet with her sisters. She tried to imagine herself wearing a big rock of a ring like Nell had but that vibe felt all wrong.

Could she really marry Lucas?

He caught her staring at him and he smiled.

Her heart did a tiny cartwheel and then a happy dance.

She wasn't making up her mind today, but she'd certainly consider it.

He slid on his sunglasses and nodded toward the hall. "Ready to rock and roll?"

It was mild but brisk mid-September weather, and windy, so both wore pullover sweaters with their jeans. Misty picked up the picnic basket and grinned. "Ready!"

She followed him down the stairs but was surprised when he headed for his truck, instead of toward Kittery. She'd thought they'd take the stone steps to the beach from there. That was the closest stretch of sand. "We're driving?"

"I thought we'd head north of town."

Misty knew he lived up that way.

"The beach is a little more private up there."

"Ooh, we'll be needing privacy, will we?"

He laughed. "If you kiss me again like you did this morning, we might."

She blushed, warming to the idea. "Lucas Reyes," she said as she climbed into the truck and set the picnic basket on the floor. "You won't be taking advantage of me?"

He got behind the steering wheel and cocked an eyebrow. "Not unless you want me to…take advantage."

She play-punched his arm. "Careful, big boy. I know karate."

"Noted," he said and she knew he knew that she was lying. "Will you tie me up with one of your black belts?"

Misty gasped. "Lucas! You're so naughty."

He chuckled at her mock offense. "Just wait until we're married."

Her heart hammered.

"I mean." He tilted his head. "If it works out that way."

"You're doing very well in convincing me of your strengths."

"Am I now? Good. Because I already know all of yours." He started his engine.

"Not so."

"True." His eyes sparkled. "I'm still learning." He set his gaze on the road driving them out of Majestic. "What kind of ring would you like, just in case?"

She shot him a sassy pout. "I'm not sure I'd want one."

"I bet Aidan produces a huge rock."

"That's fine." She folded her arms. "He won't be producing one for me."

He stopped at a stop sign, then pulled out onto Highway One after looking both ways and checking his mirrors. "What if the diamond wasn't from Aidan?"

"Who says I'd want diamond, anyway?"

"No?" He shot her a sidelong glance. "Ruby maybe? Pearl? Emerald?"

"No precious stones. I…I'm not sure that feels right." She pondered this. "I like the promise ring idea."

"I'm not sure what you mean."

"The man and woman exchange wedding bands when they become engaged, but wear them on their right hands. When they're officially married, they switch them over to the left. My mom and dad did that."

"But I thought that was because—"

"Dad couldn't afford a diamond? Yeah, that was part of it. But actually I think the concept's kind of cool. I mean, if I'm wearing a ring showing I'm spoken for, my man's sure going to be doing the same."

His neck colored. "Your man, huh?" he asked huskily.

"Didn't necessarily say it was you."

"Also didn't say it wasn't."

"Noted," she said, sitting back in her seat. *My man, Lucas*. Yeah, that had a nice ring to it, and made her smile so, so big.

He peered in his rearview mirror. "Looks like Grant's ad is back up."

Misty spun in her seat, staring behind them. The "Marry me: Misty!" billboard had been completely removed and Grant's Blue Sky Adventures' advertisement restored.

Misty sighed. "That's at least one thing Charlotte did right."

They drove for a while and then Lucas turned onto a narrow paved road. The next one after that was just gravel. It meandered through sandy hills and lush underbrush until they finally reached a gray shake-siding beach house perched by some dunes overlooking the ocean. A worn white picket fence teeming with roses surrounded the charming cottage with a white-painted brick chimney and shutterless windows. Rose vines crept up a trellis framing the door, and—everywhere she looked—pale pink roses were in bloom.

"What's this?"

He turned to her and grinned. "My place."

• • •

Lucas led Misty through his garden gate and in through the front door.

She paused to examine his rose-covered trellis. "It's beautiful, Lucas. How did you get them to grow that way?"

"I trained them."

"Trained?"

"Ever hear the phrase clinging vine? Roses love to climb, especially this variety."

She stared around at his living room. He had a two-seater blue sofa and a couple of blue-checkered arm chairs with a few end tables, some recessed lighting, and a standing lamp. His TV screen was a decent size and you couldn't beat the sound system he'd installed himself. You could sit on the seaside deck and still hear music if you wanted because he'd placed additional speakers outside.

His kitchen was small but functional with a tiny table, but he mostly ate at the island that divided it from the living room with its white brick hearth. He had one large bedroom and another small one, and just one bathroom, but you couldn't beat the view. It was home. And, for whatever reason, he'd wanted Misty to see it. It was important to him.

"This is an amazing house." Her admiration warmed him. "Especially with all the roses."

He shot a glance at the rose tattoo on her wrist. "You should feel right at home."

She chuckled. "I do." She walked toward the door to the deck. "Mind if I peek outside?"

"Be my guest."

She unlocked the door and pushed it open and a blast of ocean air whipped into the house. "Oh!" She giggled in surprise, wrestling with the door.

Lucas went to help her. "The winds can get a little fierce."

"Bet so," she said.

"That's what the fireplace is for." In the colder months, he liked keeping it going when he was home, because it made everything so cozy. This cottage would feel even cozier with Misty here to warm it with her smile, the way she was doing now.

He followed her onto the deck where they both observed the view. It was a gorgeous September day with the first official day of autumn just around the corner. Clouds pranced above the windswept beach and waves crashed and curtsied toward each other. There was not another soul in sight. That's why he'd chosen this property. A wildlife refuge sat to the north of his acreage and a marshy area to the south, making that section of beach basically unbuildable.

"If I lived out here," she said, "you'd never drag me into work. I'd just stay and stare at the ocean all day."

"Trust me." He sank his hands into his jeans pockets. "Some days I've been tempted." He'd be even more tempted if she was living here with him. If she were snuggled in his arms, he'd never want to get out of bed. "The moment I found this cottage, I knew it was for me. I put in an offer the next day."

"I remember your saying you'd gotten a place outside of town." She turned his way. "I just didn't know you'd bought it."

"Yeah." He sighed. "I'd been saving up for a while living at my mom's. Finally I decided it was time to move on. You know, cut those old apron strings."

Misty chuckled. "You and your mom seem to have a really good relationship."

"Yeah. We get along." He snickered. "When she's not telling me what to do."

"I know bossy females." Misty rolled her eyes. "But honestly, your mom doesn't seem that bad."

"She's not. She's a sweetheart."

She frowned sympathetically. "Must have been hard on her losing your dad."

"Yeah. It was hard on everybody, but we've got some great memories."

Misty turned toward him, the wind whipping her ponytail sideways. "You've also got his trumpet."

His heart warmed, because it was one of the few concrete mementos of his dad that he had. "Sure do."

"Is it here?" She glanced back toward the cottage.

"Uh. No. Still back at my mom's. Why?"

"Maybe you should polish it up? Start playing again?" Her eye sparkled in the sunlight, and he felt suddenly inspired to do that.

"I just might."

She gazed down at the beach. "So we're legit eating down there? Or…"

"Of course!" He steered her back inside. "I'll get a blanket, you grab that picnic basket."

"Lucas," she said as they were leaving, "I'm glad you showed me your house." She touched his arm. "It's interesting like you."

"Interesting, not a man of mystery?"

She chuckled. "Is that what you'd rather be?"

He rubbed his chin. "Maybe."

She laughed again, then said, "Noted." It charmed him that she'd picked up one of his signature expressions and was now using it with him. It was like they were developing their own private language together. A couple's code. "Although maybe you're not as mysterious as you used to be."

They strode companionably down the path that crossed the dunes. "How so?"

She leaned toward him. "Maybe I'm figuring some of your mysteries out."

"That makes two of us."

She grinned and his heart felt light. "Nothing like the joy of discovery."

• • •

"This is probably one of the best beach picnics I've ever had," she said as they finished their sandwiches. They'd had a great time talking about retro music and classic movies, discovering they enjoyed many of the same things. It was okay that she didn't like to read and preferred podcasts. He might check a few of those out himself.

Lucas relaxed back on his elbows, stretching out his legs. "Me too." Misty assumed the same pose and both were staring at the ocean. "So, you're a modern-day woman," he quipped, "who appreciates old-fashioned things."

Her hazel eyes danced. "I guess you could say the same for yourself."

"That I'm a modern-day woman?"

She thumped his chest and he laughed. "You know exactly what I meant." She took a long while to appreciate the view. "I really love the ocean." She glanced up and down the beach. "Looks like great seashell territory out here."

"You're welcome to bring your pail and shovel out any time you'd like."

She chuckled. "I don't have a plastic shovel."

"Bet you did as a kid, though."

She cocked her head and her ponytail swished behind her. "Bet you did, too."

"No. My parents made us dig with our hands."

"Lucas."

"My dad said it would make us turn out tougher. Hard-knuckled."

"Stop." She giggled when he showed her his fingers.

"See? Nice and strong."

"That's probably from all that coffee roasting and working the machinery."

"No. It was from all the sand-digging."

She elbowed him. "You are one big tease."

He chuckled, scanning the waves. "So. You collected shells as a kid?"

"Some, but not like I do now."

"Built sandcastles?"

"Who didn't?"

He shrugged. "Some people whose parents wouldn't give them a shovel." She pushed his shoulder and he grinned. "What was your favorite summer activity growing up?"

"Going to the carnival. You know that traveling one where they set up rides?"

"Yeah. Some of them were cool, if you were eight or something."

She rolled her eyes. "I thought we were talking about when we were kids?"

"Okay." He nodded. "So you liked, what? The Ferris wheel?"

"Uh, no. Being up high kind of scared me. Nell and Charlotte would always go, though. I stayed down with Mom."

"Guess you're over your fear of heights now, judging by the lighthouse."

"Yeah, but it took some time."

"What was so great about the carnival in that case?"

"Are you kidding? Cotton candy!"

He pulled a face. "Yuck."

"No judgments, please." She set her chin in a haughty manner and then confessed. "What I really, really loved were the games where you could win something. Only." She frowned. "I never did."

"Which kinds of games?"

"The one I liked was that ball toss. There was a low metal table that sort of looked like pinball but not. It had metal rings surrounding these holes—"

"And you tried to get the ball into the higher scoring ones."

"Exactly."

He studied her forlorn face. "But you didn't?"

"Not even once!" She heaved a breath. "For three whole years, I lusted after that giant purple panda."

He blubbered out a laugh. "A what?"

"A panda, Lucas! It was so darn cute with big sad eyes and everything. I swore it was begging, 'Misty!'" She put on a high shrill voice. "'Misty, take me home!'"

Lucas shook his head. "You poor deprived child. I had no idea life had been so rough on you."

"It *was* rough." She crossed one ankle over the other, the tip of her boot angled toward the waves. "In many ways, I'm still not over it."

"Noted."

She wryly twisted her lips. "I like you, Lucas Reyes," she said. "Like you a lot."

"Good to hear," he answered. He met her gaze and held it. "I like you a lot, too."

Misty checked her watch. "Wait. How is it after three o'clock?"

"After three?" The time had totally escaped him. "What?"

"If we're going to make that movie…" She scooted onto her knees and started packing things up. "Before Charlotte beats us at that too—"

"Wait!" She stared at him and her pretty eyes took his breath away. "Our selfie."

"Good thing you remembered." She took out her phone and they snapped a few posed shots with them smiling over the picnic basket with the beach in the background. Misty leaped to her feet and Lucas stood, too, folding the blanket.

"You think we can still make the three-thirty show?"

He tucked the blanket under his arm. "They always run trailers first."

"Right," she said, hustling up the dunes beside him.

Lucas's heart felt warm and full. He was going to the movies with Misty, after showing her his house—and his world, and she'd seemed to love both.

He couldn't have imagined a happier day.

CHAPTER NINETEEN

Misty and Lucas crept into the movie theater hand in hand, their heads bowed as they scooted down a row to minimize blocking the screen from others behind them. It was amazing to her they'd almost missed the movie. The picnic had been so much fun, she'd totally lost track of time. They found a stretch of empty seats about three-quarters of the way back. Other than those, the place was packed, except for the very first row, which had several openings. Majestic had been waiting for this superhero flick and it seemed like half the town was here.

The main feature had just started with the beginning credits rolling, so they luckily hadn't missed anything important. "How 'bout here?" Lucas glanced at an empty seat and Misty nodded, dropping down into a red velvet chair. It had polished wooden arms with its seat number embossed on a small brass plaque. Its soft cushiony seat rocked back and forth when you pushed back with your feet a little. So comfy and cool.

She loved this place and it was extra great being here with Lucas. It had been so much fun seeing his little cottage, and just the thought of him tending to those pretty roses filled her heart with wonder and joy. He'd had a few personal touches in his house, too. Photos of him with his family, and a nice shot of his parents alone together. Her favorite had been a pic of him as a kid, maybe age ten or so, standing beside his dad on a fishing boat. He held up a fish that was nearly half his size and beamed at the camera.

Lucas was such a multifaceted guy. There were so many things about him she'd never known, and the more she learned about him, the more she liked him. She was falling for him for real, and maybe it *was* on account of Nell's silly list. It was hard to say if she'd already be feeling this way if they hadn't done all those romantic adventures together. Then again, the trumpet playing and him showing her his house hadn't been scripted. Neither had Lucas finding that conch shell. Each of those events had been serendipitous. Happy coincidences that had drawn them closer together.

Or maybe they weren't coincidences at all.

Misty held her breath.

Now she was starting to think like Mei-Lin and Nell. Believing in signs and fated matches.

Lucas had joked about the whole "being fated" idea.

Was he starting to believe in it, too?

Three teenage girls scooted into their theater row, snagging the remaining seats next to them. A few other stragglers walked up and down the aisles holding snacks and hunting for a spot. They'd probably have to sit at the very front and develop cricks in their necks from looking up at the too-close screen. Misty was glad she and Lucas didn't have to contend with that, and relieved they hadn't wasted time by getting popcorn. She'd offered to slip out for some later in the show.

The music swelled in a dramatic crescendo and all eyes locked on the screen. A wildly exciting opening unfolded with a heart-pounding car chase involving the female action-hero. Lucas squeezed Misty's hand, the tension mounting as they became thoroughly engrossed in the plot. There was one twisty turn after another, keeping the audience riveted in place.

Now wasn't the time for making out. The film was too exciting. Lucas must have sensed that, too. He put his arm around her shoulders and gave her an affectionate squeeze. "Doing all right?" he whispered.

She grinned and nodded, and he gave her cheek a peck.

Happiness coursed through her as they settled back to enjoy the show.

Finally, the roaring action passed and a quieter scene showed the heroine bonding with her sidekick. "Still want popcorn?" she asked Lucas in low tones.

"Yeah." He dug for his wallet but she stayed his hand. "This is on me." He'd gotten the tickets. She couldn't let Lucas buy everything for her. "Want anything else?"

He made a motion like he was drinking from a cup, but the drinks here were always so huge. "Want to share one?"

"Sure."

Someone shushed them from the back and Misty glared in that direction. She was being as quiet as she could and was on her way out. Some people had such little tolerance for distraction.

Wait. That woman on the aisle in the very last row looked a lot like Charlotte.

It was kind of hard to tell with her having her arms wrapped around the guy beside her. He clung to her, too, and they were kissy-face making out. Gross!

Charlotte was twenty-eight, not fourteen. Misty inched out of her row, stepping over feet and avoiding toes.

She reached the aisle, storming back toward Charlotte.

Yep. That was her sister all right. She recognized Charlotte's gleaming dark hair and those fancy cowgirl boots in an instant. Not to mention that necklace made from an energy crystal, which seemed to be working overtime about now.

Misty was kind of surprised heated sparks were flying off the couple's bodies.

What was her sister thinking? She was in a public place.

Seriously, Charlotte? Get a room.

Misty strode right up to Charlotte in the darkened space and tapped her shoulder.

Charlotte's chin jerked up and her eyes widened in surprise. "Misty!" she gasped. Colorful light ribbons bouncing off the movie screen cut across her pale face.

The guy beside her was wide-eyed, too. Only he wasn't Dave. He was a ginger, with wavy reddish hair and lighter eyes. It was hard to tell exactly what shade they were in the shadows.

"Who's this?" Misty demanded.

"Uh. Hello." He grinned awkwardly. "I'm Steve."

"Hi, Steve. I'm Misty," she said matter-of-factly before turning her gaze on Charlotte. "What happened to Dave?"

The guy warily eyed Charlotte. "Who's Dave?"

Charlotte gave Misty the stink-eye, then someone in front of them spun around. "Do you mind?" It was a dad in his forties with his wife and kids. He blinked at Misty. "Oh, hey! It's you."

His little girl turned around and got up on her knees, speaking over the back of her chair. "Look!" She pointed at Misty and movie-theater patrons whirled around and stared. "It's feeling-the-wind girl!"

Shushes sounded all around them and Misty winced. "Sorry."

She waved at the child, who waved back before her mom settled her down in her seat.

Misty placed her hand on her hip, speaking quietly. "We need to talk," she said, glowering at Charlotte. "*Now.*"

Charlotte stood, smoothing down her short peasant skirt. "Really, Misty. Way to interrupt."

"*Way to put on a show,*" Misty growled under her breath.

"I won't be a minute," Charlotte told her date. He sat there too stunned to do anything but stare at Charlotte and nod.

Misty fumed, following Charlotte out of the theater. If Charlotte wasn't still with Dave, had she made the whole thing up about almost winning their bet? Maybe she really wasn't getting serious with any guy. Clearly not with Dave! Where had he disappeared to, anyway? This had to be another one of Charlotte's tricks. She'd totally invented the Dave thing. Staged all those photo ops, causing Misty to develop ulcers unnecessarily. *Grrr.*

Charlotte must have sensed her hostility because she paused on a step, like she might change her mind and bolt—racing back into the protective custody of her seatmate.

But no. Charlotte wasn't going anywhere until she confessed about what she'd actually been doing. With—and without—Dave in the picture.

"Stop shoving!" Charlotte's husky whisper made her sound very annoyed.

What right did she have to be irritated? She's the one who'd left Misty in a panic, thinking she might get saddled with marrying Aidan Strong, when Charlotte had totally inflated her successes in the nailing-down-a-groom department.

"Then keep walking," Misty whispered back. From the corner of her eye, she saw Lucas's curious gaze trained on them. Whatever Charlotte's story was, he needed to hear it too and Misty would be happy to share. First, though, she wanted to hear it herself.

Misty corralled Charlotte in the movie theater's lobby on the far side of the divider rope and away from the concession area. "Want to tell me what's going on?"

Charlotte stuck out her bottom lip. "Way to be rude and ruin a date, Misty."

Misty huffed out a breath. "Way to totally mess up my outing with Lucas!"

"Hey."

"Where did Steve come from, anyway?"

Charlotte swished her skirt. "The waitlist. What do you think?"

Misty crossed her arms in front of her. "I think you've been hinting nonstop that you're making progress with Dave, and that you've been lying to me and Nell the entire time. Whatever on earth happened to him?"

Charlotte bit her lip. "We had a little problem when he saw the list."

"The waitlist? Maybe he was scared to know he had so much competition?"

"No, not that one. The other one. Nell's romantic must-dos."

Misty rubbed the side of her nose. "I thought you'd already shown him that?"

"Um. Not exactly? I told him about the contest, though." Her face brightened. "He was all on board with that."

"So what exactly was the problem then?"

Charlotte drew in a breath then exhaled it. "Dave was *all about* sharing secrets."

"What?"

"That had to do with stargazing."

"Stargazing? I don't get it."

Her shoulders sank. "It had to do with aliens."

"Aliens? What? From different worlds?"

Charlotte shook her head. "Galaxies."

He had to have made that up just to dump Charlotte. "So, Dave's what?" Misty asked. "Afraid of being abducted?"

"No." Charlotte pursed her lips. "That's kind of just it. He *wants* to be taken up in the mothership."

Misty didn't know what to say to that. Finally, she ventured, "Seriously?"

Charlotte lowered her voice. "I do think he was serious. That was the scary part. He wanted us to wear outfits and everything."

Misty's jaw dropped. "Outfits?"

Charlotte's eyebrows knitted together. "You apparently have to look nice for alien abduction. Or at least suitably appealing to be chosen."

Misty threw back her head and roared. "Nooo. Charlotte!" She stared at her wide-eyed. "Do you really think he meant it?"

Charlotte winced. "I thought he was kidding around until he started quoting all these strange statistics."

"Oh gee."

Charlotte rolled her eyes. "That's what I said, exactly."

Misty hugged her older sister. "I'm sorry, Char. Really I am. How did you end things?"

"Very firmly." Charlotte set her chin. "I said I'd miss my family too much by leaving this universe." She sighed. "In a very strange way, I think Dave understood."

Misty pulled back to look in Charlotte's eyes. Her sister looked a little sad. Disillusioned, even. "When did all this happen?"

"It was the same night we watched the sunset. He found the list in my kitchen drawer when he went looking for a corkscrew. Things had all been going really great until then. But when he started talking about stars, his eyes took on this glossy sheen and I don't know, Misty." She shrugged. "Honestly, it was a little weird."

That sounded a lot weird to her. Misty did some mental calculations. "Hang on. Are you saying you and Dave stopped seeing each other that night?"

Charlotte stepped back, clearly guessing where Misty was going with this. "Maybe?"

Misty gawked at her. "So then the pic of your breakfast in bed...you dancing in the rain?"

Charlotte's forehead wrinkled. "I'm sorry, Misty. I couldn't admit that things had gone south. Especially in such a bizarre way. Not with you getting together with Lucas, who's so grounded and normal and everything." She searched Misty's eyes. "By the way, how's all that going?" She grinned tentatively. "Looks like, pretty well? I saw you two enter the theater together holding hands."

"Things are going very well. Lucas is special."

"Have you completed Nell's list?"

"We should get there shortly." Misty squared her shoulders. "Evidently a lot sooner than you. And here's the thing. We haven't cheated."

Charlotte blinked and Misty's heart went out to her. Maybe she'd been too harsh. Railing at Charlotte for fudging on the list. "So. What's the deal with Steve?"

"He's fine with Nell's list and the bet. Only." Charlotte sighed. "I'm finding it hard to fall in love on a dime."

"I can see that's a challenge." It was so different with her and Lucas. They had a history as coworkers and friends. A foundation to build on. Mutual admiration and trust. And Nell had been crushing on Grant for years.

"Misty," Charlotte said, and her tone was sincere. "If things work out for you and Lucas, I want you to know." Her voice trembled. "I'll be very happy for you. Happy for both you guys."

Misty choked up a little herself, because she knew what Charlotte was saying.

"Believe it or not, I believe in true love." Charlotte's blue eyes misted over. "Nell's with Grant now, and I want you to have the same with Lucas."

Misty's heart thumped and all at once, she knew that's what she wanted, too. She wanted a romantic relationship with Lucas, hopefully an amazing and endless one. But she didn't want to have to sacrifice Charlotte's happiness to get there. Poor Charlotte. Getting relegated to London and a loveless, in-name-only marriage. "Charlotte. About you and Aidan."

"No, seriously," she said. "It will be okay. I'll be okay."

"But what about Steve?"

Charlotte shrugged. "He's an awfully good kisser."

"So you're going to keep doing Nell's list?"

"I don't see why not," she said. "He's on board with it, and I suppose my feelings could change."

Misty guessed she was right, but somehow she didn't quite think that they would. "Well, good luck then, with Steve. Maybe it can still work out."

"You're the lucky one," Charlotte said. "You and Lucas? I think you're written in the stars."

"You really think so?"

"Uh-huh, yeah. Yes, I do."

In a strange way, Misty was starting to think that herself. Maybe RISD had just been a pipe dream, maybe that was never bound to happen. She'd been fooling herself by hoping it might. Misty loved Majestic and she loved her family. If by some miracle of miracles she and Lucas fell legit in love with each other, would this really be such a terrible place to stay?

No, it could actually be fantastic.

"So, what do you say?" Misty asked, motioning toward the concession stand, which was experiencing a lull at the moment. "Want to get some popcorn to take back to the guys?"

"Yeah," Charlotte said. "Great idea." She gave a shaky grin and pulled herself together, and Misty latched onto her arm.

"I'm sorry, Charlotte. Really I am. About Dave. I thought there were…" She glanced Charlotte's way. "Possibilities."

Charlotte patted Misty's hand. "You know. For a fleeting instant, I thought so, too."

When Misty returned to her seat, Lucas whispered, "Get everything straight with your sister?"

Misty nodded. "I'll tell you all about it when we get home."

Home. It sounded so natural saying that to Lucas. Like he and she had a place together, a shared nest. Maybe things would be all right, and her life would work out as it was meant to. With her and Lucas becoming lovebirds and them spending their happily ever after together.

"Good popcorn," he said, digging into the bucket. "Thanks."

Misty sighed, glad to be in his company. Wanting to stay in his company more and more each day. No matter what was going on with her sisters, or in the greater world, when Lucas was by her side, everything felt right. "You're welcome."

His smile warmed her through and through.

He leaned toward her and gave her a soft kiss on the lips. "I love you," he said in a husky whisper. "You know that?"

Warmth spread through her chest.

"Yeah," she said, because she felt it with her

whole heart. Emotion welled up within her until she was bursting with her truth. "I love you, too."

Misty bit into her bottom lip and stared at the movie screen, her cheeks burning with her confession. In all her years and with all the guys she'd dated, she'd never said that to anyone romantically. Not even once. Maybe because she hadn't loved any of the others.

Not deeply.

Not seriously.

Not in the way her heart was opening up to Lucas.

Like a new rosebud blooming under the end-of-summer sun.

He placed his arm around her shoulders and held her close, and she snuggled up against him. The movies, popcorn, and her and Lucas at the Majestic Theater…

Yeah, this was perfection.

About as close to heaven as you could get.

CHAPTER TWENTY

Lucas floated on air as they drove back to Misty's apartment.

She loves me.

He'd spent so many years waiting for this to happen. Lucas understood now these delayed results were in large part his fault for not making a move earlier. Then again, maybe the timing hadn't been right until now.

"Great flick," he said as they drove along. He didn't dare mention their expressions of love for fear he might jinx things. In a way, his heart wouldn't fully believe it until he heard it again and out of the dim lights of the theater.

"Yeah," she said. "It was fun."

"You didn't let that popcorn ruin your dinner, did you?"

She laughed. "Nope. Not at all." Misty turned to him. "Still up for takeout?"

"You bet."

"Chinese sound good?"

"Only if I can get Lo Mein."

She chuckled and sat back in her seat. "You can have anything you want."

She was so right about that, because all he wanted was her, and amazingly this was working out. "Want to eat on the roof?"

"What?"

"We can watch the sunset from there." He shrugged.

"That would be great."

"We still have some wine."

She grinned and his heart melted. "Even better."

They got back to her place and settled in. Misty put away the picnic basket after they'd emptied it out, then Lucas pulled up the restaurant menu on his phone. "By this time tomorrow, there might not be much of Nell's 'must do' list left."

"I guess we did tell each other one deep, dark secret."

He smiled. "More like one deep secret in the dark."

Her mossy green eyes sparkled and his heart soared.

He waited for her to say it again, but she didn't. Oh well. Now he was a lot more certain there'd be a next time. Especially since she'd brought it up and not him.

"Lucas," she said. "This has been the best day. I mean it. From start to finish."

He stepped toward her and took her in his arms. "It's not over yet."

She shot him a saucy look. "No, and I'm glad."

He tightened his arms around her and kissed her like he wouldn't have done in the theater. Which reminded him. "What's up with Charlotte?" he asked when they broke apart.

Misty pushed back her bangs. "She's a big phony. Dave's no longer in the picture and hasn't been for days."

He pursed his lips. "So those selfie shots?"

"You were right. It was strange they were only of her. Those last ones anyway."

Something hadn't felt right about that to him, and

now he knew why. "What happened?"

"He got cold feet. Or maybe she did. In a way, I think it was both of them. I don't think they were really suited for each other to tell you the truth."

"So, who's the new guy?"

"His name is Steve. Someone off the waitlist."

"Huh. Do you think he and she will…?"

She sighed. "I don't know, Lucas. It's so hard to tell. They've only just met each other. It's not like you and me who've been acquainted forever."

It had seemed an eternity to him before. From the time he first saw her till she'd finally said she loved him in the theater. Now though, in looking back, it was like all those years had flown by in the blink of an eye. The past seemed so fluid and inconsequential in light of his potential future with Misty.

This was finally going to happen. He could feel it.

He adored her so much. Now more than ever. He'd give her the moon if he could.

His heart jolted when he got an idea. Then it thudded again.

Yes. She would love that.

He was going to do it tomorrow.

Get her everything she needed to begin that design career.

She made him so unbelievably happy just with her smile, and he wanted to make her happy, too, by supporting her dreams.

• • •

Misty and Lucas sat on the rooftop drinking their wine and watching the sun set in the west. She paused, her chopsticks hovering over her takeout container. "How's the Lo Mein?"

"Very tasty." He took another bite. "Your Sesame Chicken?"

She grinned. "The best."

Everything seemed better after talking to Charlotte. Even though Charlotte didn't want to marry Aidan, she seemed to want Misty's happiness more. It wouldn't be right for Misty to dash off to London now. Not after admitting her feelings to Lucas. Now that she'd said it out loud, she found her love for Lucas spreading all through her, flooding each recess of her soul with bright rays of sunshine. He loved her and she loved him.

What a wonderful, wonderful world.

She thought of her trumpet playing this morning and that moment seemed eons ago somehow.

"We've had a busy day," he said, mirroring her thoughts.

"Yeah, and I'm so glad we went to your house, too. I loved it." While she'd seen all the photos of his family, he hadn't had any of former girlfriends around. Maybe he didn't hang onto those. Misty had a shoebox of pics of her exes in her bedroom closet. She wasn't sure what she was planning to do with them, or even why she'd kept them. Maybe it was time to let them go.

"I'm glad you like my house," he said. "Because I'm counting on having you over. A lot."

"I'd like that," she said and he grinned warmly.

Misty poked at her food with her chopsticks, dying to know. "Lucas, about your other girlfriends—"

He shook his head. "Never had any." But Misty

knew that was a lie. She'd seen him dating plenty, in and around town with different women.

"That's not true."

"It is true if you're asking about women I dated seriously. I might have dated some people but I wouldn't say 'seriously' about any of them."

"No?" Her eyebrows shot up. "And why's that?"

His gray gaze held her. "I suppose I was waiting for you."

Misty's cheeks heated. "I mean it, though."

"Yeah, and so do I." He twirled some noodles around his paired chopsticks and popped them into his mouth. He finished eating, then said, "It was hard to get serious about another woman under the circumstances."

"What circumstances were those?" she asked, hoping she knew.

He set down his food and held her hand. "My heart was already taken, Misty." His gaze swept over her, his adoration so clear. "By you."

She squeezed his hand. "Thank you for being so patient."

"Thank you for coming around." He lifted her hand to his mouth and gently turned it over, kissing her rose tattoo. A delighted shiver tore through her.

"You really have a way… A way with me, Lucas."

He smiled and met her eyes. "You're pretty great at making me feel special, too."

Happiness hummed through her. "More wine?" she asked, lifting the bottle.

"Yeah, that would be great."

She refilled both their glasses and they sat there enjoying their dinners and the pretty scenery. After a while, she raised her glass to his. "Here's to being mostly done with our list."

"Aren't we all the way done?"

"Let's see." Misty cocked her head. "The bikes, exercise, the picnic—"

"The movies," he said. "And dancing in the rain." Subtle warmth radiated from his gaze outshining the glory of the sunset.

"That makes five."

"Don't forget our breakfast in bed."

She chuckled. "Six."

He set his chin. "This sunset," he said, toasting to the sky. "There's seven."

"Sharing secrets." She clinked his glass again. "That's eight."

"Speaking of sharing," he said. "We've got tons of shared passions. Not sure how you're going to capture that with a pic, though."

"No worries," she said. "I texted my sisters a photo of my trumpet case, saying you were wild about playing, too, and about old movies like I am, and also that we both value family."

"What did they say to that?"

"Nell sent a bunch of heart emojis."

"And Charlotte?"

"Nothing yet. I just thought to send that with the one of the beach picnic. Charlotte already saw us together at the movies."

"Yeah. That brings us up to nine." He sat back on the loveseat. "So what are we missing?"

"Um. Just two more." She focused on remembering. "Stargazing at midnight?"

"Want to try that tonight?"

"We've already done a lot today. How about saving something for tomorrow?"

He chuckled indulgently. "Tomorrow it is, then."

Since the rush was off in beating Charlotte, Misty felt more relaxed about waiting. "Sounds good." She took a sip of wine. "I'll rest up for it."

He laughed. "That still leaves one more thing. Ahh," he said after a beat. He lowered his eyebrows and teased, "Getting frisky in the kitchen."

She flushed. "Doesn't have to be *that* frisky, Lucas." She tried to suppress the naughty image she'd had of them in aprons only. They'd been large aprons, covering nearly everything. But still. Her skin burned hotter just at the idea. Misty tightened the band on her ponytail. "Nell said maybe couples' cooking could work?"

He leaned toward her and winked. "That could be hot."

She slapped his arm, laughing. "Will you stop?"

He chuckled and held up his hands. "We can make a cold dinner if you'd like."

Misty smirked. "Hot food is fine. What did you have in mind?"

"Hmm. How about a piñón?"

"What's that?"

"It's like a Puerto Rican lasagna. It's great served with Arroz con Habicheulas. That's like Puerto Rican pink beans and rice."

"Oh no." She waved her hands in front of her. "That sounds hard."

He cocked his head. "Won't be so hard with the two of us working together. I'll help you."

The way he said it was so convincing and appealing. The notion of them tackling that sort of project together sounded kind of fun. "Okay, we can do that. Before the stargazing."

"If you'd rather pick something else."

"No, Puerto Rican cooking sounds good." She recalled the photo of him and his dad. "Do you cook much fish?"

He shrugged. "Sometimes."

"Still catch it?"

His eyebrows arched and she explained.

"I saw that old pic at your cottage of you and your dad on his boat."

"No," he said. "Fishing's really not my thing." He chuckled and then added, "I'll leave that to Grant."

She wondered about something. "When did you stop fishing and why?"

"Oh, about the time my dad died. I guess…" He pursed his lips. "It was too hard to do it without him."

She frowned feeling bad for mentioning it. "I'm sorry, Lucas."

"It's all right. Ramon took it up. Does surf fishing sometimes with his friends."

"It's okay not to fish," she told him.

"I know, but sometimes I miss it." He looked distant for a moment. "I guess like I miss my dad."

"I'm sure he's in a good place now."

"That's what I like to think, and that I'll see him again eventually."

"How do you know he's not here with you now?"

He studied her. "What do you mean?"

"In your heart, Lucas, and in your soul. You're such a good person and I know you're close to your mom. In many ways, though, I suspect you take after him."

He smiled sadly. "Thanks for saying that, Misty."

"I don't know what I would do if something happened to my parents," she said. "They haven't been perfect parents, but they've always loved us. We've never doubted that. That's one reason my sisters and I—" She bit her lip.

"Made that bet about Aidan," he said. "I know."

He held Misty's hand. "Everything will work out somehow."

She wanted to believe that, too. Only she wasn't exactly sure how that would happen with everybody winding up happy. Charlotte. Her parents. Lucas. And even her.

CHAPTER TWENTY-ONE

After Misty and Lucas finished their morning run and had breakfast, he showered and shaved, saying he needed to go into town. He wanted to pick things up for their dinner and run a few other errands, promising to return late morning. Misty saw this as the perfect opportunity to see Mei-Lin, who was going out of town tomorrow. She invited her over for coffee, so Mei-Lin took an early lunch break from Bearberry Brews.

When Mei-Lin arrived, Misty was just returning from her trip to the dumpster.

"Taking out the trash?"

"Tossing out the exes."

"Not the shoebox?"

Misty nodded, glad to have disposed of those years of useless memories.

"Well, hooray for you."

"Mei-Lin." Misty hugged her tightly. "It's so good to see you!"

"It's only been two days."

"I know," Misty said. "But a lot's happened."

"Like?" Mei-Lin asked, as they climbed the stairs.

"Like, I'll tell you inside."

Misty filled Mei-Lin in at her kitchen table while they both drank coffee.

"Misty!" Mei-Lin squealed. "You and Lucas! You actually said the words?"

"The amazing thing is, we meant them."

Mei-Lin braced Misty's upper arms. "I'm so happy for you!"

"Yeah. I'm happy for us, too. The only thing is…" Misty frowned. "Charlotte."

"What about her?"

"She was giving me a run for my money, Mei-Lin. By totally pretending to make progress on Nell's list with Dave."

"The banker?"

"Yeah, him. Turns out, he wasn't in the picture at all. Literally."

Mei-Lin leaned forward. "What do you mean?"

"She faked it. Faked those photos where she and Dave were supposedly doing all this romantic stuff together. I mean, apart from the first two pics. Those were real. But after—"

Mei-Lin cleared her throat.

"If you've got something to say, Mei-Lin—"

"I seem to recall someone who asked me to take a photo of *her* in lobster-patterned boxers." She tapped her chin. "Wouldn't have happened to be you when you were trying to beat Nell in same-said competition?" Her eyebrows arched.

"First of all, that wasn't at all the same thing."

"Yeah, it kind of was, because Nell had sent you and Charlotte a selfie of her wearing Grant's fishing-lure boxers while she was stuck at his cabin."

"And, she totally exaggerated the whole thing."

"Which you didn't?" Mei-Lin crossed her arms.

Misty sighed. "Look, it's not like me to be competitive with my sisters."

"No. Not at all."

"I mean, not usually. Once in a while they goad

me into it."

"So, what did you do to goad Charlotte?"

"Nothing! That's just it. She was born competitive. Mom says she argued with the other infants in the nursery about having the smoothest birth."

This piqued Mei-Lin's interest. "Did she?"

"Okay, she was born in four hours. No complications. Nell took longer, and I came early."

Mei-Link smirked. "Maybe you were trying to break Charlotte's record? Four hours minus however many days?"

"You are so not helping the situation."

"What situation is that?"

"About me and Charlotte!"

"Sounds like you've already got that bet in the bag to me."

"I wish I could believe that, but I still feel bad about Charlotte, in spite of her faking those photos. That only shows how desperate she is, and maybe conflicted. We all want to help Mom and Dad, but things get a little scary when you start looking London in the face."

"Nell was prepared to do it."

"I know, and she shocked all of us."

Mei-Lin shrugged. "Maybe Charlotte will be okay. She's tough and speaks her mind. She'll handle Aidan."

Misty's spirit buoyed for a second but then her heart sank. "What if she can't?"

"Then you guys call this whole thing off. Maybe when she buys her ticket, make it a round trip? Like for the following week or something. That way, if things get really bad she can hole up in a hotel room and then fly right back home."

That made Misty feel a little better but not tons. "Today's September fifteenth," she said. "We're half-way through the month."

"Leaving just fifteen more days until the month ends and your parents' loan comes due."

Misty rubbed the side of her nose. "Yeah."

"Well, if Charlotte works things out with Aidan, it will all be okay, right?"

Misty hung her head. "I don't know. Maybe."

"What about school?" Mei-Lin asked.

"Still haven't heard, which means I probably didn't get in." Misty shrugged. "Maybe it's all for the best? Don't need one more complication." She looked up, ready for a fresh topic of conversation. "So what's the deal with you and Dusty?"

"He's very special." Mei-Lin blushed. Misty didn't think she'd ever seen her do that. "And he seems to like me."

"Okay. And you like him?"

She nodded eagerly. "I do. So, so much Misty. He's like earthy and energetic and fun!"

"So you're going to his cousin's wedding as what?"

"As his girlfriend." Mei-Lin blushed again. "Guess what? We're exclusive!"

Misty felt like she was experiencing whiplash. "Wait. Already?"

Mei-Lin took offense. "You didn't say that about Nell and Grant."

"No, but—"

"And when you invented your little lovey-dovey fake setup with Lucas, I didn't blow your cover before things became real."

"I know. It's not that."

"Then what?"

Misty placed her hand on Mei-Lin's. "I just worry about you, that's all."

"No need to worry. I'm fine! And Dusty is—"

Misty's phone buzzed on the table and they both stared down at it.

"What's that?" Mei-Lin asked.

Misty's stomach clenched. "An email—from RISD." The subject heading read: Application Status. She'd convinced herself she didn't care, but now that the moment was here, she really, really did. She'd worked so hard on her application essays and her portfolio, all that financial aid nonsense, too. She couldn't bear to look.

Misty slid her phone across the table in front of Mei-Lin. "Could you please read it for me?"

Mei-Lin nodded solemnly and picked up the phone. "Listen," she said with a serious edge that oozed with compassion. "Whatever happens, you're going to be all right. If not RISD, there will be someplace else. Okay?"

Misty nodded, although she didn't feel okay at all.

Mostly, she felt like she was going to hurl her whole entire breakfast.

Lucas had made pancakes and sausages and she kind of wished he hadn't.

Mei-Lin swiped at her phone. "Ready?"

Misty's muscles tensed and she held her breath.

"Misty," Mei-Lin said with deadpan seriousness and bile rose in Misty's throat. Then Mei-Lin grinned. Not just any old grin, either. A megawatt one. "You got in!"

Misty exhaled sharply. "What?"

"Not only that." Mei-Lin bounced in her chair. "You're under consideration for some fancy scholarship deal! They want you to come up to Providence for an in-person interview!"

"What? When?" Misty felt like her head was exploding. This was such great news. But what about Lucas? Oh no.

"Monday," Mei-Lin said.

"This Monday?" Misty's head spun. If she went away to school, she couldn't marry Lucas. But maybe if they had a long engagement... No. What would he think? Would he wait? He'd already waited so many years. And what about the Aidan bet, and Charlotte, and her parents? Misty clutched her belly. "That's so soon."

"I'll be back from Bar Harbor by then," Mei-Lin said. "I'll drive you."

• • •

Lucas drove back into Majestic wearing a grin. The forty-minute drive to the nearest artists' supply store would have been so worth it when he saw the look of happy surprise on Misty's face. At least he hoped she'd be happily surprised, and not think he was overstepping. He'd gotten her a great drafting table with an ergonomic working stool to go with it. These had to be an improvement over the card table and metal folding chair she had in her spare room now. With the clip-on lamp he'd bought and the collection of other supplies recommended by the knowledgeable salesperson, she'd be outfitted like a professional.

If Misty thought the gift was too elaborate, she could consider it an early Christmas present. Lucas was used to saving up. He'd tucked money away religiously when saving for a down payment on his house, and had never really gotten out of the habit. He didn't have any expensive hobbies to splurge on, or a family to think of supporting—yet. His heart warmed at the idea of him and Misty having kids together. She would make such a fun mom and he couldn't wait to become a dad with her. But he would wait. He wanted her to pursue her dreams first, and give things a shot with design. He'd checked it out online and the community college offered some courses that she could take in the evenings to get her started.

Lucas knew the Delaneys well and he was sure they'd be supportive of Misty's private ambition. He didn't blame her for wanting to do something more than run the register at the café. She'd already done that job for eleven years and had done it really well. But Misty had other talents, and she owed it to herself to explore them. Lucas turned onto a side road and slammed on his brakes, then carefully backed up his truck. No way! The used bookstore was going out of business. A big sign in its window said LIQUIDATION SALE.

Lucas thumped his steering wheel, thinking. He was all for encouraging Misty to pursue her dreams, but what about his? Misty wasn't the only one who'd worked at Bearberry Brews forever. He had, too, and he loved the job. Still, he wanted more. He wanted to open that book café he'd talked about. He also wanted to marry Misty. Maybe the right way for them to

start off their new union together would be with both
of them pursuing their dreams. Yes. That could be so
excellent. Misty would admire him for bravely taking
this step, too.

He had to talk to the Delaneys about timing. They
were going through a rough patch and he didn't want
to make things worse for them by abandoning ship in
their time of need. But first, he wanted to speak with
Carlisle Jones, the man who ran this shop, and ask
him about the particulars. What kind of rent he paid
and what his expenses were so Lucas could come up
with a business plan. No way was Misty moving to
London now. She'd be staying right here in Majestic
with Lucas, where they'd give their futures a bright
start.

• • •

An hour later, Lucas parked on the street near
Bearberry Brews. Mr. Jones had given him all the
necessary details on his operation. He was closing his
shop because he was ready to retire and didn't have
anyone in mind to take it over for him. He seemed
pleased by Lucas's interest in revamping the place
into a book café, but Lucas hadn't made any commit-
ments. He needed to work out a budget, and get a few
contractors in for estimates. The space would require
structural updating and also a decent kitchen and
coffee bar area.

Lucas figured he could do a lot of the renovating
himself. Of course, he'd need approval from the building's landlord before making any changes. A buzz of
excitement hummed through him. He could really do

this. Start his own business. He'd learned a lot about how small businesses ran from his job managing the café, and he'd also taken those business courses in accounting and such.

But he didn't want to let the Delaneys down. It's not like he'd be leaving his job as manager immediately, though. Getting his new place ready to become operational would take some time. He'd also probably have to get bank loans approved in order to make some of the improvements.

He could keep working for the Delaneys while he got all of that in place, and also help them hire and train a new manager. He wanted to fly all this by them to get their thoughts. He particularly valued Mr. Delaney's advice. He was the closest thing to a dad Lucas had had since losing his own father.

He pushed open the door to Bearberry Brews, wearing a smile.

"Lucas! Hey!" Nell said, grinning brightly. "What a fun surprise." She scrunched up her face. "You're not coming in to work, though? You're supposed to be spending time with Misty."

"That's my ultimate goal," he said. "Your dad around?"

CHAPTER TWENTY-TWO

Lucas returned from his errands in a really great mood. He had two paper grocery bags in his arms and Misty relieved him of one of them when he entered the kitchen. She'd been making them lunch to quell some of her nervous energy. Staying busy helped.

"Thanks for doing the shopping!" She peeked into a bag and set it on the counter. "Got any more in your truck?"

"Nope. This is it for now."

For now? She wasn't sure what that meant.

He began unloading groceries and putting things away. His gaze fell on the two plates on the kitchen counter. "Great! You made us sandwiches. I'm starved."

"You like egg salad BLTs?"

"I don't think I've ever had one."

"Well, you're having one today." She grinned, hoping her lips didn't tremble. The RISD acceptance was such great news and she wanted to tell him, but when? Nothing was certain without that scholarship, so maybe the whole thing would blow apart anyway.

"I thought you didn't cook?" he teased.

"I can slap two pieces of bread together."

"Yeah. But you made egg salad."

"Nell taught me how to do that."

She'd added potato chips to their plates and pickle spears. "Well, it all looks delicious."

He stared down at the sink which contained two coffee mugs. "Wait. Did you have someone over?"

"Mei-Lin stopped by."

"I just saw her at the café."

"It was earlier. I wanted to tell her about—" Wait. "What were you doing at the café?"

"I'll tell you about it shortly."

"Everything okay?"

He grinned. "Really okay. Fantastic."

"Well, that sounds good," she said, curious about what he was hiding.

They finished with the groceries and then each grabbed a plate, setting it on the table.

"What did Mei-Lin have to say about Charlotte?" he asked, fixing them some waters.

Misty shrugged as they took their seats. "She wasn't surprised by Charlotte's competitive nature." She picked up her sandwich. "She was pretty happy about us, though."

"That we're no longer pretending?" He winked and her heart fluttered. "That's good."

It *was* good that their relationship had become authentic. It also made the whole RISD dilemma so much tougher. It would be hard to be away from Lucas, and he probably wouldn't want to move there. Not with his job and mom in Majestic.

He bit into his sandwich. "Mmm, Misty! Really good. I like this combo."

She nibbled on a chip, suddenly not as hungry as she normally was. "Yeah, it's tasty!"

He observed her plate. "Then why aren't you eating yours?"

She picked her sandwich back up, making an effort. "I am. See?"

His forehead wrinkled. "You feeling okay?"

"Ah, yeah! Really super." She set down her sandwich and went back to the chips. With her stomach so tense it was easier to nibble on something crispy and salty. And smaller. "You were gone a while."

"I know. I had to do some…things."

"Things?"

"I'll fill you in soon enough." He gave her a warm smile. "It doesn't feel right keeping secrets from you."

Misty felt like she'd been socked in the gut.

But she wasn't keeping—

Okay, she really was.

But she was going to tell him.

He'd maybe even be happy for her.

"I was thinking we might take a walk after lunch," he said. "It's a really gorgeous day."

Getting some fresh air sounded good. Maybe she could tell him about RISD on their walk. "Great idea."

He stared at her plate. "I don't want to rush you, though." He'd already nearly finished eating. "Take your time."

"It's okay," Misty said, standing up. "I'll just wrap my sandwich for later."

His eyebrows arched. "Are you sure?"

"One hundred percent."

But when they exited Misty's apartment building, they didn't head toward the ocean like she thought they might. He led her in the opposite direction and away from his truck. It looked like there were some big boxes in its bed. "Uh, did you buy something?"

He grinned mysteriously. "Not saying."

She shoved his arm. "Lucas! What is it?"

"Patience, little one."

She chuckled. "Fine." She took longer strides to keep up with him. Wherever he was headed, he seemed in a huge hurry. "We're not going to the beach?"

He shook his head. "I want to show you something."

Misty was flummoxed as they ambled along. "Okay." She had no idea what Lucas was doing until he reached the front of the used bookstore and paused. She stared at the sign in the window. "Oh no! They're going out of business?"

He slowly cracked a grin. But how could he be about happy about this?

Misty blinked. "Lucas! What is it?"

"Misty." He took her in his arms. "I think this is another sign."

"Yeah, and the sign says 'Liquidation—'"

"No." He stopped her. "I'm not being literal. Come on." His eyes twinkled. "I mean a bookstore! In Majestic."

"Yeah." She wrinkled up her nose. "It's kind of the only one." Then she frowned. "Was. Soon enough, I guess."

"That's just it." He jostled her in his arms. "It's the perfect opportunity for us."

"Us?"

"I can start that book café I've always dreamed about, and you can work on your designs. Even take night classes if you want. Maybe we can work out a way for you to go to school full-time, once I get this business up and running."

Her head reeled. What was he saying?

"I already talked to your parents."

Wait. He what?

"And they're all for it. They say we have to follow our own paths, just like they did when they were our age. They wished you'd told them about wanting to design things but they weren't completely surprised, with you always having been so artistic." He was going at a million miles per minute. She could barely catch her breath. "Plus, they know that we're together. I mean, we told them that when we told your sisters. So they've never thought any differently, and still believe that you and I are a—"

His sunny face collapsed in a frown because she was crying. "What's wrong?"

Hot tears leaked from her eyes. "Lucas, I…"

"Is it us? You're having second thoughts? Because when you said you loved me—"

"I do, Lucas, I do!" Her voice cracked shrilly and her throat burned raw.

He ran his thumb across her cheek and stroked back a tear. "Then, honey. What's the problem?" He glanced at the storefront window. "I thought this could be so good for us. A fresh start." He swallowed hard. "As husband and wife." He peered into her eyes. "Don't you want that, too?"

She did, she really did want the husband and wife part. She knew that in her soul. But if he opened his shop, he'd never come to Rhode Island. Then she couldn't go there, either, not without breaking his heart. "Yeah, but…" Her voice quivered.

He stared at her.

"I applied to school in Rhode Island."

He couldn't have appeared more gobsmacked. "The state?" he asked in a daze. "But what's—"

"The Rhode Island School of Design," she told him. "They've got a fantastic reputation and I applied and got in!"

He blinked. "When did all of this happen?"

"I applied early admission in late August, way before the Aidan thing and the bet with my sisters, and I've only just now heard."

"Oh. Well. That's…um." He shifted on his feet. "So great, then. Congratulations."

"I'm still waiting on the scholarship decision. I meet with the committee on Monday."

"Three days from now, on Monday?"

She nodded, crying again. "I'm sorry."

"Sorry? No. Misty. That's…that's awesome." He gazed back at the bookstore with a pained look, like his dreams were ebbing away. "You should totally do it." He braced her shoulders. "Absolutely."

She wiped back her tears with her hands. "I don't want to leave you."

"We can make it work." But even as he said it, he sounded doubtful, and that tiny shred of doubt broke Misty's heart. "I mean, maybe. If we—"

Misty broke out of his embrace and hurried down the street.

"Misty, wait!" He took off after her, so she ran faster to the one place that still felt like home. Moments later, she went barreling through the door to Bearberry Brews. She entered the back way through the alley, so she wouldn't disturb their paying customers.

Nell saw her pass by the office and looked up from the computer on her desk. "Misty?"

Charlotte exited the storeroom carrying a stack of

coffee filters and Misty nearly bowled her over. "Oh no." Charlotte's whole face hung in a frown. "What's wrong?"

Nell hurried out of her office and Misty dashed into the storeroom, while her sisters followed her.

"Hon?" Nell asked in her tender, motherly way. "Did something happen with Lucas?"

Misty's life was such a mess. She couldn't marry Lucas, then move away.

What about his dreams and this new opportunity?

But if she wasn't marrying Lucas, then she might have to marry Aidan and move to London after all. Maybe she could go back to her earlier plan about attending design school there. She blubbered through her tears when Mei-Lin crowded into the storeroom.

"Lucas is out there asking for Misty," Mei-Lin said sadly, "and looking like he's just lost his best friend."

That only made Misty cry harder.

CHAPTER TWENTY-THREE

Misty spilled everything to Mei-Lin and her sisters. She even told Nell and Charlotte about how she and Lucas hadn't really been dating at first. They'd only made that up to get her away from the billboard guys and give her time to sort things out. All these days later, they weren't sorted at all. Instead, everything was one great big jumble.

Lucas had come into the café asking if the others had seen Misty. Since Mei-Lin hadn't seen her sneak in the back way, she'd been able to truthfully say no. She told Lucas she'd tell Misty that he was looking for her, though, so now she'd done that.

Misty dabbed her eyes with a napkin. "I've made such a mess of everything," she said, wrapping up what had happened in front of the bookstore so bringing them up to date.

Charlotte laid a hand on her shoulder. "There's still time to make things right."

"Sure." Kindness shimmered in Nell's goldish hazel eyes. "You can talk to Lucas about RISD. The two of you can work out a way."

Misty sniffed and blew her nose. "Then what about his dream of opening the book café?"

Mei-Lin frowned. "Maybe he can postpone that?"

"If he wants retail space in Majestic, though," Charlotte said, "the options are pretty limited."

Nell elbowed her. "Maybe some other place will open up?"

Charlotte bit her lip. "Yeah. Like here."

"Hang on, ladies," Mei-Lin said. "No one's saying that Bearberry Brews is going under."

"We've got just two more weeks now," Charlotte said, looking desperate. "Fourteen days." She took out her phone. "I'm texting Aidan."

Misty and Nell both said "No!" at once.

"To say what?" Nell asked her.

"Well, that I'm coming." Charlotte stubbornly set her chin. "We can't let Misty go, not after what she just told us. She loves Lucas, and he loves her. We pretty much all know he's worshiped her forever."

Misty's face grew hot. "Somehow I didn't know that."

Mei-Lin shook her head. "We all tried to tell you."

"That's not the point," Nell said. "The point is you and Lucas?" She stared at Misty. "You're written in the stars, all right? Definitely meant to be. So, it's happening. You going to London makes zero sense. You *are* going to RISD on Monday," Nell continued sternly. "This is the opportunity of a lifetime and you should grab it."

Misty's shoulders sank. "I don't even know if I'll get the scholarship though."

"You know you got into the school." Mei-Lin grinned. "That's a really big achievement."

"A really expensive achievement," Misty said. "Potentially."

Charlotte rubbed her chin. "Maybe I can help you! Once I'm married to Aidan and in London."

"True," Nell said to Charlotte. "You'll be rich."

"You won't have all the money yet," Misty protested. "Aidan's only promised to help Mom and Dad pay off their loan right away. Other than that, the bulk of the money won't get divided until after five years."

Charlotte lowered her eyebrows. "Maybe I can work out something with Aidan. An allowance."

"An allowance?" Nell asked, aghast.

"Okay, fine. Call it something different, but maybe a monthly payment for me posing as his wife."

"Uh," Misty said. "You're kind of forgetting he's doing this for us."

Mei-Lin grimaced. "Must be super geeky if he couldn't come up with a wife of his own."

"He is super geeky," Misty assured her. "At least *was*."

"We're sure he still is," Nell chimed in. "That's why he's photograph-phobic."

Charlotte addressed the group. "I haven't found a husband, and it hasn't been for lack of trying."

"Yeah, but," Misty said, raising the obvious point. "You've only been looking recently."

"Didn't stop you and Nell from finding your ones."

Nell's face softened. "Misty and I both had a head start, hon."

"In a way that's true," Mei-Lin agreed. She turned to Charlotte. "So, seriously. You're going to do it?"

"If not me, then who?"

Mei-Lin shrank back. "Oh no. Not me! I'm not even in the family. I'm also seeing Dusty. Exclusively."

Nell's mouth fell open. "Mei-Lin! Congrats!"

Charlotte blinked. "Wow. Since when?"

"Since a few days ago," Mei-Lin said, sounding breathy. She blushed glancing at Nell. "It's kind of your fault, really."

Nell thumbed her chest. "What?"

"Remember all those cowboy romance novels you sneaked me?"

Charlotte gawked at Nell. "Wait. When was this?"

"A long time ago." Nell giggled. "I guess I can see it now. Mei-Lin and Dusty."

"Okay," Charlotte said, bringing them back on topic. "So, we've agreed. Nell is marrying Grant and Misty's going to marry Lucas."

Misty held up a shaky hand. "One small thing." She had their full attention. "He hasn't asked me."

Nell blinked. "But I thought he said that thing."

"Yeah. The husband-and-wife thing," Mei-Lin confirmed. "Outside the bookstore."

Charlotte nodded. "You told us so yourself."

"He did say it, but he didn't *ask me*." She lifted a shoulder. "Didn't actually propose or anything."

Charlotte crossed her arms in front of her, looking fierce. "Okay then, you ask him."

"What?" Misty asked weakly. "Now?"

"Maybe she should wait," Mei-Lin said. "Until after Monday. So she knows what's going on with the school and what her options are."

That sounded reasonable to Misty, but one option she didn't want to sacrifice was Lucas. She loved him, she really did. So, so much. More than she'd ever expected. Thinking of being without him, made her realize it even more.

"Okay. Monday. Ooh." Charlotte's brow furrowed. "That's the eighteenth, though, so cutting things kind of tight. Maybe I should go ahead and text Aidan. Give him a heads-up."

"Not yet!" Nell said.

"She's right," Misty said. Still Charlotte's fingers moved across her phone keys. "Not yet."

Charlotte nodded without looking up. She was actually willing to do this, bite the bullet and marry Aidan so Misty wouldn't have to.

"Oh Charlotte," Misty said, growing sentimental. "I love you so much." Charlotte was so take-charge. She always knew what to do. Even when she did the wrong things, she went back and fixed them. "And thanks for taking that billboard down."

Charlotte dropped her phone back in her apron pocket. "You were right. It was a menace." She sensed Mei-Lin's gaze on her. "With a few important exceptions."

Nell worriedly studied Charlotte. "Are you sure? Sure about you and Aidan?"

Charlotte heaved a sigh. "Why not me? I always kind of guessed that it would be. I mean, I did try with your list, Nell. And, Misty, even though I wanted to help you at first, I admit to getting jealous of you always having luck fall your way."

Luck? Misty had never felt particularly lucky, but maybe she had been.

Just look at her wonderful family and Mei-Lin.

Look at Lucas, the guy of her dreams, who'd been right under her nose just like that conch shell had been right under her feet. "I guess I have been lucky," Misty said. "Luckier than I knew."

"And that luck's going to hold," Mei-Lin promised. "That meeting will go great on Monday. You'll see."

Misty's confidence surged. "And then I'll propose to Lucas! We'll work out some sort of compromise and all will be good."

Mei-Lin smiled. "All will be awesome."

Nell nodded happily but Charlotte gnawed on her lip.

"Charlotte?" Nell asked her. "You all right?"

"Yeah. I'm just wondering what I should wear to London."

Her phone *dinged* in her apron and they all jumped.

"Who's that?" Mei-Lin asked.

Nell plugged her ears. "And why do you have your alerts set so loud?"

"So I can hear my phone above all the noise at the counter."

"You're supposed to keep it on vibrate," Nell scolded and Charlotte play-scowled.

"OMG." Charlotte checked her phone and stared around the group wide-eyed. "It's him! Aidan!"

"Aidan?" Misty felt herself blanch. "What?"

Nell gaped at Charlotte. "You didn't text him already? We asked you not to!"

"What's the point in delaying? I've got to prepare!" Charlotte straightened her spine. "And maybe, you know. He should prepare himself, too."

Mei-Lin chuckled under her breath and whispered to Misty, "I almost feel sorry for Aidan. He's not going to know what hit him with Charlotte."

Misty shushed her.

"So, come on," Nell prompted. "What did he say?"

Charlotte's jaw unhinged as she read. "*Don't buy that ticket. I'm coming there.*"

"*Here*, here?" Misty asked her.

"To Majestic?" Nell gasped.

Mei-Lin scrunched up her face and her glasses

went askew. "Why?" she asked, setting them straight.

"He wants to meet the family." Charlotte blinked. "Again, I mean, before our, uh…wedding."

"Sounds fair," Mei-Lin said.

"Maybe it's good for all of us to see him, too." Nell turned to Charlotte. "Is his mom coming?"

"He didn't say anything about her." Charlotte swallowed hard. "Just him. And…wait." She kept scrolling and reading. "Something about his assistant."

"When?" Nell asked.

Charlotte looked like she'd been picked up by aliens then transported back into her body. Without her brain.

"Charlotte?" Nell waved her hands in front of Charlotte's eyes.

Charlotte blinked. "Wednesday."

"Next Wednesday?" Nell fell back a step. "As in five days from now?"

Misty covered her mouth with her hands. This was all becoming so real. "Who's going to tell Mom and Dad about which of us is marrying Aidan?"

"Uh. Not me," Nell said. "I had to tell them last time."

"With our help," Charlotte corrected.

"We can all go in and tell them now," Misty suggested.

"No." Nell set her chin. "They're working. They might hurt themselves with the roaster or something."

"After work then?" suggested Mei-Lin.

Charlotte got that sneaky gleam in her deep blue eyes. "Maybe we shouldn't tell them at all? I mean, not until we're one hundred percent sure that he's really coming."

"Fair point," Nell said. "He could change his mind."

"You did," Mei-Lin said, glancing at Nell.

Nell sighed. "That was a little different."

They all stared at each other, thinking.

"Okay," Misty said at last. "I'll go through with my interview on Monday and we'll wait to alert Mom and Dad about the marriage after that. In the meantime, I'm going home to try to patch things up with Lucas. Apologize for running off the way I did. See if I can smooth the waters." She turned to Charlotte. "Charlotte, are you sure? Sure you want to do this? Because I can't give Lucas false hope if it winds up being me."

"It will never wind up being you, Misty," Charlotte said. "You've found your forever love."

It was true. She had. So had Nell. Even Mei-Lin was dating someone. It was only Charlotte who was out there drifting.

Misty wished she could toss her a life raft but didn't know how.

Maybe things would be okay.

Maybe Aidan wouldn't be so bad.

It said something that he wanted to see the family.

Hopefully, it was something good.

The rest of them frowned at Charlotte, but she set her chin.

"Don't worry about me," she said stoically. "I'll be all right."

• • •

Lucas finished unloading his truck with a heavy heart. Then he told himself not to be sulky. Misty needed his support right now, not him feeling sorry for himself. Besides, nothing said they still couldn't find a way to make things work. He wanted to talk things through with her this evening, if she was up for it.

He'd decided to go ahead and set up her surprise in her office anyway. She could probably use the supplies more than ever after her acceptance to design school. He'd looked RISD up online and found it very impressive. It was also tough to get into and he was proud of Misty for her achievement. She was so talented, his bet was she'd get that full scholarship, too. Then she'd have her dream. Maybe he could put his on hold. It would just be for four more years. Five really, since she wouldn't be entering school until a year from now.

He sighed. Charlotte would be back from London by then, after her five-year arranged marriage with Aidan and things at Bearberry Brews would be getting back to normal. Maybe that would be a better time to resign as manager anyway.

He'd just finished attaching the clip-on lamp to Misty's new drafting table when he heard her come in the front door.

"Lucas?"

He stood in the threshold facing the living room. "Hey."

"Hey." Her face drooped. "Lucas, I'm so, so sorry. I didn't mean to run off that way."

His heart hurt because she looked so sad. "It's okay. You had a shock." He laughed sadly. "I guess we both did."

"Yeah, but I shouldn't have reacted the way I did when you told me about the bookstore. You were so stoked about it, then I totally burst your bubble. I didn't mean to." Her eyes grew moist.

He sank his hands in his jeans pockets. "I'm sorry, too. I should have found a better way to tell you about the bookstore. Probably should have talked to you before your parents."

"Yeah, maybe so."

"I wanted to clear things with them, because of me possibly leaving my job."

"I do understand."

"And Misty?"

"Huh?"

"I am so, so proud of you. You don't know." He beamed at her. "For getting into RISD? Are you kidding me?" His voice rose in congratulations. "That's amazing! Go you!"

She gave a small smile but not a full-blown one. "Thanks, Lucas."

"I had no clue that you'd applied."

"Yeah. So…about that." She clucked her tongue. "It was wrong of me not to tell you. I'm sorry about that, too."

"Why didn't you?"

She locked on his gaze. "I guess I was afraid to. I hadn't really told anybody except Mei-Lin. Not even my sisters or parents. Nobody knew. I felt like if I blabbed, I might jinx it. Part of me never really believed I'd get in."

"If I'd known, I would have supported you."

Gratitude flooded her face. "I know that now."

He walked toward her and she took a few steps toward him.

"I know Mei-Lin is your best friend, and you also

have your sisters. But Misty? I'd like to think of us as friends, too."

"We *are* friends," she said. "You've always been there for me."

"And I want to continue to be. Though I want to be more than friends."

Her eyes sparkled warmly. "I get that part. That's what I want, too."

"So then, we can do this, yeah?" he asked, hoping. "You have your dreams and I've got mine. There's nothing stopping us from both having what we've wanted, because mostly, Misty, I want you."

She tugged him into a hug. "I want you, too, Lucas."

"Good." He kissed her firmly on the lips. "Then here's the deal. Neither of us is ever running away from the other again. All right? You got a problem with me, you stay and talk it through. I'll promise to do the same. Because we're smart. We're adults. We can do this."

She gazed up at him. "You've got yourself a deal."

His heart swelled with affection. "One more thing." He pressed his forehead against hers and whispered, "I love you."

She kissed him softly. "I love you, too."

"I'm very glad you said that," he teased, "because it makes me that much more juiced about giving you your surprise."

She gasped happily. "You got me a— Wait." Her eyebrows knitted together. "Juiced? This doesn't have to do with smoothies and blenders?"

He belly laughed, thankful the tension between them was gone. He didn't like it when things between them felt wrong, because most of the time they went so exactly right. "Nope." He grinned. "No blenders. Even better. It's something for your work."

"Running the register at the café?"

He chuckled at her puzzled look. "No, honey. Not for that job, for your future career. It might also prove useful at RISD."

She held both his hands. "I don't see how I can go there without you."

"Why don't we take things one step at a time? Let's wait and see what that scholarship committee says on Monday. Until then, you can have fun breaking in your new toys."

"Toys?" Now she really looked lost.

Lucas gently latched onto her shoulders, turning her toward the spare room she used as her work space. "Santa came early."

"What?"

He guided her gently toward the door. "Go on. Take a peek."

She grabbed onto the doorframe and goggled at the room. "Lucas! Oh wow! It's…it's…" She glanced back over her shoulder. "You did all this?"

He grinned and crossed his arms. "I hope it isn't too much?"

"Are you kidding?" She squealed like an excited little kid and bounded into the room, picking up and looking at everything. Her new box of colored pencils, the canvas tote bag, the top-of-the-line design ruler. She even unclipped the lamp from the drafting board and then put it back. "Wow, wow, and wow!"

She sat down on the swivel stool and gave herself a push off the drafting table, spinning completely around. "Weee!" She gawped at the drafting board. "This is all too much. It looks brand new and must have cost a fortune."

"I'm glad it makes you happy."

"So, wait. You got all this before you knew about RISD?"

He nodded. "That's what I was talking about outside the bookstore. I thought you could focus more on pursuing design, and I wanted to help in some small way."

"This is not small," she countered. "This is enormous!" She leaned forward and spread her hands on the drafting table, laying her fingertips on its smooth surface. "Lucas," she said with a loving grin. "Thank you."

"You're welcome."

He didn't need a camera to take a picture of her happy face. His heart had captured this memory forever.

"I have news," she said, sitting up straighter. "Charlotte's going to marry Aidan."

You could have bowled him over with a feather. "Hang on. She said that?"

Misty nodded. "She knows now about me and you, how we're a couple for real. And, of course, there's Grant and Nell."

"So, she called the bet?"

"She called the bet."

Lucas whistled. "That's kind of hard to imagine. Charlotte giving up."

"I know. I was a little stunned, too, but she really means it. She's already texted Aidan and he's coming over."

"To Majestic?"

"Yes! Isn't that wild? Something about wanting to see the Delaneys again before tying the knot."

"When?"

"He's coming Wednesday," Misty said.

"That's soon."

"Yeah, but just ten days before the month is up and my folks' loan comes due."

"That's true." Lucas processed this and then he asked, "So what made Charlotte want to throw in the towel now? What tripped her switch?"

"She said she had no choice. There was no point in keeping up the contest, not when it was a losing battle for her. She'd tried with guys from that waitlist, but nothing really clicked. Checking in with her old boyfriends didn't pan out, either."

"A few more dudes meandered into town after hearing about the billboard."

"Oh no! But it's already been taken down."

"Yeah, but apparently word is still getting around."

"Where did you see them?"

"Outside of Bearberry Brews. But don't worry. I sent them packing."

"I hope you weren't too mean?"

"Mean, no. But firm. I'm pretty sure they got the message."

"You're going to be one great big protective papa bear, huh?" Her eyes danced when she said it and he laughed.

"Maybe. But not too strict."

"It's hard to think of you as being mean—ever."

"That's because you've only seen my nice-guy side."

She hopped down off her stool and raced into his arms. "I love you."

"Yeah. I love you, too." He gave her another kiss. "So, what do you say? You want to learn how to cook Puerto Rican?"

"I do!"

"We're going to make it, Misty," he said, kissing her. "Have faith."

CHAPTER TWENTY-FOUR

Lucas laid the ingredients for their meal on the counter and Misty stared in shock.

"Okay." She picked up one of the large, very ripe plantains. "This is definitely going to be too hard."

He chuckled. "Maybe that's because you haven't cooked much at all." His eyebrows rose. "You do have a frying pan, though. I used it for the bacon and eggs. Got another one?"

"Anything else?"

"A large baking dish and a measuring cup if you've got them."

She nodded and hauled the items out from the charity box in the hall closet. He set the skillet on the cooktop when she returned, and she produced the cutting board for him as well as a small sharp knife. "I'll chop the onion and the green pepper. You can open cans."

"Yay!" Relief washed through her. "I can handle that."

She located her can opener and opened the diced tomatoes and tomato sauce. She noted a jar of olives with pimentos in them, too. "Want me to open the olives?"

He nodded and checked his phone where he'd pulled up the recipe. "We'll need a half cup of those, drained and chopped, and also a half cup of tomato sauce. Can you measure that out? We'll use the whole can of tomatoes."

That sounded easy enough. She got that ready while he sauteed ground beef in the skillet. He added the onions and green peppers to it, then salt, pepper, a couple of bay leaves and the contents of a small seasoning packet called Sazón. Flavorful aromas filled the air. She picked up the empty packet and read its ingredients, which seemed to be a mix of seasoning.

"Is this spicy?"

"Spicy?" He looked surprised by the question. "No. Not in the hot sense."

"So it's not *caliente* then?" she said, thinking she'd show off some Spanish. She'd only taken it for two years and had forgotten almost everything.

"You mean *picante*?" He grinned. "That's how you say spicy in Spanish. Caliente is hot as in temperature."

"Or," she said. "As in you're a *caliente* boyfriend?"

He laughed. "I'm not sure that has the right connotation, either. *Caliente* means, um, like ready for action there."

"Oh." She blushed.

"You can call me *guapo,* though."

"All right, Señor Guapo."

She took out another cutting board and began chopping up the olives, while he stirred the browning beef mixture on the stove. "Bet you're pretty good at Spanish, huh?"

His neck colored slightly. "Not exactly. I mean, I took it in school because my parents gave me no choice." He shrugged. "And got decent grades because I've got an ear. I mean, I know what sounds right, but don't always know exactly why."

He indicated the can of tomatoes and she dumped them into the skillet. Then he pointed to the tomato sauce she'd measured out and she poured that in next.

"So you and Ramon didn't speak it growing up?"

He shook his head. "Nope. Once in a while my parents spoke it to each other, but mostly when they were arguing and not wanting us kids to know what they were saying."

She chuckled at this, trying to imagine his parents at odds with each other. They'd always seemed compatible when she'd seen them, but all couples had their moments. She understood.

"They also sometimes used Spanish talking to relatives back in Puerto Rico, but not much to us. When they talked to me in Spanish, I answered in English. When Ramon came along, they didn't even try."

"It's cool you learned to cook the food, though."

"That's because I like to eat it."

While they were talking, he cut up some French green beans. He added those to the skillet, too, and a big splash of vinegar. "I think we're ready for those olives," he said.

She scraped them off the cutting board into the frying pan and he stirred it all together.

"Now what?" she asked, looking up.

He checked his watch. "We let this simmer a half hour or so and get the plantains ready."

She couldn't believe they'd already made so much progress. This was actually kind of fun. With him talking her through it and them making other conversation besides, it hadn't felt like work at all.

He began peeling a plantain so she followed his

lead and did another. There were six of them altogether. "What are we going to do with these?" she asked him.

"Cut them diagonally into third-inch slices, like so." He demonstrated on his cutting board. "Then we'll sauté them in olive oil to get them ready to add to the casserole. Can you get out that second frying pan?"

She nodded and helped him ready the plantains, then watched them turn a golden brown color on either side as he flipped them in the pan. "If you can put some paper towels on a plate, we'll drain these. Then we can start the assembly. Oh! And can you preheat the oven to three fifty?"

She set the oven temperature and rolled out some paper towels. "I've never made anything this complicated before." She tore off the paper towels, placing them on a large plate. "Seems kind of like Charlotte's chicken parmigiana."

He glanced at the large casserole dish he'd placed on the counter. "If you'll bring that over," he said, setting the plantains aside to drain, "we can get started."

He took the two eggs he had ready and used a fork to whip them together. "Can you oil the casserole dish while I'm doing this? Just use a little oil on a paper towel and rub it in."

She nodded and went to work while he grabbed the grated parmesan cheese measuring out half a cup. He checked the meat mixture in the skillet. "Ah just right." He glanced at what she was doing and his gray eyes sparkled. "You're doing great."

Misty felt so proud of herself. Accomplished in the

kitchen! Even though she'd done almost nothing except for follow his directions.

"Thanks. I'm having fun."

"You know what?" He grinned. "So am I."

She was also learning a ton. "What do we do now?"

"Now…" He poured about half of the beaten eggs into the baking dish. "We assemble!"

He showed her how to lay the browned plantains along the bottom and across the sides of the dish, then encouraged her to add the meat mixture, which she ladled in. He was right behind her, helping her along, his steady reassurance so affirming. "Excellent job!"

She chuckled. "I'm not doing this all alone, you know." She peeked over her shoulder and he closed in for a kiss.

"That's why they call it teamwork," he said, giving her another peck on the lips.

They sprinkled half the grated parmesan into the dish and added more plantains then beef and cheese, finishing with a final plantain layer and crowning the top with the remaining eggs. "Ta-da!" she said, tipping up the bowl after drizzling the egg topping over the casserole. "We're done."

"Almost." He picked up some tin foil and covered the baking dish. "Now this goes in the oven for a while, and we start on the Arroz con Habichuelas."

Misty's shoulders sank. "There's more?" But she was only play complaining. She loved every minute of this.

"If you need to take a break," he said, "I can continue."

She set a hand on her hip. "Lucas Reyes, are you

call me a cooking wimp?"

He wiped his hands on a dishtowel. "No. I actually think you've been a champ!"

This whole *piñón* thing had been kind of like completing a marathon. Now they were up for another run. Hopefully, this one would be more of a sprint.

"Is the arroz as complicated as the *piñón*?"

He chuckled. "Easy peasy compared to *piñón*. I promise."

Misty picked up a tall narrow jar of a tomato-ish looking paste labeled Sofrito. "Does this go in it?"

"It does."

"Then I'll uncap the jar." She tried but it was brand new and definitely stuck. She applied more muscle, cranking hard with her hand but the lid didn't budge.

Lucas held out his hand and she passed it to him. He removed the lid with one quick turn.

"I loosened it for you." She smirked.

"Did not." His eyes held a teasing glimmer. He set down the jar. "I'm just stronger than you are."

"Oh no, you're not." She charged at him and he caught her by the wrists, holding up both hands.

He chuckled. "Who's stronger now?"

She wiggled out of his grasp and tickled his ribs. "Oof! Hey!" He laughed so hard his whole face turned red. "Stop it."

He grabbed for her but she jumped back, taking care not to bump into the stove.

He held out his arms on either side of him, bending his knees and attempting to corral her. But she dashed by him with a giggle and flew into her bedroom.

"Misty!"

He pushed on the door from the hall and she shoved back. "Not letting you in here."

He pressed his shoulder against the door. "Why not?"

"I don't trust you!"

He was about to slam through when the door flew open wide and she attempted to race past him. He caught her by the elbow and then around the middle. "Now who's going to get a tickling?"

"Lucas, no!" He hauled her back toward her bed as she kicked her feet in the air screaming and laughing. "Wait!"

He threw her down on the bed and prowled on top of her. "Really?"

"Yes!" She was panting hard and her eyes darted everywhere like she was looking for an escape or maybe plotting revenge.

"Okay." He sat back on his knees and released her. Then she reached up and tickled his ribs. He growled and pinned her back to the bed. "Very tricky," he said, hovering on top of her.

"Sorry." She licked her lips. "Didn't mean it."

He lowered his mouth to hers. "Oh, I think you did."

She tugged her arms free, sliding them around his neck, and grinned. "Maybe."

"You're going to get yourself in trouble, Misty Delaney."

"Oh, I hope so," she said, tugging him into a kiss.

The kitchen timer went off what seemed like eons later.

Misty sat up, pushing Lucas aside on her bed. The

covers were all rumpled and so were their clothes, and Lucas's curls went every which-way.

Her ponytail holder had slid halfway out of her hair.

"That was some *caliente* kissing," she said, catching her breath.

He winked. "Things got a little frisky."

She laughed so hard. "Yeah, in the kitchen—and here."

"There's one more item on the list," he declared.

"Yep. We're champions!" She kissed him quickly and hopped out of the bed. He caught her by the elbow. "Lucas, we have to make dinner."

The timer still beeped in an annoying fashion.

Still the sultry look in his eyes was tempting.

"Why don't you turn off the oven and come back to bed?" he murmured.

Misty's whole body heated, but it didn't burn half as hot as it had just seconds before. "I…think I need some water. Maybe you do, too."

He sat up and grabbed a pillow, holding it against his middle. He had a lovesick look about him and his face was all flushed. Misty was sure she looked basically the same way.

"Water?" she asked, heading out the door to turn off the timer.

He reluctantly got to his feet. "All right."

Misty turned off the timer and the oven and spun around to find Lucas behind her.

He blinked, seeming to return to his senses. "Misty, I'm…sorry if things got carried away in there." All they'd done was kiss but it had been a lot of heavy kissing and they'd been physically close.

Dangerously close. Her knees shook at the memory.

"It was both of us, Lucas." She placed her hands on his cheek. "It's okay."

"Yeah, but maybe we should…" He swallowed hard. "Be more careful. At least until. You know. Things are more settled?"

"I agree," she said because she didn't want to make things any more complicated than they already were for her, or him, or the two of them.

• • •

Lucas finished making the dinner with Misty's assistance. He didn't know what had happened in the bedroom but they'd both kind of lost control. He didn't need to be taking chances like that with Misty, not until their future had been worked out. What if she opted to go away to school and break up with him? What if she had a last minute change of heart and decided that she should be the one of her sisters to marry Aidan after all?

Lucas couldn't risk getting that close to Misty if it didn't mean forever. He didn't want to hurt her. And if things somehow didn't work out between them, he'd be even more torn apart.

"Um, Misty," he said, setting their plates on the table. Dinner was finally ready and the dishes looked and smelled great. "I've been thinking. With those billboard guys no longer a problem and your sisters knowing the truth about our relationship, maybe I shouldn't go on staying here."

Her face sagged in disappointment. "You mean because of what happened?" She glanced toward the bedroom but he didn't want to say yes and embarrass her.

Maybe embarrass them both.

"I just think it might be better." He ran a hand through his hair. "You'll want to be clearheaded for Monday and—"

"That's just it. I need you here." She held his hand. "Please, Lucas. Say you'll stay. At least until Monday. I agree that maybe you're right." She avoided looking at the bedroom but still she blushed. "Maybe we should be more careful right now about certain things. But I'd really like your support until I find out about RISD."

She did have his support and would continue to have it for a lot longer than that.

As long as she needed.

"I'm here for you, you know that."

"So you'll stay until Monday?"

A melancholy took hold inside. He didn't honestly want to go but knew he had to. He had his house to return to and they both needed to get back to work for now. He sighed. "Of course. If that's what you want."

She eyed him gratefully. "It is. Thank you." She took a bite of food and moaned. "Lucas," she said. "This is to die for."

He chuckled at her euphoric expression. "I'm glad that you like it. You did half the work."

"One quarter."

"A third."

She giggled and rolled her eyes. "Whatever. The important thing is we did it together."

He leaned across the table and kissed her on the lips. "Yeah. We did."

CHAPTER TWENTY-FIVE

Misty had the best Saturday ever with Lucas. They went for their morning run, which was now becoming part of their routine, then had breakfast. While Misty loved hearty meals, she told Lucas they didn't have to go that overboard every day. Sometimes toasted bagels or cereal was fine. That would also be easier once they both went back to work. They'd been away from the café for a while but were going back in on Tuesday after Misty's trip to Rhode Island.

It felt good having his company. Calming. Lucas always soothed her spirit and made her feel more positive about every outcome.

Though he'd done the opposite of calm her during that steamy make-out session in her bedroom. But he was right about pulling back and being careful. They both needed to exercise good judgment about things, and Misty had a looming conflict to resolve right in front of her: what her fate would be regarding going to design school. By mutual agreement, they decided not to talk too much about RISD or the future until they saw how Misty's interview went. Afterward, when they knew more, they'd make their plans.

She spent the whole afternoon playing with her new equipment in the fancy office Lucas had set up for her. He had such a good heart and was so great with her. She wished she could do something special for him, too. But Lucas lived pretty basically and, if there was something he wanted, like an electronic gadget or whatnot, he tended to buy that for himself.

Then she got an idea. A really great gift idea. Stellar.

She pulled up the website for a local business on her phone and checked its hours. They closed at six o'clock and weren't open on Sunday. But she still had an hour and a half left today, and it wasn't very far away. Just a short walk, like pretty much everything in Majestic.

"Lucas?" she called as she headed toward the door. "I'm going out for a bit!"

"Where you going?"

Um. Yeah. What should she say? She wanted to keep this a surprise. "I thought I should check in on Charlotte. Make sure she's not freaking out."

"Good idea." He was on his laptop in the kitchen, coming up with some new choices for movies. They'd watched another fun one after their Puerto Rican dinner last night. The recipe had made a ton, though, so they'd decided to heat up leftovers for tonight. "See you in a few!"

Misty slipped out the front door, giggling to herself.

Yeah, this was going to be perfect.

A plan was falling into place in her mind.

One way or another, she knew just what she intended to do and say.

First things first. She was going to the jewelry store straightaway.

Then, she was checking on Charlotte.

When Misty reached Bearberry Brews, Charlotte was locking up. The others had already gone and Mei-Lin had the day off since she'd gone to Bar Harbor.

"Misty?" She buttoned up her sweater and stepped onto the sidewalk. "Is everything all right?"

"With me? Just perfect. I wanted to check on you."

"Oh, I'm okay." Charlotte shrugged. "Resigning myself to it."

"Hear any more from Aidan?"

"He sent his flight information."

"You going to the airport?" Misty asked.

"Might as well face the music."

"I'll go with you."

"Nell's coming."

"Then I'll go, too."

Charlotte frowned. "This is going to be very weird."

Misty touched her arm. "Maybe you shouldn't do it."

"Mist-y, come on." She blew out a breath. "Plans have been made and airplane tickets bought. It's already been decided."

"But no one's told the parents."

"Not yet." Charlotte pursed her lips. "Once he's here on U.S. soil. Then. For sure."

"Er. Maybe we should give them a little more warning?"

"You're right." Charlotte nodded. "We'll tell them once I've got confirmation he's boarded his plane and it's in the air."

Misty couldn't help but worry inside. "Do you want to grab a drink or something?"

"Wish I could, but I'm meeting Steve at Mariner's."

"Steve?" Misty asked in shock.

"Not like that. Give me some credit." Charlotte rolled her eyes. "I'm meeting him to break things off."

"Poor Steve."

"He'll probably be fine with it." Charlotte shrugged. "There are lots of fish in the sea."

While that was true, Misty wished Charlotte had found the right fish for her. Somebody truly special to love and cherish, and someone who would love and cherish her.

"What are your plans tonight?" She gazed at Misty. "And why aren't you with Lucas?"

"I'm headed home now. We're eating leftovers and watching movies."

Charlotte chuckled. "Already sounding like an old married couple."

Misty patted her purse, which contained her new purchases. "Yeah," she said happily. "I guess we are."

• • •

Misty relaxed on the sofa next to Lucas, snuggling close to him and enjoying her dinner. This was just what she needed tonight. Something to take her mind off Monday.

Lucas put the film on pause and they carried their plates to the kitchen.

"I guess it's time for dessert." He reached for a box on top of the fridge that she hadn't noticed before. It was turquoise and white and stamped with the Dolphin Donuts & More logo. He grinned at her look of surprise.

"When did you get that?"

"When you were out checking on Charlotte. My mom sends her congratulations on RISD." He handed her the box and Misty peered inside, seeing two adorable cupcakes decorated to look like ice cream sundaes with hot fudge and maraschino cherries on top. "Oh yum, these look delicious!"

He took the box from her and set it on the counter. Then he removed the cupcakes and set them on two plates, handing one to her. "Want to eat these in here or out there?"

Lucas was always doing things like this. Thinking of her. He was going to make the best forever partner. And she was going to work every day to be wonderful to him. "Let's take them to the living room."

Misty settled down on the sofa, believing all was right with the world. Even if she didn't get that scholarship to RISD, she'd still find a way to pursue design. She had Lucas in her corner to support her. Just like she planned to support him in starting his book coffee shop.

She still worried about Charlotte and Aidan, but it was better that he was coming here. That way, if he was really awful, Misty and Nell could convince Charlotte to cancel the deal. Their parents would want that, too.

"You know," she said, biting into her cupcake. Oh wow, its chocolatey creamy custard center was sooo good. "I'm going to really miss having you around here."

"I know, but I do eventually have to get back to my place." His eyes sparkled when he joked. "My roses miss me."

Misty poked out her bottom lip. "Well, I'm going to miss you more when you're not here."

"All good things come to those who wait." He

quirked a grin. "Just look at me. I waited for you."

"Yeah, but it's fun having you here as a roommate. I like eating together and being together. Even running with you in the morning." It was hard to believe she'd actually said that. Misty had hated exercise before. It didn't really feel like exercise with Lucas, though. It was more like they were keeping each other company, in a healthy way. She stared down at her cupcake and chuckled. Okay. Not all of their choices were healthy. But once in a while, treats were okay.

"I like those things, too." He lightly thumbed her nose. "That's why we're talking about making things more permanent. But Misty. Sweetie." His eyebrows rose. "You know I can't stay here in your guest room indefinitely. I want to do things right."

He didn't say much more and she knew why. They were trying to avoid talking about the impact RISD's financial decision might have on their futures. "You have a beautiful cottage. I can see why you miss it."

He shrugged. "I haven't really. I'd much rather be here with you. But, like I said, I want to do this right." He sighed and shook his head. "It took me some work to explain to my mom about how we weren't living in sin and that my intentions were honorable. Now that she knows we've fallen in love, she's very happy about the whole thing. My mom likes you a lot."

Misty's eyebrows rose. "Yeah?"

"Yeah. She always has and says we're a great match. Ramon said so, too. He thinks you're cool."

"Ramon? When did you see him?"

"He was at the bakery helping my mom move

some heavy stuff in back. So I filled them both in."

"Well, you don't even have to ask if my family likes you," she said lightly. "My dad already thinks of you like a son and my mom loves you, too."

"And your sisters and Mei-Lin?"

She nudged him. "You're a shoo-in for everyone's approval. They all knew you liked me way before I did."

He ran a hand through his hair. "Was I that obvious?"

She chuckled. "I guess not to me."

They finished eating their cupcakes, then Lucas said, "Cooking together last night was fun. We'll have to do that again."

"Definitely." She smiled at him. "More than once."

"You know," he said. "It's occurred to me. We've done nearly every item on Nell's list. All except one."

Her eyes sparkled. "Stargazing at midnight."

"Yeah." He stared out the window. "Tonight's pretty clear."

She yawned. "I'm not sure I can make it until midnight. I've always been early-to-bed and early-to-rise."

He laughed warmly. "So you're not much of a date at New Year's, huh?"

"Oh no. I make an effort then."

His eyebrows arched and she was on the spot.

"Okay." She giggled. "You've got me. Stargazing at midnight it is. But maybe can we try to be done by then?"

Lucas checked his watch. "This movie's almost over. We could see another one after this one. Or."

"Or what?"

"Go up on the roof and make out?"

She swatted his arm. "That's not stargazing."

"It is if you look up at the sky once in a while."

Being under the stars with Lucas did sound kind of dreamy.

He leaned toward her and whispered, "I can point out some constellations."

"You know constellations?"

"A few." His husky breath tickled her ear and shivers of delight raced through her.

"Can we bring a bottle of wine?"

He grinned. "How about champagne?"

"Champagne?"

"We've got a lot to celebrate, Misty. You getting into RISD. You *not* going to London." His eyes danced. "You falling in love with me."

His smile warmed her heart. "So you bought champagne?"

"I did." He gazed into her eyes. "You were gone a long time, checking on Charlotte. So I ran my errands too."

"Where's the champagne?"

He hopped up. "In the fridge, but I'll stick it in the freezer while we finish the movie so it gets icy cold."

"I wish you'd told me you'd make such an amazing boyfriend," she said. "I probably would have dated you sooner."

"I'm not so sure about that."

She cocked her head. "You might have asked me out."

"You were always with somebody else."

"Not always. Come on." Curiosity got the best of her. "So when was the first time, you know. You ever thought of asking?"

He didn't hesitate. "Back in high school."

"What? Seriously?"

"I'm glad we waited until now. If we'd dated then, who knows if it would have lasted? We were kids, but we're adults now."

"That's true. Although some people meet when they're young and stay together."

"We did meet when we were younger," he said.

She grinned. "And we're together."

"Let me take care of that champagne, then we'll get back to our movie." He picked up their dessert plates. "Deal?"

Misty crossed her arms, totally happy and content. "Deal."

CHAPTER TWENTY-SIX

Lucas and Misty sat on the two-seater rocker chair on gliders. Its worn cushions had dried out from the rain a few nights ago due to a couple days' sunny weather. They settled down under the pair of sofa blankets they'd brought along. Due to the chilly wind they both wore their jackets, but Lucas wasn't cold snuggled up beside Misty.

He doubted she was, either.

He reached for the bottle of champagne on the table in front of them. He'd also brought two short plastic cups, which he handed Misty to hold. She appreciated the view, taking in the panorama of the ocean. Its dark drama thundered onto the blackened beach in tumbling waves.

"This is nice up here."

"Pretty quiet at this hour."

Her eyes sparkled in the shadows. "A lot quieter than the other morning when we were playing trumpet."

"I'll give you that. I'm surprised nobody complained."

"The neighbors are pretty chill around here." She laughed. "Meaning very few residents on this street. Mostly businesses."

He twisted the champagne cork with the dishtowel in his hands and steadily popped it open, catching the cork in his palm.

"You're very good at that," she teased. "Had practice?"

"Not too much." He poured her a glass and she settled back against a cushion.

"I could get used to this."

"So could I." He fixed himself a glass and they toasted to the view.

"I loved hearing you play that *Jungle Book* song," she said. "That really took me back. My sisters and I watched it over and over growing up." She gazed up at him in the moonlight and her beauty took his breath away. "What else can you play on the trumpet?"

He shrugged. "Pretty much everything. If I've heard a tune, I can generally pick it up. I guess I inherited that from my dad. He used to let me tinker around on his horn when I was a kid, and taught me a few things. A lot of it came naturally to me, I guess. Like some of those catchier tunes."

"Like 'When the Saints—'"

"'Go Marching In'?" He laughed. "Oh yeah."

"Ever been to New Orleans?"

"No. You?"

She shook her head. "Might be a fun place for two trumpeters to visit someday. Maybe for a jazz festival."

"Now that would be really cool."

She gazed up at the stars. "Do you have a favorite song to play?"

"I guess I've got lots of favorites, but one of 'em is 'Songbird.'"

"Lucas!" She gasped and spilled her champagne. He helped her wipe it off the blanket with his napkin while she dabbed at it, too. "That's one of my absolute favorites." She met his eyes. "I mean, possibly my all-time favorite."

"It is very sweet." But not half as sweet as her. Man, he was toast. He'd fallen so hard. He hoped RISD wouldn't change things in a bad way. Still, he knew he needed to encourage Misty to take this chance and spread her wings.

"Will you play it for me sometime?"

His gaze washed over her. "Maybe."

She shot him a smug grin. "Which is just as good as yes."

They both drank from their champagne some more, then she looked up at the sky. Majestic was the kind of place that shut down early, so there weren't too many ambient lights to interfere with the twinkling of the distant stars.

"Do you really know your constellations?"

"My dad taught me. Working the sea and understanding the sky seem to go hand in hand." He held her hand when he said that and she sighed.

"Show me one."

"All right. It's mid-September. So, hmm." He motioned with his cup. "Look up and in the direction of Bearberry Brews."

"What's that bright one? The North Star?"

"Yep. Good job."

"It's a little early yet. But wait. There it is!" He squinted and motioned to a dark section of the sky boxed in by four faint stars.

"The Big Dipper?" she guessed.

He shook his head. "That's Pegasus."

"Doesn't look like a winged horse."

"The square is its hindquarters. He's on his back."

She craned her head to try to make out what he

was seeing and he used the opportunity to wrap his arm around her shoulders. She snuggled in against him, just as he'd hoped.

"Imagine a long line connected to the square and running through those stars," he said, pointing out three others. "That's the horse's neck. Then, when the line tips up again forming an obtuse angle—that's the horse's head."

"Wait." She squealed excitedly. "Yeah. I think I get it. I can imagine. But where's the rest of his body?"

He laughed. "Sometimes these things are imprecise. Want to know something cool, though? That star in the northeast corner of the big square is officially also in Andromeda."

"Oh. I've heard of that."

"It sits on the border of both constellations, so often gets included in Pegasus. In Greek mythology, Pegasus was the son of Poseidon—"

"The god of the sea?"

"And also of horses."

"Oh really? Hmm. Interesting."

"So this Poseidon was a rascal. He seduced this mortal Medusa in Athena's temple, but Medusa got all the blame. She was beautiful and vain, especially of her pretty long hair. So in punishment for her going astray, Athena made her super ugly. Her face was made into scales and her hair became coils of snakes."

"Oh no! What happened to Poseidon?"

He gently squeezed her shoulders. "Nothing. But poor Medusa became so hideous that any man who looked at her turned to stone."

"How unfair!"

"I know. But finally this hero named Perseus put her out of her misery by chopping off her head."

Misty's eyes went wide. "That's horrifying!"

"I know, but it's a myth. The story of how Pegasus was born."

"From a chopped-off head?"

He shrugged. "Basically. The winged horse flew out of her blood and up to the heavens. He's there to this day, thundering across the sky and carrying lightning bolts for Zeus."

She stared up at the constellation in awe. "That's quite a story."

He grinned, holding her closer. "Yeah."

"Where's Andromeda?"

He pointed out the elongated V-shaped apparition in the sky.

"Who was she?"

"She was a beautiful princess. Her mom was super beautiful, too, but a little boastful to be honest. This ticked off Poseidon when she claimed she and her daughter were better looking than any of the sea nymphs in Poseidon's court."

She laughed. "Not Poseidon again?"

He laughed, too. "Yeah. The guy gets around."

They both stared at the ocean, captivated for a moment by its tousling waves.

"Anyway," Lucas went on. "Back to the stars… Poseidon decided to dole out punishment to Andromeda and her mom by sending a sea monster to ravage their kingdom. Somehow Andromeda got blamed for the drama. Her parents chained her to a rock when the sea monster was coming to serve as a sacrifice and save the kingdom."

Misty gasped. "No. What happened?"

"Our hero, Perseus. Remember him from before?"

"The head chopper, yeah."

Lucas nodded. "Well, he saved Andromeda by setting her free. But the man had his price."

Misty's forehead rose and he could tell she was into this tale, maybe even more engrossed than she'd been in those classic movies. And having her rapt attention warmed his heart. "Which was?"

"He told her parents that he'd slay the beast and free her under one condition. He could have her hand in marriage."

"Oh no. Poor Andromeda didn't have a choice?"

Lucas shook his head. "Not really." At least Misty and her sisters each had a say about marrying Aidan, and had all been given a fighting chance to escape that fate. He could only hope Misty was getting further and further away from considering London as any kind of possibility, because—more than anything in the world—he wanted her staying in Majestic right here with him.

Misty shifted in his hold to scan his eyes. "So," she asked, clearly into the tale, "did Andromeda marry Perseus?"

"Reluctantly. Yeah. Then later the goddess Athena placed her in the heavens to join her parents, who already had constellations of their own."

She relaxed her pose, settling back against him, and he caught the light minty scent of shampoo in her hair. He'd spotted her bath products in the one bathroom and they all seemed to be made of eucalyptus, which seemed organic and fresh, like her.

"Wow. Who knew?" She studied the elongated

vee. "I'm somehow not getting a woman."

"She's uh, like lying upside down almost. With her legs up that way in a gown and her arms spread out forming the points of the vee down here."

Misty giggled. "If you say so." After a moment, she asked, "Whatever happened to that sea monster? Did he ever get a constellation?"

Lucas grinned at her interest. "It's right there. That's Cetus," he said, motioning to a grouping of stars sitting low on the horizon. "His name technically means 'whale' in Latin, but most drawings I've seen make him look like a seafaring dragon."

"Like the Loch Ness Monster?"

"With hotter breath."

She laughed. "This is amazing. I never knew you knew so much about the stars."

Warmth spread through his chest at the adoring look in her eyes.

"I'll tell you more any time you ask."

"Noted," she said, giving him a kiss, and his heart grew wings just like Pegasus galloping up through the sky.

CHAPTER TWENTY-SEVEN

Monday morning, Mei-Lin texted that she was waiting downstairs in her SUV. Misty's nerves dialed up to a frantic pitch.

Lucas sensed it, of course, and held Misty tightly, staring into her eyes. "I wish I could go with you, but understand this is something you need to do yourself."

"Yeah. Plus I promised Mei-Lin."

"I'm glad you'll have her with you."

Misty gave a shaky laugh. "She'll probably have to hang out at a coffee shop somewhere."

Lucas grinned. "At least she's had practice."

She kissed him one last time, then slipped out the door.

Before she closed it, he sent her a sunny thumbs-up.

She couldn't help but be nervous as she hurried down the stairs, a few steps at a time. She could get this scholarship! Wind up going to school in Providence! So many possibilities could open up, but then there was Lucas. She couldn't ask him to sacrifice his dreams, and she didn't plan to. While he hadn't made any further moves on assuming the bookstore rental space, he had spent hours and hours developing his business plan over the weekend. He went and talked it over with her dad yesterday afternoon, and her dad had given him some tips.

Everything was on hold until they had news from

the committee, but Misty didn't intend to let Lucas down. She had a strategy up her sleeve.

She climbed into Mei-Lin's SUV. "Hi, thanks for picking me up."

"Glad to do it." Mei-Lin gave her a dopey grin, like she was totally besotted or something. Misty could guess with whom.

Misty buckled her seatbelt. "So. How was the wedding?"

"Excellent. I met Dusty's family." Her eyes grew huge. "There are so many of them!"

"How many?"

Mei-Lin shook her head and began to drive. "I honestly lost count. They were very nice, though. Accepting."

"Of you as his girlfriend?"

"Yeah." Mei-Lin chuckled. "Funny how I was going to go as his faux date, then we made things real before that."

Misty knew all about making things real. Her heart thumped just thinking of Lucas. "I'm glad you're happy. Just don't rush things, okay?"

"Who's rushing?" Mei-Lin sent her a sidelong glance. "We're taking our time."

"Uh-huh."

Mei-Lin squealed. "I'm going to see his ranch next week!"

"What?" Misty stared at her, gobsmacked. "Mei-Lin! That's not exactly taking things slow."

"They've got horses and everything." She tightened her grip on the steering wheel. "He's going to teach me to ride."

"Er. Careful with that."

"Of course I'll be careful. Misty!" She sighed happily. "He's such a cool guy. Rugged. Charming. And his muscles…ooh."

Misty shook her head. She'd never seen Mei-Lin like this. Beside herself with giddiness. "Just as long as you don't do anything rash. Like decide to stay out there forever."

"I won't," Mei-Lin said. "Without consulting with you first." She turned to Misty and grinned. "So. How was your weekend?"

Misty slumped back against her seat and sighed. "Pretty amazing. Lucas and me? We just work."

"Yeah. You two are very cute together."

"I don't know quite how to say this, but it's easy being around him. With all the other guys I dated, it felt almost like a chore at times."

Mei-Lin rolled her eyes. "It's a good thing Lucas spared you from going through that again. So, what did you guys do while I was away?"

Misty giggled. "Finished up Nell's list. We did some stargazing supposedly, but we spent a lot of the time kissing."

"Doesn't sound too bad."

"Lucas bought champagne!"

"For the stargazing? Nice!"

"In congratulations for me getting into RISD. He was incredibly cool about the whole thing, Mei-Lin. Even bought me a cupcake."

"Aww. So I guess you patched things up after your bookstore ordeal."

"Yeah. We talked it out."

Mei-Lin quirked an eyebrow. "How grown up of you, Misty."

"Lucas makes me want to be grown up. Handle things maturely. I've never been in a relationship like that. I mean, never. With the other guys, there was always some kind of drama or misunderstanding. Weird stuff like jealousy. But no. Lucas isn't like that. He's a straight-talker and he's asked me to be one, too." She sighed happily. "I mean how could I not be totally head over heels for a guy like that?"

"Exactly." Mei-Lin grinned. "How could you not?"

They were on the highway now and moving along.

By the end of today, Misty would know so much more about her future.

"I'm really pulling for you," Mei-Lin said. "To get this scholarship. If anyone deserves a full ride, it's you."

"Thanks, Mei-Lin."

"If you get it, do you think Lucas will move to Providence?"

"I'm hoping he won't have to."

Mei-Lin shot her a puzzled stare.

But Misty wasn't ready to share any more just yet. She needed to see how this interview went.

"You're not going to believe what else Lucas did." She bounced a little in her seat. "He redid my little workspace into this really primo office with a new drafting table, fancy swivel stool, and everything."

"Man. He's not wanting you to get away."

With any luck, he wouldn't have to worry about that.

• • •

Lucas grabbed his jacket off a hook in the kitchen at Bearberry Brews.

"Thanks for coming in this morning," Mrs. Delaney said.

Mr. Delaney nodded, shutting down the roaster. "Things always run so much smoother when you're here."

"I'm sorry if I've let you down," Lucas said, "by not being around."

Mrs. Delaney shook her head. "At our insistence. We wanted you spending time with Misty."

"Yes," her husband agreed. "All of us did." He glanced toward the register. "Sean's been a big help. He's done a nice job learning the ropes and we've appreciated having him here with business booming."

"Won't be enough to dig us out of the financial hole we're in," Mrs. Delaney said. "But every little bit helps."

"Yeah, I'm sure it does."

Lucas was glad Sean seemed engaged and willing to learn the business. Maybe he hadn't been the right fit with Misty—Lucas heaved a sigh of relief over that—but he'd picked up running the register right away and had seemed interested in doing more. Sean had never stuck with any job for long, but Lucas had an inkling this one would be different. Which could work out really well for Lucas, if he was able to launch his own venture soon.

He stepped out the door and was greeted by Mr. Mulroney, who was headed inside for coffee.

"Morning, sir."

"Good morning." The older man nodded. "Back to work again, I see?"

"Just helping out this morning. I'll be back full-time tomorrow."

"Nell told Grace that Misty's applied to art school."

"Yes, sir. She has."

"She's always had that talent."

"That's what I believe, too," Lucas said. He started to walk away but Mr. Mulroney touched his sleeve.

"She's also had a blind spot when it comes to you, you know." He grinned softly. "And the way that you feel about her."

"Yeah. Well." Lucas cleared his throat. "Hopefully, we've cleared that all up now."

Mr. Mulroney's eyebrows arched. "Have you?"

"Sir?"

Mr. Mulroney leaned into his cane and studied Lucas. "Sometimes a woman needs to hear the words, boy. As bright as she is, you can't expect her to be a mind reader."

Words? But he'd already told Misty that he loved her, and she'd said the same.

"I'm not talking about admitting some gushy feelings," Mr. Mulroney said. "I'm talking about laying it on the line. Showing her once and for all just how very far you'll go to make her yours—and you hers. Because she's your forever one."

"But I've already—"

"Search your heart, Lucas."

An older lady scuttled toward them checking her cell phone and then dropping it in her shoulder bag. She wore a swishy skirt and Birkenstock sandals and her shoulder-length gray hair was in pigtails. She looked up after stumbling over Mr. Mulroney's cane. "Uh-oh! Sorry!"

Mr. Mulroney pulled his cane aside. "My apologies." He smiled. "Didn't mean to trip you up."

She grinned and her large purple peace sign earrings danced. "I should have been looking." She peered at Lucas, then Mr. Mulroney. "I've got an appointment here shortly," she said, checking her smartwatch. "Thought I'd arrive early to prep."

Mr. Mulroney considered her a moment. "You're new in Majestic, aren't you?"

"Brand new. My daughter and son-in-law just had their first child and I want to live closer."

"How nice," Mr. Mulroney said. "What are their names? It's likely we know them."

"Delilah and Kent Wilcox."

"Oh yeah," Lucas said. "They run Mariner's," he said, glancing down the street.

Mr. Mulroney rubbed his chin. "New owners, yes? Less than a year?"

"That's right," the woman said. "They moved over from Belfast." She hesitated, then smiled. "I'm Crystal."

Mr. Mulroney nodded. "Matthew."

"And I'm Lucas," he offered with a wave.

The woman lowered her voice in a whisper. "I'm applying for a receptionist position at the Majestic B&B. Maybe the two of you can tell me if I've got anything to worry about? Like if the innkeeper's an ogre? I hear he's very old-fashioned."

Mr. Mulroney tapped his cane. "I am the ogre."

"Oh!" Pink dots formed on her cheeks. "Oh boy."

"No harm done." He pulled a pocket watch from his jacket and flipped it open, checking the time. "As long as we're both here," he said, tucking his timepiece away again, "why don't we grab some coffee and go ahead with that interview?"

Her eyes darted to Lucas and then back to Mr. Mulroney. "You mean, I haven't blown it already?"

Mr. Mulroney chuckled, putting her at ease. "No, dear. You haven't blown a thing." He held open the café's front door for her to enter and peered back at Lucas. "Think about what I said, son. When you've got a good thing going, you need to lock it down— tight, and not let it get away." He surprised Lucas with a saucy wink. "There's a reason that Beyonce says 'put a ring on it.'"

• • •

After leaving Bearberry Brews, Lucas went to see his mom. The bakery was closed, so he knew she'd be home. He was surprised to find Ramon on the couch lounging in his sweat clothes and watching reality TV.

"Oh, hey Lucas."

"What?" Lucas challenged. "No school today?"

Ramon held up the remote. "Teacher workday."

"Ah."

"Lucas? Is that you?" His mom came in from the dining room. She'd been sitting at the table with her checkbook and laptop paying bills. Lucas still helped her out with a small direct deposit to her account each month to augment Ramon's education, but Ramon didn't know that. Ramon had stayed at the same Catholic school that Lucas had attended through his middle school years. His mom got a tuition discount for working there as the school nurse, but she didn't receive a full ride for either kid.

So when Ramon became eligible for the private preschool program, Lucas had volunteered to enter public school. His mom had hesitated at first, but no way could she afford to pay two private school educations, even at a discount. Lucas hadn't minded the change. He'd made friends easily at his new school and had been a soccer star. Most of his buddies were on the team, and he'd never lacked for female interest.

Although the only girl's interest he'd ever wanted was Misty's.

Now, he finally had it and his heart couldn't feel any lighter.

They'd work this RISD situation out, one way or another. He really hoped she'd get that scholarship. She deserved it so badly.

"I'm so happy to see you." His mom smiled warmly. "How's Misty?"

"She's doing great. Down in Rhode Island today."

"Rhode Island?"

At the mention of the state, Ramon scrambled off the sofa, shutting off the TV. "Oh yeah, dude!" he said excitedly to Lucas. "I've got news."

"It's true. He does." His mom's eyes sparkled and Lucas wondered what this was all about. Maybe another one of Ramon's college applications had come through.

Ramon dashed up the stairs, then returned with a letter on fancy stationary from his room. It was embossed with the seal of Brown University. He waved it in Lucas's face. "Premed, baby! Premed! I got in, early decision."

"Wait." Lucas snagged away the letter reading it over. "Ramon!" he cried with joy. "They're paying your way?"

Ramon's whole face was a rainbow of happiness.

"At least the first year." He nodded. "I've got to bust my chops and get good grades. If I do, the money will hold."

Lucas's heart felt like a hot air balloon soaring through the firmament. He bear-hugged his baby brother. "I'm so proud of you."

Ramon patted his back. "If it hadn't been for you and all that tutoring—"

"You would have done it regardless."

Ramon braced Lucas's shoulders. "No. I don't think so."

"I'm so proud of both my boys," their mom said. When he'd seen her about the cupcakes, Lucas had told her a bit about the closing bookstore and his hopes to open a book café.

"So." Lucas grinned at Ramon. "I guess you're going to Brown." This was by far the best offer he'd had. It was hard to imagine another school topping this.

"Yeah." Ramon's smile filled the whole room. "I guess I am."

"So, why is Misty in Rhode Island?" his mom asked. "Is this about her application to design school?"

"That would be cool," Ramon said. "Misty and I being in school in the same town."

"That *would* be cool," their mom said. "And convenient. When you're visiting Misty," she told Lucas, "you can also see Ramon."

Ramon held up his hands, teasing him. "Who says I'll want my big brother poking around in my Ivy League business?"

They all laughed, then their mom addressed Lucas. "Did you come to see me about something, or just check in?"

"A little of both?" He sank his hands in his pockets. "I did want to ask you about something. It has to do with rings."

Ramon's ears perked up. "Ooh, rings?" He chuckled. "I guess I wouldn't mind getting a new sister-in-law. Not one as cool as Misty." He spoke to their mom. "She's got tats and a nose stud. Plus she's an artist."

Lucas interceded. "One tattoo, technically."

His mom nodded at Ramon. "Yes. Yes, I know." She turned her gaze on Lucas. "Rings now? This sounds very serious."

"It is serious, Mom," he said and her eyes sparkled.

Then she broke into a grin. "Okay. So. What would you like to know?"

• • •

When Lucas returned from his mom's there was still no word from Misty.

She'd texted when they'd gotten there, but she apparently had a full day planned with the scholarship committee, including lunch with them and the other candidates. Mei-Lin was busying herself exploring the quaint downtown area.

He was restless but determined about what he was going to do. He just needed Misty to get done with her appointments and get back here. He paced around her small apartment, thinking maybe he should have gone back in to work. All this nervous energy was driving him nuts.

He carried his coffee mug to the kitchen, passing Misty's open bedroom door.

That pretty conch shell sat on her dresser.

Maybe a walk on the beach would do him good.

Better yet, he'd go for a run.

Lucas was halfway down the beach to his turn-around mark, when he stopped short.

Look who was here. That cute little family from the lighthouse.

Those parents with their two kids. They were gathering shells and Lucas wondered about the kids being out of school. Then he remembered. Teacher workday. Other schools, besides Ramon's, might have had one, too. But it wasn't the sight of the kids that stopped him.

It was what the little girl had clutched in her arms. She held an oversized pink and white stuffed panda with goofy-looking black eyes. It was nearly as large as her torso as she trudged along giving commands to her younger brother to pick up certain shells and drop them in his plastic pail. "That one, Scotty! No, not… Yeah! Oh. And there!"

Their parents walked slightly behind them, engaged in conversation between themselves. The mom saw Lucas first, recognizing him. "Hello again."

"Hi there." Lucas's forehead rose. "No school today?"

"Teacher workday," their dad said. "Where's your friend?"

"Yeah." The little girl grinned. "Your feeling-the-wind friend."

Lucas chuckled. "She's out of town for today."

His eyes roved over her bear. "Great panda." Next he addressed her parents. "Do you mind me asking where you got it?"

The mom thumbed toward the pier. "The arcade now has them as prizes."

Lucas hadn't been in the arcade in ages. Not since his teen years probably. "Oh wow. Really?"

The dad chuckled. "You in the market for a bear?"

It would have never occurred to him until now. Wasn't that the one thing Misty had said she'd wanted from the fair as a kid, but had never been able to have? It was never too late to fulfill your dreams. He knew that now because he was with Misty.

Now, he wanted all of her wishes to come true.

No matter how long ago she'd made them, or how small.

"I might be," Lucas said. "For a friend." He winked at the parents and they got it.

"You'd better hurry then," the mom said. "They only had a few more left."

Lucas thanked them and took off running in that direction, hoping one of those remaining panda bears was purple.

A short time later, Lucas texted Mei-Lin. Last she'd heard, Misty was headed out to lunch with her group and would wrap up mid-afternoon, three or four o'clock. If he got on the road right now, he could be there when she was done with her meeting. Mei-Lin was excited that he was coming and filled in on his plan. She said she'd help him and Misty meet up, promising to keep his arrival a surprise.

CHAPTER TWENTY-EIGHT

Misty sat in front of the scholarship panel, her heart pounding. The lunch had gone great and the morning activities, too. She'd received a tour of the design school with a small group of others, then they'd broken out with potential mentors one-on-one. Everyone had reconvened for lunch at a local restaurant and now the hardest part was almost over. Answering a battery of questions from the cadre of instructors and administrators seated in front of her at a big, long table. Misty was grateful now she'd never had any problems with speaking up. She also had years of customer service experience so was used to fielding questions of almost every kind.

She was doing awesome, sailing through every answer.

Then the last question threw her, even though it shouldn't have. "And why do you want to come to RISD?"

Misty thought long and hard about this. She had an instant answer prepared about receiving an excellent education and training for her future career. The outstanding reputation of the school and so much more. But all she could think of was Lucas and leaving him behind. She loved him so, so much, with her whole heart, so how could she? This wasn't like a summer vacation. It meant going away to school for four whole years.

Misty blinked when the realization hit her.

She couldn't do this.

"I'm so sorry for wasting your time."

The faces in front of her drew blanks as Misty stood.

"I thought this was what I wanted, a design career—"

"But your slides are excellent," one instructor said.

"Top of the line," another commented.

"Ms. Delaney," the financial-aid person said, "we're about to offer you the scholarship."

Misty sank back in her chair. "What?"

A woman stood and walked over, handing her a glossy folder. "All the details are in here for you to look over. You'll receive summer placements and internships during the year."

Which only meant more work and spending time away from Majestic.

"But I…I think I've changed my mind."

The school officials stared at each other and one man asked, "Why?"

Misty licked her lips. She didn't dare say Lucas. They might read that wrong and take him to be some super-controlling boyfriend, or something. Which he absolutely wasn't. The program here looked amazing, but also very competitive. She'd have to work hard. Burn the midnight oil just to keep up. She'd been a bit intimidated during the slideshow highlighting the work of all the scholarship applicants. Her designs had been decent, but not as great as some of the others. "I'm sorry," she said, standing again. "I've got to go."

Misty sucked in a breath, then found herself hyperventilating as she fled the room.

The woman who'd handed her the folder followed her out into the hall. "You don't have to decide to-day." She passed Misty the folder that she'd left behind. "Just by the deadline." Her eyes sparkled. "But I really hope you'll say yes. You'd be a real asset here."

Misty took the folder and nodded, but still her head spun. This was too much. She couldn't do it. Three hours from Majestic might as well have been three thousand miles. She missed home already. She missed her family. And Lucas. She wanted to sit out on the beach and close her eyes and feel the wind.

How had she ever thought she'd make it in London?

Her sisters and Mei-Lin had been right. Charlotte erecting that billboard hadn't been as farfetched as it had seemed. They'd all known what she hadn't: Misty was a great big chicken and could never leave her hometown.

She wanted to stay safe and protected—with Lucas.

She didn't need RISD or Rhode Island!

She dashed out of the administration building, hurrying down the stairs, dividing her attention between her phone and her feet so she wouldn't trip. She texted Mei-Lin.

Done!

Mei-Lin wrote back.

Coming!

But when Misty lifted her gaze, it wasn't Mei-Lin

standing on the path.

It was Lucas.

And wait. What was he holding?

A giant purple-and-white panda bear?

She threw herself into his arms and he caught her as the big stuffed animal squished between them. She'd never been happier to see anybody in her life. "Lucas! Where did you come from?" She was hugging him and crying, sobbing onto his shoulder. If ever she needed him to hold her it was now. She'd nearly made such a big mistake.

"Misty? Hey?" He held her tighter. "What's going on?"

"I'm not…" She briefly met his eyes, then collapsed in tears again. "Not going to RISD."

He gave her a steadying gaze. "Listen. It's going to be okay. Maybe this wasn't meant to be, but there will be other opportunities."

"No, that's not what I meant." She drew in a shaky breath. "I got it."

His gray eyes widened. "The scholarship? What? That's fantastic!" She glanced down at the folder she'd dropped on the ground and his eyebrows knitted together. He released her and picked it up, handing her the panda bear.

He flipped through the pages and glossy pie charts, then met her eyes. "This looks like an offer you can't refuse."

Her chin trembled. "I already did."

"What? Why?"

"It's too much, Lucas. All too much. My sisters and Mei-Lin were right. Majestic is what I know and where my home is. I can't go back to school now.

That's ridiculous. I've been out of the classroom for eight years!"

"Yeah, but this will be different. It's college and design school."

"And about a billion times harder." She squeezed the panda bear to her chest. "What if I fail? What if I flunk out?"

"Misty. You won't."

But it didn't matter. It had taken coming here to Rhode Island for her to fully understand what she didn't want to do, and that was leave her family and Lucas behind in Maine. She held up the giant panda, turning it toward him. "Where did you get this?"

Lucas blinked, clearly thrown. "At the pier in Majestic."

"And you bought it for *me*?" Her voice rose and he nodded. She glanced around the courtyard where they were. "I can't wait to show Mei-Lin. Where is she?"

"Waiting at a coffee shop."

He probably knew what this was. A stall tactic. But she didn't want to talk about RISD or the scholarship anymore. All she wanted was for Lucas to take her home. Assuming Mei-Lin was okay with that, and Misty was pretty sure she would be.

"So she knows that you're here?"

"Yeah. I texted her earlier and she's giving us some space. I couldn't wait, Misty. Couldn't wait to tell you so many things. I talked to my mom today and Ramon, too."

"You did?"

"He's gotten into Brown! On a full ride."

She grinned, feeling lighter-hearted. "Great for him."

Lucas shoved his hands in his pockets. "I talked to Mr. Mulroney." He shrugged. "Or, it's more like he talked to me. Kicked some sense into me."

"What?"

"And then I saw that kid on the beach. The kid who called you feeling-the-wind girl."

Misty laughed.

"She had a panda bear almost like that one." He nodded at the toy in her arms. "I knew then and there I had to get one for you. Because, Misty. I want *all* your wishes to come true."

Nerves fluttered in her belly and a song played in her heart. Because she wanted that for him absolutely. She wanted him to open that book café and make it a raging success.

"Yeah, well. I have things to tell you, too," she said, still squeezing the bear. "Like I love you, Lucas Reyes. Love you so much. And I want to marry you and stay in Majestic. Not run away here."

"Hang on." He wore a pleased grin. "You want to marry me? That's pretty great, because I want to marry you." He gently cupped her cheek. "So then, what's all this business about running away?"

"I don't want to run. That's what I'm saying. I want to stay in Majestic with you."

He rubbed the side of his neck. "And pass up the scholarship? The chance of a lifetime?"

"*You're* my chance of a lifetime."

He shook his head. "No, Misty. I'm not going to be that guy. Not going to be the one who derails you from your dreams and you come to resent years later."

But she couldn't imagine ever resenting him.

"Misty." He locked on her gaze. "You have to take it. You have to tell that scholarship committee yes."

"But I can't." Panic seized her and for an instant she couldn't breathe.

"Why not?"

Her voice trembled with the truth she was just now admitting to herself. "I'm afraid. Afraid that I'll fail. Afraid that I'll miss my family. Afraid of losing you."

"Honey," he said. "You're never losing me." He stepped closer and continued. "Here's what I think. You should try it. Only for a year, okay? Give things a shot. If you hate it more than ever, you can throw in the towel, but at least you'll know you tried."

He latched on to her wrist with the rose tattoo and brought it to his lips, kissing it warmly. "Life isn't any bed of roses you know." His voice was husky as he stared into her eyes. "It's thorny. Do you think for a minute that successful people didn't fight for what they've got? I mean, sure. Yeah. Maybe there are a lucky few who have things fall in their lap. But that's not the real world most of the time. Most days, people have to struggle, take chances, put themselves out on a limb for what they want most. Because if you never stretch yourself you'll never know what might have been if you didn't."

He was making so much sense. Was so sage. But what about his ambitions? "If that's true, then what about you? What about that business you want to start?"

"I don't see why I can't delay a year or two."

"Sure," she said stubbornly. "But not for four, or five. I'm not letting you move out of Majestic to come here."

He set his jaw. "And I'm not letting you refuse that scholarship."

"You can't tell me what to do."

"No," he said. "But I can give you advice."

"Yeah, and I can give you some, too. I want you to lease that space that's opening up and take a shot on your shop. I could see how excited you were about the idea. At first when you told me, and all weekend long when you worked on those business plans."

"I am excited about that, but it can wait."

"No." She placed a hand on one hip, holding the panda bear on the other. "It can't."

He blew out a breath. "So. What do you propose we do?"

She stared down at her purse, then said, "I don't know about school, but I do know one thing. I want to be with you." She set the panda bear on the ground and held up a finger. "I'll just be a minute," she told its pudgy face. "Or okay, maybe a moment longer."

She opened her purse and took out a small paper bag from the jewelers. "Lucas," she said. "I didn't know I'd change my mind about school before I came here, but I was really certain about one thing." She opened the flap of the bag and dug out two wedding bands. "That I want to be with you."

He raked both hands through his hair and stared at her. "Are those what I think they are?" His expression was both stunned and pleased.

"They're promise rings," she said, extending her palm. "I want us to wear them on our right hands until we're married."

"Then move them to our left," he said hoarsely. "Misty." He pulled a jewelry box from his pocket and flipped it open.

She clasped her hands over her mouth. "Lucas." He'd gotten her wedding bands, too, only the design on the band was different. His set had an intricate rose pattern engraved and hers were patterned after Celtic knots.

They grinned broadly, chuckling at each other.

"I can't believe it!" she wailed.

"I swear to goodness, Misty. This has got to be a sign."

"Okay, all right." She laughed heartily. "Maybe I finally believe in them." The universe was certainly telling her something. And that something was she'd made absolutely the right choice with Lucas. No man on earth could make her happier.

She slid the Celtic knot men's band on his right-hand ring finger.

Then he placed the rose-patterned women's band on hers.

His eyes twinkled with love. "You think we should stay with the mismatched set?"

She hugged him around the neck. "I think it's perfect. Individual. You picked yours out for me, and I got yours for you."

He arched an eyebrow and a million happy tingles resonated inside her. "So you'll give one year of school a try?" He was so smart to see through her. She really did want to take this chance but had lost her nerve at the last minute, totally freaking out. Lucas was good for her. He made her want to take chances and to be her best self.

She liked believing she had the same effect on him.

She nodded. "And you'll open up your shop?"

"I can't ask you to be brave if I won't take risks myself. And anyway." He held up his hand. "I guess if I'm wearing this all the women in Majestic will know that I'm taken."

She laughed, feeling happy and free. "You are taken. You're my forever man."

"And you're my forever woman." He gave her a deep kiss.

"So?" she asked when they pulled apart. "How are we going to do this?"

"I can come down on my days off," he said. "And you can come home sometimes on weekends. Meaning." His gray eyes danced. "We're going to make this work."

"Yeah, we are."

She smiled and kissed him again, finally believing this could happen.

With patience, love, and forbearance, and lots of hard work—she and he could build a wonderful life. Just like the one Louis Armstrong sang about.

"So!" He gave her a firm peck on the lips and picked up the panda. "Should we go find Mei-Lin?"

She took the panda from him, her heart so happy and full.

"Most definitely. I can't wait to tell her our news."

EPILOGUE

Misty held the precious baby bundle in her arms, tiny puffs of breath warming the side of her neck. Little Jessica was just three months old and this had been the most amazing autumn of Misty's life. She danced slowly around the living room, cradling Jessica in her arms and moving to the low lulling tune of Lucas playing his dad's trumpet with a mute. The mute muffled the sound to a soft murmuring melody.

He played sitting on the sofa in a relaxed stance, his feet propped up on the coffee table. Beyond him, ocean waves tumbled into the sea and brisk fall winds swept across the sandy beach. It was a lazy Sunday at the rose-covered cottage that Misty now called home. Lucas had built his business "Epilogue" into a raging success and it was a mecca for couples and young families in Majestic. Singles liked to hang out there, too. A few pairs had even started dating after meeting at the cute book café.

On a memorable note, Dusty had popped the question to Mei-Lin there after reading her romantic poetry at a small table in the street-side window. They married and moved to Jackson, Wyoming, where Mei-Lin taught ESOL and Dusty ran the family ranch. Mei-Lin had learned to ride horses and had a collection of her very own Stetsons, which she wore proudly.

Misty and Lucas had been out west to visit them a few times, and they returned to Majestic once in a while to see friends and Mei-Lin's family. Nell took credit for the happy union saying it had all happened on account of her lending Mei-Lin those early romance novels.

Lucas finished up the final notes of the song and Misty's heart swelled with the music as she sang along in a hoarse whisper. "I love you, I love you, I love you like never before—ore—ore." Jessica sagged in her embrace, a heavy weight of sweet smelling soap and baby shampoo. She had her daddy's dark curls and Misty's hazel eyes, and had the very best disposition. Misty had been a colicky baby herself, so maybe she didn't deserve such a perfect kid. But Lucas did. He deserved everything.

To him, she would give the world. And what a wonderful world it was. She'd not hesitated at all in saying "I do" to Lucas and when they'd moved their wedding bands from their right hands to their left, she'd never felt so whole. She and Lucas completed each other in such a unique way, it had to be fate. Misty had thought she'd known love with her family and then she experienced a whole new level of love with Lucas, her incredible forever man. Then along came this child and her heart had grown from full to bursting with boundless adoration.

She spied the drafting table by the hearth and under an ocean-facing window. After five years of commuting to her design job in Portland, her home-office business had taken off with her freelance base built up. One thing was certain. The aesthetics were amazing.

She sometimes took Jessica into Epilogue with her and caught up on business details on her laptop there. She'd started a parent support group with some other work-from-home parents, and when Lucas was able, he joined them for coffee and conversation. He had a full staff now, so had a little more freedom around the shop. Bearberry Brews was still thriving, too, but under different management.

Misty's parents had retired and spent most of their time vying over babysitting for their various grandchildren, whom they spoiled no end. Misty smiled at Lucas. "I think I'll take her to her crib and tuck her in." It was Jessica's afternoon naptime and when they were both home with her, Lucas and Misty occasionally took a "nap" of their own, too, snuggling under the covers and basking in their affection for each other.

Misty positioned Jessica in her crib, appreciating the nursery's decor. It was all *Jungle Book* themed, with a cute jungle animal mobile dangling over the crib. When you wound up the music box, it played "The Bare Necessities" and Misty's heart always leaped with joy as she recalled that first time Lucas had played the trumpet for her. He played a lot at home now, but wasn't interested in performing publicly. Misty felt the same way, and they sometimes enjoyed playing together. Lucas had showed her the Louis Armstrong house in Queens when they'd vacationed in New York for their honeymoon. They'd also toured museums and had taken in a Broadway show. The entire trip had been perfection.

And now she lived with perfection in their beautiful daughter every day. She stared at Jessica's dozing profile, wondering if she'd become musical. She definitely had the genes. Misty tilted the blinds to keep bright rays of sunshine from beaming onto Jessica's face, and her arm brushed the giant purple panda bear positioned in the rocker. Lucas had named him "Mr. Nightly" and given him the job of watching over the nursery when everyone was sleeping. That was so like Lucas, still such a sweetly protective guy.

Misty loved Mr. Nightly and planned to keep him forever, or at least until Jessica grew big enough to want to take him over and claim him for herself. Misty foresaw tea parties, beach picnics, and other fun adventures in Jessica and Mr. Nightly's future, suspecting they'd become fast friends.

Misty felt so lucky to have such a great friend in Lucas, her valued partner and lover, too. She returned to the living room and he pulled her into his lap.

"Beautiful singing," he said.

She smiled at the love of her life. "Beautiful playing."

"This has kind of worked out, huh?" he asked with a teasing lilt.

She swished her ponytail. "You told me that it would."

"And who was right?" He kissed her.

Misty sighed. "You were."

She was glad things had worked out for her sisters, too, and that they were all doing well in their separate lives. It was hard to imagine their one daring bet had achieved so many different and interesting outcomes.

Nell had found her perfect match in Grant first.

Then Misty got together with Lucas.

In retrospect, Nell and Misty had obtained their HEAs relatively easily.

Charlotte, though?

She was another story.

ACKNOWLEDGMENTS

Thanks to the many people who helped make this book a reality, starting with my talented agent, Jill Marsal, for her amazing support of this trilogy. Much appreciation as well to the entire Entangled Publishing team for seeing *Second Bride Down* from its initial synopsis stage through editorial, to final galley proofs, and ultimately publication.

Special thanks to my editor, Heather Howland, Chief Executive Officer and Publisher Liz Pelletier, Associate Publisher and Marketing Director Jessica Turner, Editorial Director Stacy Abrams, Senior Production Editor Curtis Svehlak, Art Director Bree Archer, Relationship Manager Heather Riccio, Publicity Manager Riki Cleveland, Social Media Manager Meredith Johnson, Contracts Manager Aida Wright, and Subsidiary Rights and Finance Director Katie Clapsadl for their important contributions. I couldn't have done it without any of you.

To my enduring husband and family, you have my forever love for sticking with me through yet another series of deadlines, despite the inevitable frustrations that come from your having to pose simple questions more than once when this writer's deep in her fictional realm. Your tolerance and good humor mean everything. Thanks for your listening ears, thoughtful ideas, and open hearts in supporting my author journey. I owe you all a million hugs!

My gratitude as well to every bookseller or

librarian who's generously selected this book to sit on their physical or virtual shelves, delivering *Second Bride Down* into the world for others to find. To the reviewers and bloggers who've written about *Second Bride Down*, thank you for kindly spreading the word about Misty's story. And to my dear readers, thanks for coming back to Majestic, Maine, where seagulls soar overhead and the ocean lies a stone's throw away from the tiny café in which Misty's tale began. I'm so happy you returned and hope you fell in love with Misty and Lucas as a pair just as much as I did.

Warmly,
Ginny

*Find something luckier than catching
the bouquet in this delightful small-town
romance perfect for fans of* Virgin River...

The
MATCHMAKER
and the
COWBOY

ROBIN
USA TODAY BESTSELLING AUTHOR
BIELMAN

Callie Carmichael has a gift for making bridesmaid
dresses—some even call them *magical*. Somehow,
every person who's worn one of her dresses has
found love. *Real* love. And as long as that happily-
ever-after is for someone else, Callie is happy.
Because she's fully over getting her heart broken...
which is why her new roommate is *definitely* going to
be a problem.

After being overseas for six months, Callie's only
choice is to stay with her best friend's ridiculously hot
brother, Hunter Owens. Cowboy, troublemaker, and
right now, the town's most coveted bachelor. Only,
Hunter isn't *quite* the player she thought. And if it
weren't for her whole "no more love" thing, their setup could get confusing *really* fast.

Now, Hunter wants Callie to make him a best man
suit—a "lucky for love" kind of suit. But what happens if she makes the suit and he finds true love...and
it isn't her?

Old crushes reignite when they join forces to restore an old B&B in this charming small-town romance.

A Lot Like
LOVE

JENNIFER
USA TODAY BESTSELLING AUTHOR
SNOW

When Sarah Lewis inherits a run-down B&B from her late grandmother in coastal Blue Moon Bay, common sense tells her to sell it and return to her life in L.A. But when the new owners decide to tear down the old place, Sarah's plan changes in an instant. Now she's determined to return the charming-but-run-down property to its former glory...even if it means hiring her old high school crush to help.

Wes Sharrun's life feels like it's unraveling. After losing his wife three years ago, he can't seem to balance his struggling construction company afloat *and* be a great dad to his nine-year-old daughter. Working on Sarah's B&B might be the perfect opportunity to get back on his feet. But keeping his distance is tough when even his daughter can't resist Sarah's warmth and charm...

As Sarah and Wes work together to transform the old place—and discover some of its secrets—the spark between them only grows brighter. But is this a labor of love...or a second chance at it?

The chance of a lifetime requires a leap of faith…and only one dollar.

it takes a
VILLA

USA TODAY BESTSELLING AUTHOR
KILBY BLADES

For the reasonable price of $1, Natalie Malone just bought herself an abandoned villa on the Amalfi Coast. With a detailed spreadsheet and an ancient key, she's arrived in Italy ready to renovate—and only six months to do it. Which seemed reasonable until architect Pietro Indelicato began critically watching her every move…

From the sweeping ocean views to the scent of the lemon trees, there's nothing Pietro loves more than his hometown. And after seeing too many botched jobs and garish design choices, he's done watching from the sidelines. As far as he's concerned, Natalie should quit before the project drains her entire bank account *and* her ridiculously sunny optimism.

With Natalie determined to move forward, the gorgeous architect reluctantly agrees to pitch in, giving her a real chance to succeed. But when the fine print on Natalie's contract is brought to light, she might have no choice but to leave her dream, and Pietro, behind.